LIZ PRINCE • AMANDA KIRK • HANNAH FISHER

COADY
AND THE CREEPIES
™

BOOM! BOX™

COADY AND THE CREEPIES, October 2017. Published by BOOM! Box, a division of Boom Entertainment, Inc., 5670 Wilshire Boulevard, Suite 450, Los Angeles, CA 90036-5679. Coady and the Creepies is ™ & © 2017 Amanda Kirk & Elizabeth Prince. Originally published in single magazine form as COADY AND THE CREEPIES No. 1-4. ™ & © 2017 Amanda Kirk & Elizabeth Prince. All rights reserved. BOOM! Box™ and the BOOM! Box logo are trademarks of Boom Entertainment, Inc. All characters, events, and institutions depicted herein are fictional. Any similarity between any of the names, characters, persons, events, and/or institutions in this publication to actual names, characters, and persons, whether living or dead, events, and/or institutions is unintended and purely coincidental. BOOM! Box does not read or accept unsolicited submissions of ideas, stories, or artwork.

BOOM! Studios, 5670 Wilshire Boulevard, Suite 450, Los Angeles, CA 90036-5679. Printed in China. First Printing.

ISBN: 978-1-68415-029-8, eISBN: 978-1-61398-706-3

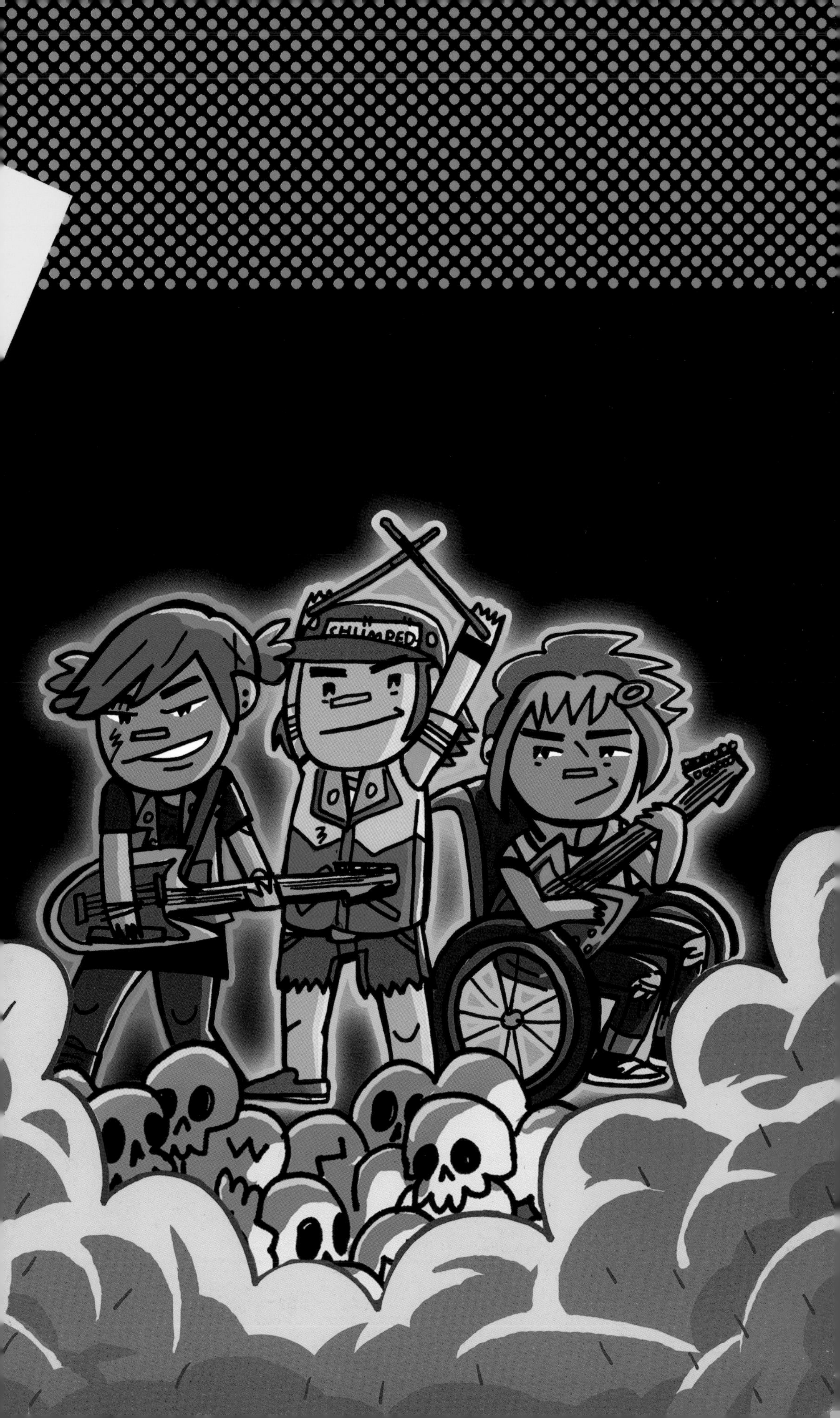
CHUMPED

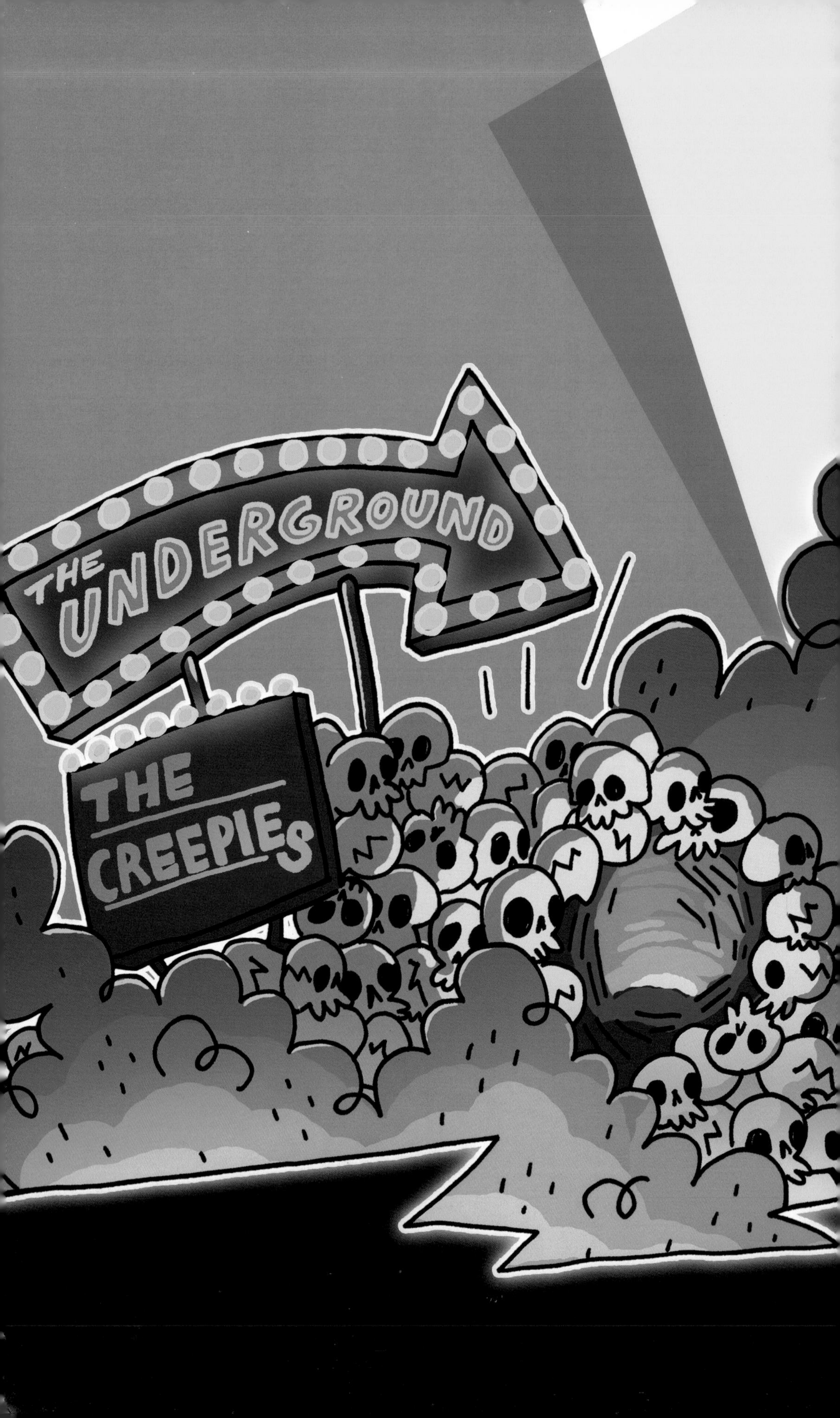
THE UNDERGROUND
THE CREEPIES

COADY AND THE CREEPIES ™

CREATED BY
LIZ PRINCE & AMANDA KIRK

WRITTEN BY
LIZ PRINCE

ILLUSTRATED BY
AMANDA KIRK

COLORS BY
HANNAH FISHER

LETTERS BY
JIM CAMPBELL

COVER BY
KAT LEYH

DESIGNER
MICHELLE ANKLEY

ASSISTANT EDITOR
SOPHIE PHILIPS-ROBERTS

EDITOR
SHANNON WATTERS

CHAPTER
ONE

BLACKWATER
BAR
PORTLAND, OR
→

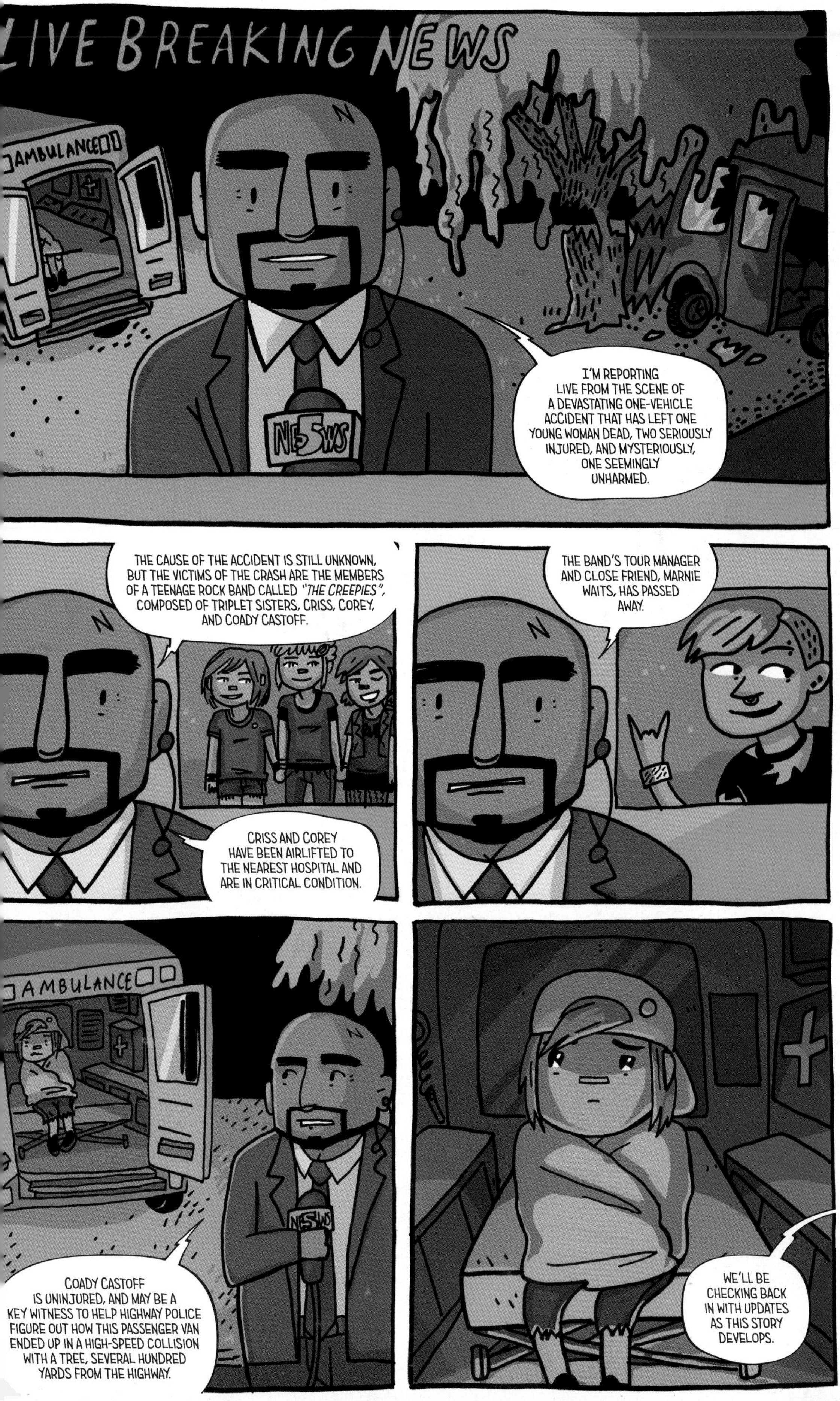
LIVE BREAKING NEWS
AMBULANCE
I'M REPORTING LIVE FROM THE SCENE OF A DEVASTATING ONE-VEHICLE ACCIDENT THAT HAS LEFT ONE YOUNG WOMAN DEAD, TWO SERIOUSLY INJURED, AND MYSTERIOUSLY, ONE SEEMINGLY UNHARMED.
THE CAUSE OF THE ACCIDENT IS STILL UNKNOWN, BUT THE VICTIMS OF THE CRASH ARE THE MEMBERS OF A TEENAGE ROCK BAND CALLED *"THE CREEPIES"*, COMPOSED OF TRIPLET SISTERS, CRISS, COREY, AND COADY CASTOFF.
CRISS AND COREY HAVE BEEN AIRLIFTED TO THE NEAREST HOSPITAL AND ARE IN CRITICAL CONDITION.
THE BAND'S TOUR MANAGER AND CLOSE FRIEND, MARNIE WAITS, HAS PASSED AWAY.
AMBULANCE
COADY CASTOFF IS UNINJURED, AND MAY BE A KEY WITNESS TO HELP HIGHWAY POLICE FIGURE OUT HOW THIS PASSENGER VAN ENDED UP IN A HIGH-SPEED COLLISION WITH A TREE, SEVERAL HUNDRED YARDS FROM THE HIGHWAY.
WE'LL BE CHECKING BACK IN WITH UPDATES AS THIS STORY DEVELOPS.

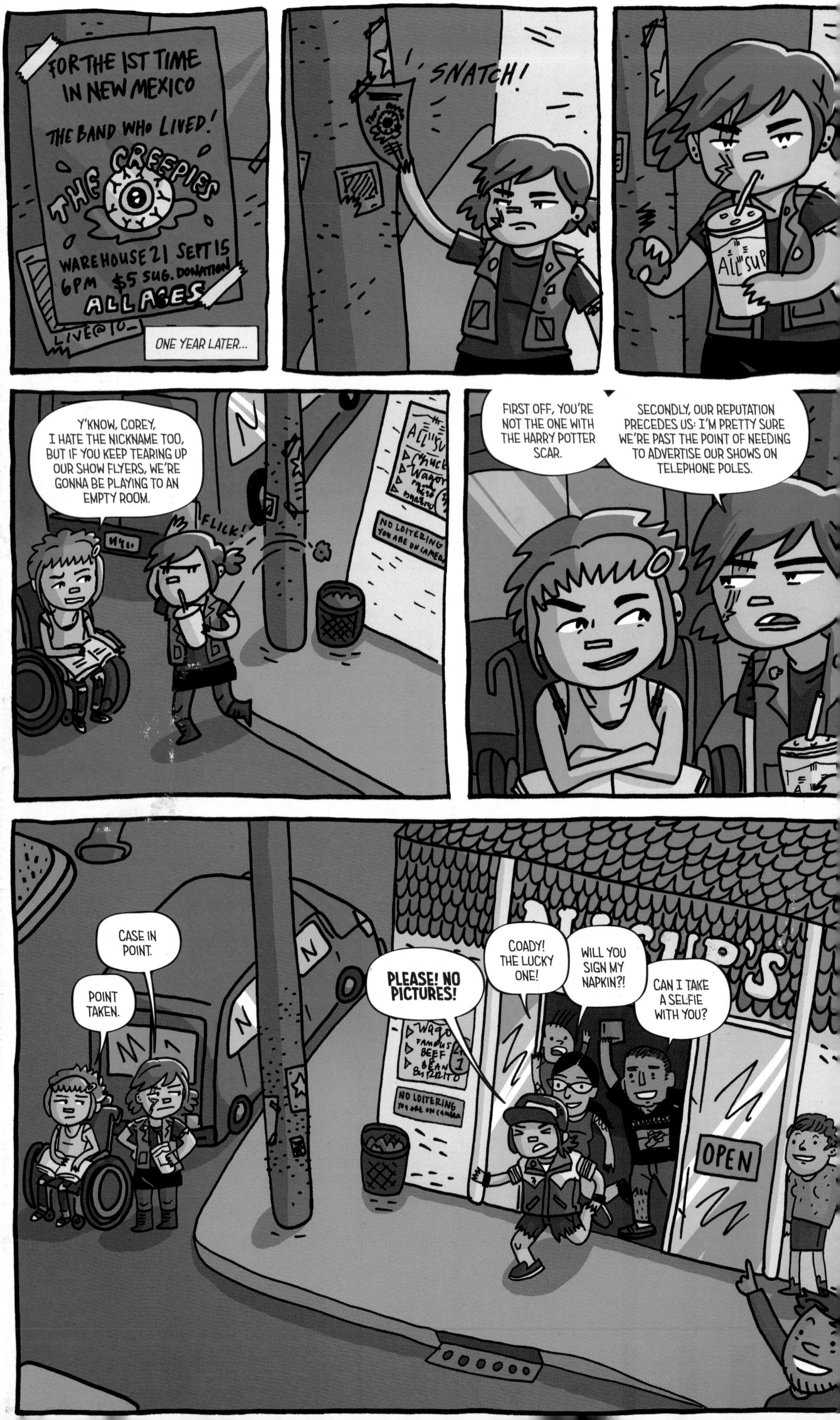

FOR THE 1ST TIME IN NEW MEXICO
THE BAND WHO LIVED!
THE CREEPIES
WAREHOUSE 21 SEPT 15
6PM $5 SUG. DONATION
ALL AGES
ONE YEAR LATER...
SNATCH!
ALL SUP
Y'KNOW, COREY, I HATE THE NICKNAME TOO, BUT IF YOU KEEP TEARING UP OUR SHOW FLYERS, WE'RE GONNA BE PLAYING TO AN EMPTY ROOM.
FLICK!
NO LOITERING YOU ARE ON CAMERA
FIRST OFF, YOU'RE NOT THE ONE WITH THE HARRY POTTER SCAR.
SECONDLY, OUR REPUTATION PRECEDES US: I'M PRETTY SURE WE'RE PAST THE POINT OF NEEDING TO ADVERTISE OUR SHOWS ON TELEPHONE POLES.
CASE IN POINT.
POINT TAKEN.
PLEASE! NO PICTURES!
COADY! THE LUCKY ONE!
WILL YOU SIGN MY NAPKIN?!
CAN I TAKE A SELFIE WITH YOU?
FAMOUS BEEF & BEAN BURRITO
NO LOITERING YOU ARE ON CAMERA
OPEN

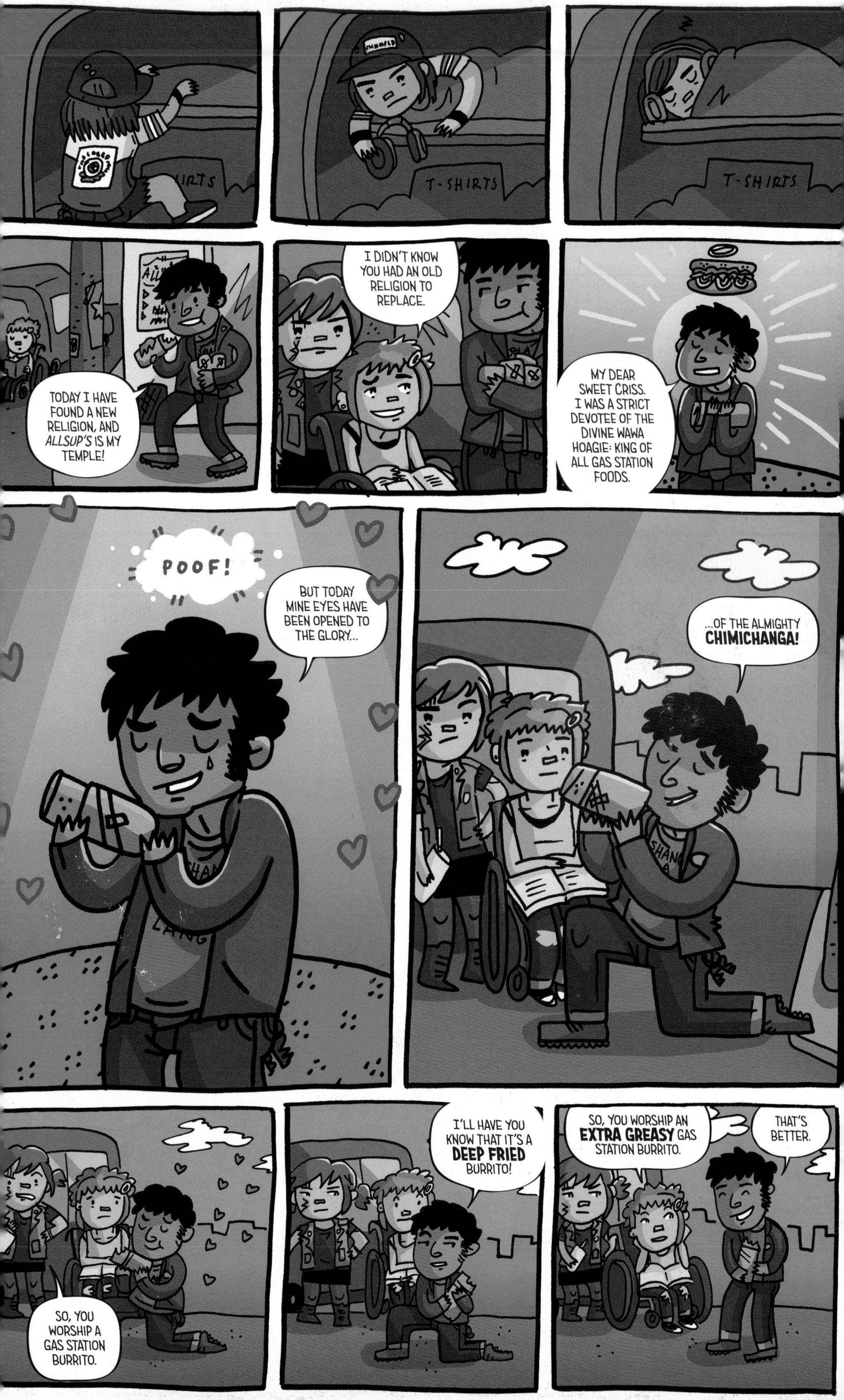
T-SHIRTS
T-SHIRTS
TODAY I HAVE FOUND A NEW RELIGION, AND *ALLSUP'S* IS MY TEMPLE!
I DIDN'T KNOW YOU HAD AN OLD RELIGION TO REPLACE.
MY DEAR SWEET CRISS. I WAS A STRICT DEVOTEE OF THE DIVINE WAWA HOAGIE: KING OF ALL GAS STATION FOODS.
POOF!
BUT TODAY MINE EYES HAVE BEEN OPENED TO THE GLORY...
...OF THE ALMIGHTY **CHIMICHANGA!**
SO, YOU WORSHIP A GAS STATION BURRITO.
I'LL HAVE YOU KNOW THAT IT'S A **DEEP FRIED** BURRITO!
SO, YOU WORSHIP AN **EXTRA GREASY** GAS STATION BURRITO.
THAT'S BETTER.

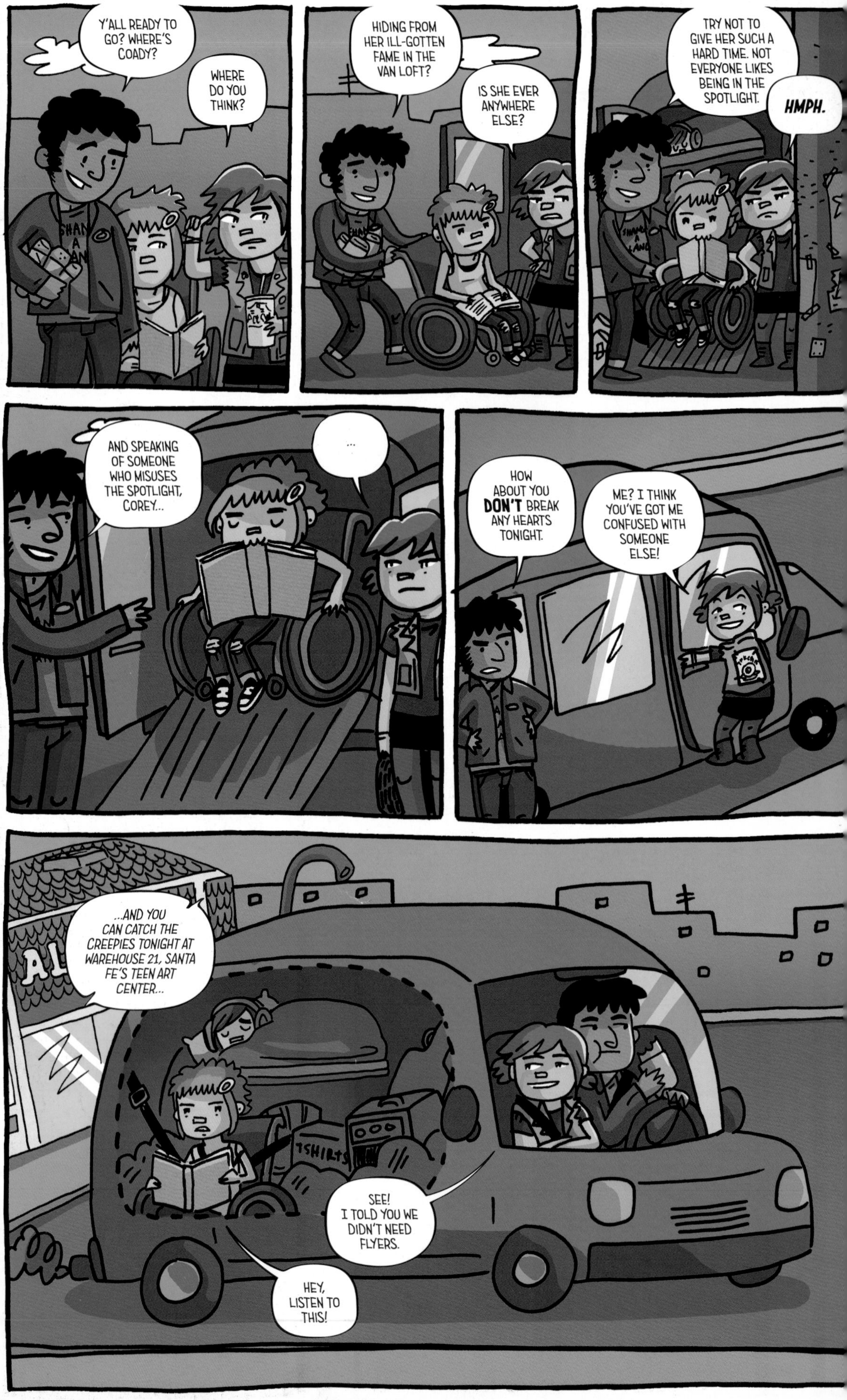
Y'ALL READY TO GO? WHERE'S COADY?
WHERE DO YOU THINK?
HIDING FROM HER ILL-GOTTEN FAME IN THE VAN LOFT?
IS SHE EVER ANYWHERE ELSE?
TRY NOT TO GIVE HER SUCH A HARD TIME. NOT EVERYONE LIKES BEING IN THE SPOTLIGHT.
HMPH.
AND SPEAKING OF SOMEONE WHO MISUSES THE SPOTLIGHT, COREY...
...
HOW ABOUT YOU **DON'T** BREAK ANY HEARTS TONIGHT.
ME? I THINK YOU'VE GOT ME CONFUSED WITH SOMEONE ELSE!
...AND YOU CAN CATCH THE CREEPIES TONIGHT AT WAREHOUSE 21, SANTA FE'S TEEN ART CENTER...
T-SHIRTS
SEE! I TOLD YOU WE DIDN'T NEED FLYERS.
HEY, LISTEN TO THIS!

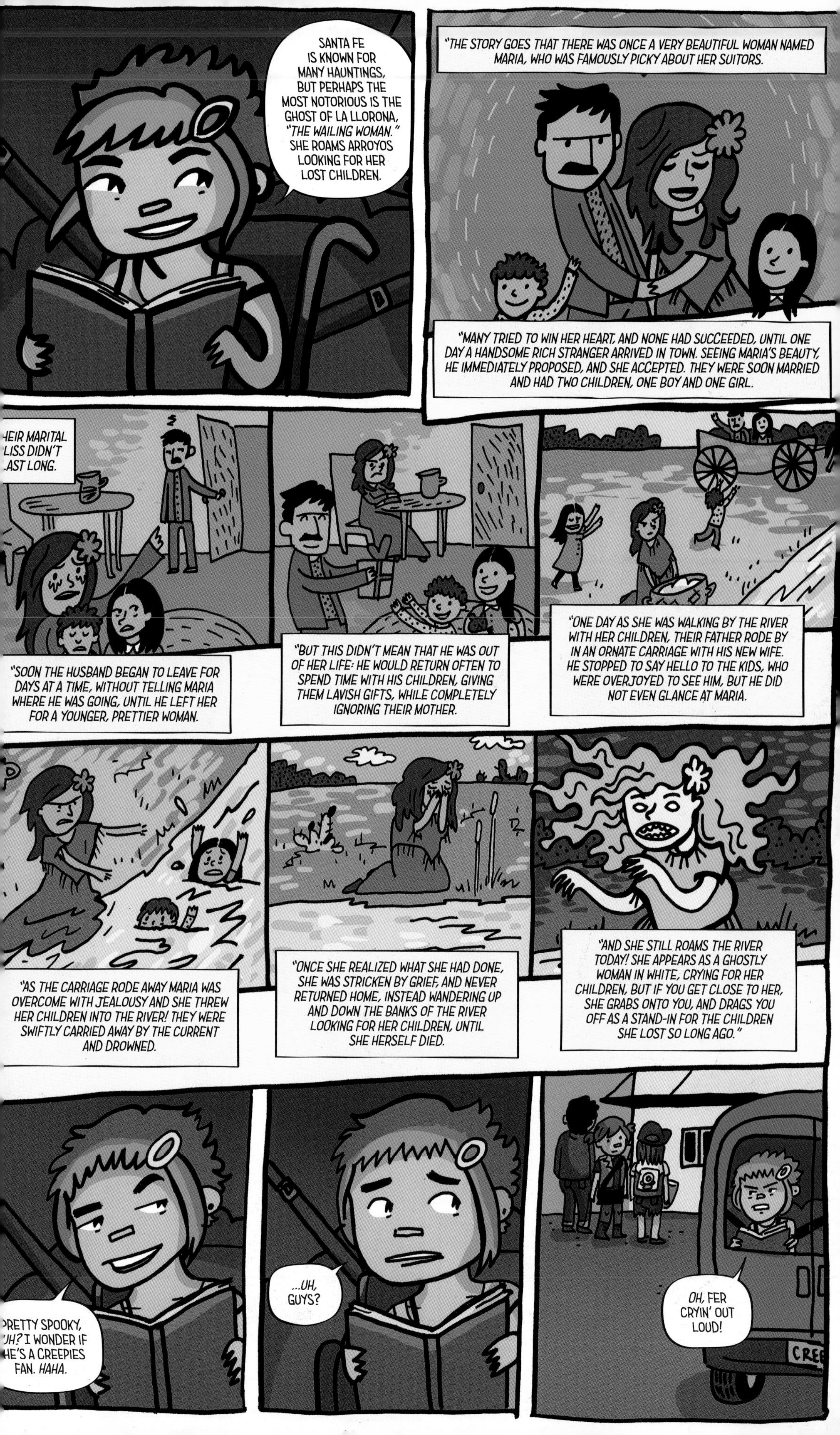
SANTA FE IS KNOWN FOR MANY HAUNTINGS, BUT PERHAPS THE MOST NOTORIOUS IS THE GHOST OF LA LLORONA, "THE WAILING WOMAN." SHE ROAMS ARROYOS LOOKING FOR HER LOST CHILDREN.
"THE STORY GOES THAT THERE WAS ONCE A VERY BEAUTIFUL WOMAN NAMED MARIA, WHO WAS FAMOUSLY PICKY ABOUT HER SUITORS.
"MANY TRIED TO WIN HER HEART, AND NONE HAD SUCCEEDED, UNTIL ONE DAY A HANDSOME RICH STRANGER ARRIVED IN TOWN. SEEING MARIA'S BEAUTY, HE IMMEDIATELY PROPOSED, AND SHE ACCEPTED. THEY WERE SOON MARRIED AND HAD TWO CHILDREN, ONE BOY AND ONE GIRL.
HEIR MARITAL LISS DIDN'T LAST LONG.
"SOON THE HUSBAND BEGAN TO LEAVE FOR DAYS AT A TIME, WITHOUT TELLING MARIA WHERE HE WAS GOING, UNTIL HE LEFT HER FOR A YOUNGER, PRETTIER WOMAN.
"BUT THIS DIDN'T MEAN THAT HE WAS OUT OF HER LIFE: HE WOULD RETURN OFTEN TO SPEND TIME WITH HIS CHILDREN, GIVING THEM LAVISH GIFTS, WHILE COMPLETELY IGNORING THEIR MOTHER.
"ONE DAY AS SHE WAS WALKING BY THE RIVER WITH HER CHILDREN, THEIR FATHER RODE BY IN AN ORNATE CARRIAGE WITH HIS NEW WIFE. HE STOPPED TO SAY HELLO TO THE KIDS, WHO WERE OVERJOYED TO SEE HIM, BUT HE DID NOT EVEN GLANCE AT MARIA.
"AS THE CARRIAGE RODE AWAY MARIA WAS OVERCOME WITH JEALOUSY AND SHE THREW HER CHILDREN INTO THE RIVER! THEY WERE SWIFTLY CARRIED AWAY BY THE CURRENT AND DROWNED.
"ONCE SHE REALIZED WHAT SHE HAD DONE, SHE WAS STRICKEN BY GRIEF, AND NEVER RETURNED HOME, INSTEAD WANDERING UP AND DOWN THE BANKS OF THE RIVER LOOKING FOR HER CHILDREN, UNTIL SHE HERSELF DIED.
"AND SHE STILL ROAMS THE RIVER TODAY! SHE APPEARS AS A GHOSTLY WOMAN IN WHITE, CRYING FOR HER CHILDREN, BUT IF YOU GET CLOSE TO HER, SHE GRABS ONTO YOU, AND DRAGS YOU OFF AS A STAND-IN FOR THE CHILDREN SHE LOST SO LONG AGO."
PRETTY SPOOKY, UH? I WONDER IF HE'S A CREEPIES FAN. HAHA.
...UH, GUYS?
OH, FER CRYIN' OUT LOUD!

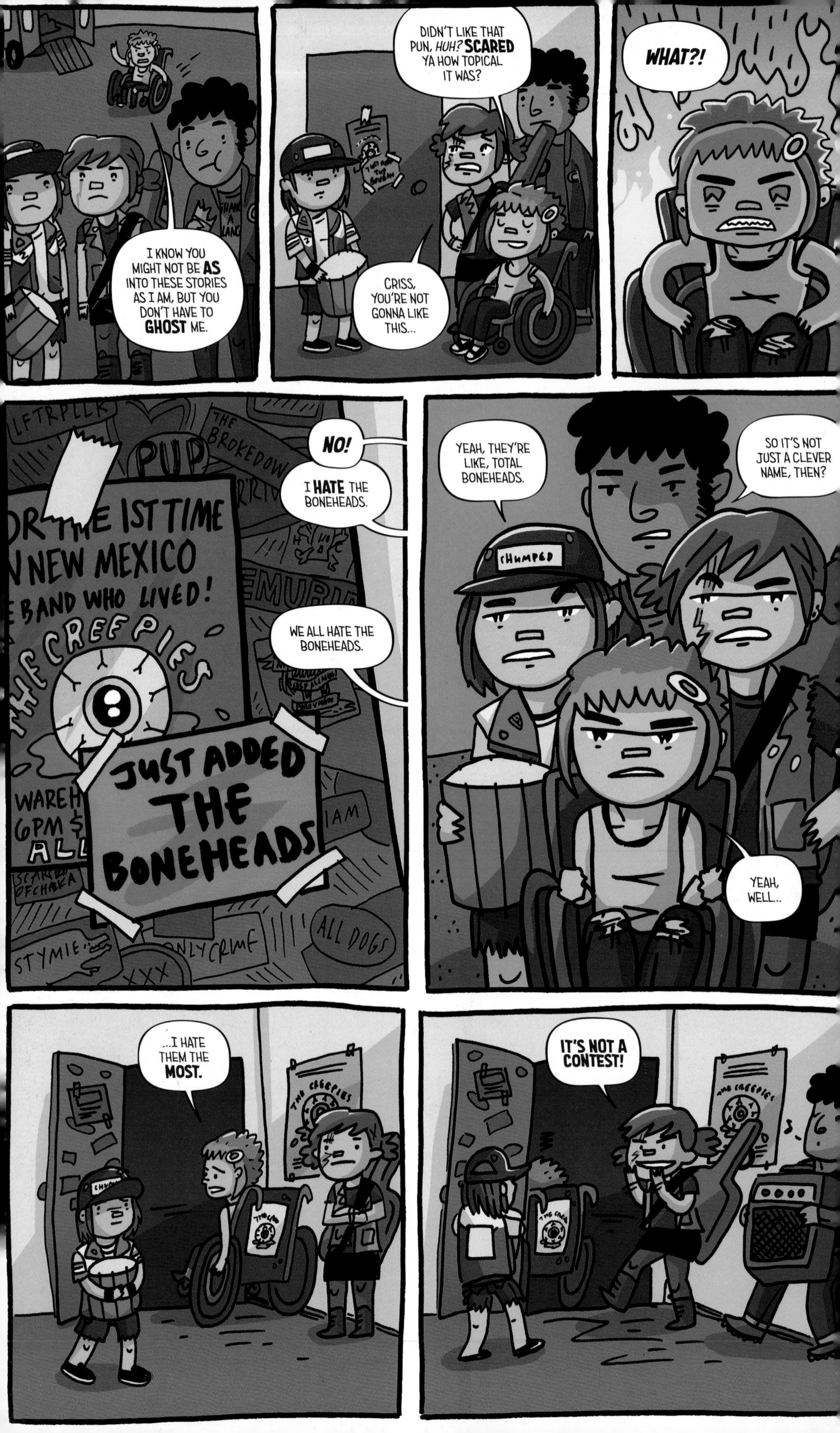
I KNOW YOU MIGHT NOT BE **AS** INTO THESE STORIES AS I AM, BUT YOU DON'T HAVE TO **GHOST** ME.
DIDN'T LIKE THAT PUN, *HUH?* **SCARED** YA HOW TOPICAL IT WAS?
CRISS, YOU'RE NOT GONNA LIKE THIS...
WHAT?!
JUST ADDED THE BONEHEADS
NO!
I **HATE** THE BONEHEADS.
WE ALL HATE THE BONEHEADS.
YEAH, THEY'RE LIKE, TOTAL BONEHEADS.
SO IT'S NOT JUST A CLEVER NAME, THEN?
YEAH, WELL...
...I HATE THEM THE **MOST.**
IT'S NOT A CONTEST!

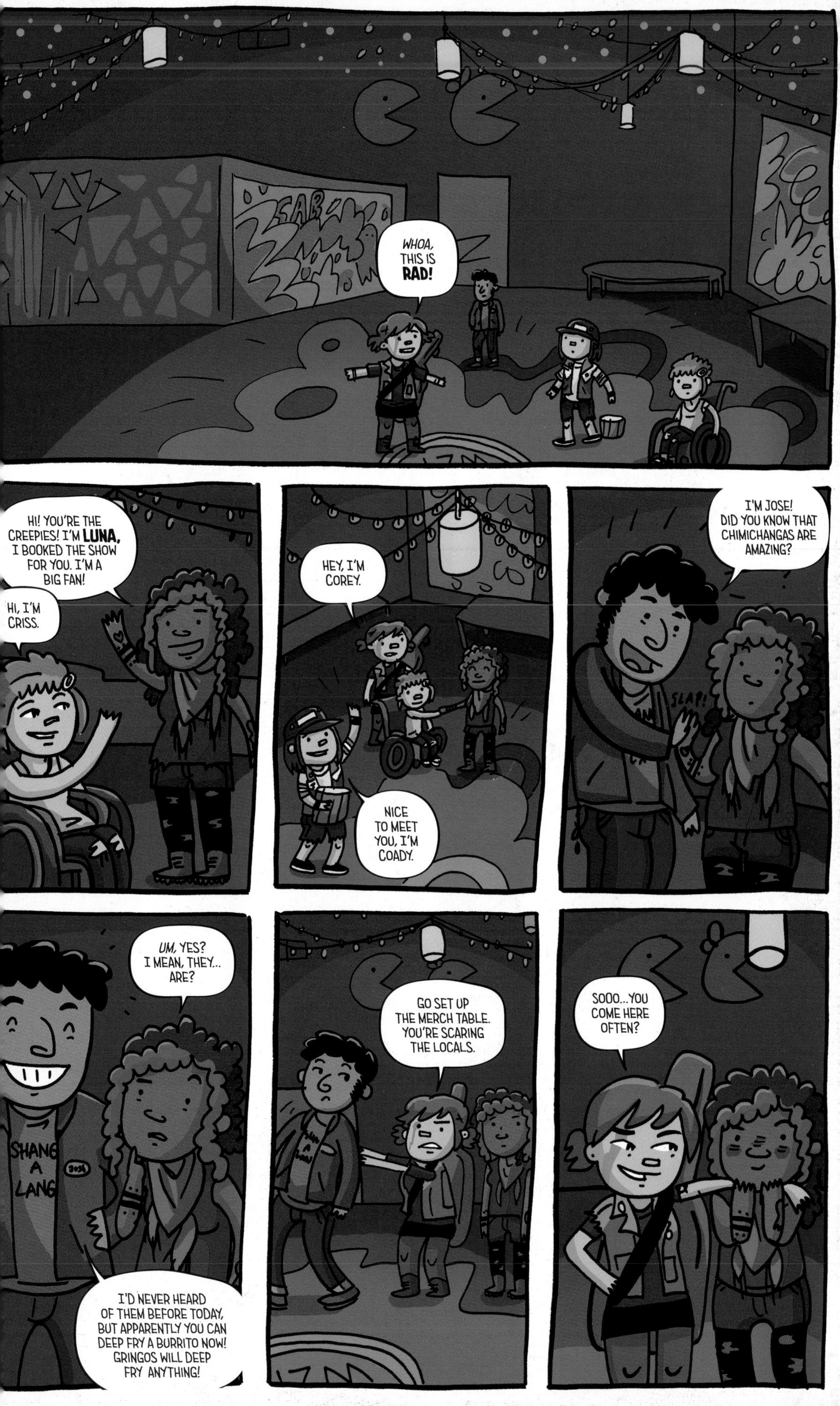
WHOA, THIS IS **RAD!**
HI! YOU'RE THE CREEPIES! I'M **LUNA,** I BOOKED THE SHOW FOR YOU. I'M A BIG FAN!
HI, I'M CRISS.
HEY, I'M COREY.
NICE TO MEET YOU, I'M COADY.
I'M JOSE! DID YOU KNOW THAT CHIMICHANGAS ARE AMAZING?
SLAP!
UM, YES? I MEAN, THEY... ARE?
SHANG A LANG
I'D NEVER HEARD OF THEM BEFORE TODAY, BUT APPARENTLY YOU CAN DEEP FRY A BURRITO NOW! GRINGOS WILL DEEP FRY ANYTHING!
GO SET UP THE MERCH TABLE. YOU'RE SCARING THE LOCALS.
SOOO...YOU COME HERE OFTEN?

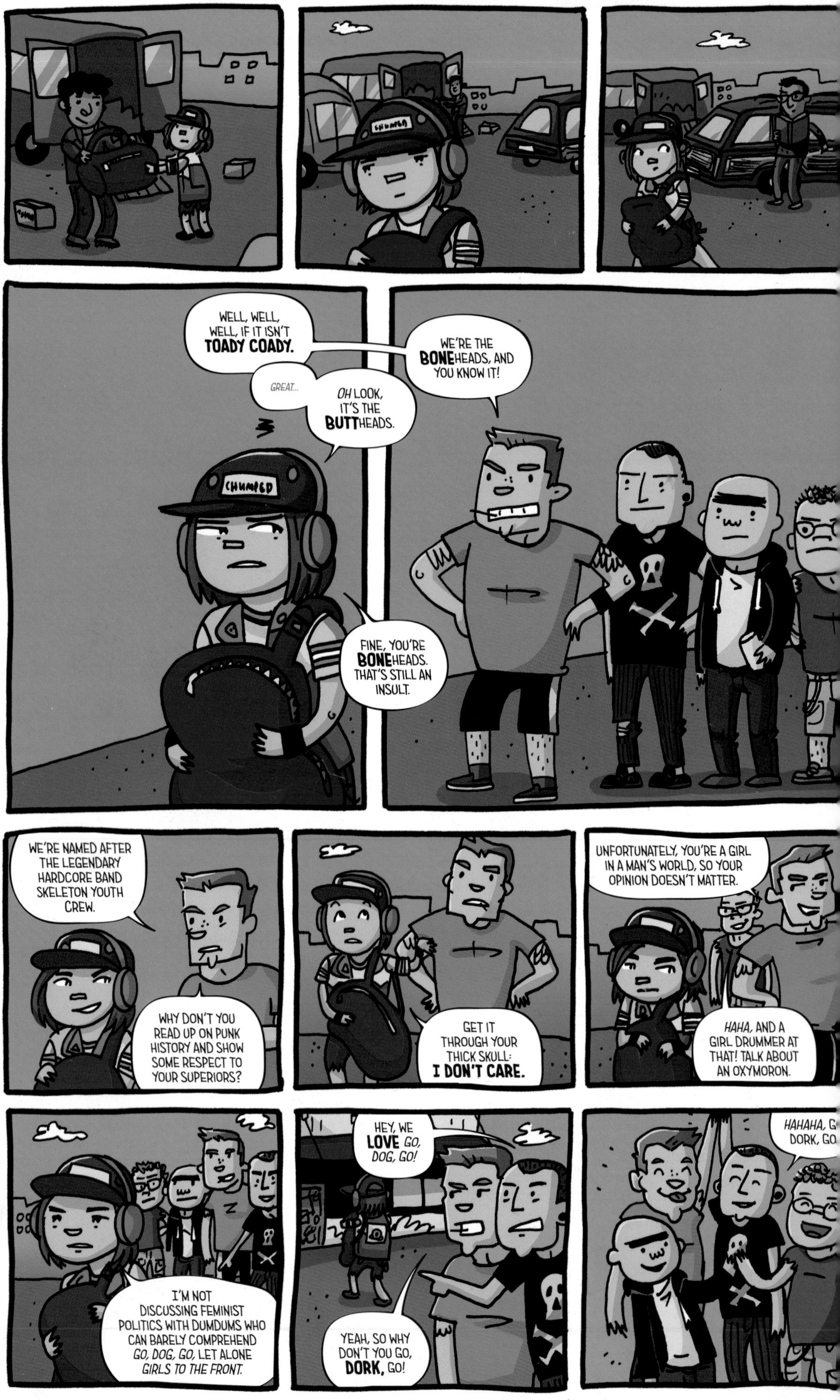

WELL, WELL, WELL, IF IT ISN'T **TOADY COADY.**
GREAT...
OH LOOK, IT'S THE **BUTT**HEADS.
WE'RE THE **BONE**HEADS, AND YOU KNOW IT!
FINE, YOU'RE **BONE**HEADS. THAT'S STILL AN INSULT.
WE'RE NAMED AFTER THE LEGENDARY HARDCORE BAND SKELETON YOUTH CREW.
WHY DON'T YOU READ UP ON PUNK HISTORY AND SHOW SOME RESPECT TO YOUR SUPERIORS?
GET IT THROUGH YOUR THICK SKULL: **I DON'T CARE.**
UNFORTUNATELY, YOU'RE A GIRL IN A MAN'S WORLD, SO YOUR OPINION DOESN'T MATTER.
HAHA, AND A GIRL DRUMMER AT THAT! TALK ABOUT AN OXYMORON.
I'M NOT DISCUSSING FEMINIST POLITICS WITH DUMDUMS WHO CAN BARELY COMPREHEND *GO, DOG, GO,* LET ALONE *GIRLS TO THE FRONT.*
HEY, WE **LOVE** *GO, DOG, GO!*
YEAH, SO WHY DON'T YOU GO, **DORK,** GO!
HAHAHA, G
DORK, GO

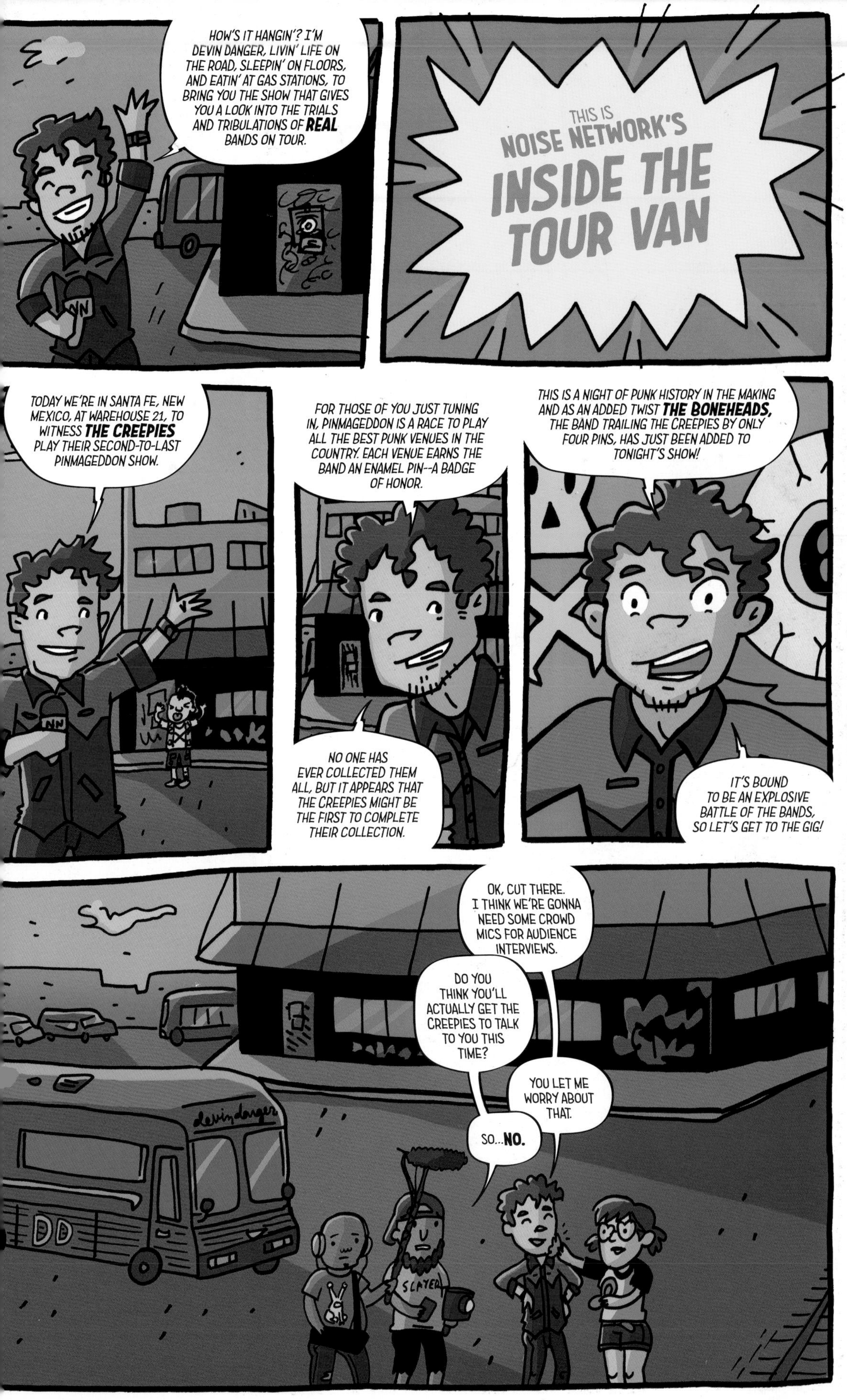
HOW'S IT HANGIN'? I'M DEVIN DANGER, LIVIN' LIFE ON THE ROAD, SLEEPIN' ON FLOORS, AND EATIN' AT GAS STATIONS, TO BRING YOU THE SHOW THAT GIVES YOU A LOOK INTO THE TRIALS AND TRIBULATIONS OF **REAL** BANDS ON TOUR.
THIS IS NOISE NETWORK'S INSIDE THE TOUR VAN
TODAY WE'RE IN SANTA FE, NEW MEXICO, AT WAREHOUSE 21, TO WITNESS **THE CREEPIES** PLAY THEIR SECOND-TO-LAST PINMAGEDDON SHOW.
NN
FOR THOSE OF YOU JUST TUNING IN, PINMAGEDDON IS A RACE TO PLAY ALL THE BEST PUNK VENUES IN THE COUNTRY. EACH VENUE EARNS THE BAND AN ENAMEL PIN--A BADGE OF HONOR.
NO ONE HAS EVER COLLECTED THEM ALL, BUT IT APPEARS THAT THE CREEPIES MIGHT BE THE FIRST TO COMPLETE THEIR COLLECTION.
THIS IS A NIGHT OF PUNK HISTORY IN THE MAKING AND AS AN ADDED TWIST **THE BONEHEADS,** THE BAND TRAILING THE CREEPIES BY ONLY FOUR PINS, HAS JUST BEEN ADDED TO TONIGHT'S SHOW!
IT'S BOUND TO BE AN EXPLOSIVE BATTLE OF THE BANDS, SO LET'S GET TO THE GIG!
OK, CUT THERE. I THINK WE'RE GONNA NEED SOME CROWD MICS FOR AUDIENCE INTERVIEWS.
DO YOU THINK YOU'LL ACTUALLY GET THE CREEPIES TO TALK TO YOU THIS TIME?
YOU LET ME WORRY ABOUT THAT.
SO...**NO.**
devin danger
DD
SLAYER

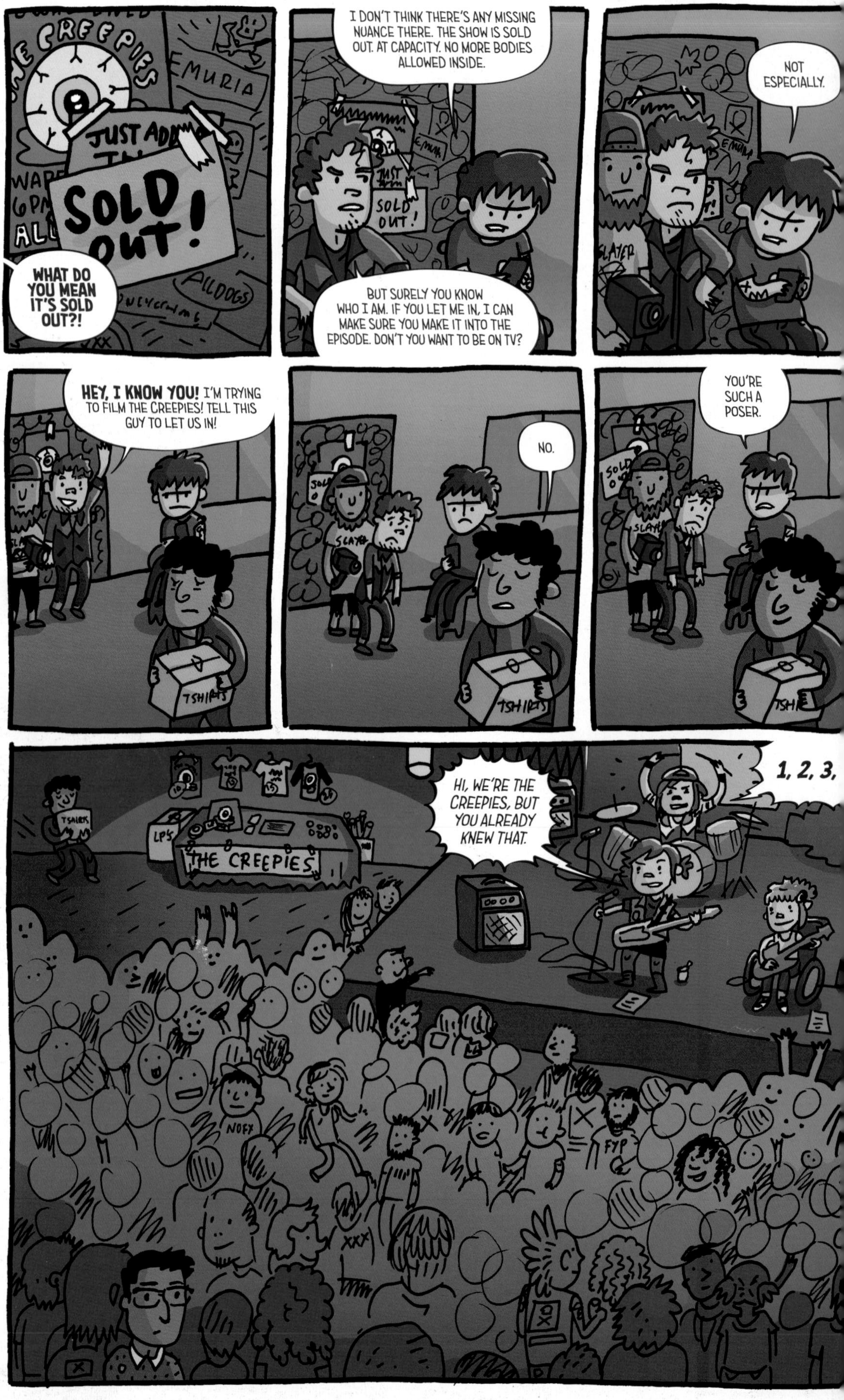
THE CREEPIES
EMURIA
JUST ADD
SOLD OUT!
WHAT DO YOU MEAN IT'S SOLD OUT?!
I DON'T THINK THERE'S ANY MISSING NUANCE THERE. THE SHOW IS SOLD OUT. AT CAPACITY. NO MORE BODIES ALLOWED INSIDE.
BUT SURELY YOU KNOW WHO I AM. IF YOU LET ME IN, I CAN MAKE SURE YOU MAKE IT INTO THE EPISODE. DON'T YOU WANT TO BE ON TV?
NOT ESPECIALLY.
HEY, I KNOW YOU! I'M TRYING TO FILM THE CREEPIES! TELL THIS GUY TO LET US IN!
NO.
YOU'RE SUCH A POSER.
HI, WE'RE THE CREEPIES, BUT YOU ALREADY KNEW THAT.
1, 2, 3,
THE CREEPIES
LP'S
NOFX

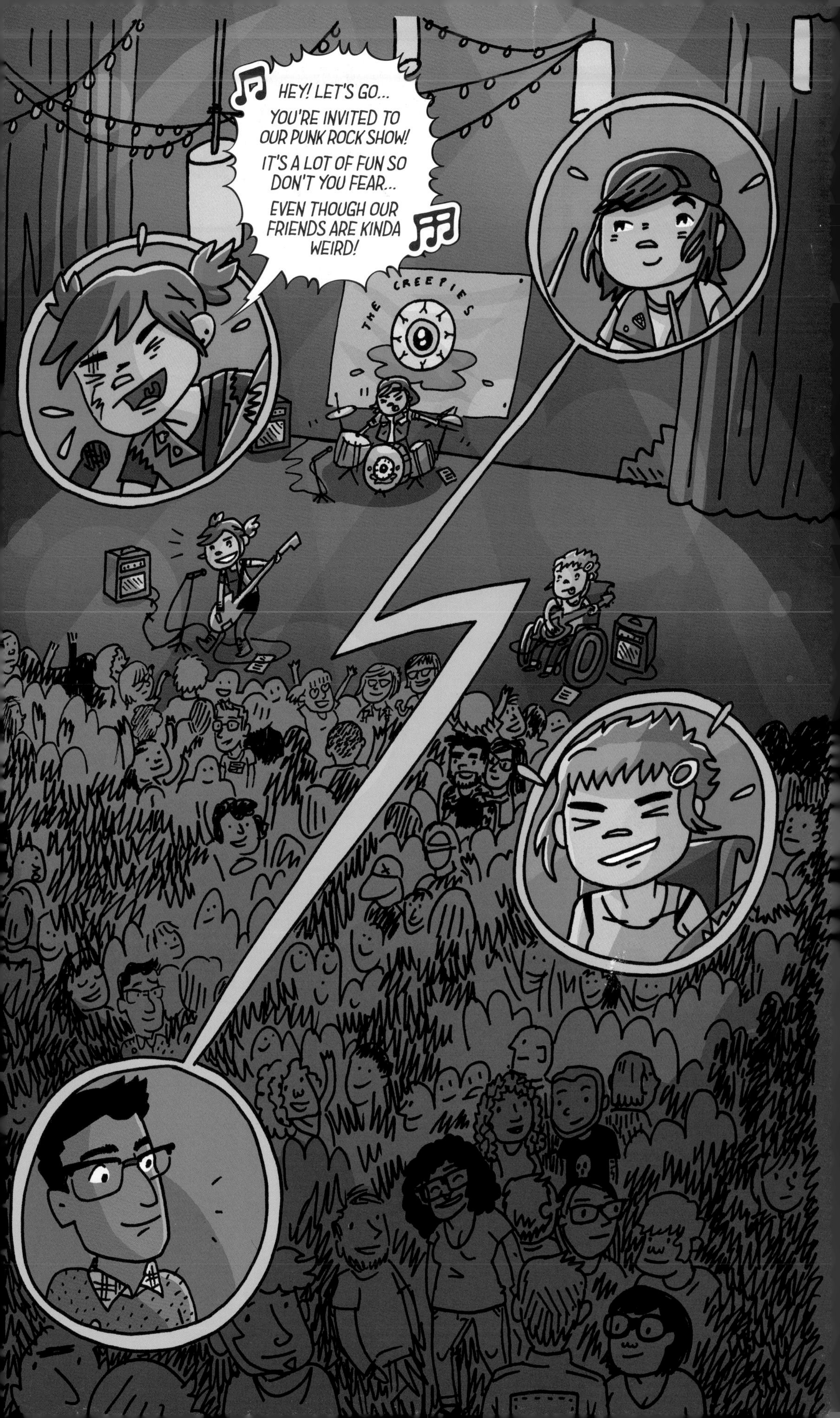
HEY! LET'S GO...
YOU'RE INVITED TO OUR PUNK ROCK SHOW!
IT'S A LOT OF FUN SO DON'T YOU FEAR...
EVEN THOUGH OUR FRIENDS ARE KINDA WEIRD!
THE CREEPIES

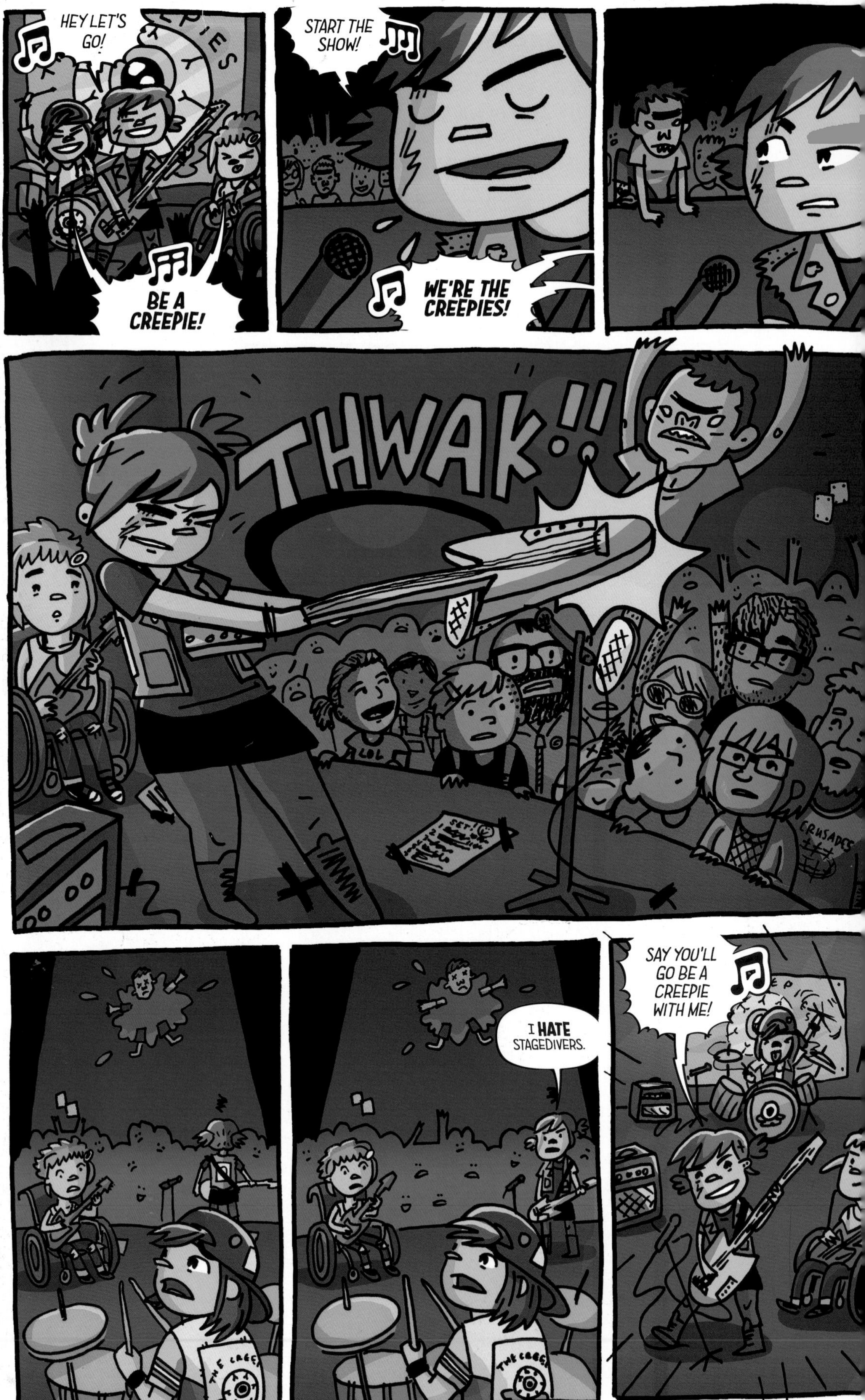
HEY LET'S GO!
BE A CREEPIE!
START THE SHOW!
WE'RE THE CREEPIES!
THWAK!!
SET!
LOL
CRUSADES
I HATE STAGEDIVERS.
SAY YOU'LL GO BE A CREEPIE WITH ME!

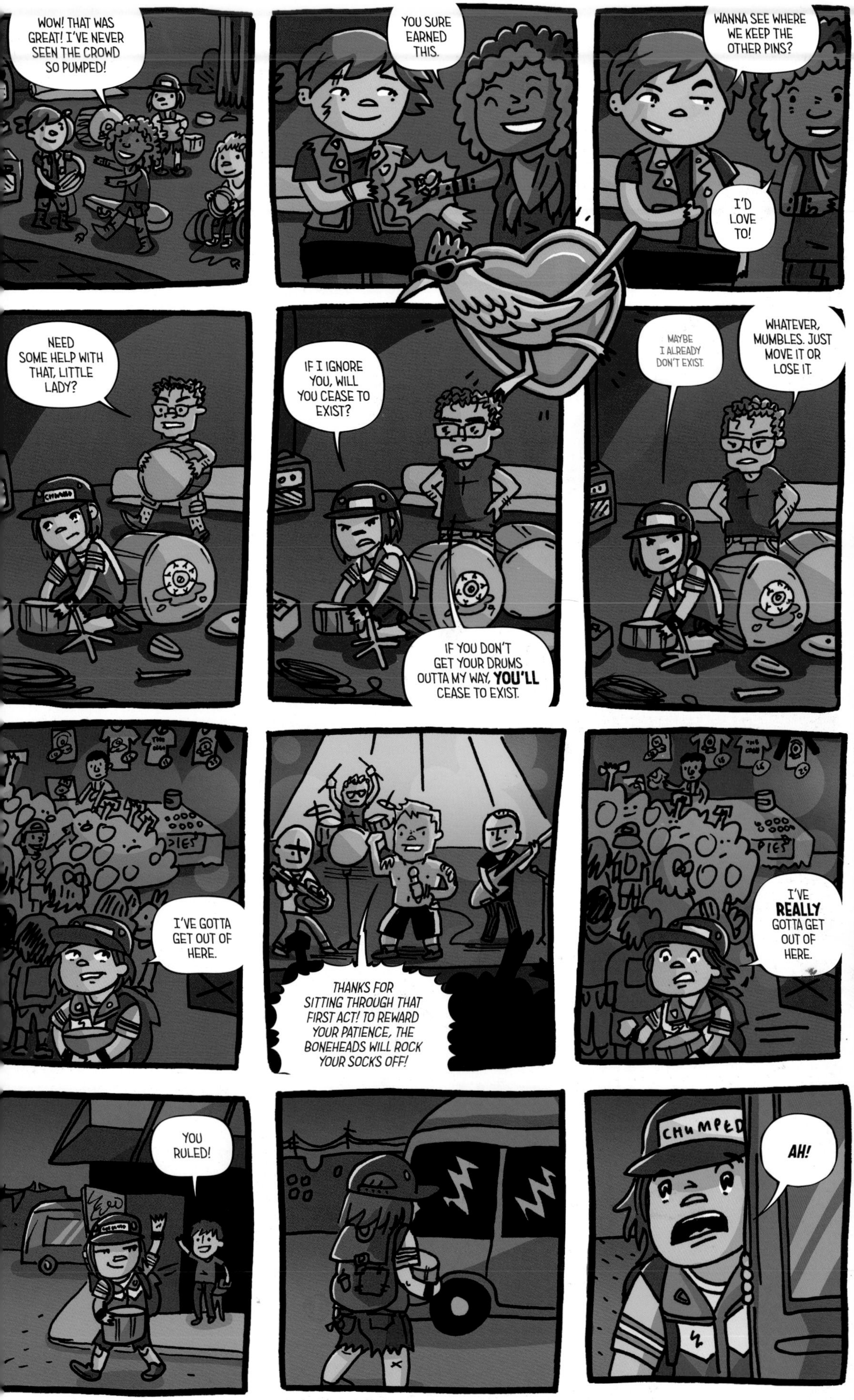
WOW! THAT WAS GREAT! I'VE NEVER SEEN THE CROWD SO PUMPED!
YOU SURE EARNED THIS.
WANNA SEE WHERE WE KEEP THE OTHER PINS?
I'D LOVE TO!
NEED SOME HELP WITH THAT, LITTLE LADY?
IF I IGNORE YOU, WILL YOU CEASE TO EXIST?
IF YOU DON'T GET YOUR DRUMS OUTTA MY WAY, **YOU'LL** CEASE TO EXIST.
MAYBE I ALREADY DON'T EXIST.
WHATEVER, MUMBLES. JUST MOVE IT OR LOSE IT.
I'VE GOTTA GET OUT OF HERE.
PIES
THANKS FOR SITTING THROUGH THAT FIRST ACT! TO REWARD YOUR PATIENCE, THE BONEHEADS WILL ROCK YOUR SOCKS OFF!
PIES
I'VE **REALLY** GOTTA GET OUT OF HERE.
YOU RULED!
CHUMPED
AH!

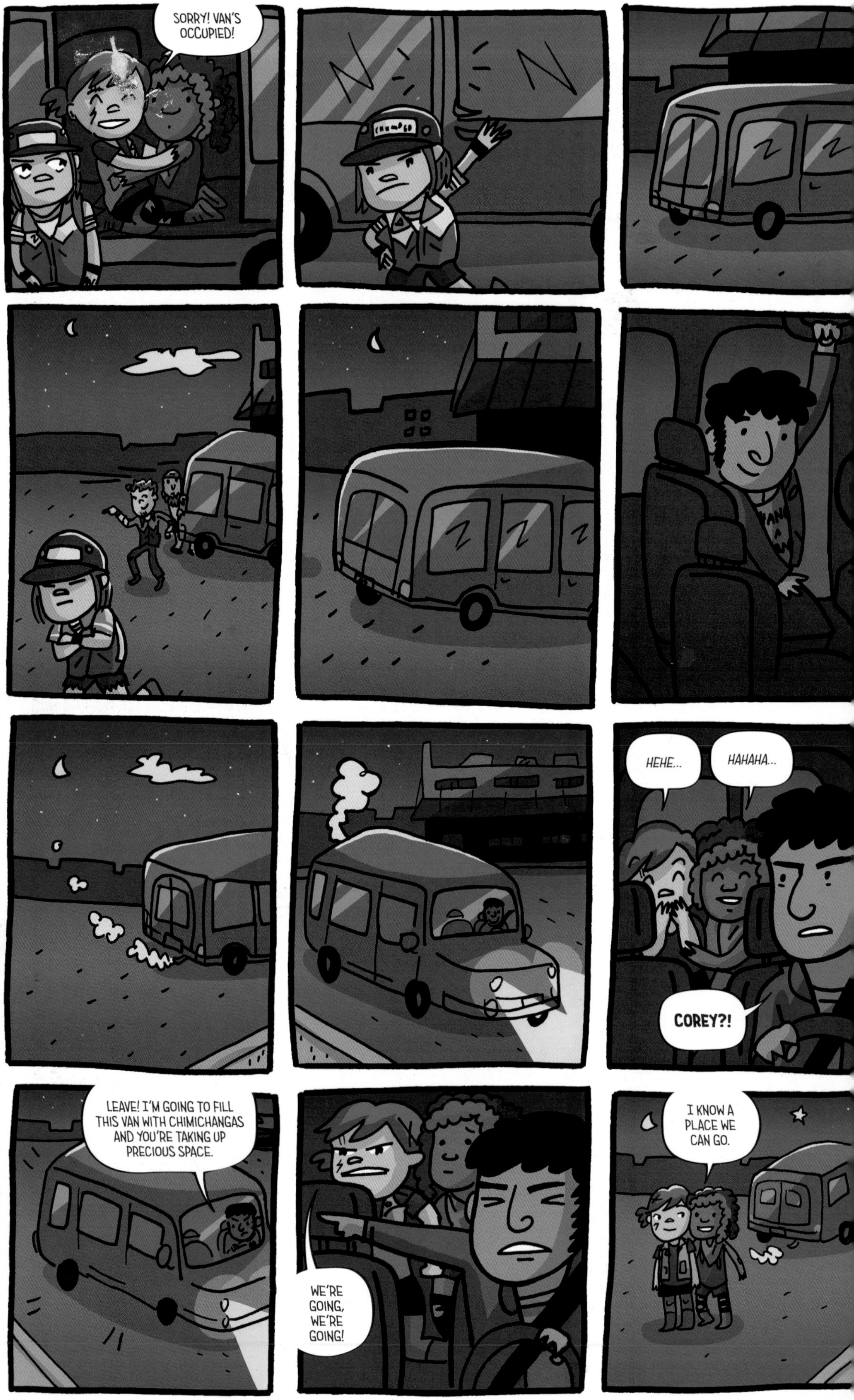
SORRY! VAN'S OCCUPIED!
HEHE...
HAHAHA...
COREY?!
LEAVE! I'M GOING TO FILL THIS VAN WITH CHIMICHANGAS AND YOU'RE TAKING UP PRECIOUS SPACE.
WE'RE GOING, WE'RE GOING!
I KNOW A PLACE WE CAN GO.

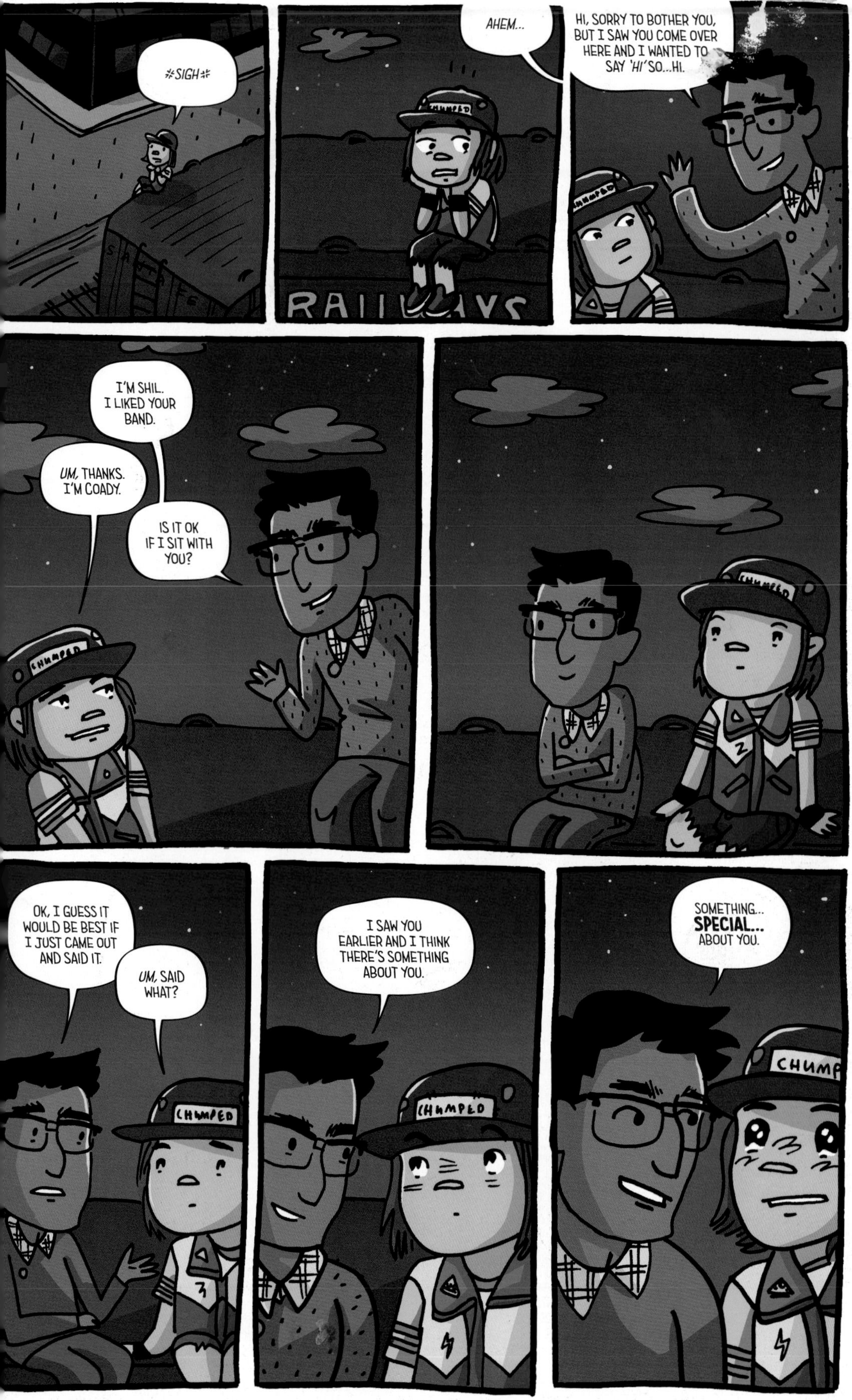

SIGH
AHEM...
RAILWAYS
HI, SORRY TO BOTHER YOU, BUT I SAW YOU COME OVER HERE AND I WANTED TO SAY 'HI' SO...HI.
CHUMPED
I'M SHIL. I LIKED YOUR BAND.
UM, THANKS. I'M COADY.
IS IT OK IF I SIT WITH YOU?
CHUMPED
CHUMPED
OK, I GUESS IT WOULD BE BEST IF I JUST CAME OUT AND SAID IT.
UM, SAID WHAT?
CHUMPED
I SAW YOU EARLIER AND I THINK THERE'S SOMETHING ABOUT YOU.
CHUMPED
SOMETHING... **SPECIAL...** ABOUT YOU.

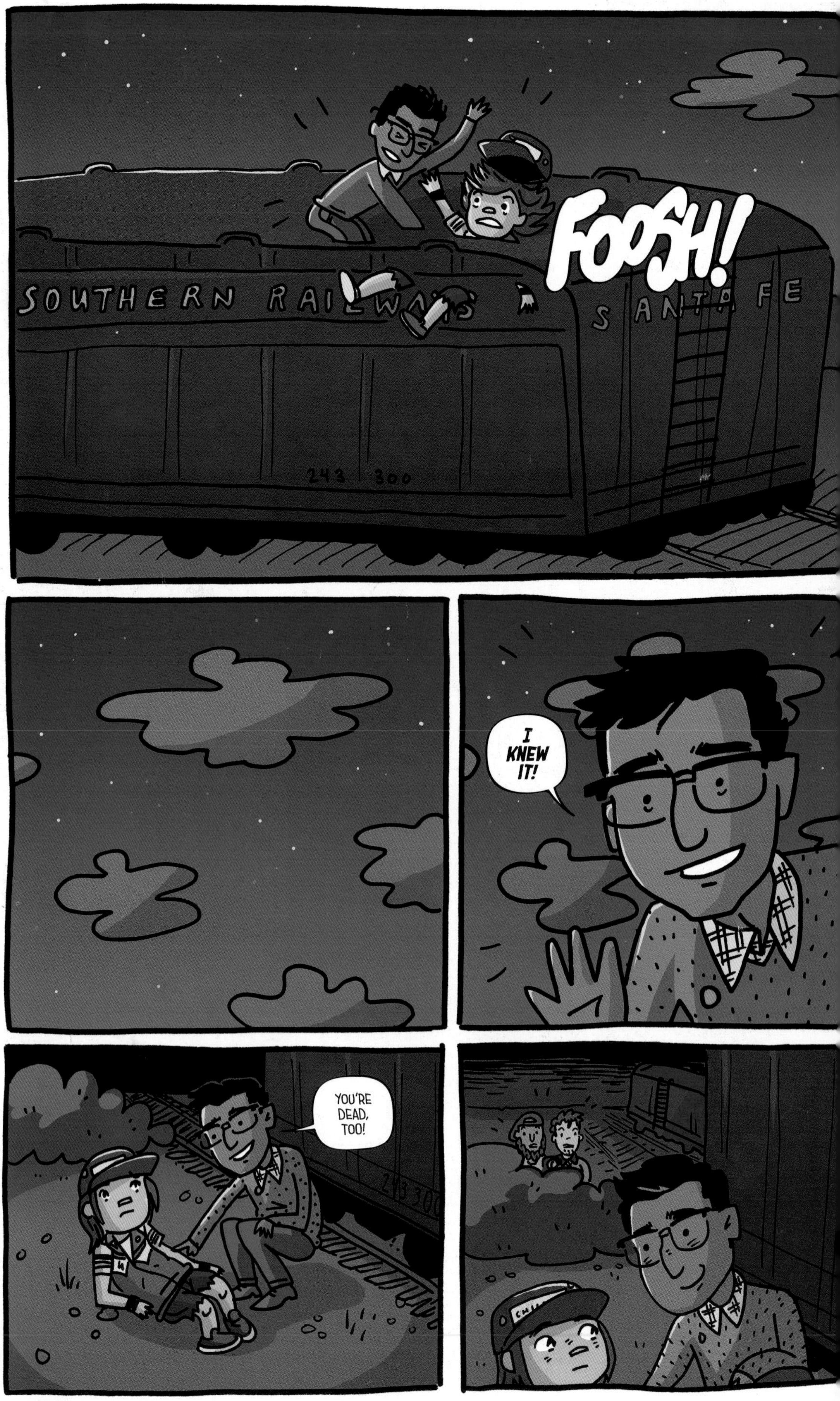
SOUTHERN RAILWAYS
SANTA FE
FOOSH!
243 300
I KNEW IT!
YOU'RE DEAD, TOO!

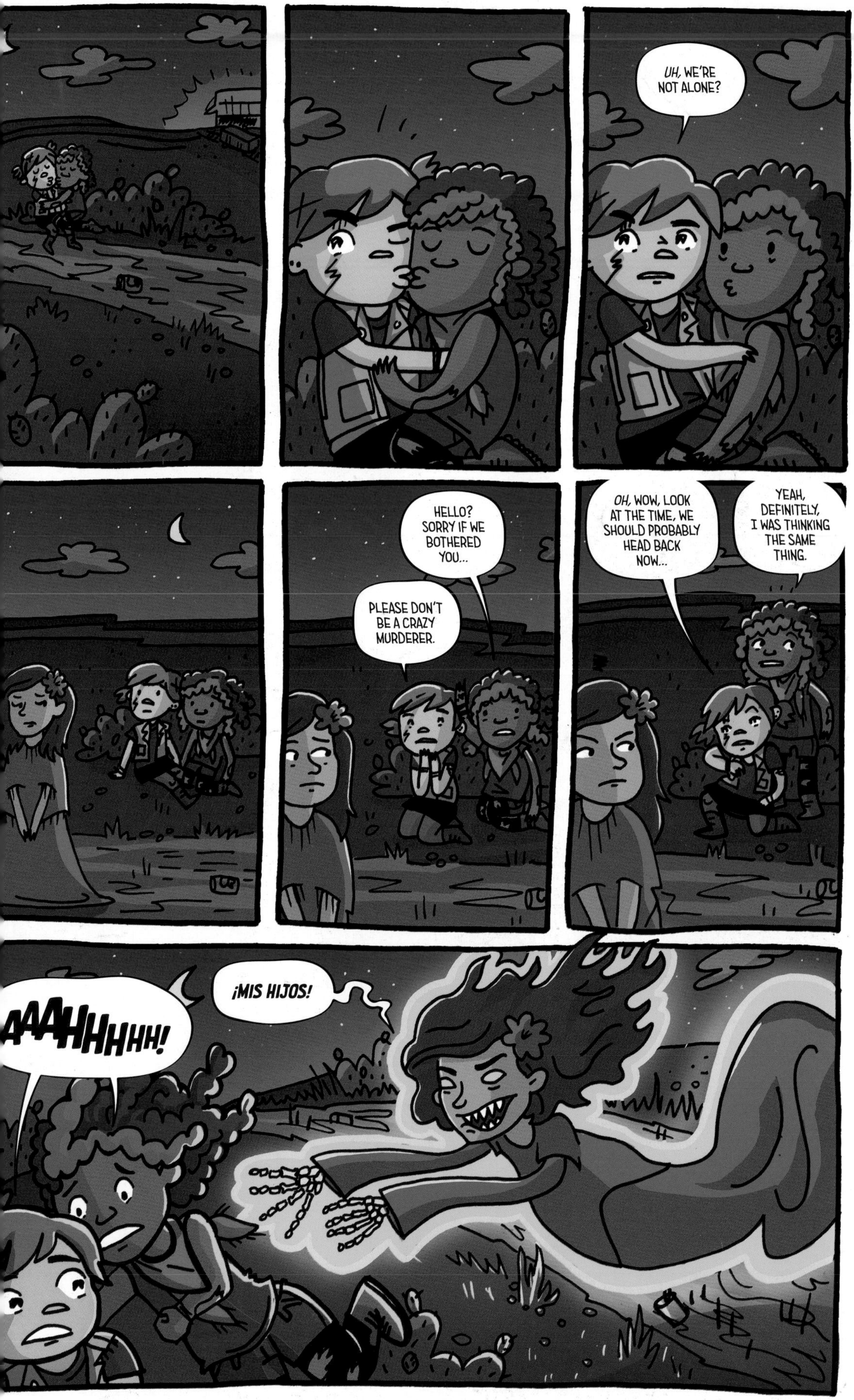
UH, WE'RE NOT ALONE?
HELLO? SORRY IF WE BOTHERED YOU...
PLEASE DON'T BE A CRAZY MURDERER.
OH, WOW, LOOK AT THE TIME, WE SHOULD PROBABLY HEAD BACK NOW...
YEAH, DEFINITELY, I WAS THINKING THE SAME THING.
AAAHHHHHH!
¡MIS HIJOS!

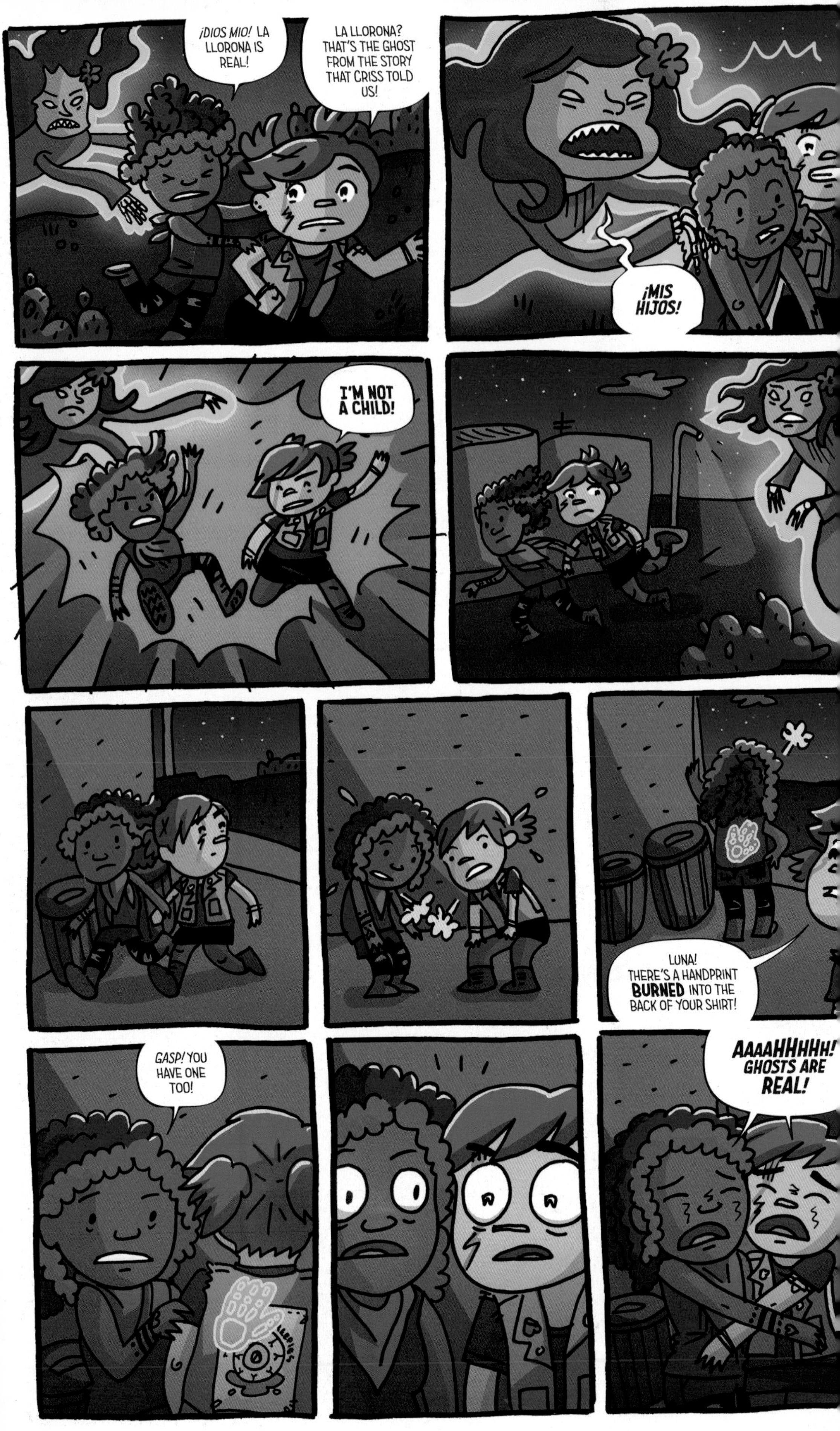
¡DIOS MIO! LA LLORONA IS REAL!
LA LLORONA? THAT'S THE GHOST FROM THE STORY THAT CRISS TOLD US!
¡MIS HIJOS!
I'M NOT A CHILD!
LUNA! THERE'S A HANDPRINT **BURNED** INTO THE BACK OF YOUR SHIRT!
GASP! YOU HAVE ONE TOO!
AAAAHHHHH! GHOSTS ARE REAL!

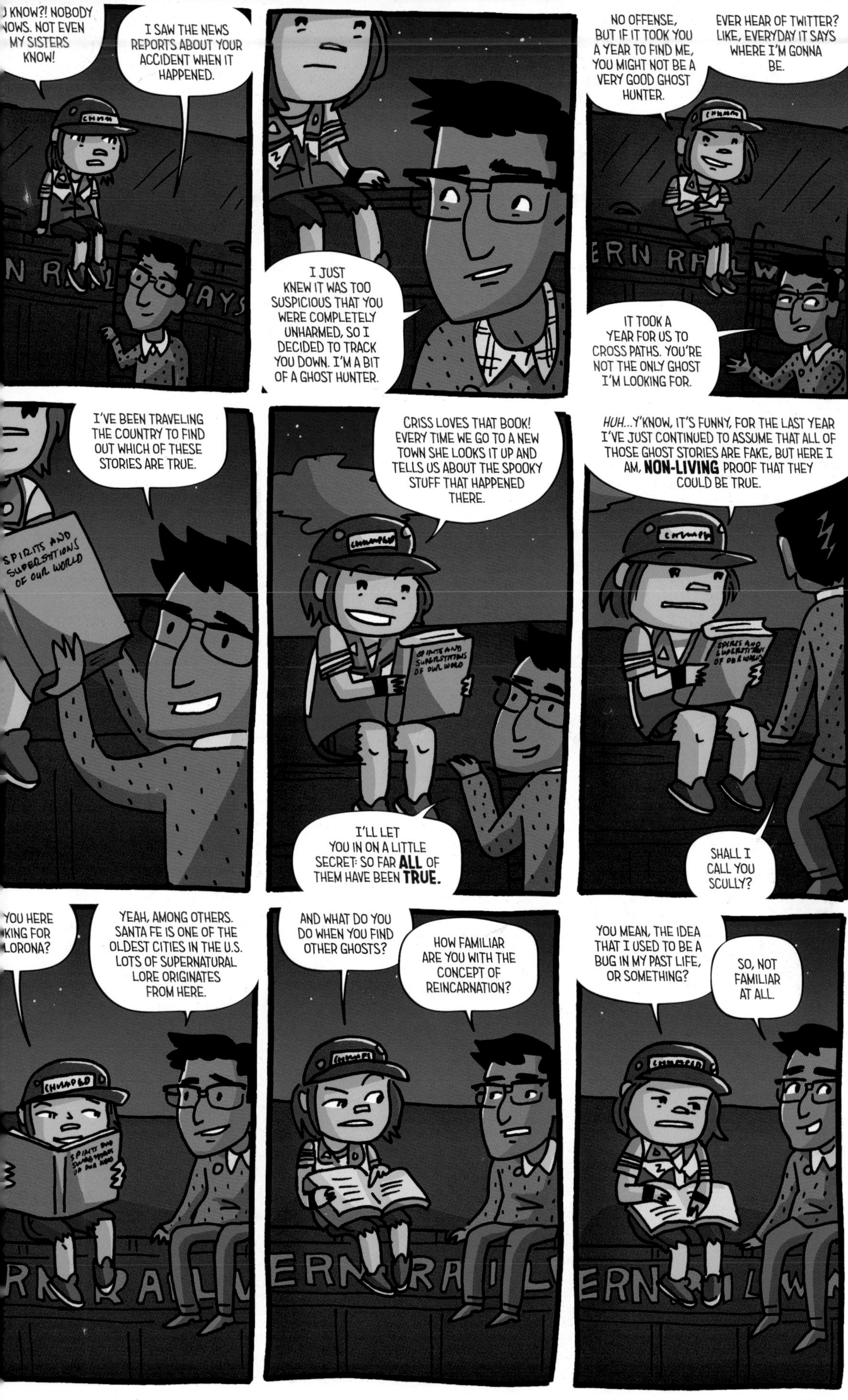

KNOW?! NOBODY
NOWS. NOT EVEN MY SISTERS KNOW!
I SAW THE NEWS REPORTS ABOUT YOUR ACCIDENT WHEN IT HAPPENED.
I JUST KNEW IT WAS TOO SUSPICIOUS THAT YOU WERE COMPLETELY UNHARMED, SO I DECIDED TO TRACK YOU DOWN. I'M A BIT OF A GHOST HUNTER.
NO OFFENSE, BUT IF IT TOOK YOU A YEAR TO FIND ME, YOU MIGHT NOT BE A VERY GOOD GHOST HUNTER.
EVER HEAR OF TWITTER? LIKE, EVERYDAY IT SAYS WHERE I'M GONNA BE.
IT TOOK A YEAR FOR US TO CROSS PATHS. YOU'RE NOT THE ONLY GHOST I'M LOOKING FOR.
I'VE BEEN TRAVELING THE COUNTRY TO FIND OUT WHICH OF THESE STORIES ARE TRUE.
SPIRITS AND SUPERSTITIONS OF OUR WORLD
CRISS LOVES THAT BOOK! EVERY TIME WE GO TO A NEW TOWN SHE LOOKS IT UP AND TELLS US ABOUT THE SPOOKY STUFF THAT HAPPENED THERE.
I'LL LET YOU IN ON A LITTLE SECRET: SO FAR **ALL** OF THEM HAVE BEEN **TRUE.**
HUH...Y'KNOW, IT'S FUNNY, FOR THE LAST YEAR I'VE JUST CONTINUED TO ASSUME THAT ALL OF THOSE GHOST STORIES ARE FAKE, BUT HERE I AM, **NON-LIVING** PROOF THAT THEY COULD BE TRUE.
SHALL I CALL YOU SCULLY?
YOU HERE
KING FOR
LORONA?
YEAH, AMONG OTHERS. SANTA FE IS ONE OF THE OLDEST CITIES IN THE U.S. LOTS OF SUPERNATURAL LORE ORIGINATES FROM HERE.
AND WHAT DO YOU DO WHEN YOU FIND OTHER GHOSTS?
HOW FAMILIAR ARE YOU WITH THE CONCEPT OF REINCARNATION?
YOU MEAN, THE IDEA THAT I USED TO BE A BUG IN MY PAST LIFE, OR SOMETHING?
SO, NOT FAMILIAR AT ALL.

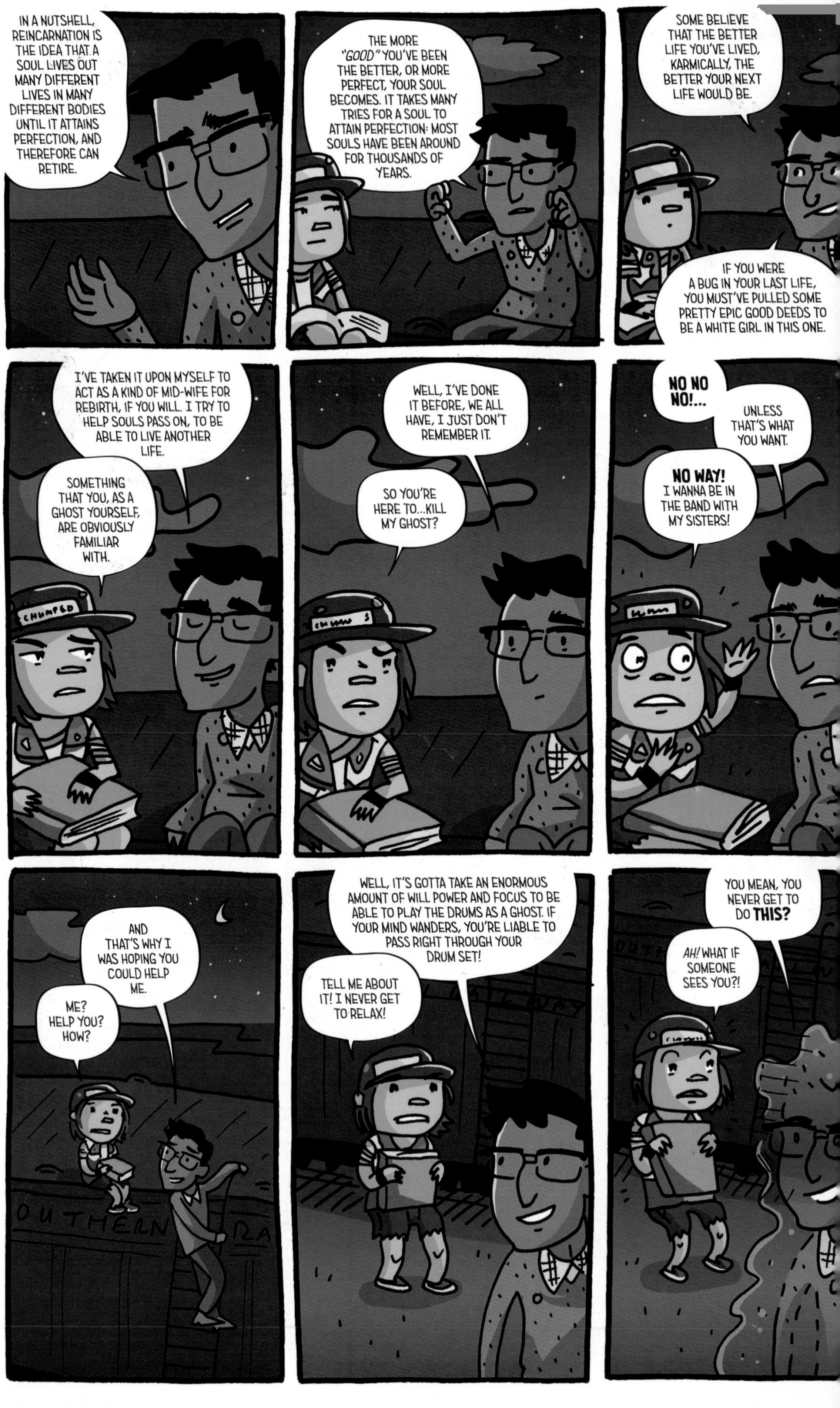

IN A NUTSHELL, REINCARNATION IS THE IDEA THAT A SOUL LIVES OUT MANY DIFFERENT LIVES IN MANY DIFFERENT BODIES UNTIL IT ATTAINS PERFECTION, AND THEREFORE CAN RETIRE.
THE MORE "GOOD" YOU'VE BEEN THE BETTER, OR MORE PERFECT, YOUR SOUL BECOMES. IT TAKES MANY TRIES FOR A SOUL TO ATTAIN PERFECTION: MOST SOULS HAVE BEEN AROUND FOR THOUSANDS OF YEARS.
SOME BELIEVE THAT THE BETTER LIFE YOU'VE LIVED, KARMICALLY, THE BETTER YOUR NEXT LIFE WOULD BE.
IF YOU WERE A BUG IN YOUR LAST LIFE, YOU MUST'VE PULLED SOME PRETTY EPIC GOOD DEEDS TO BE A WHITE GIRL IN THIS ONE.
I'VE TAKEN IT UPON MYSELF TO ACT AS A KIND OF MID-WIFE FOR REBIRTH, IF YOU WILL. I TRY TO HELP SOULS PASS ON, TO BE ABLE TO LIVE ANOTHER LIFE.
SOMETHING THAT YOU, AS A GHOST YOURSELF, ARE OBVIOUSLY FAMILIAR WITH.
WELL, I'VE DONE IT BEFORE, WE ALL HAVE, I JUST DON'T REMEMBER IT.
SO YOU'RE HERE TO...KILL MY GHOST?
NO NO NO!...
UNLESS THAT'S WHAT YOU WANT.
NO WAY! I WANNA BE IN THE BAND WITH MY SISTERS!
AND THAT'S WHY I WAS HOPING YOU COULD HELP ME.
ME? HELP YOU? HOW?
WELL, IT'S GOTTA TAKE AN ENORMOUS AMOUNT OF WILL POWER AND FOCUS TO BE ABLE TO PLAY THE DRUMS AS A GHOST. IF YOUR MIND WANDERS, YOU'RE LIABLE TO PASS RIGHT THROUGH YOUR DRUM SET!
TELL ME ABOUT IT! I NEVER GET TO RELAX!
YOU MEAN, YOU NEVER GET TO DO THIS?
AH! WHAT IF SOMEONE SEES YOU?!

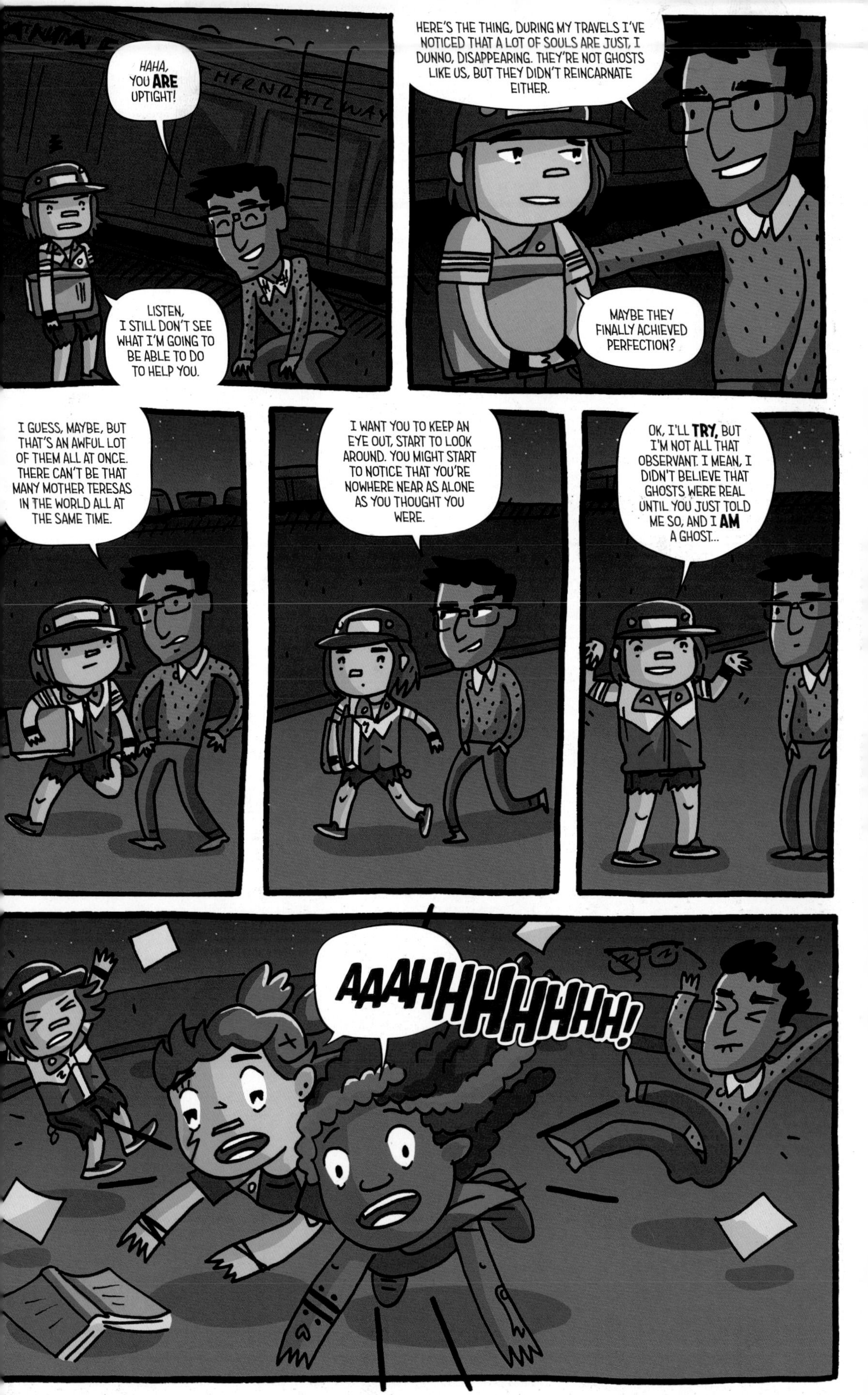
HAHA, YOU **ARE** UPTIGHT!
LISTEN, I STILL DON'T SEE WHAT I'M GOING TO BE ABLE TO DO TO HELP YOU.
HERE'S THE THING, DURING MY TRAVELS I'VE NOTICED THAT A LOT OF SOULS ARE JUST, I DUNNO, DISAPPEARING. THEY'RE NOT GHOSTS LIKE US, BUT THEY DIDN'T REINCARNATE EITHER.
MAYBE THEY FINALLY ACHIEVED PERFECTION?
I GUESS, MAYBE, BUT THAT'S AN AWFUL LOT OF THEM ALL AT ONCE. THERE CAN'T BE THAT MANY MOTHER TERESAS IN THE WORLD ALL AT THE SAME TIME.
I WANT YOU TO KEEP AN EYE OUT, START TO LOOK AROUND. YOU MIGHT START TO NOTICE THAT YOU'RE NOWHERE NEAR AS ALONE AS YOU THOUGHT YOU WERE.
OK, I'LL **TRY,** BUT I'M NOT ALL THAT OBSERVANT. I MEAN, I DIDN'T BELIEVE THAT GHOSTS WERE REAL UNTIL YOU JUST TOLD ME SO, AND I **AM** A GHOST...
AAAHHHHHHH!

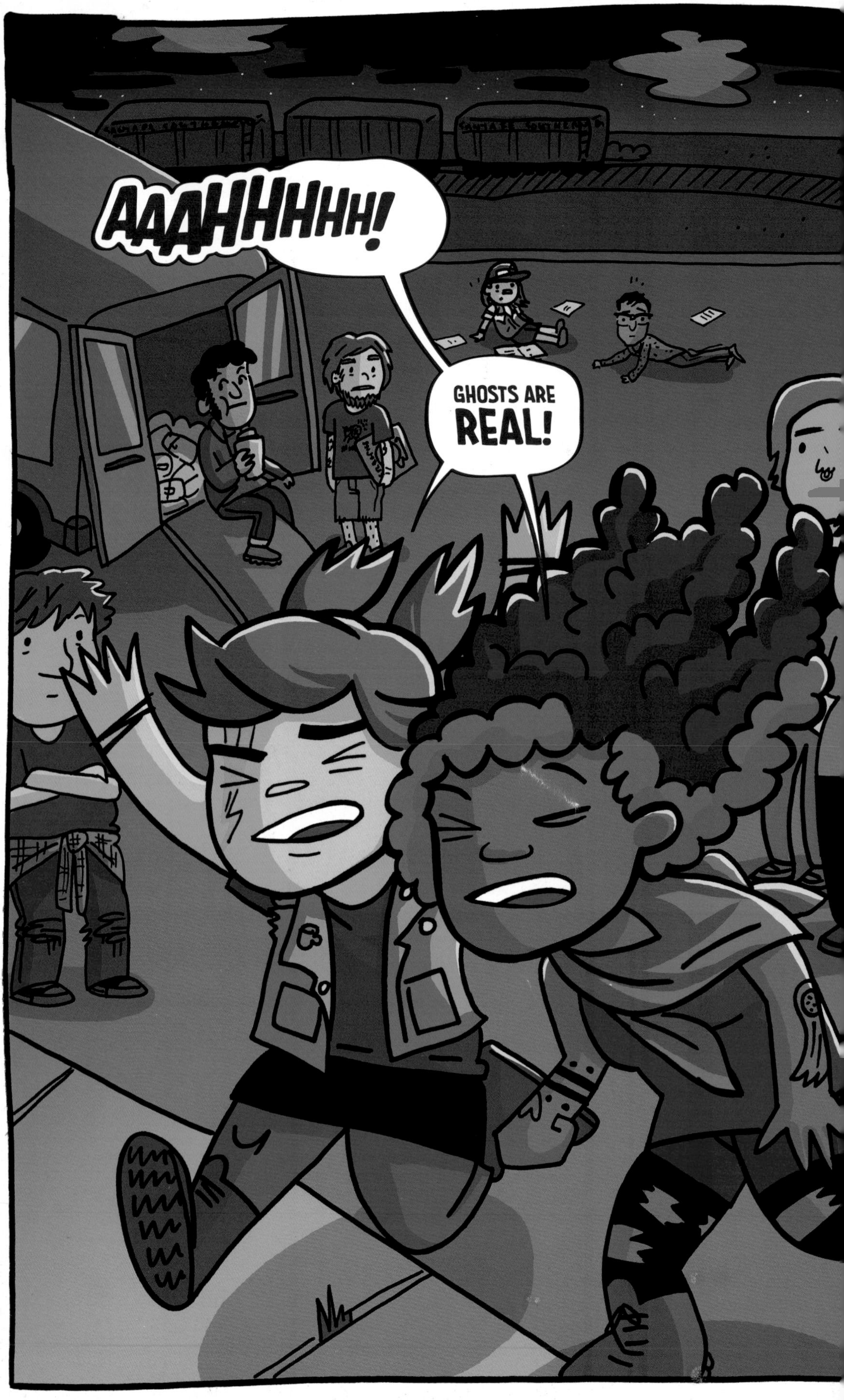
AAAHHHHH!
GHOSTS ARE REAL!

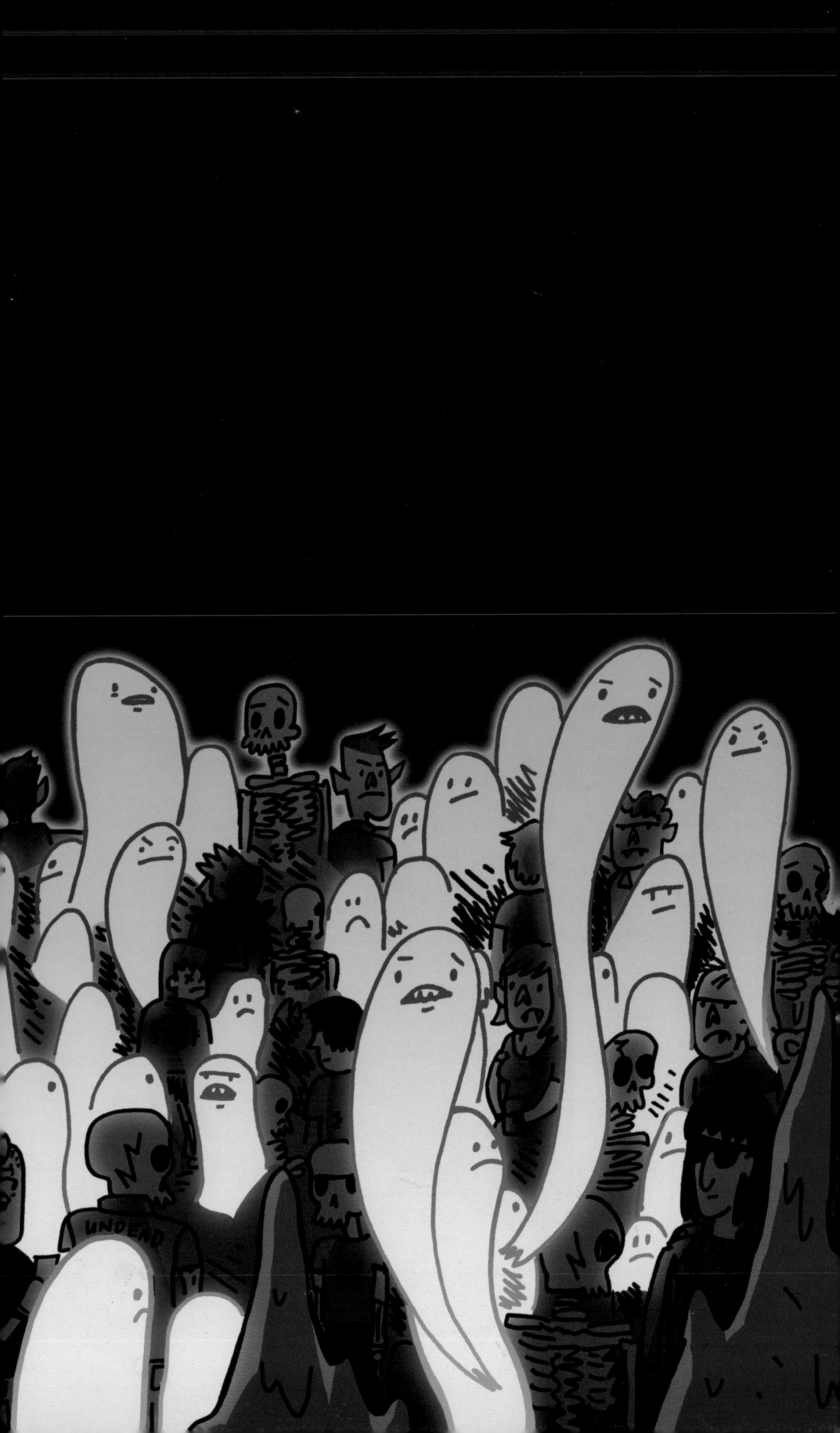
UNDEAD

CHAPTER TWO

PAPER TIGER
SAN ANTONIO, TX

TRUNK SPACE
PHOENIX, AZ

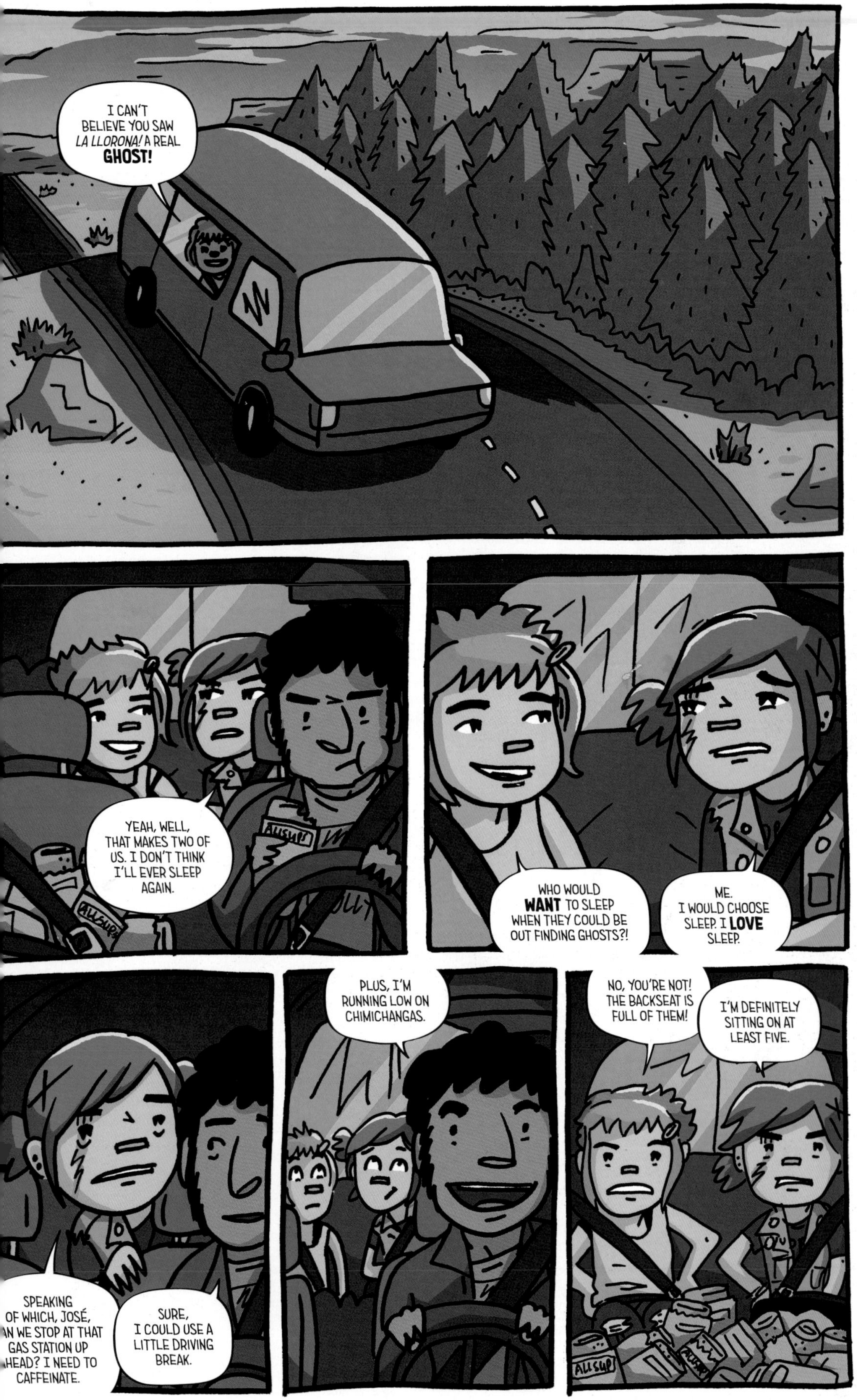
I CAN'T BELIEVE YOU SAW *LA LLORONA!* A REAL **GHOST!**
YEAH, WELL, THAT MAKES TWO OF US. I DON'T THINK I'LL EVER SLEEP AGAIN.
WHO WOULD **WANT** TO SLEEP WHEN THEY COULD BE OUT FINDING GHOSTS?!
ME. I WOULD CHOOSE SLEEP. I **LOVE** SLEEP.
SPEAKING OF WHICH, JOSÉ, AN WE STOP AT THAT GAS STATION UP HEAD? I NEED TO CAFFEINATE.
SURE, I COULD USE A LITTLE DRIVING BREAK.
PLUS, I'M RUNNING LOW ON CHIMICHANGAS.
NO, YOU'RE NOT! THE BACKSEAT IS FULL OF THEM!
I'M DEFINITELY SITTING ON AT LEAST FIVE.

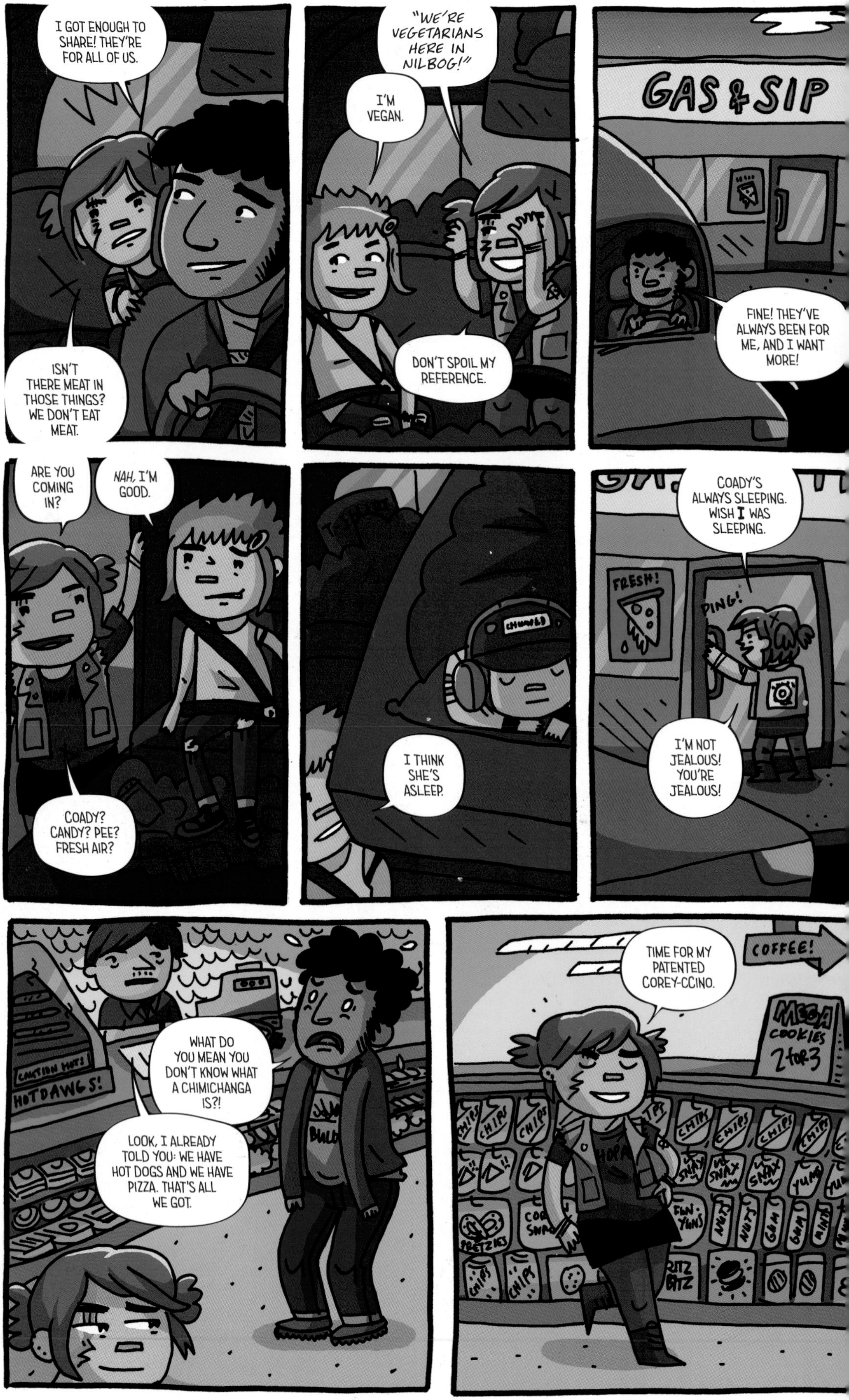
I GOT ENOUGH TO SHARE! THEY'RE FOR ALL OF US.
ISN'T THERE MEAT IN THOSE THINGS? WE DON'T EAT MEAT.
"WE'RE VEGETARIANS HERE IN NILBOG!"
I'M VEGAN.
DON'T SPOIL MY REFERENCE.
GAS & SIP
FINE! THEY'VE ALWAYS BEEN FOR ME, AND I WANT MORE!
ARE YOU COMING IN?
NAH, I'M GOOD.
COADY? CANDY? PEE? FRESH AIR?
I THINK SHE'S ASLEEP.
COADY'S ALWAYS SLEEPING. WISH I WAS SLEEPING.
FRESH!
PING!
I'M NOT JEALOUS! YOU'RE JEALOUS!
CAUTION HOT!
HOTDAWGS!
WHAT DO YOU MEAN YOU DON'T KNOW WHAT A CHIMICHANGA IS?!
LOOK, I ALREADY TOLD YOU: WE HAVE HOT DOGS AND WE HAVE PIZZA. THAT'S ALL WE GOT.
TIME FOR MY PATENTED COREY-CCINO.
COFFEE!
MEGA COOKIES 2 for 3

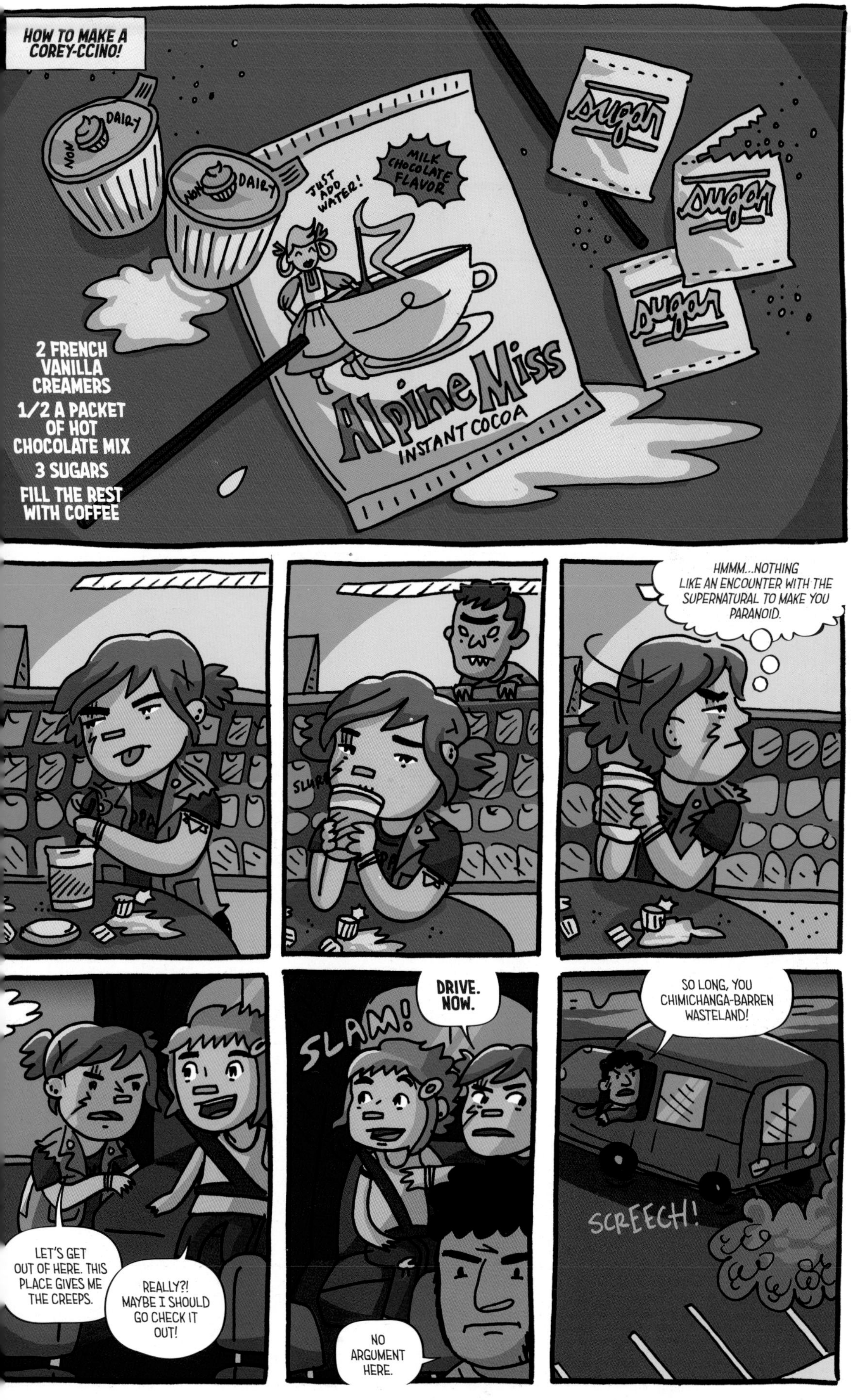
HOW TO MAKE A COREY-CCINO!
NON DAIRY
NON DAIRY
JUST ADD WATER!
MILK CHOCOLATE FLAVOR
sugar
sugar
sugar
AlpineMiss
INSTANT COCOA
2 FRENCH VANILLA CREAMERS
1/2 A PACKET OF HOT CHOCOLATE MIX
3 SUGARS
FILL THE REST WITH COFFEE
SLURP
HMMM...NOTHING LIKE AN ENCOUNTER WITH THE SUPERNATURAL TO MAKE YOU PARANOID.
LET'S GET OUT OF HERE. THIS PLACE GIVES ME THE CREEPS.
REALLY?! MAYBE I SHOULD GO CHECK IT OUT!
SLAM!
DRIVE. NOW.
NO ARGUMENT HERE.
SO LONG, YOU CHIMICHANGA-BARREN WASTELAND!
SCREECH!

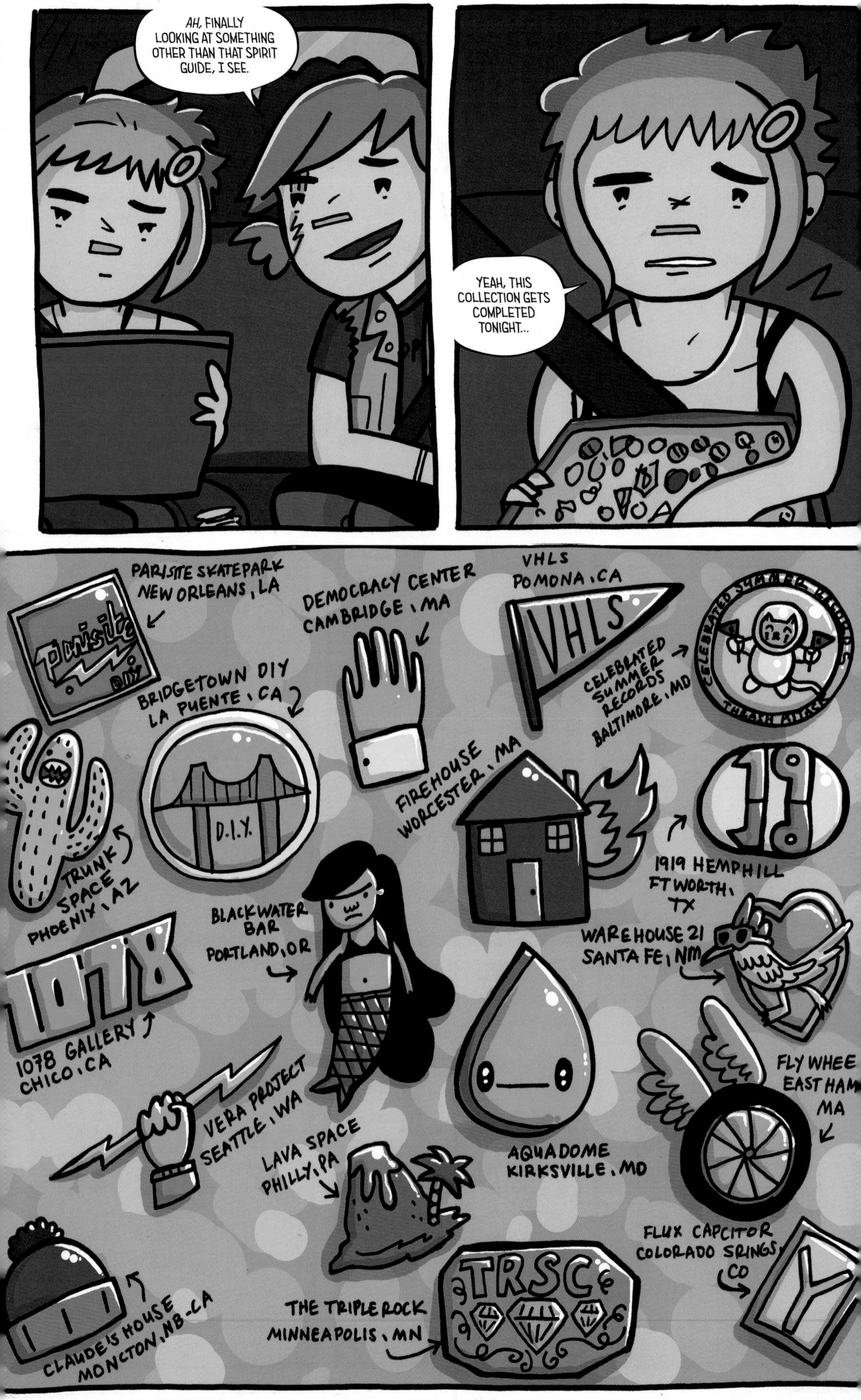

AH, FINALLY LOOKING AT SOMETHING OTHER THAN THAT SPIRIT GUIDE, I SEE.
YEAH, THIS COLLECTION GETS COMPLETED TONIGHT...
PARISITE SKATEPARK NEW ORLEANS, LA
DEMOCRACY CENTER CAMBRIDGE, MA
VHLS POMONA, CA
VHLS
CELEBRATED SUMMER RECORDS BALTIMORE, MD
BRIDGETOWN DIY LA PUENTE, CA
D.I.Y.
FIREHOUSE WORCESTER, MA
TRUNK SPACE PHOENIX, AZ
1919 HEMPHILL FT WORTH, TX
BLACKWATER BAR PORTLAND, OR
WAREHOUSE 21 SANTA FE, NM
1078
1078 GALLERY CHICO, CA
FLY WHEE EAST HAM MA
VERA PROJECT SEATTLE, WA
LAVA SPACE PHILLY, PA
AQUADOME KIRKSVILLE, MO
FLUX CAPCITOR COLORADO SRINGS, CO
TRSC
THE TRIPLE ROCK MINNEAPOLIS, MN
CLAUDE'S HOUSE MONCTON, NB - CA

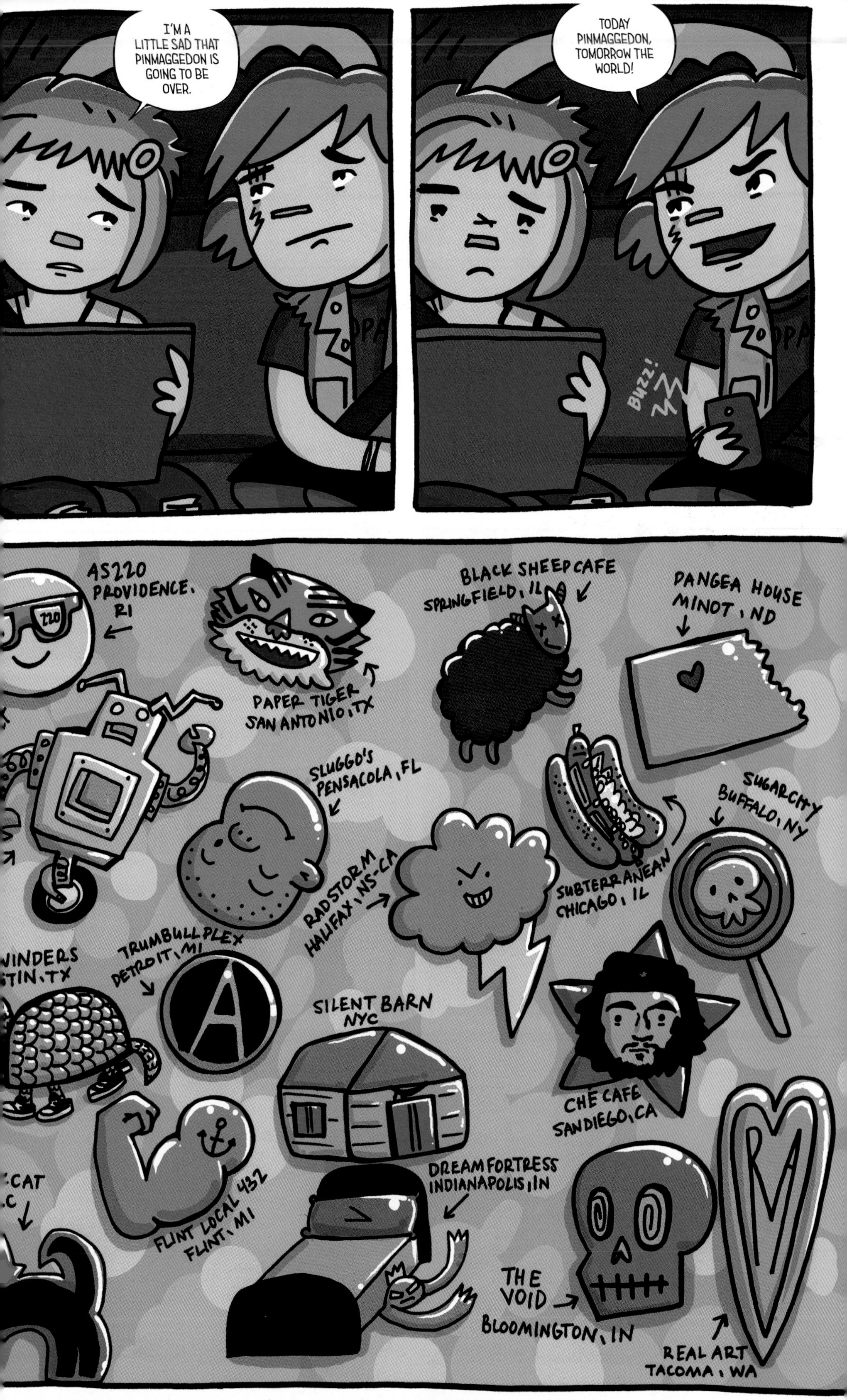
I'M A LITTLE SAD THAT PINMAGGEDON IS GOING TO BE OVER.
TODAY PINMAGGEDON, TOMORROW THE WORLD!
BUZZ!
AS220 PROVIDENCE, RI
PAPER TIGER SAN ANTONIO, TX
BLACK SHEEP CAFE SPRINGFIELD, IL
PANGEA HOUSE MINOT, ND
SLUGGO'S PENSACOLA, FL
RADSTORM HALIFAX, NS-CA
SUBTERRANEAN CHICAGO, IL
SUGARCITY BUFFALO, NY
WINDERS
TRUMBULLPLEX DETROIT, MI
SILENT BARN NYC
CHE CAFE SAN DIEGO, CA
FLINT LOCAL 432 FLINT, MI
DREAM FORTRESS INDIANAPOLIS, IN
THE VOID BLOOMINGTON, IN
REAL ART TACOMA, WA

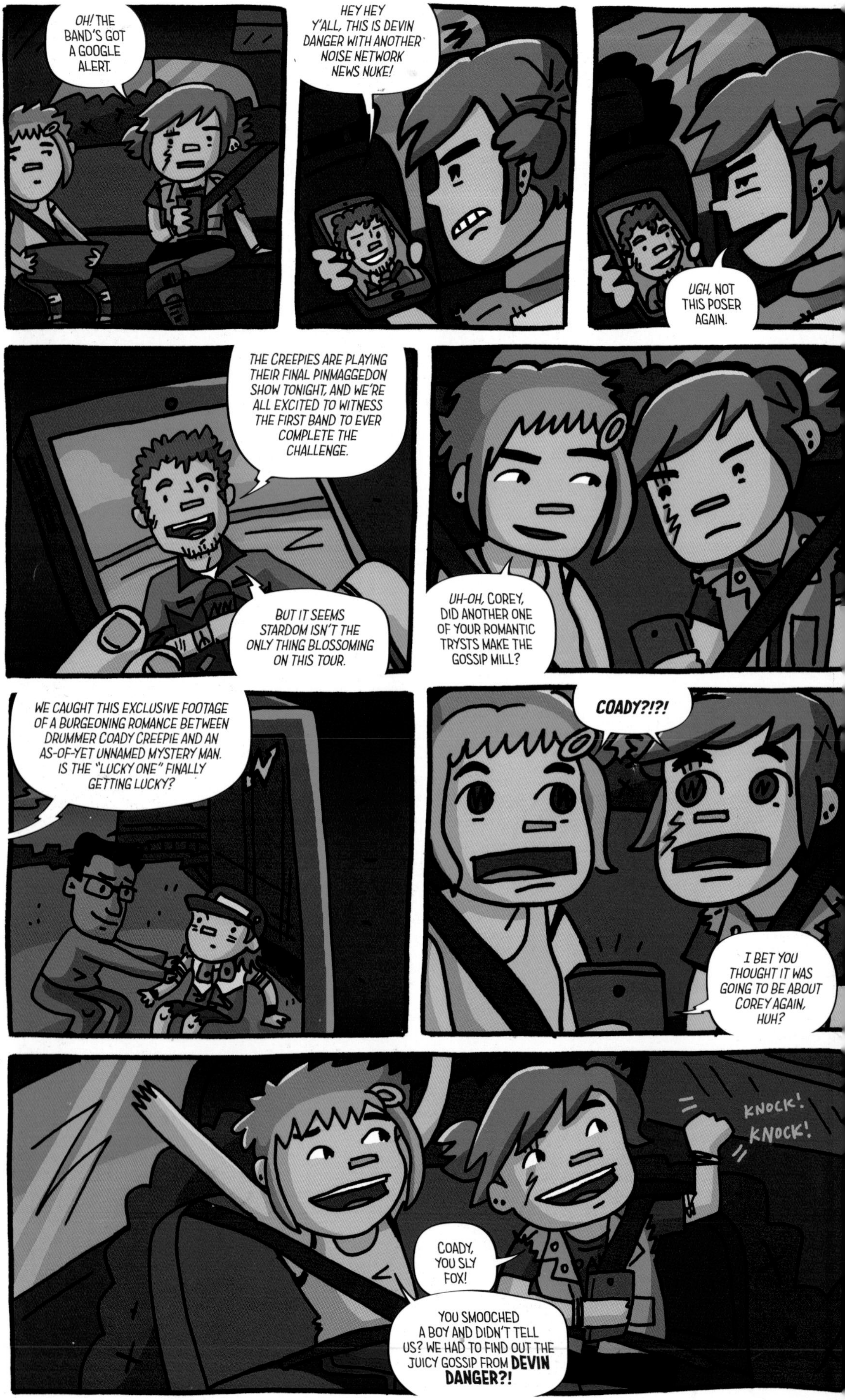
OH! THE BAND'S GOT A GOOGLE ALERT.
HEY HEY Y'ALL, THIS IS DEVIN DANGER WITH ANOTHER NOISE NETWORK NEWS NUKE!
UGH, NOT THIS POSER AGAIN.
THE CREEPIES ARE PLAYING THEIR FINAL PINMAGGEDON SHOW TONIGHT, AND WE'RE ALL EXCITED TO WITNESS THE FIRST BAND TO EVER COMPLETE THE CHALLENGE.
BUT IT SEEMS STARDOM ISN'T THE ONLY THING BLOSSOMING ON THIS TOUR.
UH-OH, COREY, DID ANOTHER ONE OF YOUR ROMANTIC TRYSTS MAKE THE GOSSIP MILL?
WE CAUGHT THIS EXCLUSIVE FOOTAGE OF A BURGEONING ROMANCE BETWEEN DRUMMER COADY CREEPIE AND AN AS-OF-YET UNNAMED MYSTERY MAN. IS THE "LUCKY ONE" FINALLY GETTING LUCKY?
COADY?!?!
I BET YOU THOUGHT IT WAS GOING TO BE ABOUT COREY AGAIN, HUH?
KNOCK! KNOCK!
COADY, YOU SLY FOX!
YOU SMOOCHED A BOY AND DIDN'T TELL US? WE HAD TO FIND OUT THE JUICY GOSSIP FROM DEVIN DANGER?!

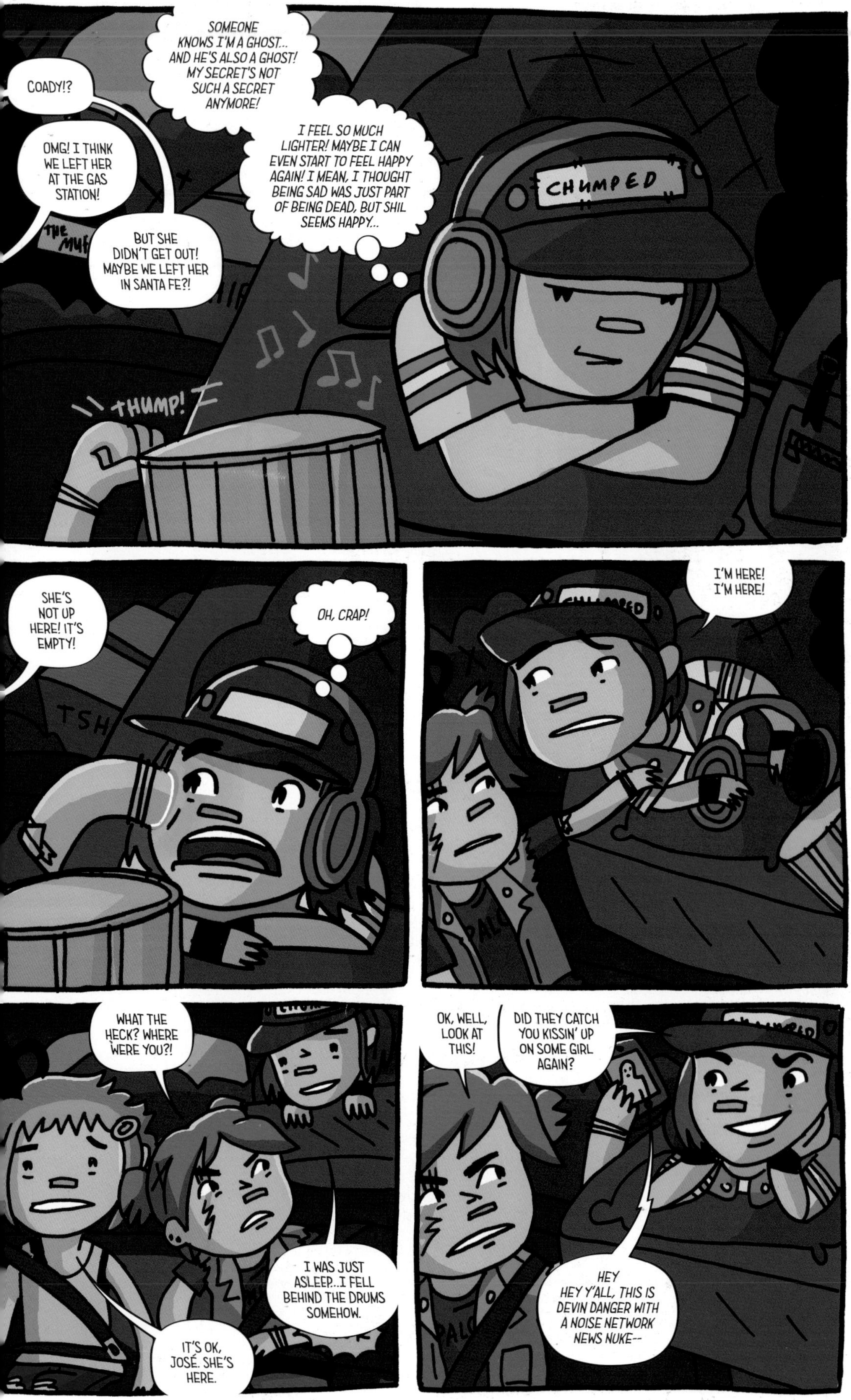
COADY!?
SOMEONE KNOWS I'M A GHOST... AND HE'S ALSO A GHOST! MY SECRET'S NOT SUCH A SECRET ANYMORE!
OMG! I THINK WE LEFT HER AT THE GAS STATION!
BUT SHE DIDN'T GET OUT! MAYBE WE LEFT HER IN SANTA FE?!
I FEEL SO MUCH LIGHTER! MAYBE I CAN EVEN START TO FEEL HAPPY AGAIN! I MEAN, I THOUGHT BEING SAD WAS JUST PART OF BEING DEAD, BUT SHIL SEEMS HAPPY...
CHUMPED
THUMP!
SHE'S NOT UP HERE! IT'S EMPTY!
OH, CRAP!
I'M HERE! I'M HERE!
WHAT THE HECK? WHERE WERE YOU?!
I WAS JUST ASLEEP...I FELL BEHIND THE DRUMS SOMEHOW.
IT'S OK, JOSÉ. SHE'S HERE.
OK, WELL, LOOK AT THIS!
DID THEY CATCH YOU KISSIN' UP ON SOME GIRL AGAIN?
HEY HEY Y'ALL, THIS IS DEVIN DANGER WITH A NOISE NETWORK NEWS NUKE--

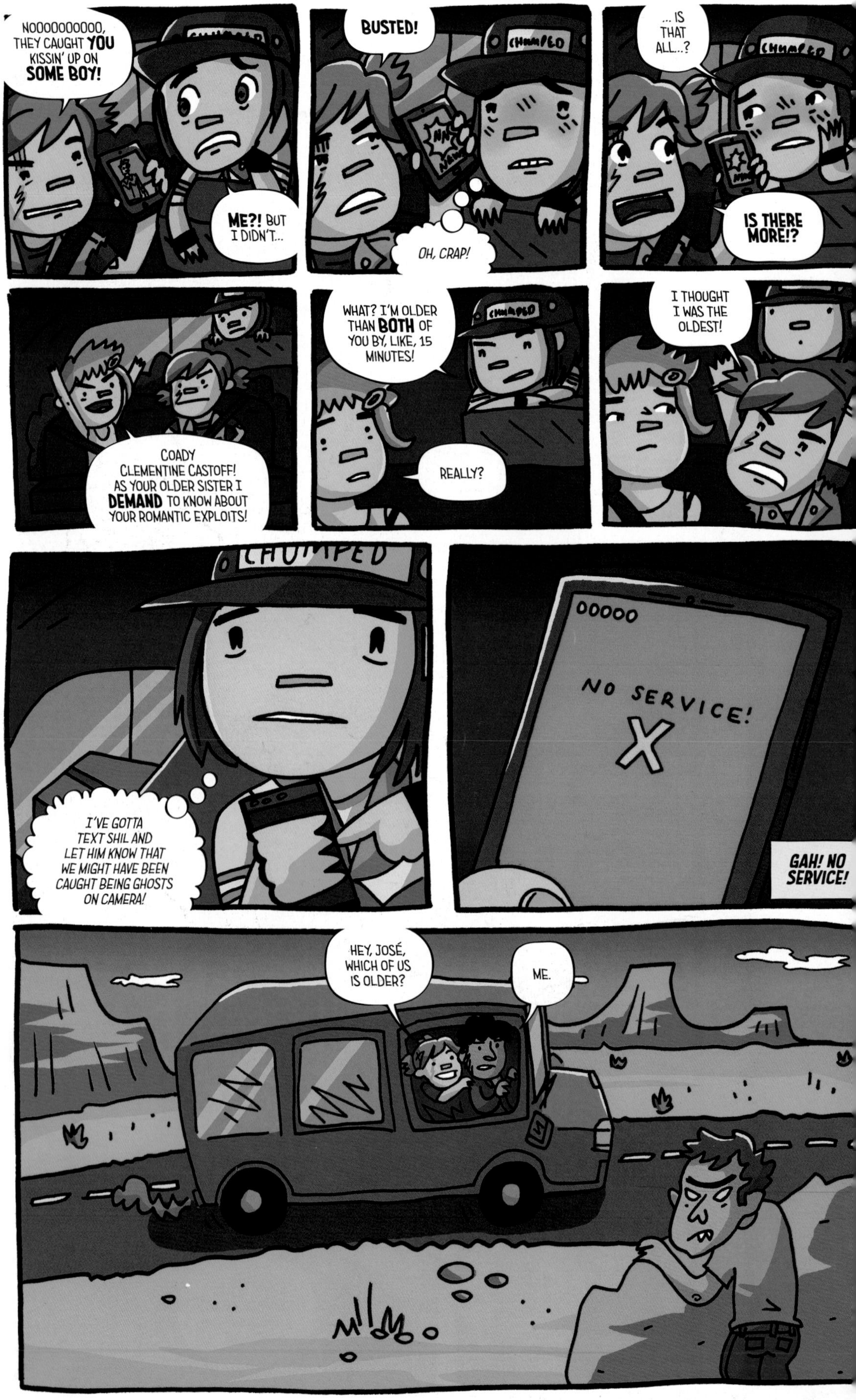

NOOOOOOOOOO, THEY CAUGHT YOU KISSIN' UP ON SOME BOY!
ME?! BUT I DIDN'T...
BUSTED!
OH, CRAP!
... IS THAT ALL...?
IS THERE MORE!?
COADY CLEMENTINE CASTOFF! AS YOUR OLDER SISTER I DEMAND TO KNOW ABOUT YOUR ROMANTIC EXPLOITS!
WHAT? I'M OLDER THAN BOTH OF YOU BY, LIKE, 15 MINUTES!
REALLY?
I THOUGHT I WAS THE OLDEST!
CHUMPED
I'VE GOTTA TEXT SHIL AND LET HIM KNOW THAT WE MIGHT HAVE BEEN CAUGHT BEING GHOSTS ON CAMERA!
NO SERVICE!
X
GAH! NO SERVICE!
HEY, JOSÉ, WHICH OF US IS OLDER?
ME.

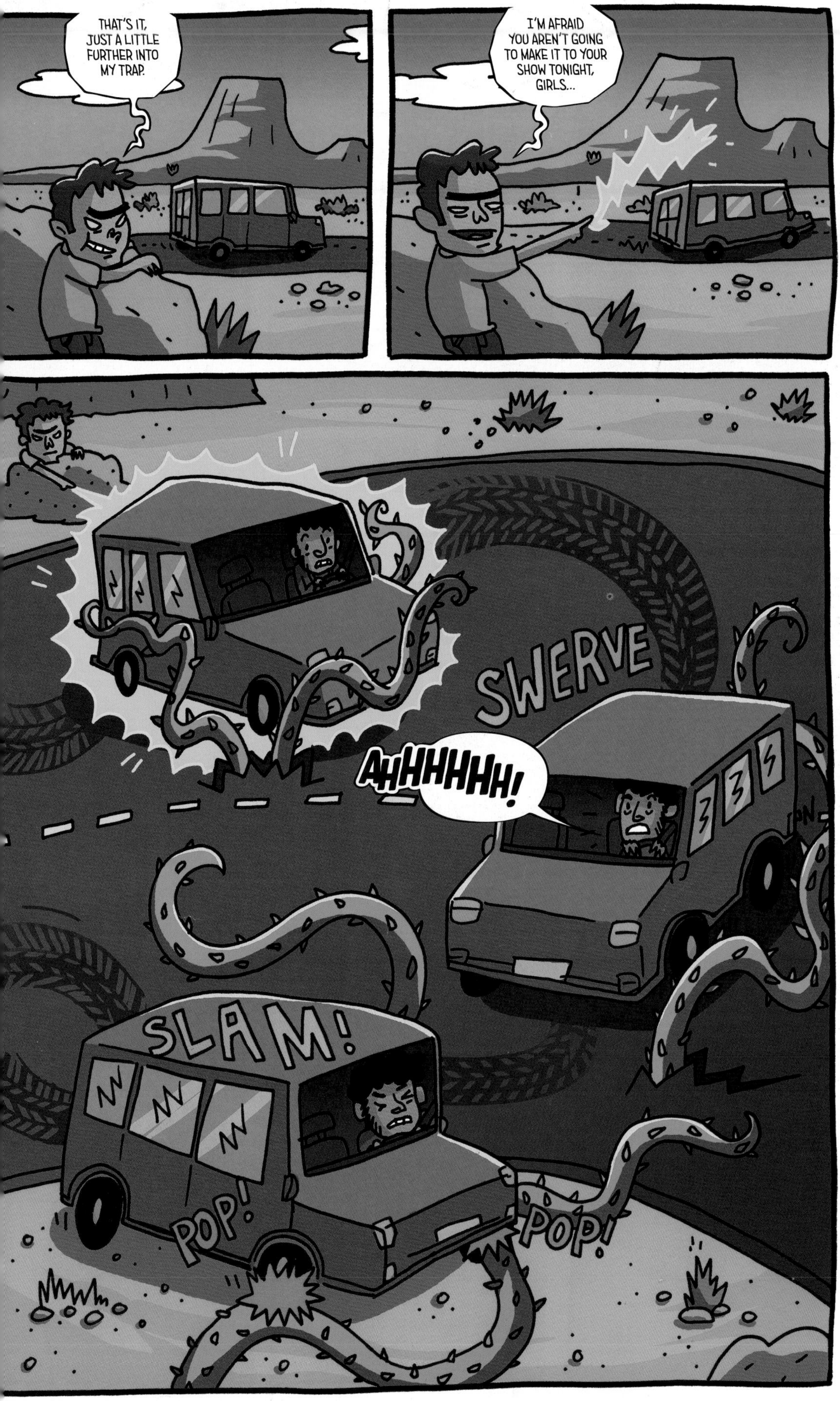
THAT'S IT, JUST A LITTLE FURTHER INTO MY TRAP.
I'M AFRAID YOU AREN'T GOING TO MAKE IT TO YOUR SHOW TONIGHT, GIRLS...
SWERVE
AHHHHHH!
SLAM!
POP!
POP!

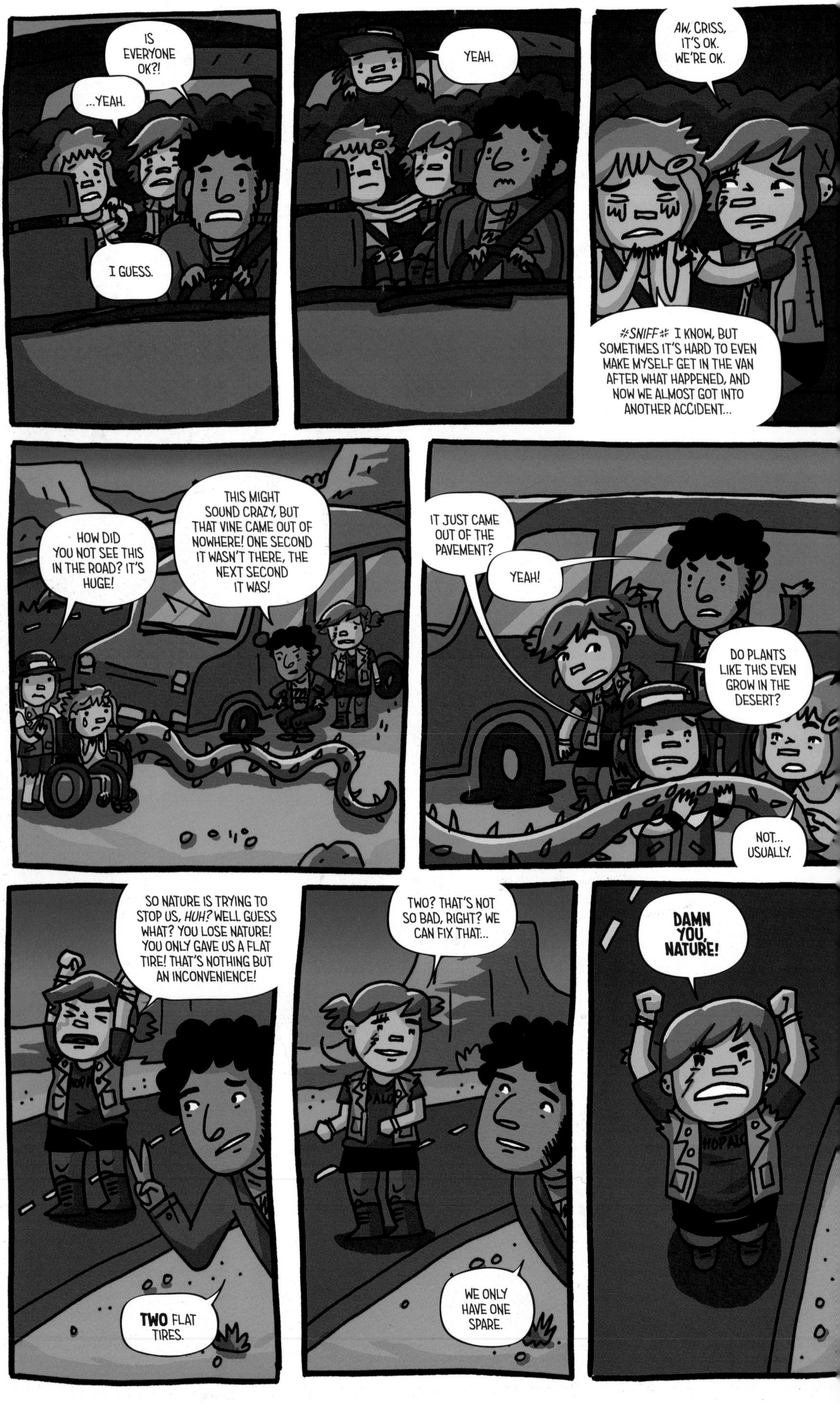
IS EVERYONE OK?!
...YEAH.
I GUESS.
YEAH.
AW, CRISS, IT'S OK. WE'RE OK.
#SNIFF# I KNOW, BUT SOMETIMES IT'S HARD TO EVEN MAKE MYSELF GET IN THE VAN AFTER WHAT HAPPENED, AND NOW WE ALMOST GOT INTO ANOTHER ACCIDENT...
HOW DID YOU NOT SEE THIS IN THE ROAD? IT'S HUGE!
THIS MIGHT SOUND CRAZY, BUT THAT VINE CAME OUT OF NOWHERE! ONE SECOND IT WASN'T THERE, THE NEXT SECOND IT WAS!
IT JUST CAME OUT OF THE PAVEMENT?
YEAH!
DO PLANTS LIKE THIS EVEN GROW IN THE DESERT?
NOT... USUALLY.
SO NATURE IS TRYING TO STOP US, *HUH?* WELL GUESS WHAT? YOU LOSE NATURE! YOU ONLY GAVE US A FLAT TIRE! THAT'S NOTHING BUT AN INCONVENIENCE!
TWO FLAT TIRES.
TWO? THAT'S NOT SO BAD, RIGHT? WE CAN FIX THAT...
WE ONLY HAVE ONE SPARE.
DAMN YOU, NATURE!

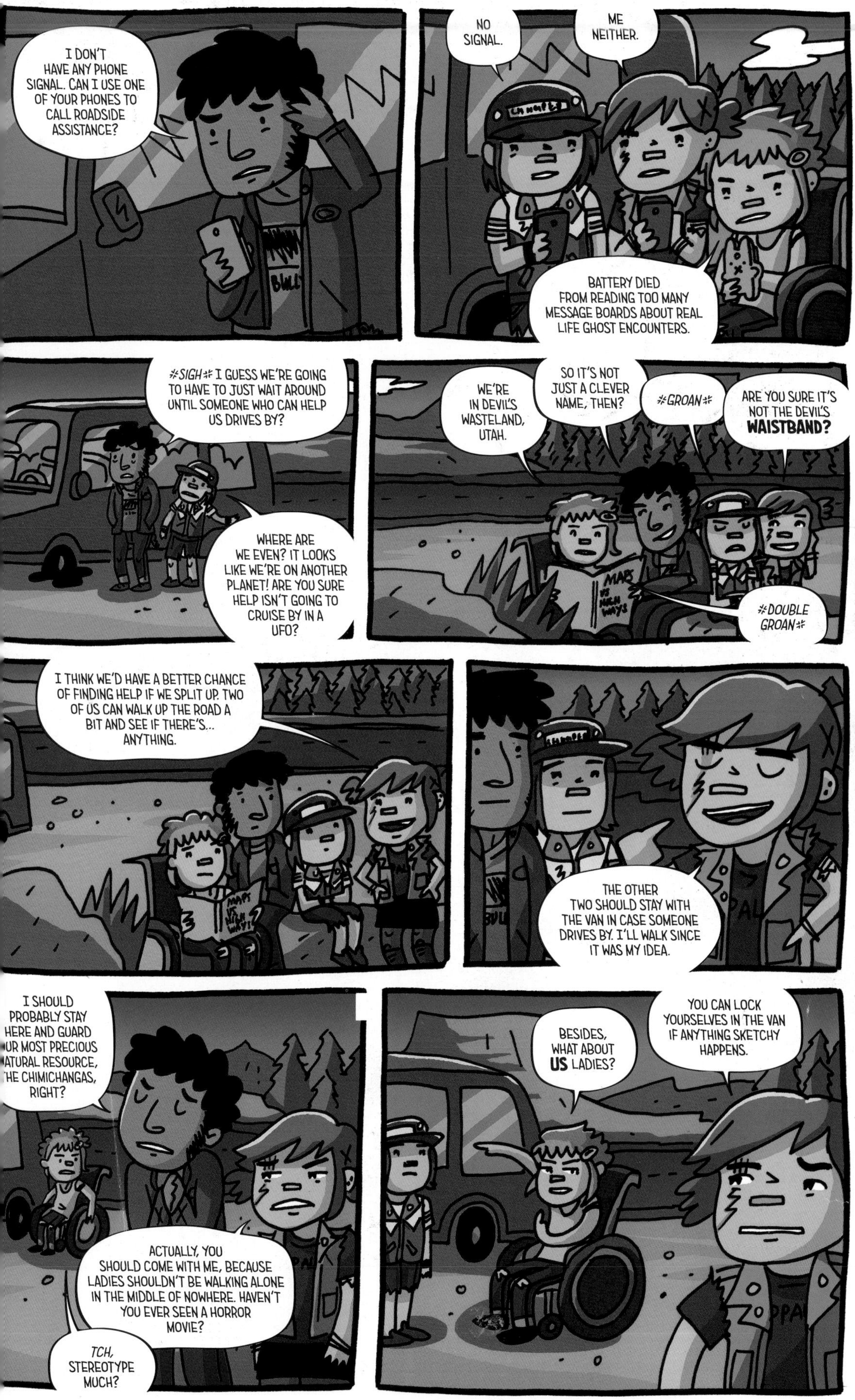
I DON'T HAVE ANY PHONE SIGNAL. CAN I USE ONE OF YOUR PHONES TO CALL ROADSIDE ASSISTANCE?
NO SIGNAL.
ME NEITHER.
BATTERY DIED FROM READING TOO MANY MESSAGE BOARDS ABOUT REAL LIFE GHOST ENCOUNTERS.
SIGH I GUESS WE'RE GOING TO HAVE TO JUST WAIT AROUND UNTIL SOMEONE WHO CAN HELP US DRIVES BY?
WHERE ARE WE EVEN? IT LOOKS LIKE WE'RE ON ANOTHER PLANET! ARE YOU SURE HELP ISN'T GOING TO CRUISE BY IN A UFO?
WE'RE IN DEVIL'S WASTELAND, UTAH.
SO IT'S NOT JUST A CLEVER NAME, THEN?
GROAN
ARE YOU SURE IT'S NOT THE DEVIL'S **WAISTBAND?**
DOUBLE GROAN
I THINK WE'D HAVE A BETTER CHANCE OF FINDING HELP IF WE SPLIT UP. TWO OF US CAN WALK UP THE ROAD A BIT AND SEE IF THERE'S... ANYTHING.
THE OTHER TWO SHOULD STAY WITH THE VAN IN CASE SOMEONE DRIVES BY. I'LL WALK SINCE IT WAS MY IDEA.
I SHOULD PROBABLY STAY HERE AND GUARD UR MOST PRECIOUS ATURAL RESOURCE, THE CHIMICHANGAS, RIGHT?
ACTUALLY, YOU SHOULD COME WITH ME, BECAUSE LADIES SHOULDN'T BE WALKING ALONE IN THE MIDDLE OF NOWHERE. HAVEN'T YOU EVER SEEN A HORROR MOVIE?
TCH, STEREOTYPE MUCH?
BESIDES, WHAT ABOUT **US** LADIES?
YOU CAN LOCK YOURSELVES IN THE VAN IF ANYTHING SKETCHY HAPPENS.

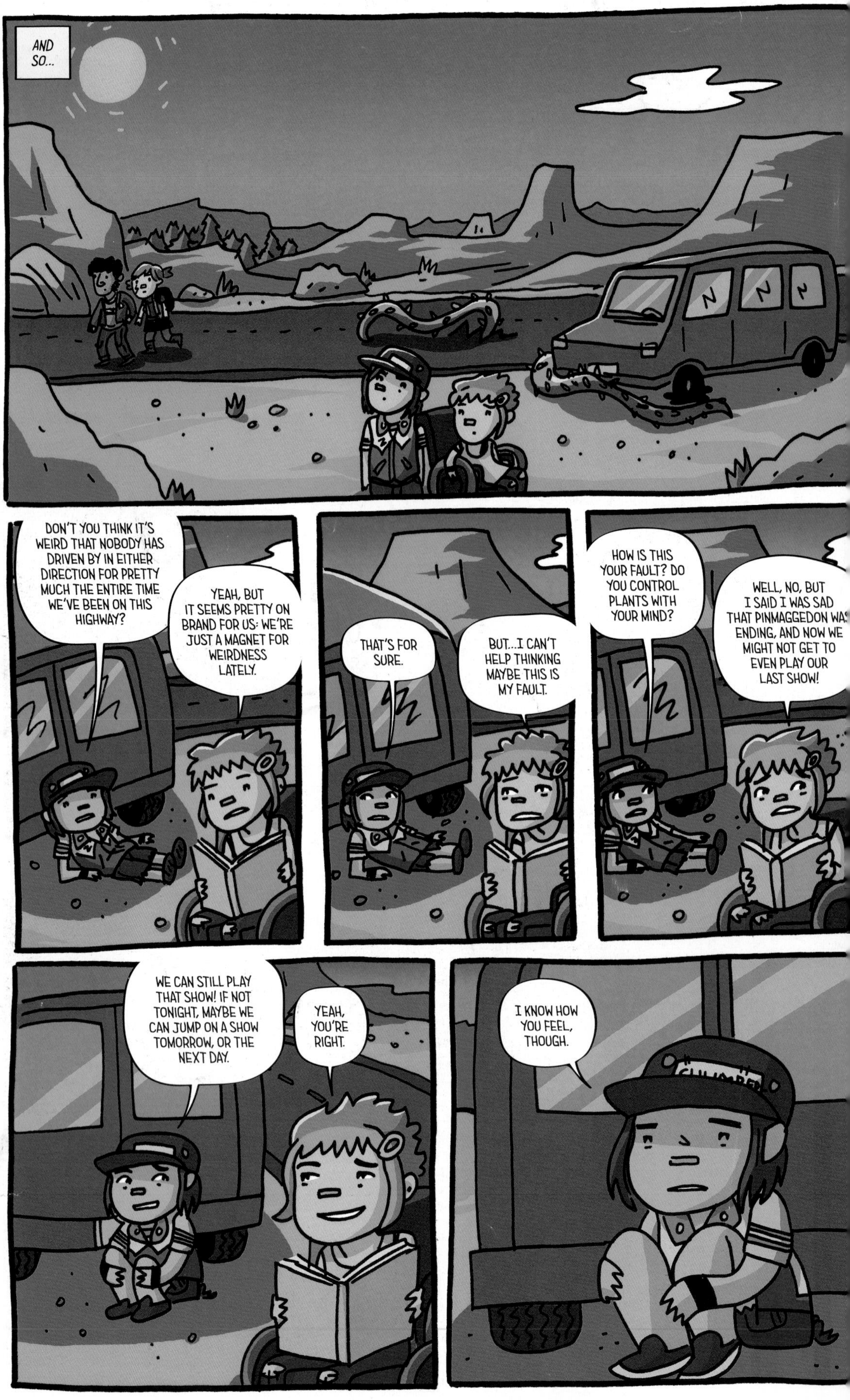
AND SO...
DON'T YOU THINK IT'S WEIRD THAT NOBODY HAS DRIVEN BY IN EITHER DIRECTION FOR PRETTY MUCH THE ENTIRE TIME WE'VE BEEN ON THIS HIGHWAY?
YEAH, BUT IT SEEMS PRETTY ON BRAND FOR US: WE'RE JUST A MAGNET FOR WEIRDNESS LATELY.
THAT'S FOR SURE.
BUT...I CAN'T HELP THINKING MAYBE THIS IS MY FAULT.
HOW IS THIS YOUR FAULT? DO YOU CONTROL PLANTS WITH YOUR MIND?
WELL, NO, BUT I SAID I WAS SAD THAT PINMAGGEDON WAS ENDING, AND NOW WE MIGHT NOT GET TO EVEN PLAY OUR LAST SHOW!
WE CAN STILL PLAY THAT SHOW! IF NOT TONIGHT, MAYBE WE CAN JUMP ON A SHOW TOMORROW, OR THE NEXT DAY.
YEAH, YOU'RE RIGHT.
I KNOW HOW YOU FEEL, THOUGH.

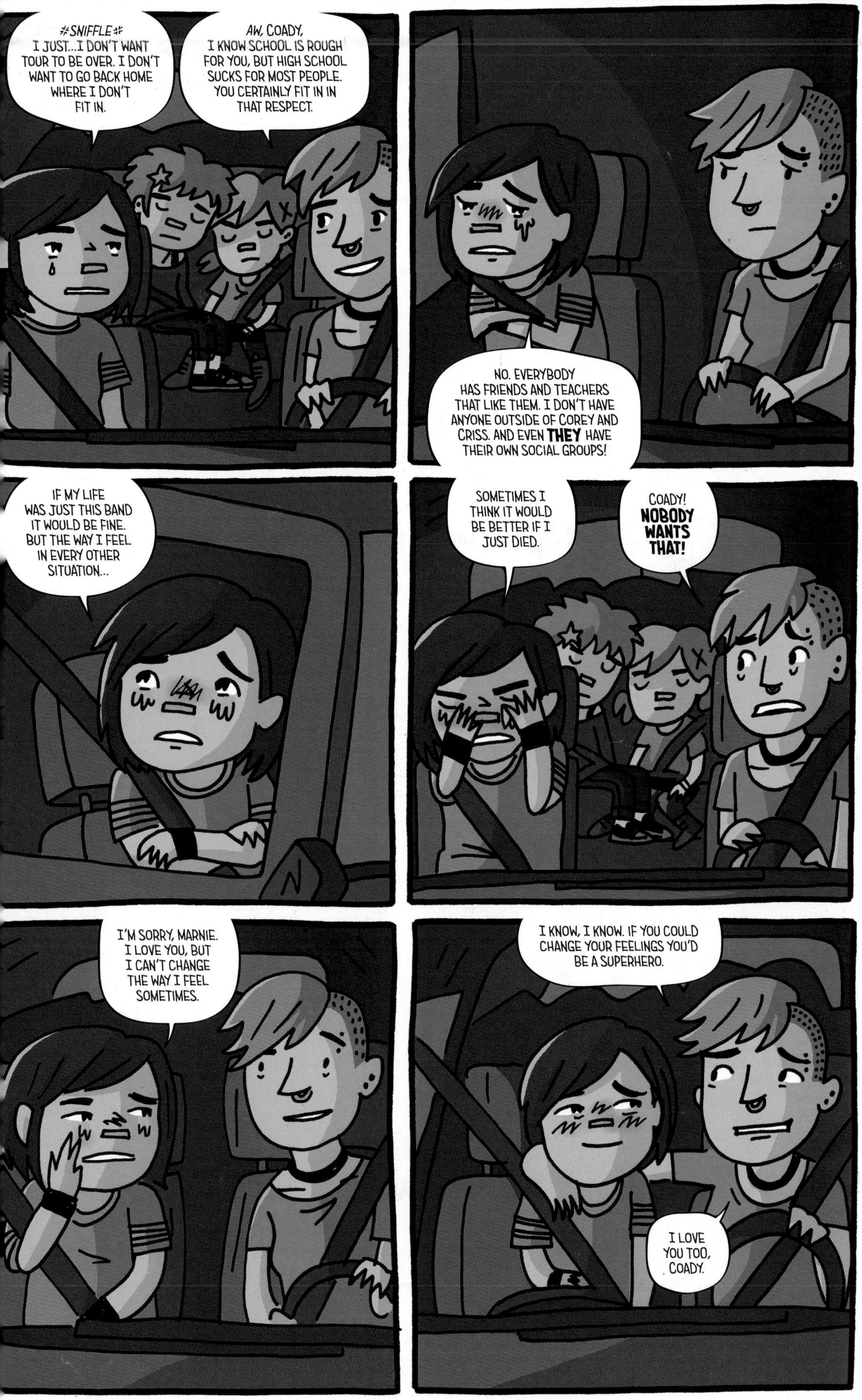
SNIFFLE I JUST...I DON'T WANT TOUR TO BE OVER. I DON'T WANT TO GO BACK HOME WHERE I DON'T FIT IN.
AW, COADY, I KNOW SCHOOL IS ROUGH FOR YOU, BUT HIGH SCHOOL SUCKS FOR MOST PEOPLE. YOU CERTAINLY FIT IN IN THAT RESPECT.
NO. EVERYBODY HAS FRIENDS AND TEACHERS THAT LIKE THEM. I DON'T HAVE ANYONE OUTSIDE OF COREY AND CRISS. AND EVEN THEY HAVE THEIR OWN SOCIAL GROUPS!
IF MY LIFE WAS JUST THIS BAND IT WOULD BE FINE. BUT THE WAY I FEEL IN EVERY OTHER SITUATION...
SOMETIMES I THINK IT WOULD BE BETTER IF I JUST DIED.
COADY! NOBODY WANTS THAT!
I'M SORRY, MARNIE. I LOVE YOU, BUT I CAN'T CHANGE THE WAY I FEEL SOMETIMES.
I KNOW, I KNOW. IF YOU COULD CHANGE YOUR FEELINGS YOU'D BE A SUPERHERO.
I LOVE YOU TOO, COADY.

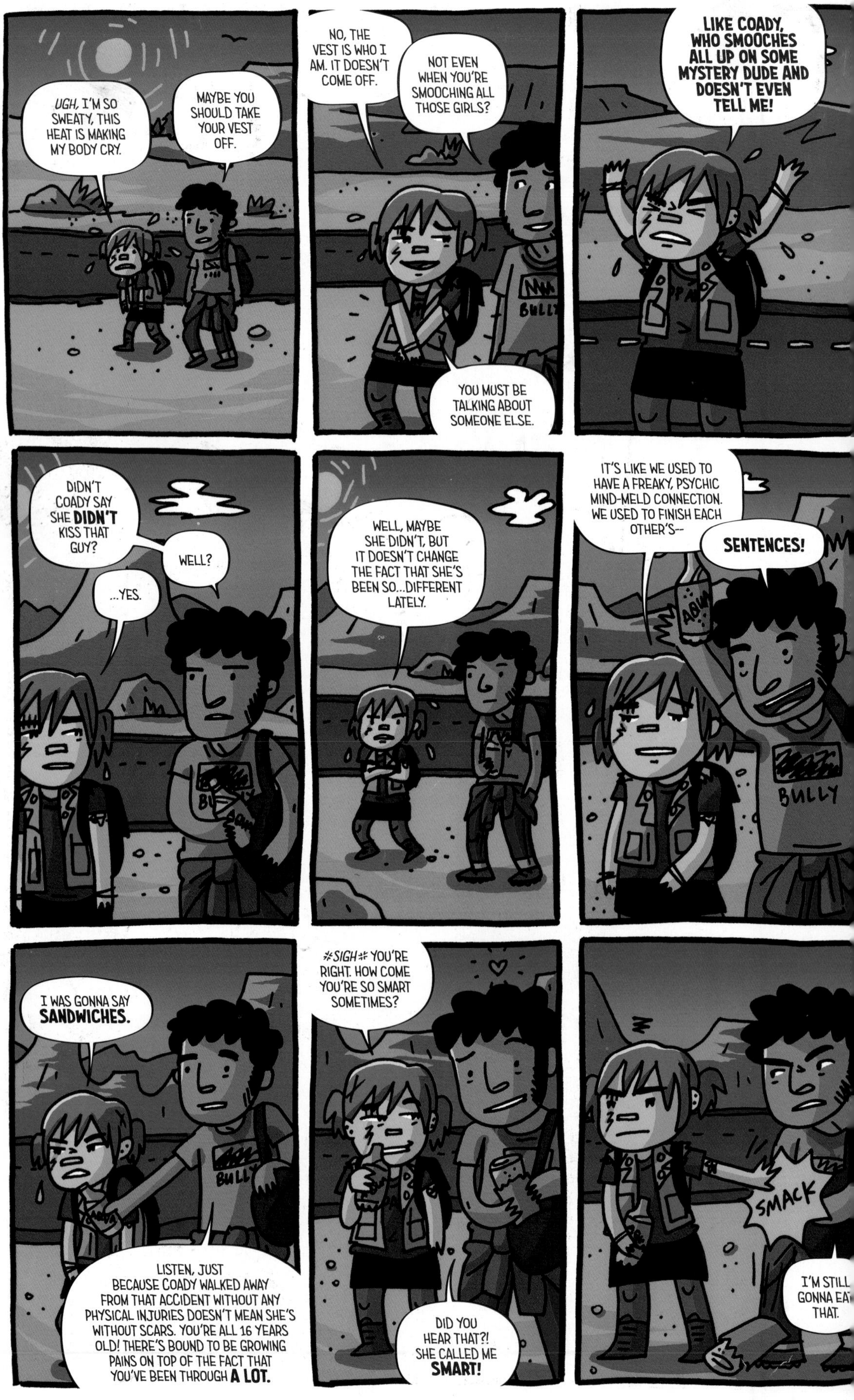

UGH, I'M SO SWEATY, THIS HEAT IS MAKING MY BODY CRY.
MAYBE YOU SHOULD TAKE YOUR VEST OFF.
NO, THE VEST IS WHO I AM. IT DOESN'T COME OFF.
NOT EVEN WHEN YOU'RE SMOOCHING ALL THOSE GIRLS?
YOU MUST BE TALKING ABOUT SOMEONE ELSE.
LIKE COADY, WHO SMOOCHES ALL UP ON SOME MYSTERY DUDE AND DOESN'T EVEN TELL ME!
DIDN'T COADY SAY SHE **DIDN'T** KISS THAT GUY?
WELL?
...YES.
WELL, MAYBE SHE DIDN'T, BUT IT DOESN'T CHANGE THE FACT THAT SHE'S BEEN SO...DIFFERENT LATELY.
IT'S LIKE WE USED TO HAVE A FREAKY, PSYCHIC MIND-MELD CONNECTION. WE USED TO FINISH EACH OTHER'S--
SENTENCES!
I WAS GONNA SAY **SANDWICHES.**
LISTEN, JUST BECAUSE COADY WALKED AWAY FROM THAT ACCIDENT WITHOUT ANY PHYSICAL INJURIES DOESN'T MEAN SHE'S WITHOUT SCARS. YOU'RE ALL 16 YEARS OLD! THERE'S BOUND TO BE GROWING PAINS ON TOP OF THE FACT THAT YOU'VE BEEN THROUGH **A LOT.**
#SIGH# YOU'RE RIGHT. HOW COME YOU'RE SO SMART SOMETIMES?
DID YOU HEAR THAT?! SHE CALLED ME **SMART!**
SMACK
I'M STILL GONNA EAT THAT.

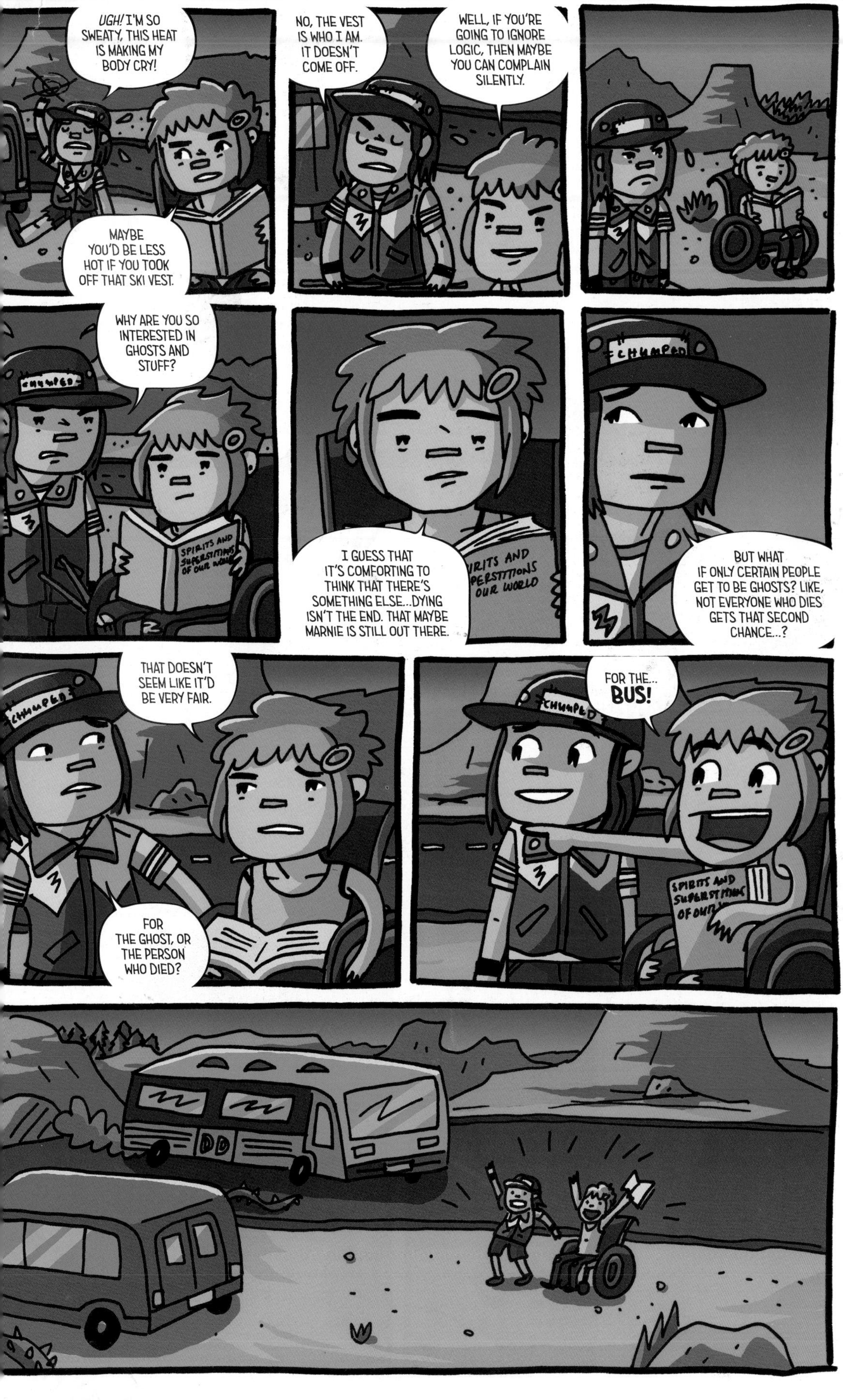
UGH! I'M SO SWEATY, THIS HEAT IS MAKING MY BODY CRY!
MAYBE YOU'D BE LESS HOT IF YOU TOOK OFF THAT SKI VEST.
NO, THE VEST IS WHO I AM. IT DOESN'T COME OFF.
WELL, IF YOU'RE GOING TO IGNORE LOGIC, THEN MAYBE YOU CAN COMPLAIN SILENTLY.
CHUMPED
WHY ARE YOU SO INTERESTED IN GHOSTS AND STUFF?
SPIRITS AND SUPERSTITIONS OF OUR WORLD
I GUESS THAT IT'S COMFORTING TO THINK THAT THERE'S SOMETHING ELSE...DYING ISN'T THE END. THAT MAYBE MARNIE IS STILL OUT THERE.
BUT WHAT IF ONLY CERTAIN PEOPLE GET TO BE GHOSTS? LIKE, NOT EVERYONE WHO DIES GETS THAT SECOND CHANCE...?
THAT DOESN'T SEEM LIKE IT'D BE VERY FAIR.
FOR THE GHOST, OR THE PERSON WHO DIED?
FOR THE... BUS!

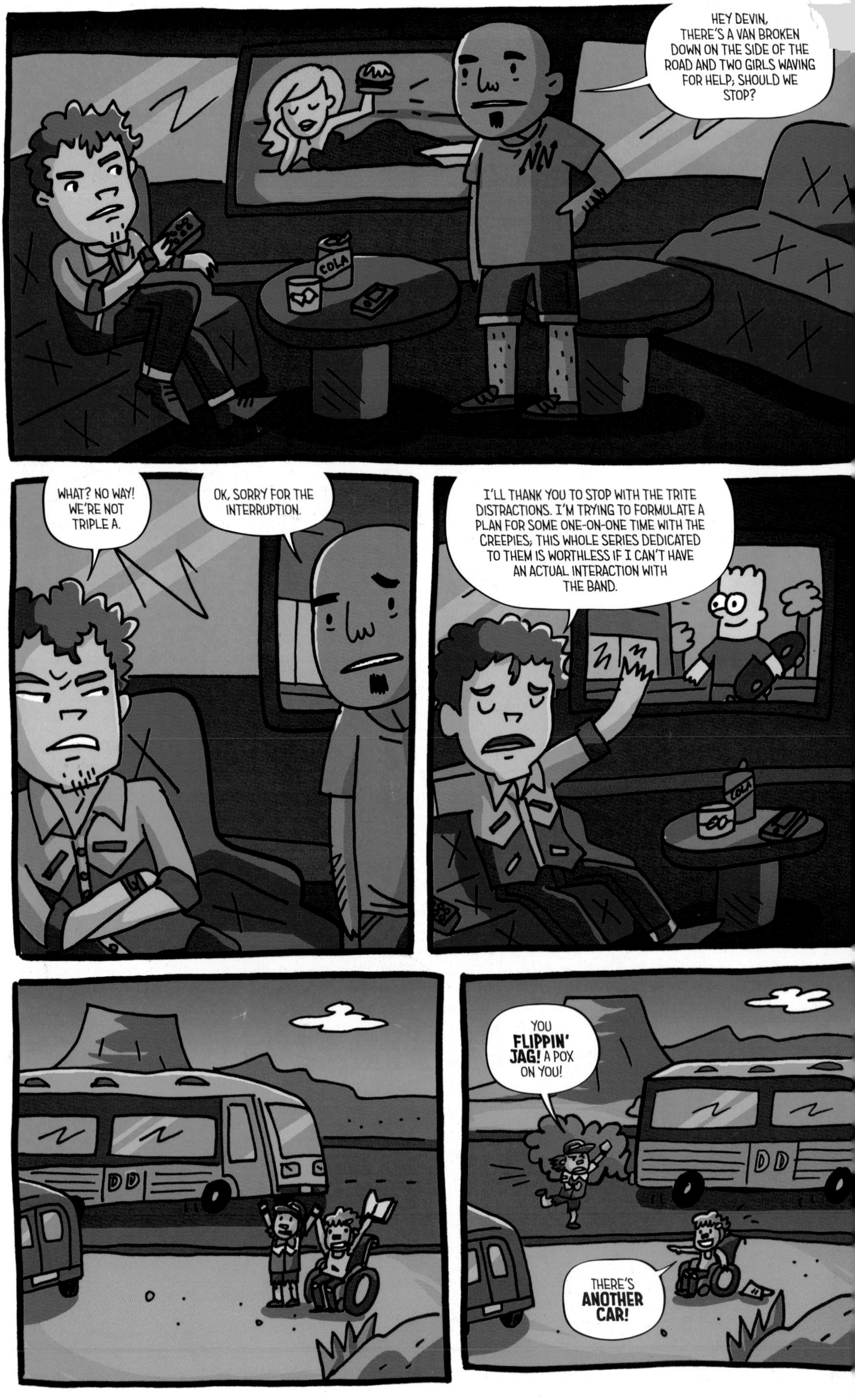
HEY DEVIN, THERE'S A VAN BROKEN DOWN ON THE SIDE OF THE ROAD AND TWO GIRLS WAVING FOR HELP; SHOULD WE STOP?
COLA
WHAT? NO WAY! WE'RE NOT TRIPLE A.
OK, SORRY FOR THE INTERRUPTION.
I'LL THANK YOU TO STOP WITH THE TRITE DISTRACTIONS. I'M TRYING TO FORMULATE A PLAN FOR SOME ONE-ON-ONE TIME WITH THE CREEPIES; THIS WHOLE SERIES DEDICATED TO THEM IS WORTHLESS IF I CAN'T HAVE AN ACTUAL INTERACTION WITH THE BAND.
COLA
DD
YOU **FLIPPIN' JAG!** A POX ON YOU!
DD
THERE'S **ANOTHER CAR!**

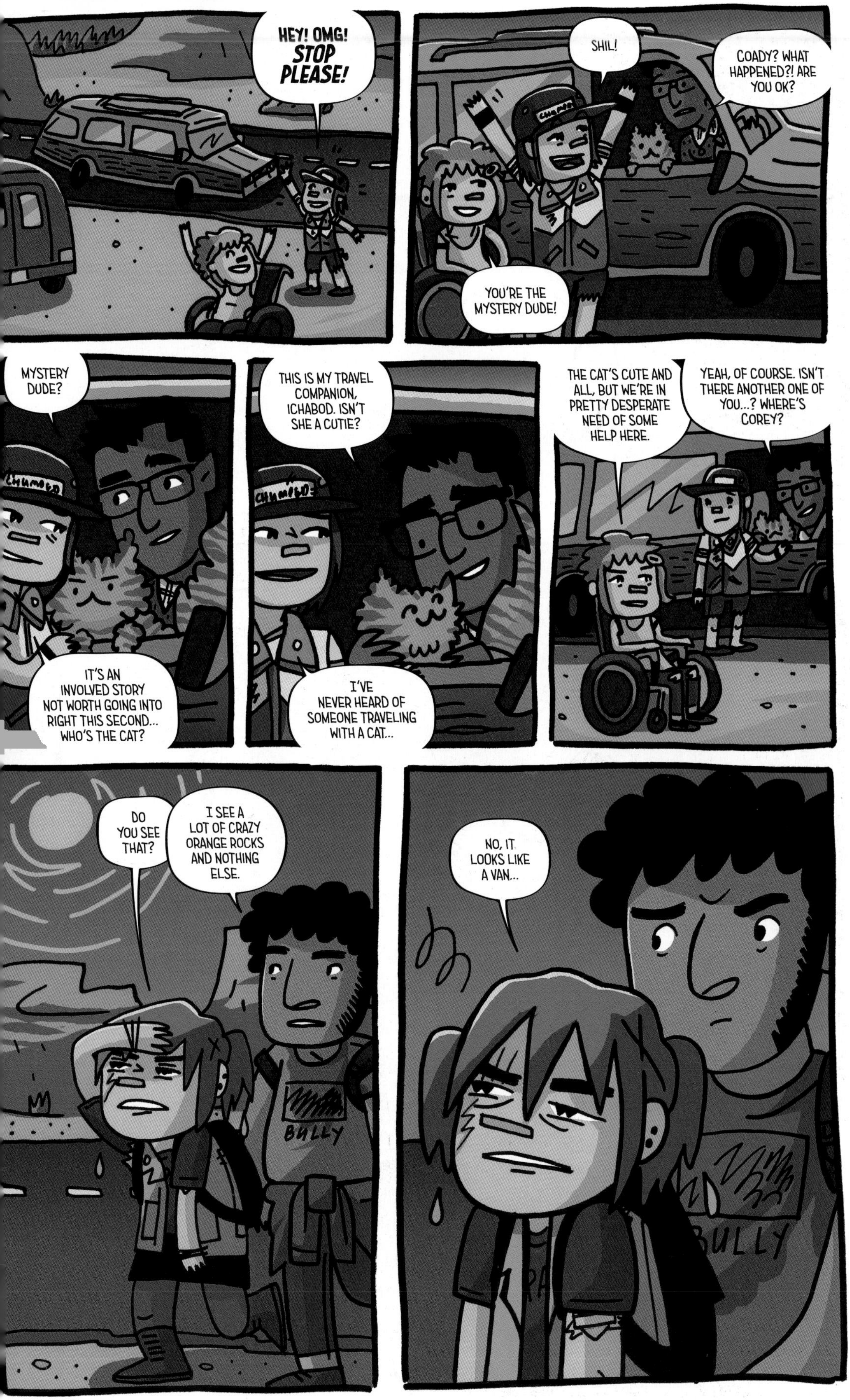
HEY! OMG! STOP PLEASE!
SHIL!
COADY? WHAT HAPPENED?! ARE YOU OK?
YOU'RE THE MYSTERY DUDE!
MYSTERY DUDE?
IT'S AN INVOLVED STORY NOT WORTH GOING INTO RIGHT THIS SECOND... WHO'S THE CAT?
THIS IS MY TRAVEL COMPANION, ICHABOD. ISN'T SHE A CUTIE?
I'VE NEVER HEARD OF SOMEONE TRAVELING WITH A CAT...
THE CAT'S CUTE AND ALL, BUT WE'RE IN PRETTY DESPERATE NEED OF SOME HELP HERE.
YEAH, OF COURSE. ISN'T THERE ANOTHER ONE OF YOU...? WHERE'S COREY?
DO YOU SEE THAT?
I SEE A LOT OF CRAZY ORANGE ROCKS AND NOTHING ELSE.
BULLY
NO, IT LOOKS LIKE A VAN...
BULLY

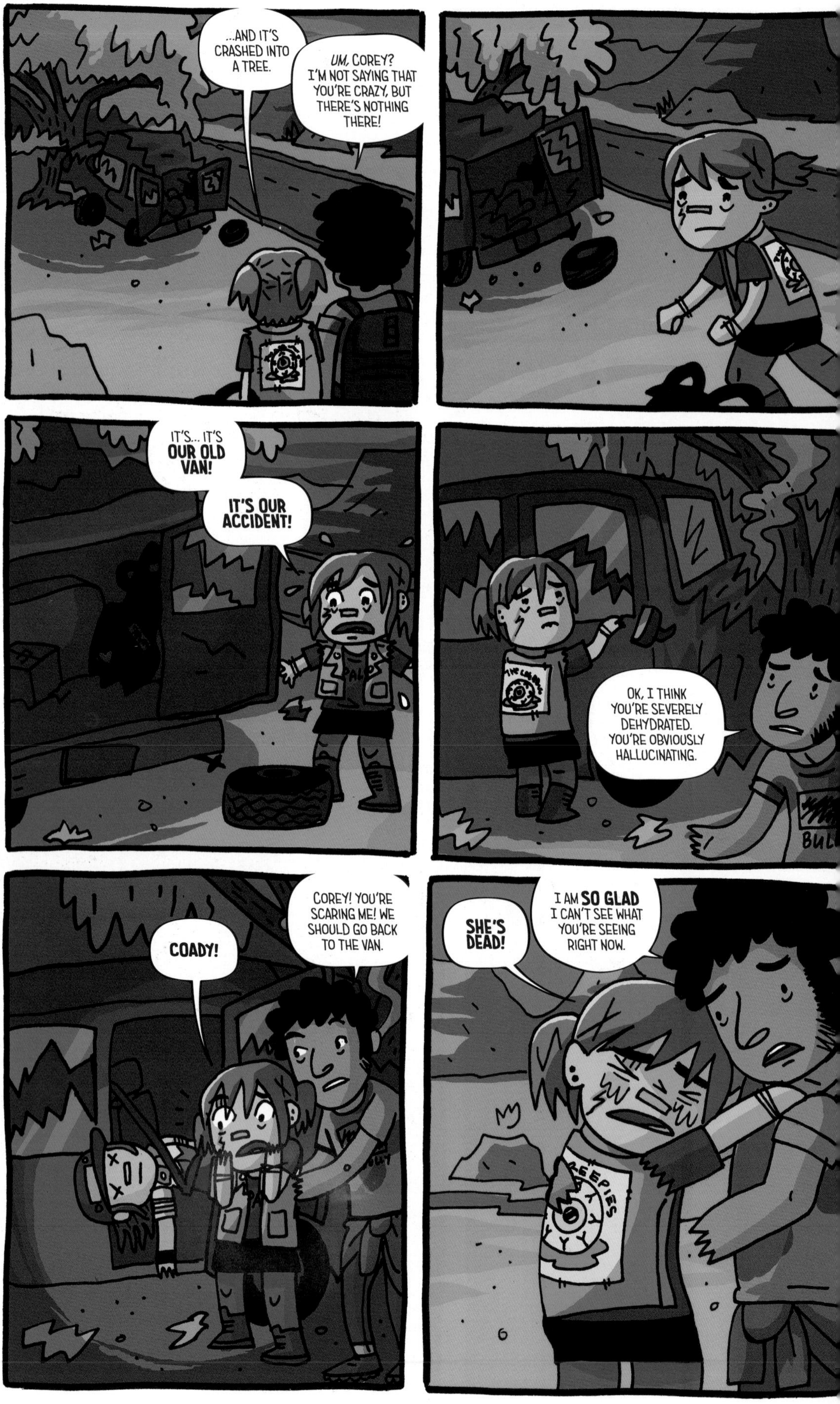
...AND IT'S CRASHED INTO A TREE.
UM, COREY? I'M NOT SAYING THAT YOU'RE CRAZY, BUT THERE'S NOTHING THERE!
IT'S... IT'S **OUR OLD VAN!**
IT'S OUR ACCIDENT!
OK, I THINK YOU'RE SEVERELY DEHYDRATED. YOU'RE OBVIOUSLY HALLUCINATING.
COADY!
COREY! YOU'RE SCARING ME! WE SHOULD GO BACK TO THE VAN.
SHE'S DEAD!
I AM **SO GLAD** I CAN'T SEE WHAT YOU'RE SEEING RIGHT NOW.

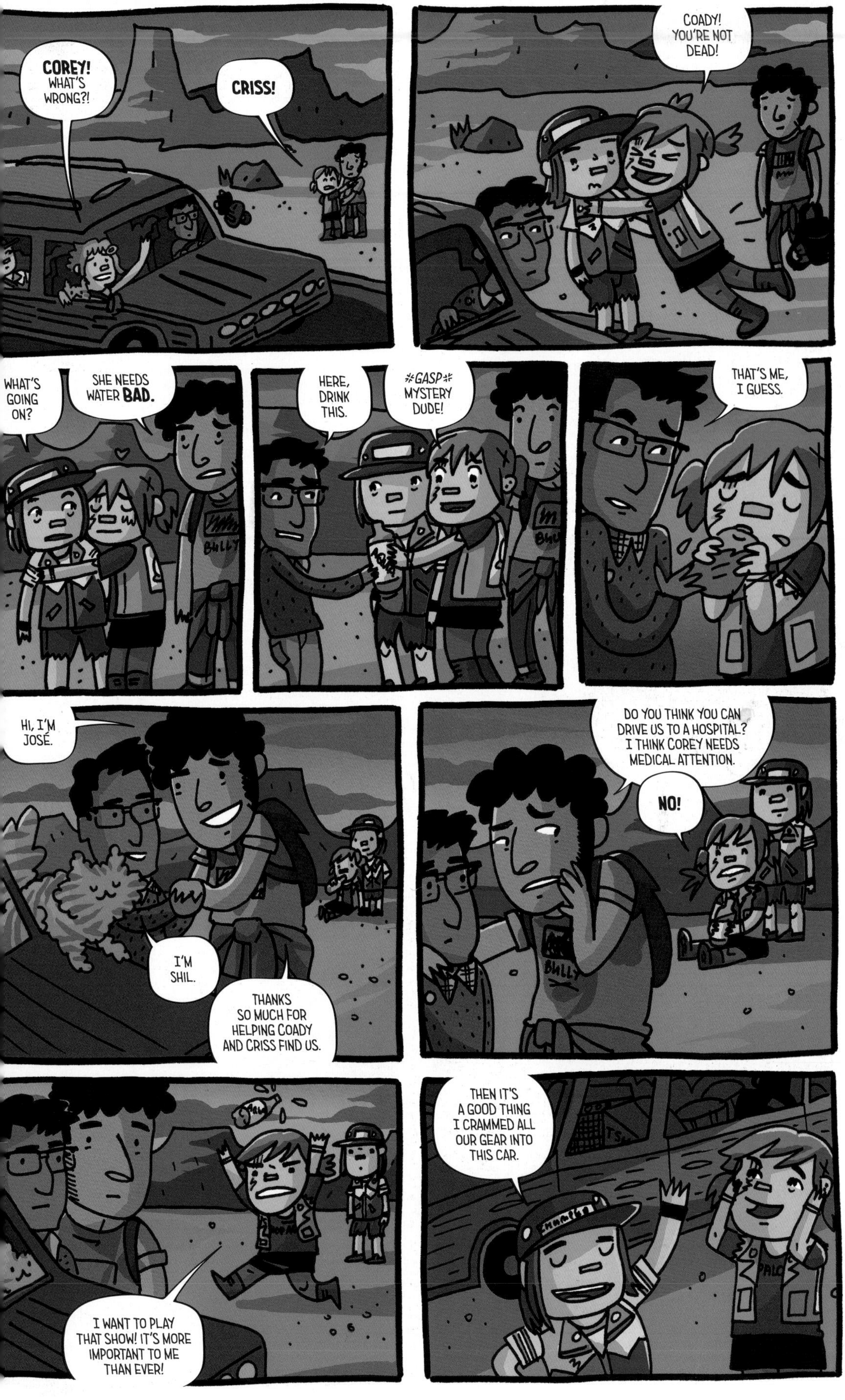
COREY! WHAT'S WRONG?!
CRISS!
COADY! YOU'RE NOT DEAD!
WHAT'S GOING ON?
SHE NEEDS WATER BAD.
HERE, DRINK THIS.
GASP MYSTERY DUDE!
THAT'S ME, I GUESS.
HI, I'M JOSÉ.
I'M SHIL.
THANKS SO MUCH FOR HELPING COADY AND CRISS FIND US.
DO YOU THINK YOU CAN DRIVE US TO A HOSPITAL? I THINK COREY NEEDS MEDICAL ATTENTION.
NO!
I WANT TO PLAY THAT SHOW! IT'S MORE IMPORTANT TO ME THAN EVER!
THEN IT'S A GOOD THING I CRAMMED ALL OUR GEAR INTO THIS CAR.

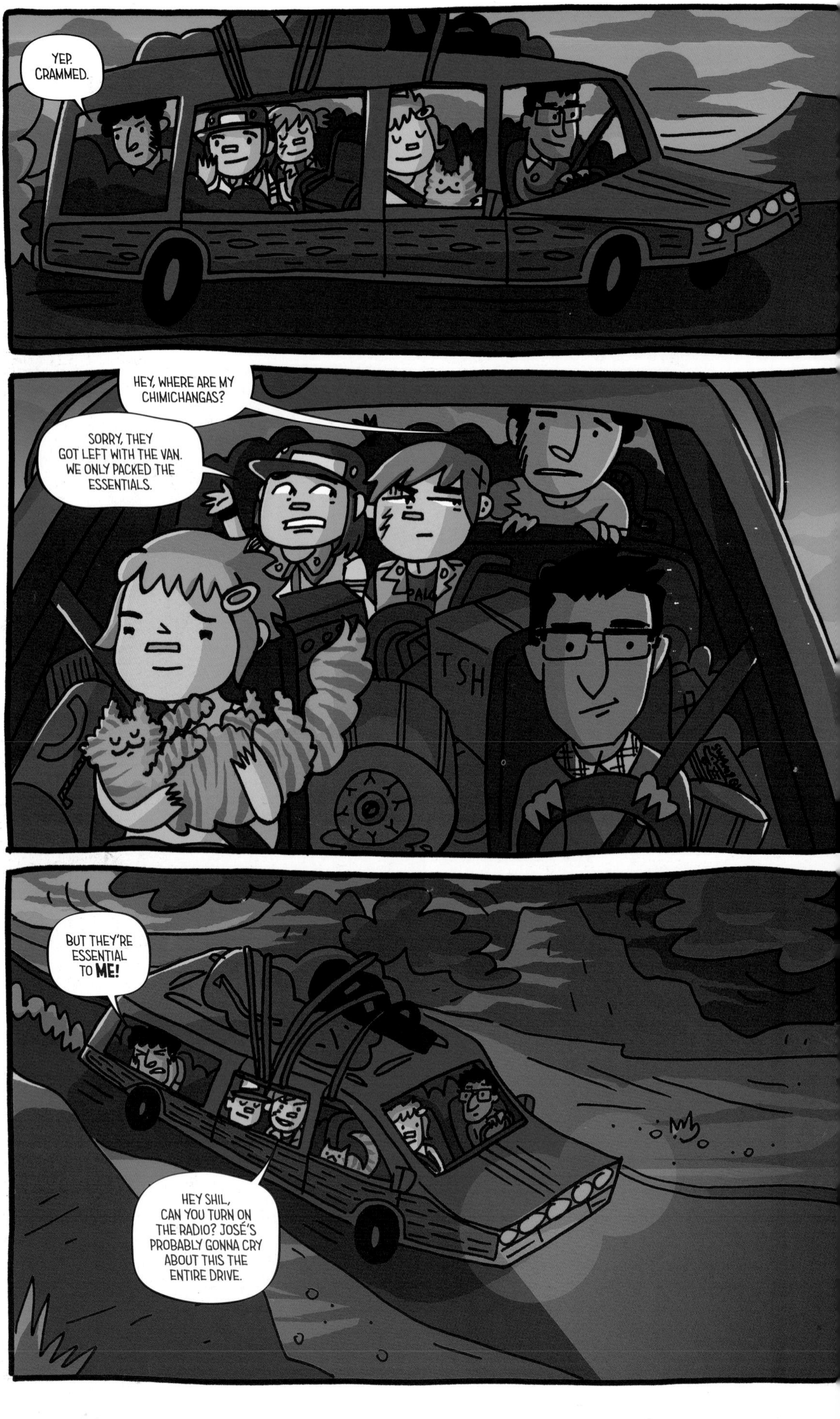
YEP. CRAMMED.
HEY, WHERE ARE MY CHIMICHANGAS?
SORRY, THEY GOT LEFT WITH THE VAN. WE ONLY PACKED THE ESSENTIALS.
BUT THEY'RE ESSENTIAL TO **ME!**
HEY SHIL, CAN YOU TURN ON THE RADIO? JOSÉ'S PROBABLY GONNA CRY ABOUT THIS THE ENTIRE DRIVE.

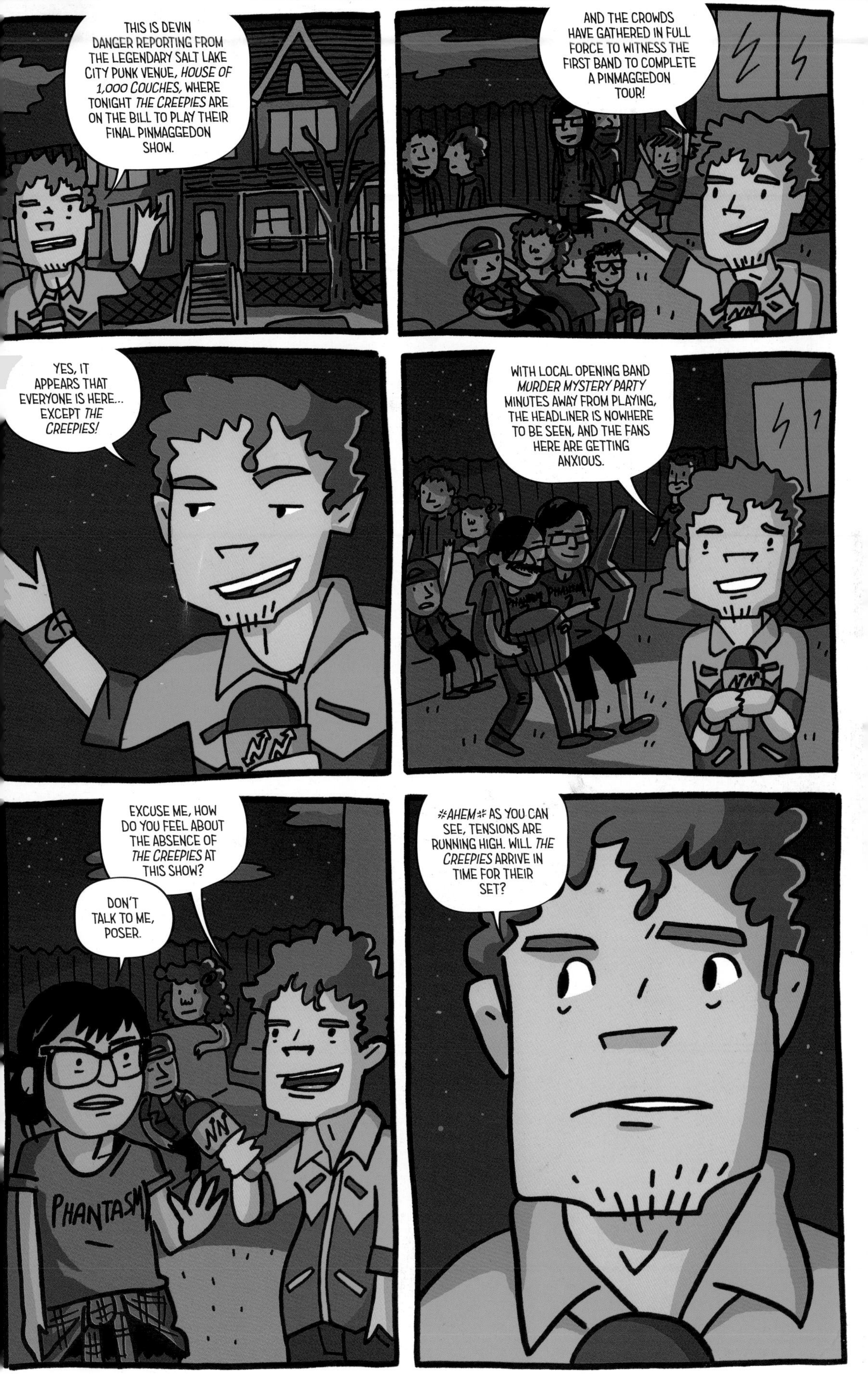
THIS IS DEVIN DANGER REPORTING FROM THE LEGENDARY SALT LAKE CITY PUNK VENUE, *HOUSE OF 1,000 COUCHES,* WHERE TONIGHT *THE CREEPIES* ARE ON THE BILL TO PLAY THEIR FINAL PINMAGGEDON SHOW.
AND THE CROWDS HAVE GATHERED IN FULL FORCE TO WITNESS THE FIRST BAND TO COMPLETE A PINMAGGEDON TOUR!
YES, IT APPEARS THAT EVERYONE IS HERE... EXCEPT *THE CREEPIES!*
WITH LOCAL OPENING BAND *MURDER MYSTERY PARTY* MINUTES AWAY FROM PLAYING, THE HEADLINER IS NOWHERE TO BE SEEN, AND THE FANS HERE ARE GETTING ANXIOUS.
EXCUSE ME, HOW DO YOU FEEL ABOUT THE ABSENCE OF *THE CREEPIES* AT THIS SHOW?
DON'T TALK TO ME, POSER.
PHANTASM
AHEM AS YOU CAN SEE, TENSIONS ARE RUNNING HIGH. WILL *THE CREEPIES* ARRIVE IN TIME FOR THEIR SET?

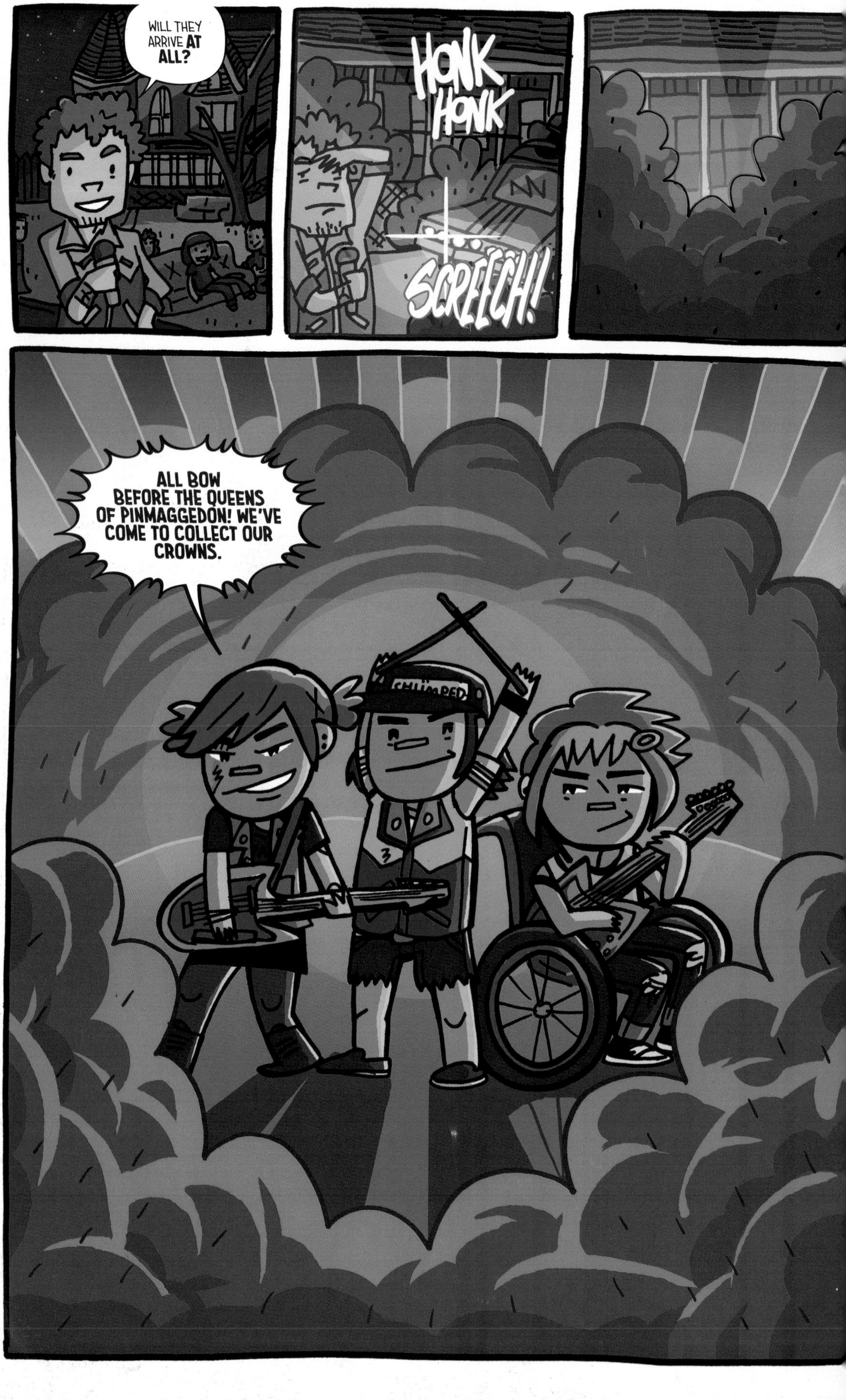
WILL THEY ARRIVE AT ALL?
HONK HONK
SCREECH!
ALL BOW BEFORE THE QUEENS OF PINMAGGEDON! WE'VE COME TO COLLECT OUR CROWNS.

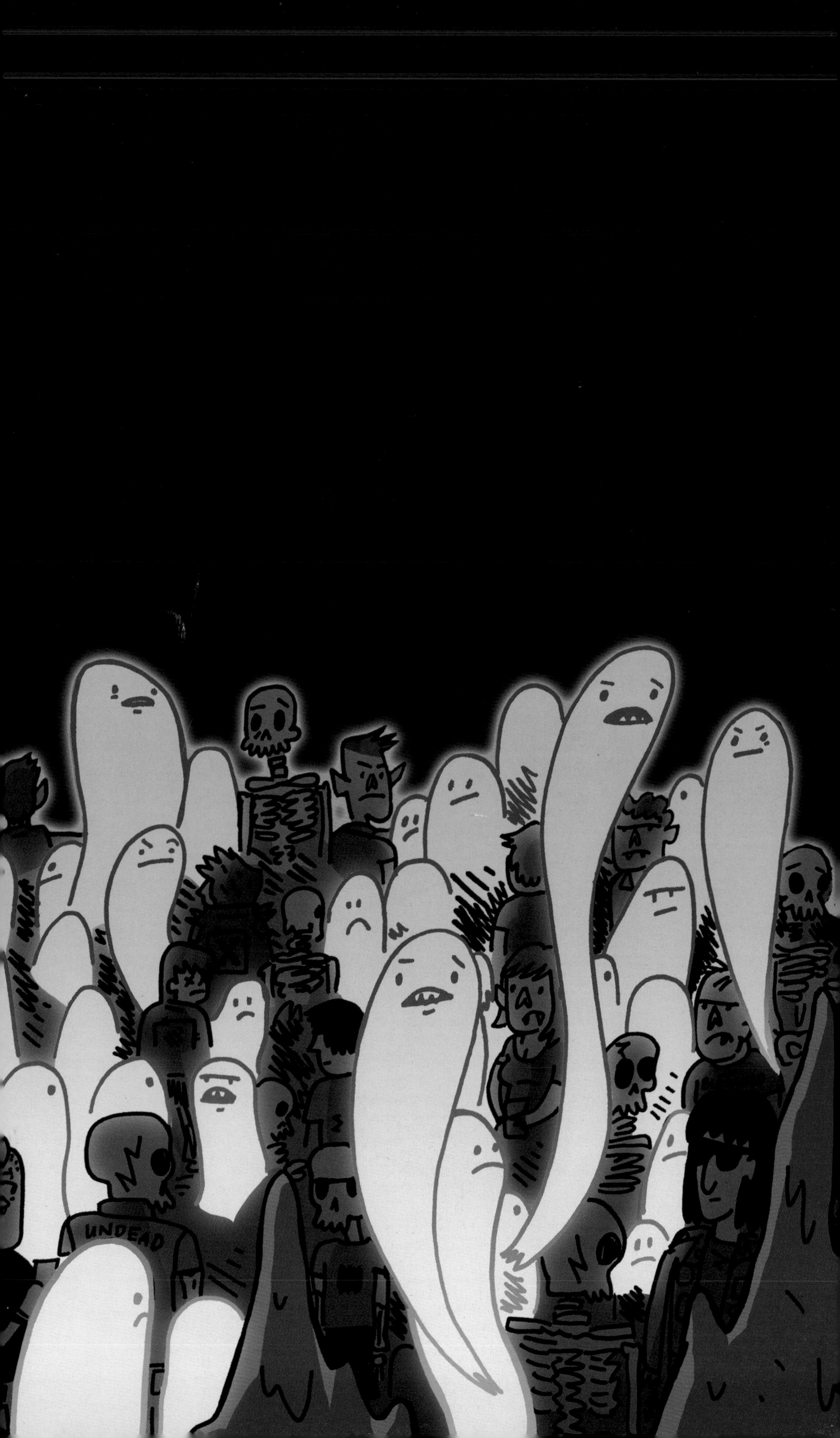
UNDEAD

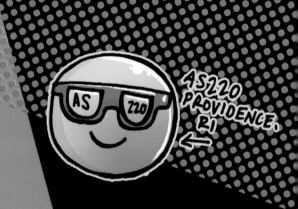

CHAPTER THREE

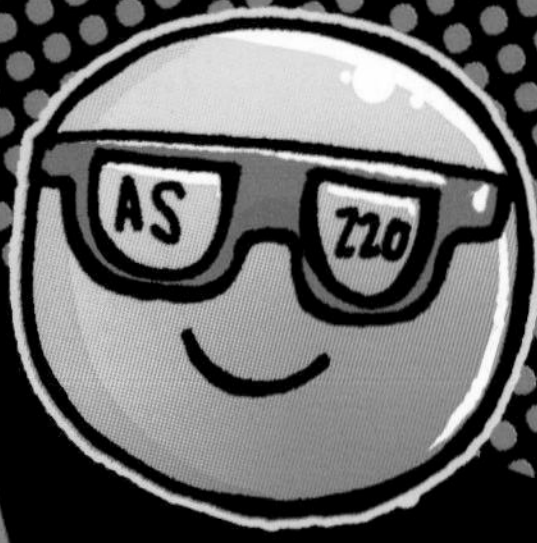
AS 220
AS220 PROVIDENCE, RI

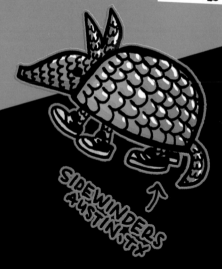

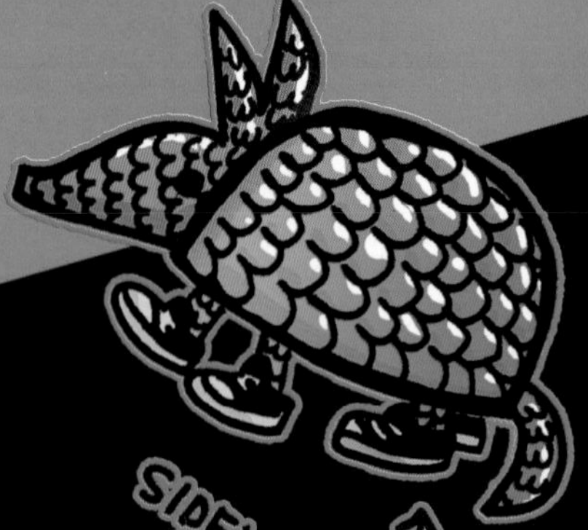
SIDEWINDERS AUSTIN, TX

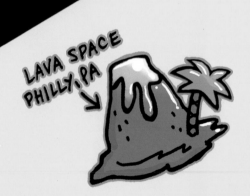

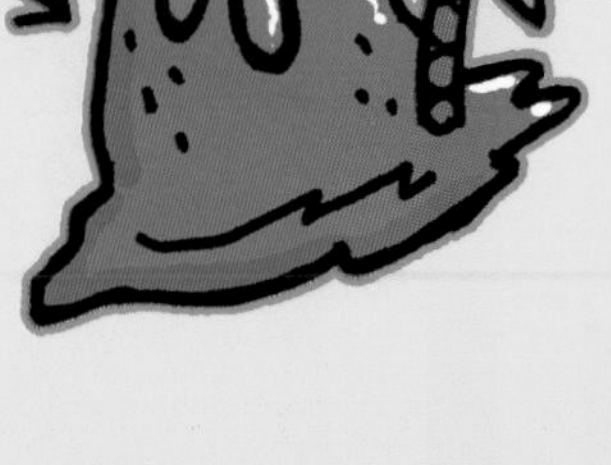
LAVA SPACE PHILLY, PA

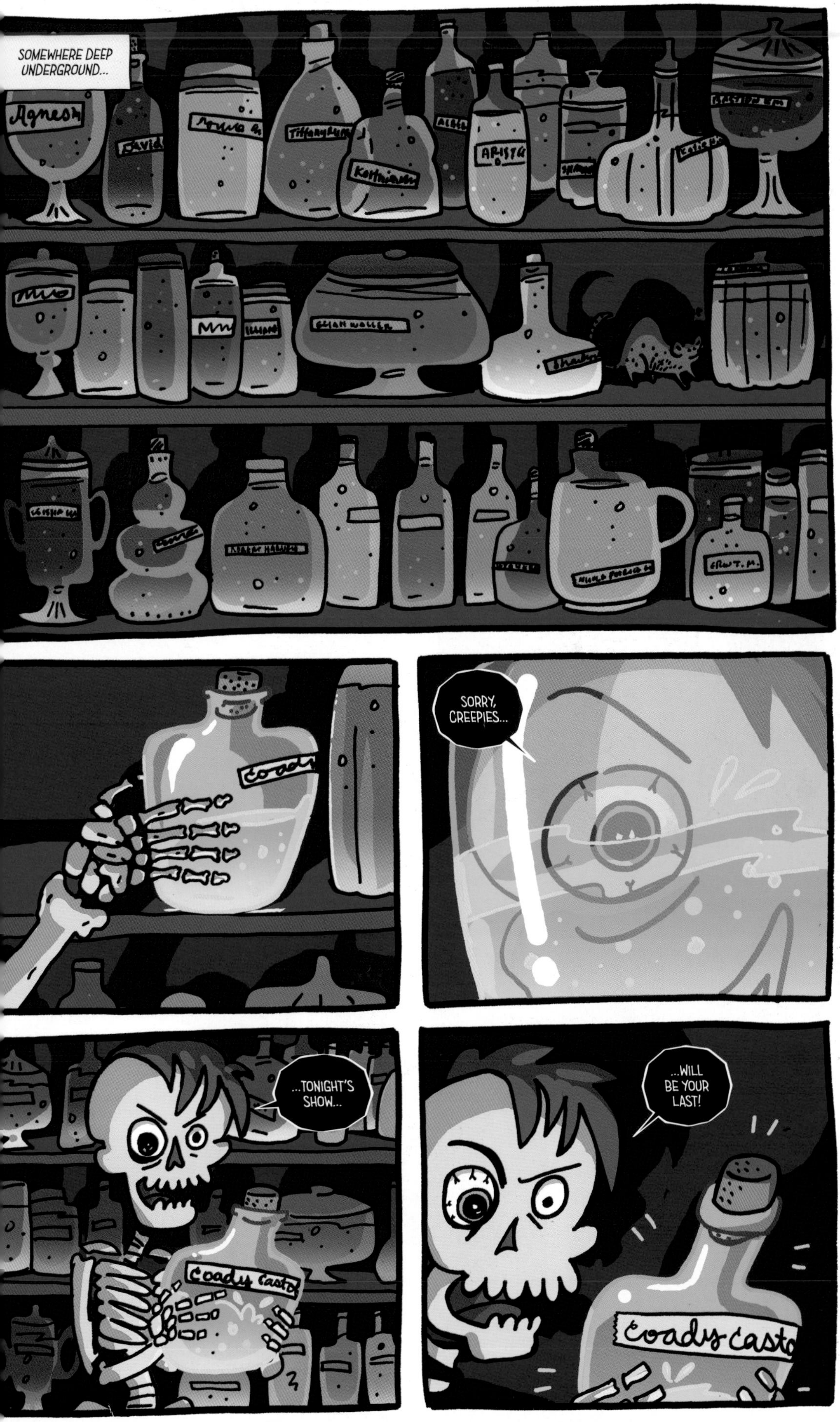
SOMEWHERE DEEP UNDERGROUND...
SORRY, CREEPIES...
...TONIGHT'S SHOW...
...WILL BE YOUR LAST!

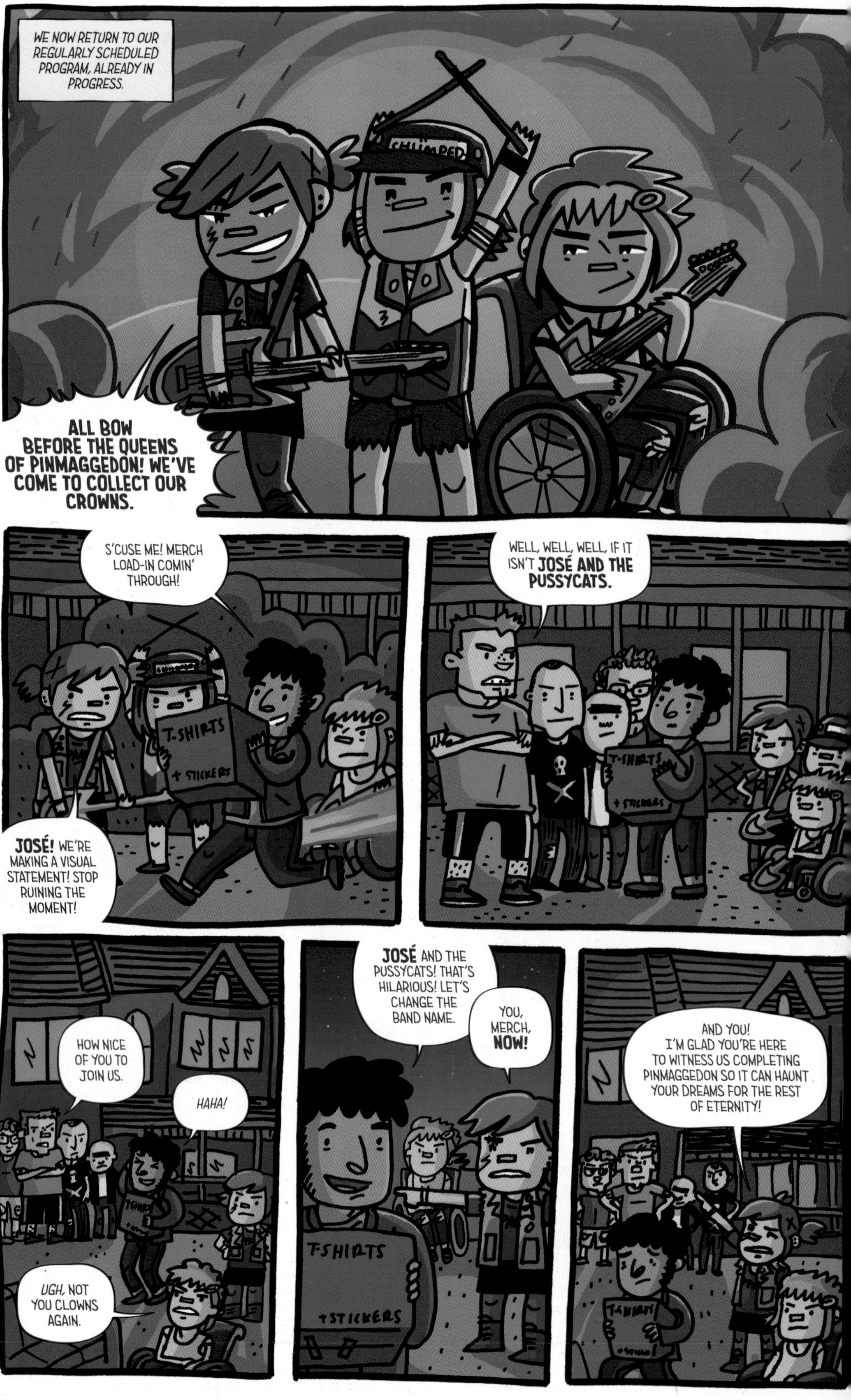

WE NOW RETURN TO OUR REGULARLY SCHEDULED PROGRAM, ALREADY IN PROGRESS.
ALL BOW BEFORE THE QUEENS OF PINMAGGEDON! WE'VE COME TO COLLECT OUR CROWNS.
S'CUSE ME! MERCH LOAD-IN COMIN' THROUGH!
T-SHIRTS + STICKERS
JOSÉ! WE'RE MAKING A VISUAL STATEMENT! STOP RUINING THE MOMENT!
WELL, WELL, WELL, IF IT ISN'T JOSÉ AND THE PUSSYCATS.
HOW NICE OF YOU TO JOIN US.
HAHA!
UGH, NOT YOU CLOWNS AGAIN.
JOSÉ AND THE PUSSYCATS! THAT'S HILARIOUS! LET'S CHANGE THE BAND NAME.
YOU, MERCH, NOW!
T-SHIRTS +STICKERS
AND YOU! I'M GLAD YOU'RE HERE TO WITNESS US COMPLETING PINMAGGEDON SO IT CAN HAUNT YOUR DREAMS FOR THE REST OF ETERNITY!

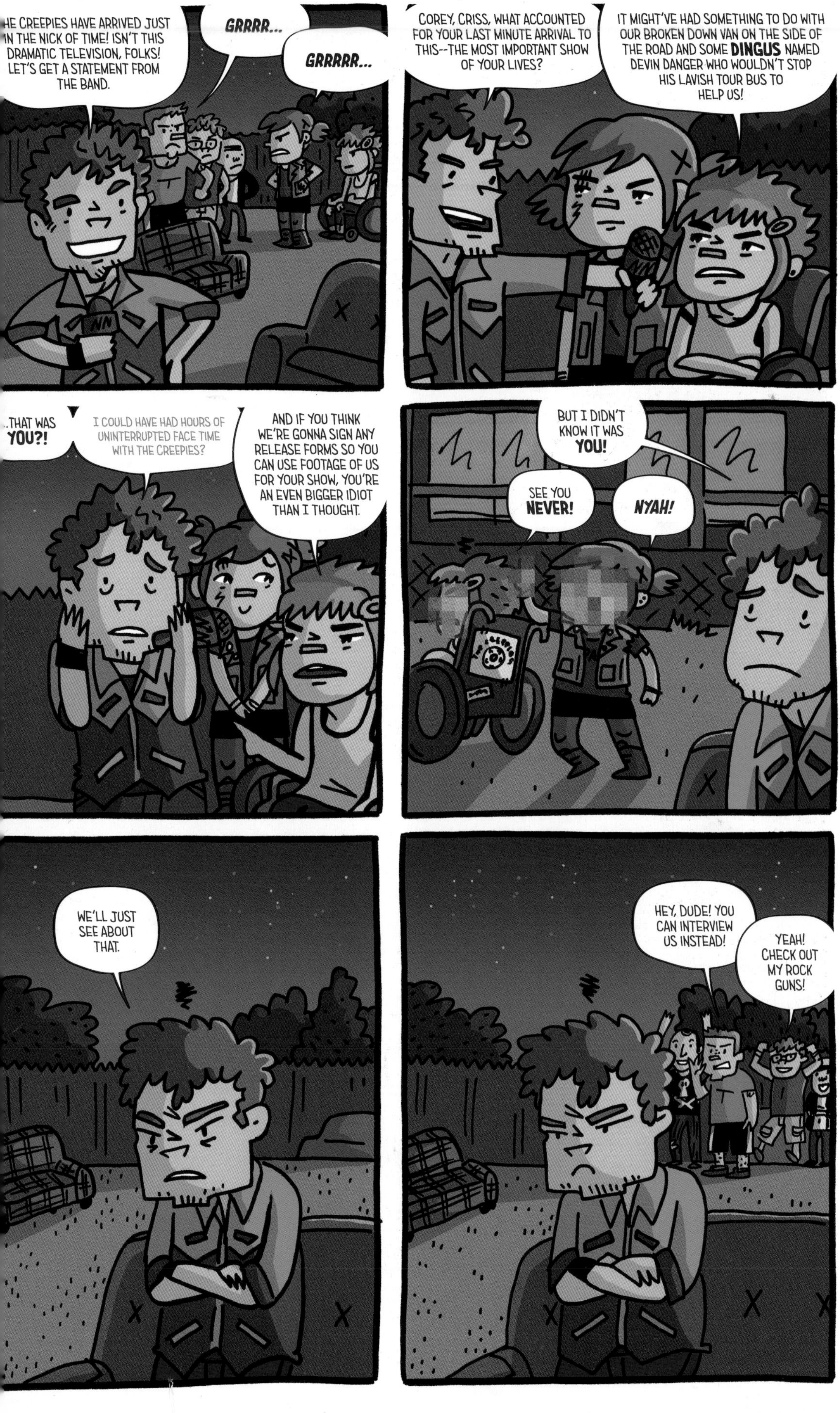
HE CREEPIES HAVE ARRIVED JUST IN THE NICK OF TIME! ISN'T THIS DRAMATIC TELEVISION, FOLKS! LET'S GET A STATEMENT FROM THE BAND.
GRRRR...
GRRRRR...
COREY, CRISS, WHAT ACCOUNTED FOR YOUR LAST MINUTE ARRIVAL TO THIS--THE MOST IMPORTANT SHOW OF YOUR LIVES?
IT MIGHT'VE HAD SOMETHING TO DO WITH OUR BROKEN DOWN VAN ON THE SIDE OF THE ROAD AND SOME DINGUS NAMED DEVIN DANGER WHO WOULDN'T STOP HIS LAVISH TOUR BUS TO HELP US!
.THAT WAS YOU?!
I COULD HAVE HAD HOURS OF UNINTERRUPTED FACE TIME WITH THE CREEPIES?
AND IF YOU THINK WE'RE GONNA SIGN ANY RELEASE FORMS SO YOU CAN USE FOOTAGE OF US FOR YOUR SHOW, YOU'RE AN EVEN BIGGER IDIOT THAN I THOUGHT.
BUT I DIDN'T KNOW IT WAS YOU!
SEE YOU NEVER!
NYAH!
WE'LL JUST SEE ABOUT THAT.
HEY, DUDE! YOU CAN INTERVIEW US INSTEAD!
YEAH! CHECK OUT MY ROCK GUNS!

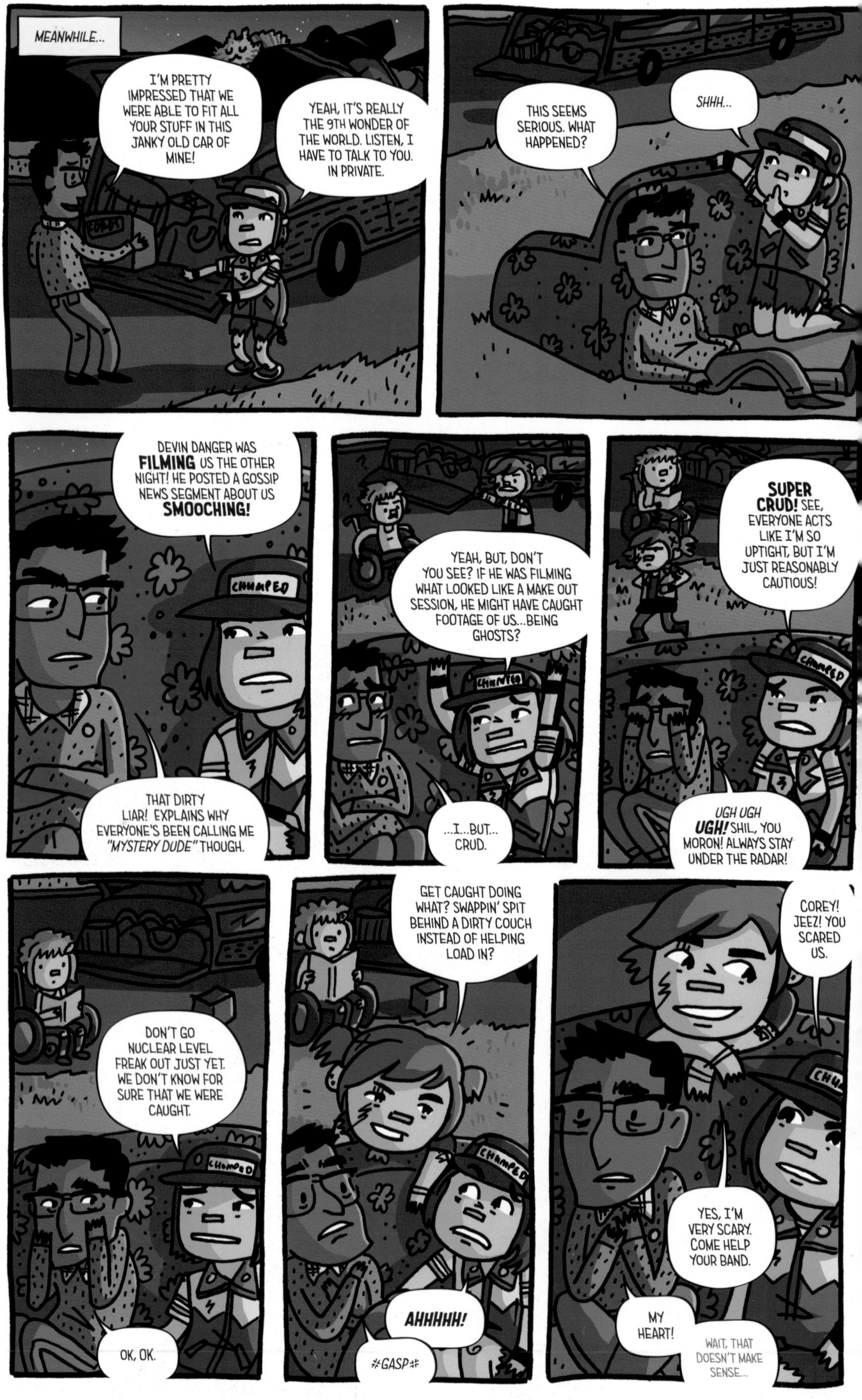
MEANWHILE...
I'M PRETTY IMPRESSED THAT WE WERE ABLE TO FIT ALL YOUR STUFF IN THIS JANKY OLD CAR OF MINE!
YEAH, IT'S REALLY THE 9TH WONDER OF THE WORLD. LISTEN, I HAVE TO TALK TO YOU. IN PRIVATE.
THIS SEEMS SERIOUS. WHAT HAPPENED?
SHHH...
DEVIN DANGER WAS **FILMING** US THE OTHER NIGHT! HE POSTED A GOSSIP NEWS SEGMENT ABOUT US **SMOOCHING!**
THAT DIRTY LIAR! EXPLAINS WHY EVERYONE'S BEEN CALLING ME *"MYSTERY DUDE"* THOUGH.
YEAH, BUT, DON'T YOU SEE? IF HE WAS FILMING WHAT LOOKED LIKE A MAKE OUT SESSION, HE MIGHT HAVE CAUGHT FOOTAGE OF US...BEING GHOSTS?
...I...BUT... CRUD.
SUPER CRUD! SEE, EVERYONE ACTS LIKE I'M SO UPTIGHT, BUT I'M JUST REASONABLY CAUTIOUS!
UGH UGH ***UGH!*** SHIL, YOU MORON! ALWAYS STAY UNDER THE RADAR!
DON'T GO NUCLEAR LEVEL FREAK OUT JUST YET. WE DON'T KNOW FOR SURE THAT WE WERE CAUGHT.
OK, OK.
GET CAUGHT DOING WHAT? SWAPPIN' SPIT BEHIND A DIRTY COUCH INSTEAD OF HELPING LOAD IN?
AHHHHH!
#GASP#
COREY! JEEZ! YOU SCARED US.
YES, I'M VERY SCARY. COME HELP YOUR BAND.
MY HEART!
WAIT, THAT DOESN'T MAKE SENSE...

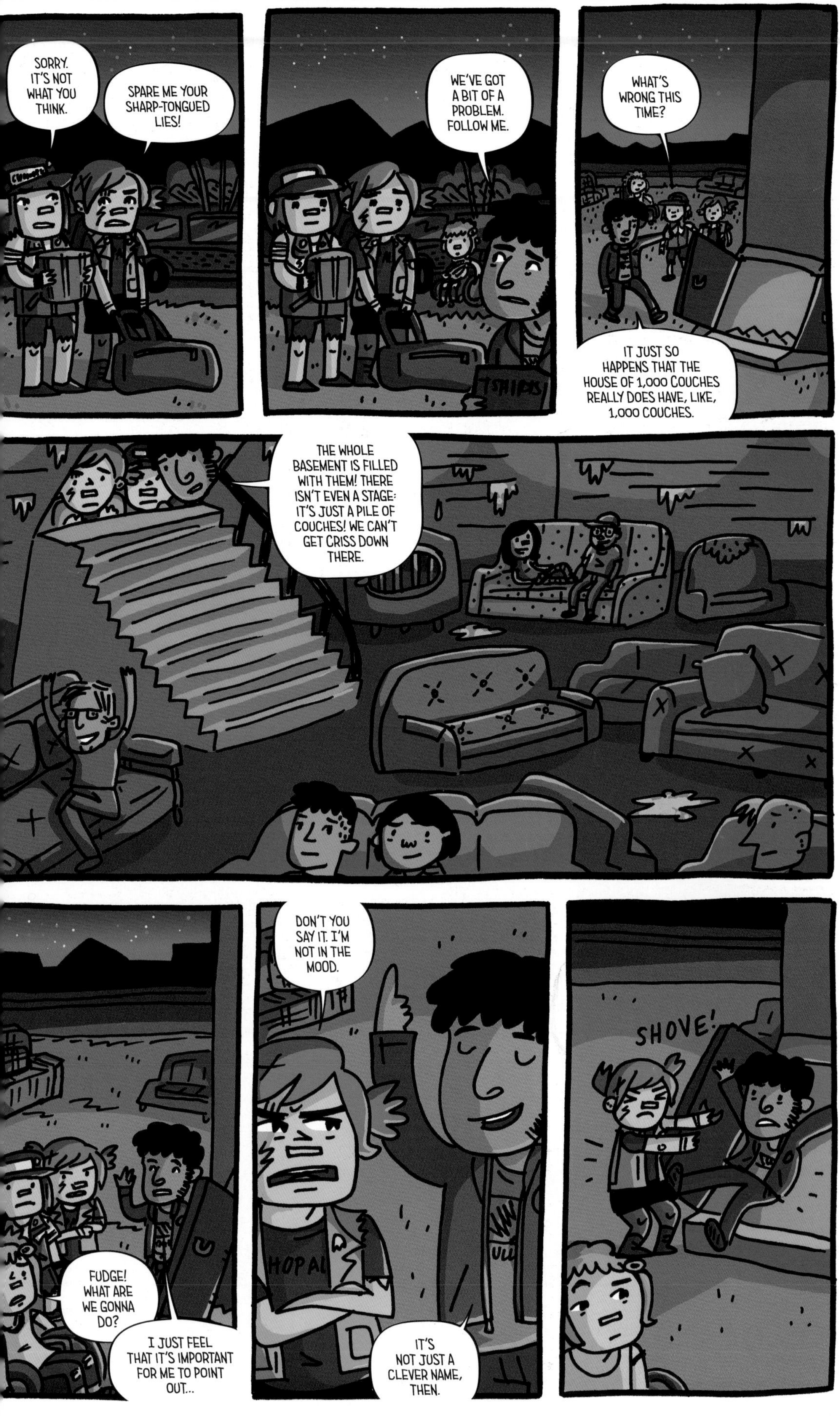
SORRY. IT'S NOT WHAT YOU THINK.
SPARE ME YOUR SHARP-TONGUED LIES!
WE'VE GOT A BIT OF A PROBLEM. FOLLOW ME.
T-SHIRTS
WHAT'S WRONG THIS TIME?
IT JUST SO HAPPENS THAT THE HOUSE OF 1,000 COUCHES REALLY DOES HAVE, LIKE, 1,000 COUCHES.
THE WHOLE BASEMENT IS FILLED WITH THEM! THERE ISN'T EVEN A STAGE: IT'S JUST A PILE OF COUCHES! WE CAN'T GET CRISS DOWN THERE.
FUDGE! WHAT ARE WE GONNA DO?
I JUST FEEL THAT IT'S IMPORTANT FOR ME TO POINT OUT...
DON'T YOU SAY IT. I'M NOT IN THE MOOD.
IT'S NOT JUST A CLEVER NAME, THEN.
SHOVE!

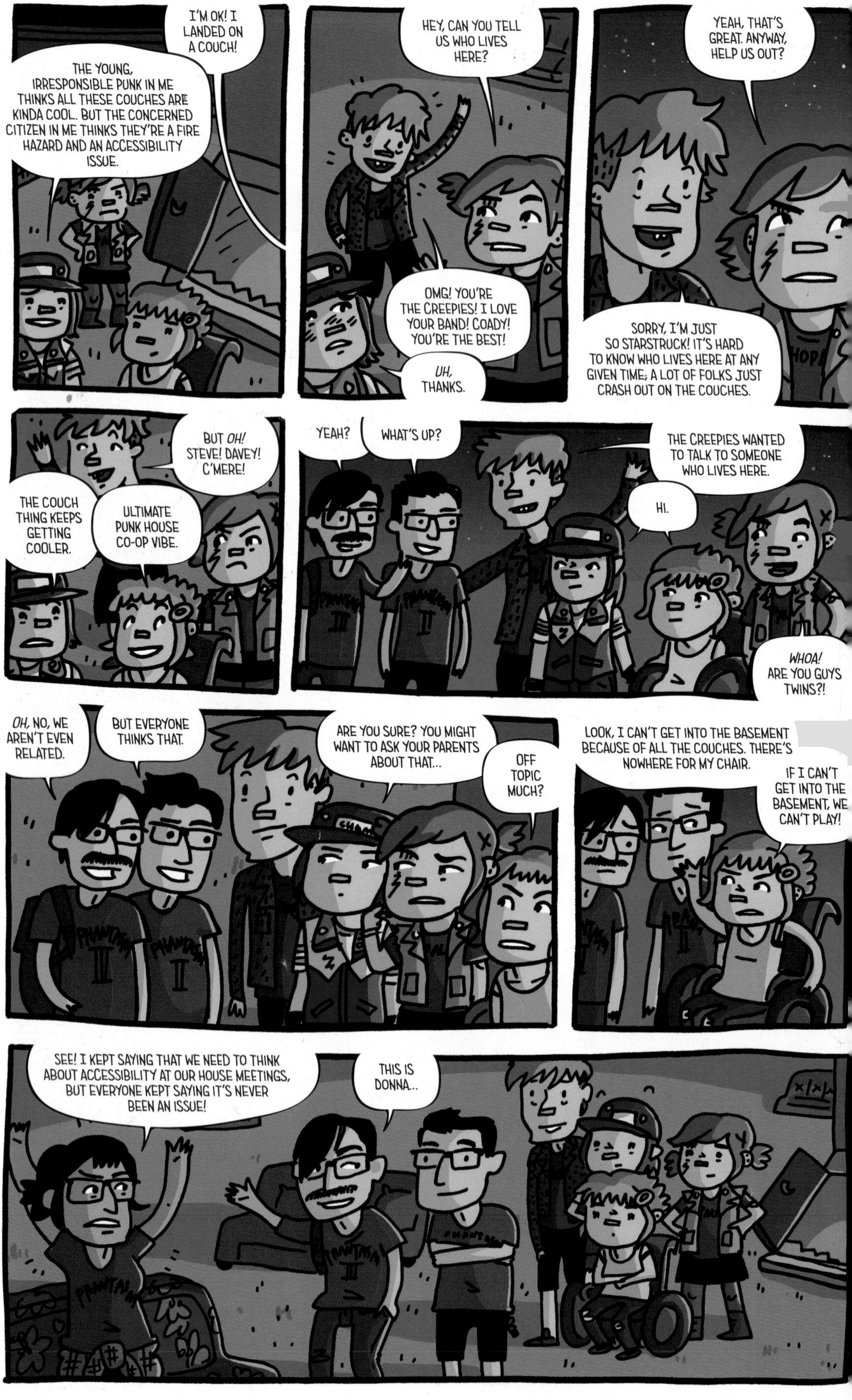
I'M OK! I LANDED ON A COUCH!
THE YOUNG, IRRESPONSIBLE PUNK IN ME THINKS ALL THESE COUCHES ARE KINDA COOL. BUT THE CONCERNED CITIZEN IN ME THINKS THEY'RE A FIRE HAZARD AND AN ACCESSIBILITY ISSUE.
HEY, CAN YOU TELL US WHO LIVES HERE?
OMG! YOU'RE THE CREEPIES! I LOVE YOUR BAND! COADY! YOU'RE THE BEST!
UH, THANKS.
YEAH, THAT'S GREAT. ANYWAY, HELP US OUT?
SORRY, I'M JUST SO STARSTRUCK! IT'S HARD TO KNOW WHO LIVES HERE AT ANY GIVEN TIME; A LOT OF FOLKS JUST CRASH OUT ON THE COUCHES.
BUT *OH!* STEVE! DAVEY! C'MERE!
THE COUCH THING KEEPS GETTING COOLER.
ULTIMATE PUNK HOUSE CO-OP VIBE.
YEAH?
WHAT'S UP?
THE CREEPIES WANTED TO TALK TO SOMEONE WHO LIVES HERE.
HI.
WHOA! ARE YOU GUYS TWINS?!
OH, NO, WE AREN'T EVEN RELATED.
BUT EVERYONE THINKS THAT.
ARE YOU SURE? YOU MIGHT WANT TO ASK YOUR PARENTS ABOUT THAT...
OFF TOPIC MUCH?
LOOK, I CAN'T GET INTO THE BASEMENT BECAUSE OF ALL THE COUCHES. THERE'S NOWHERE FOR MY CHAIR.
IF I CAN'T GET INTO THE BASEMENT, WE CAN'T PLAY!
SEE! I KEPT SAYING THAT WE NEED TO THINK ABOUT ACCESSIBILITY AT OUR HOUSE MEETINGS, BUT EVERYONE KEPT SAYING IT'S NEVER BEEN AN ISSUE!
THIS IS DONNA...

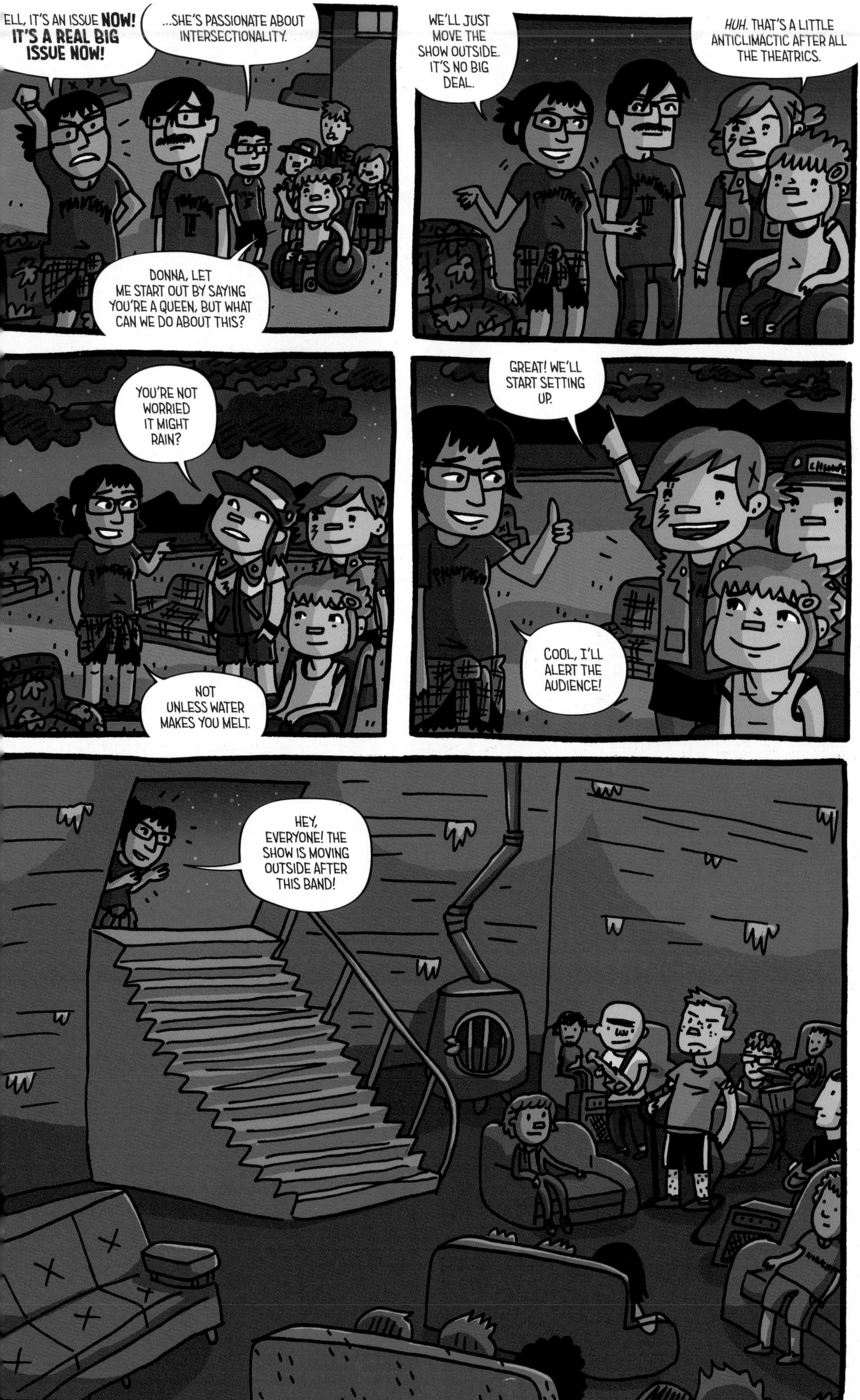
ELL, IT'S AN ISSUE NOW! IT'S A REAL BIG ISSUE NOW!
...SHE'S PASSIONATE ABOUT INTERSECTIONALITY.
DONNA, LET ME START OUT BY SAYING YOU'RE A QUEEN, BUT WHAT CAN WE DO ABOUT THIS?
WE'LL JUST MOVE THE SHOW OUTSIDE. IT'S NO BIG DEAL.
HUH. THAT'S A LITTLE ANTICLIMACTIC AFTER ALL THE THEATRICS.
YOU'RE NOT WORRIED IT MIGHT RAIN?
NOT UNLESS WATER MAKES YOU MELT.
GREAT! WE'LL START SETTING UP.
COOL, I'LL ALERT THE AUDIENCE!
HEY, EVERYONE! THE SHOW IS MOVING OUTSIDE AFTER THIS BAND!

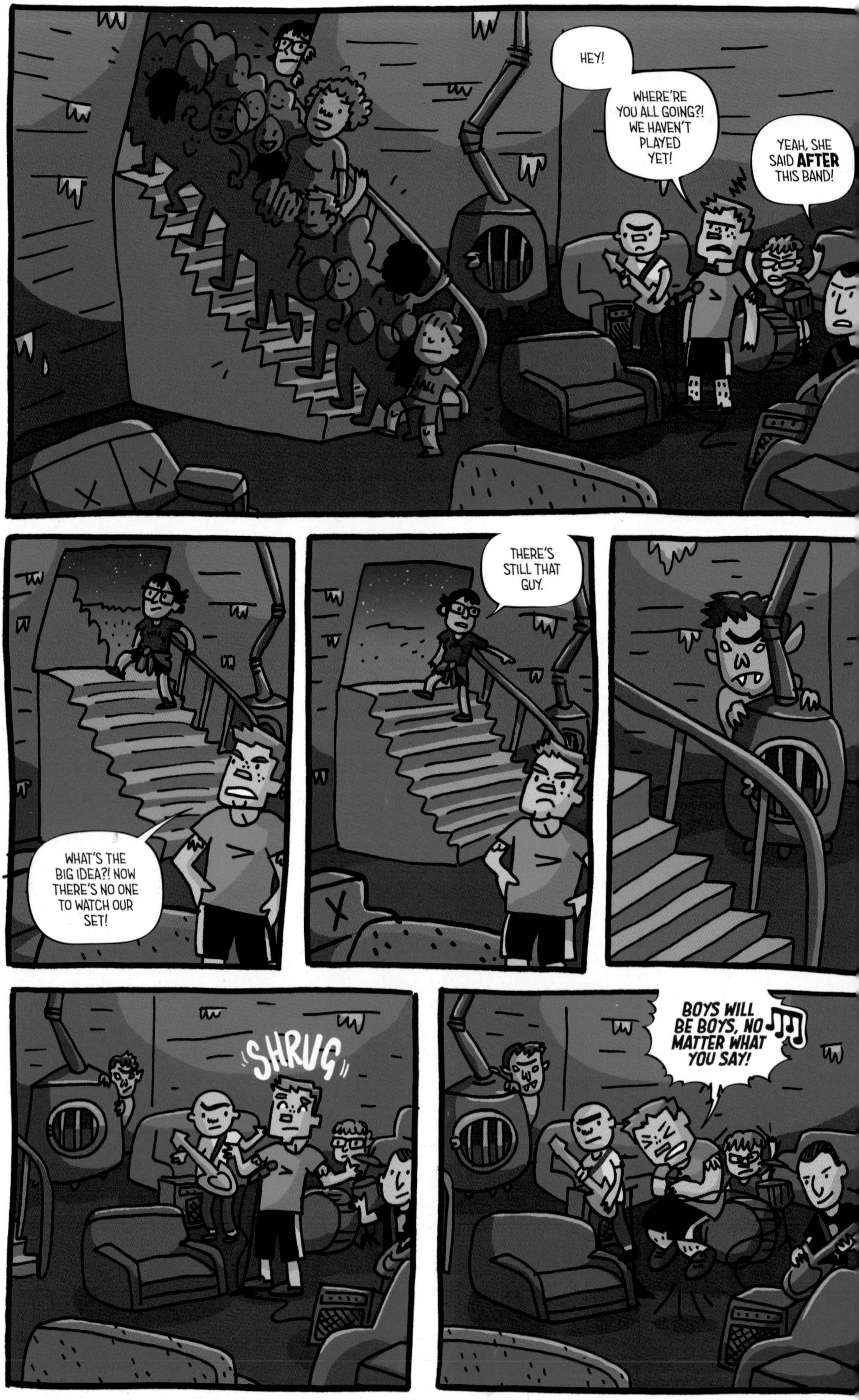
HEY!
WHERE'RE YOU ALL GOING?! WE HAVEN'T PLAYED YET!
YEAH, SHE SAID **AFTER** THIS BAND!
WHAT'S THE BIG IDEA?! NOW THERE'S NO ONE TO WATCH OUR SET!
THERE'S STILL THAT GUY.
SHRUG
BOYS WILL BE BOYS, NO MATTER WHAT YOU SAY!

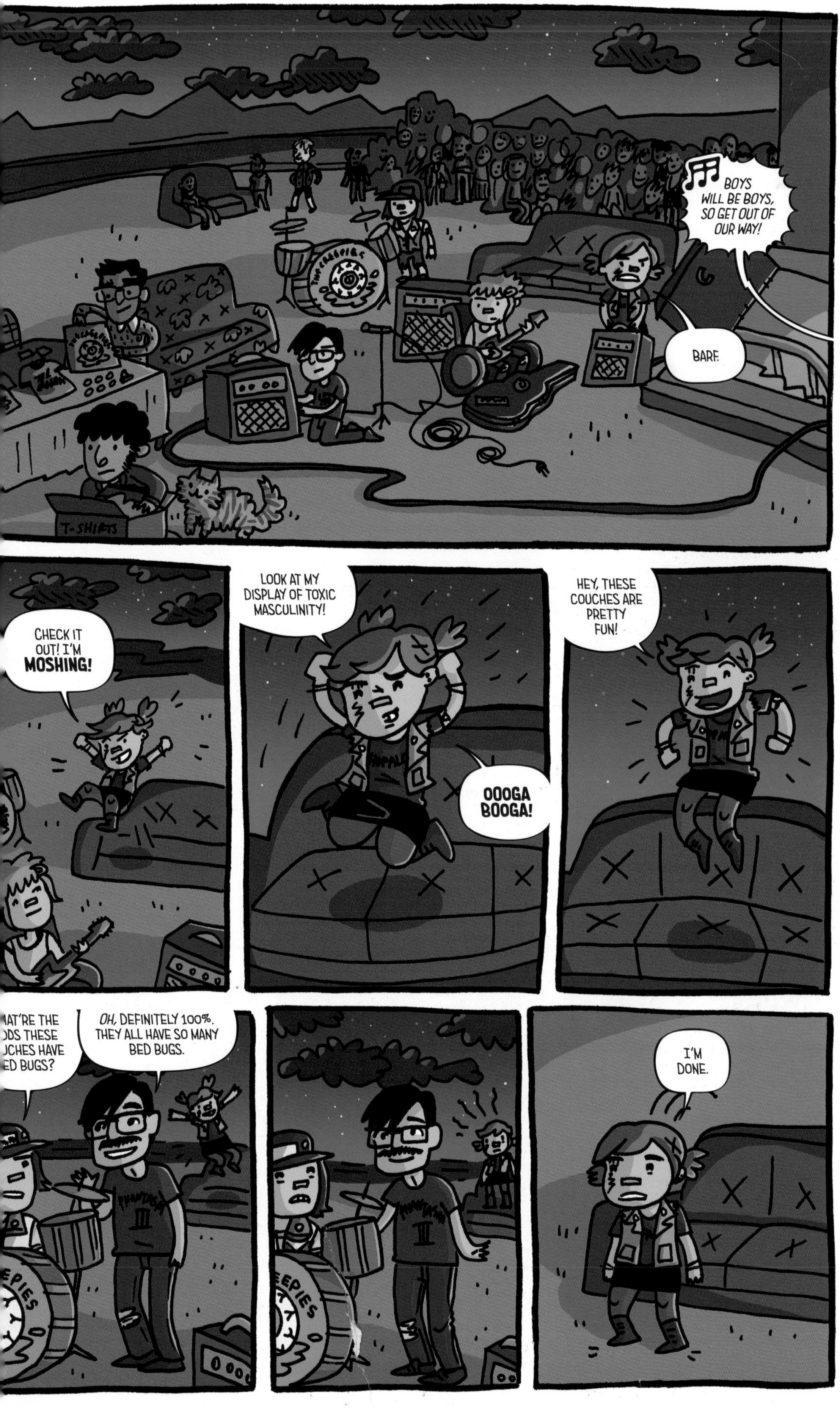

BOYS WILL BE BOYS, SO GET OUT OF OUR WAY!
BARF.
T-SHIRTS
CHECK IT OUT! I'M **MOSHING!**
LOOK AT MY DISPLAY OF TOXIC MASCULINITY!
OOOGA BOOGA!
HEY, THESE COUCHES ARE PRETTY FUN!
...HAT'RE THE ...DDS THESE ...UCHES HAVE ...ED BUGS?
OH, DEFINITELY 100%. THEY ALL HAVE SO MANY BED BUGS.
I'M DONE.

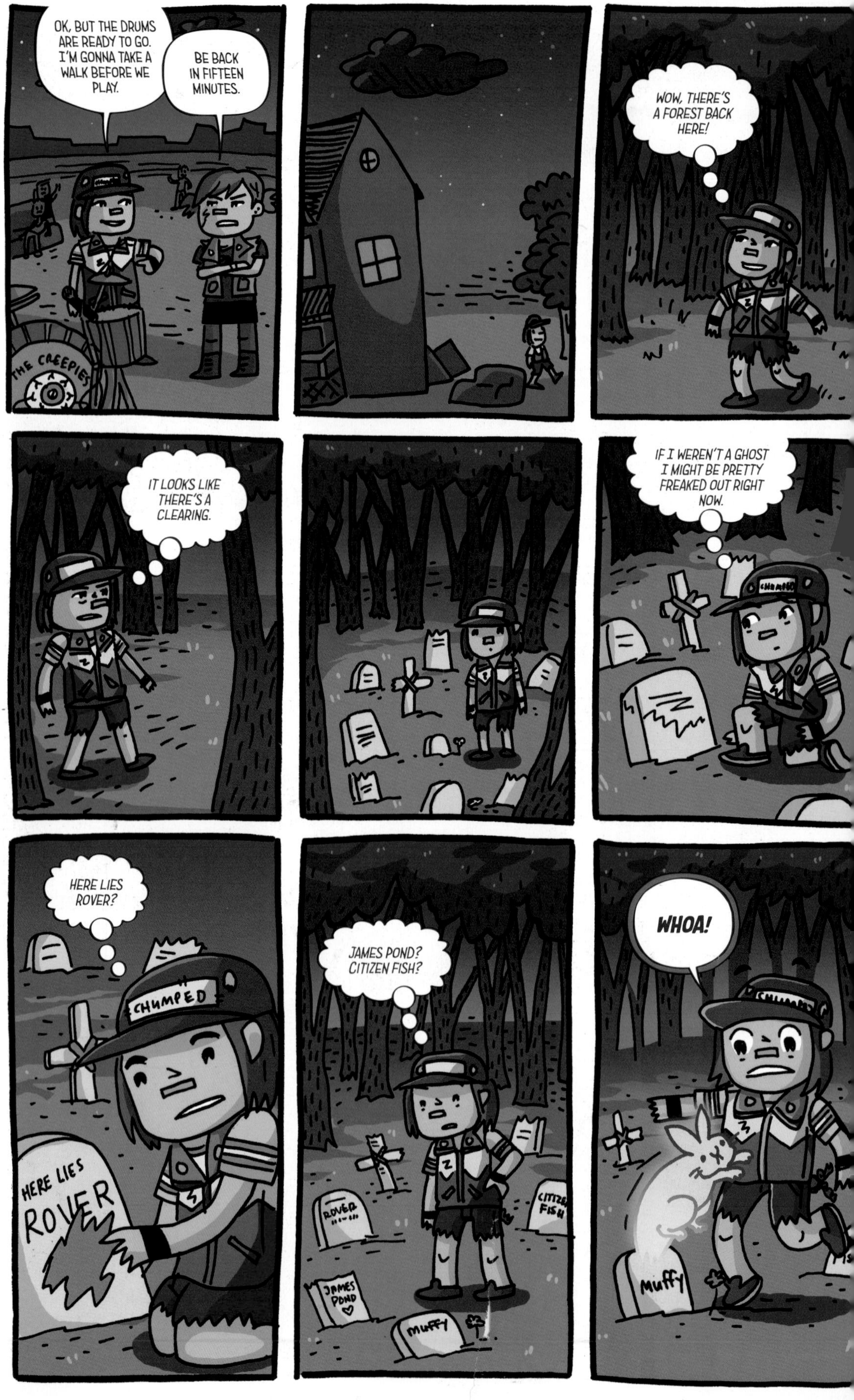

OK, BUT THE DRUMS ARE READY TO GO. I'M GONNA TAKE A WALK BEFORE WE PLAY.
BE BACK IN FIFTEEN MINUTES.
THE CREEPIES
WOW, THERE'S A FOREST BACK HERE!
IT LOOKS LIKE THERE'S A CLEARING.
IF I WEREN'T A GHOST I MIGHT BE PRETTY FREAKED OUT RIGHT NOW.
CHUMPED
HERE LIES ROVER?
CHUMPED
HERE LIES ROVER
JAMES POND? CITIZEN FISH?
ROVER
CITIZEN FISH
JAMES POND
MUFFY
WHOA!
MUFFY

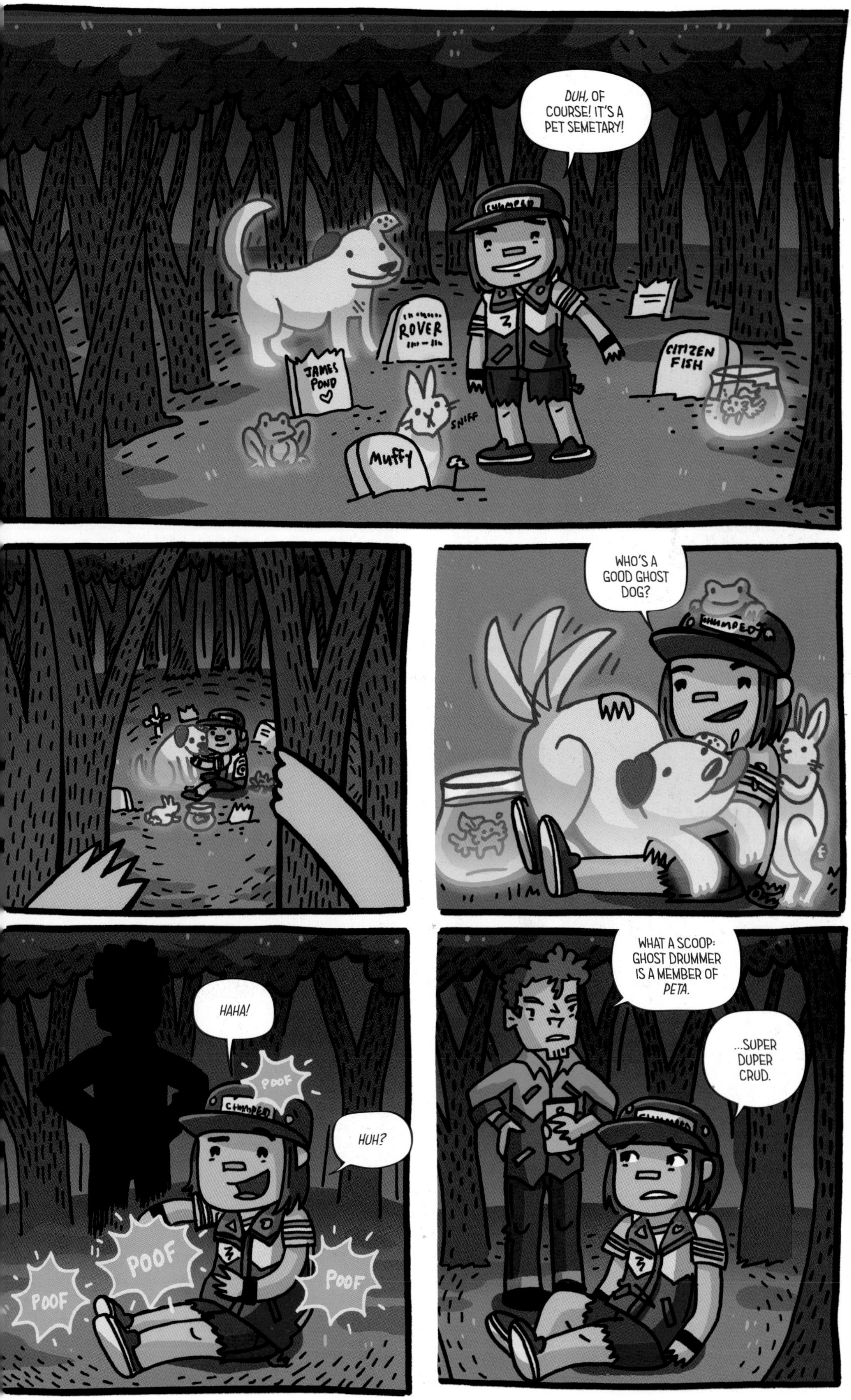

DUH, OF COURSE! IT'S A PET SEMETARY!
ROVER
JAMES POND
CITIZEN FISH
SNIFF
MUFFY
WHO'S A GOOD GHOST DOG?
HAHA!
POOF
HUH?
POOF
POOF
POOF
WHAT A SCOOP: GHOST DRUMMER IS A MEMBER OF PETA.
...SUPER DUPER CRUD.

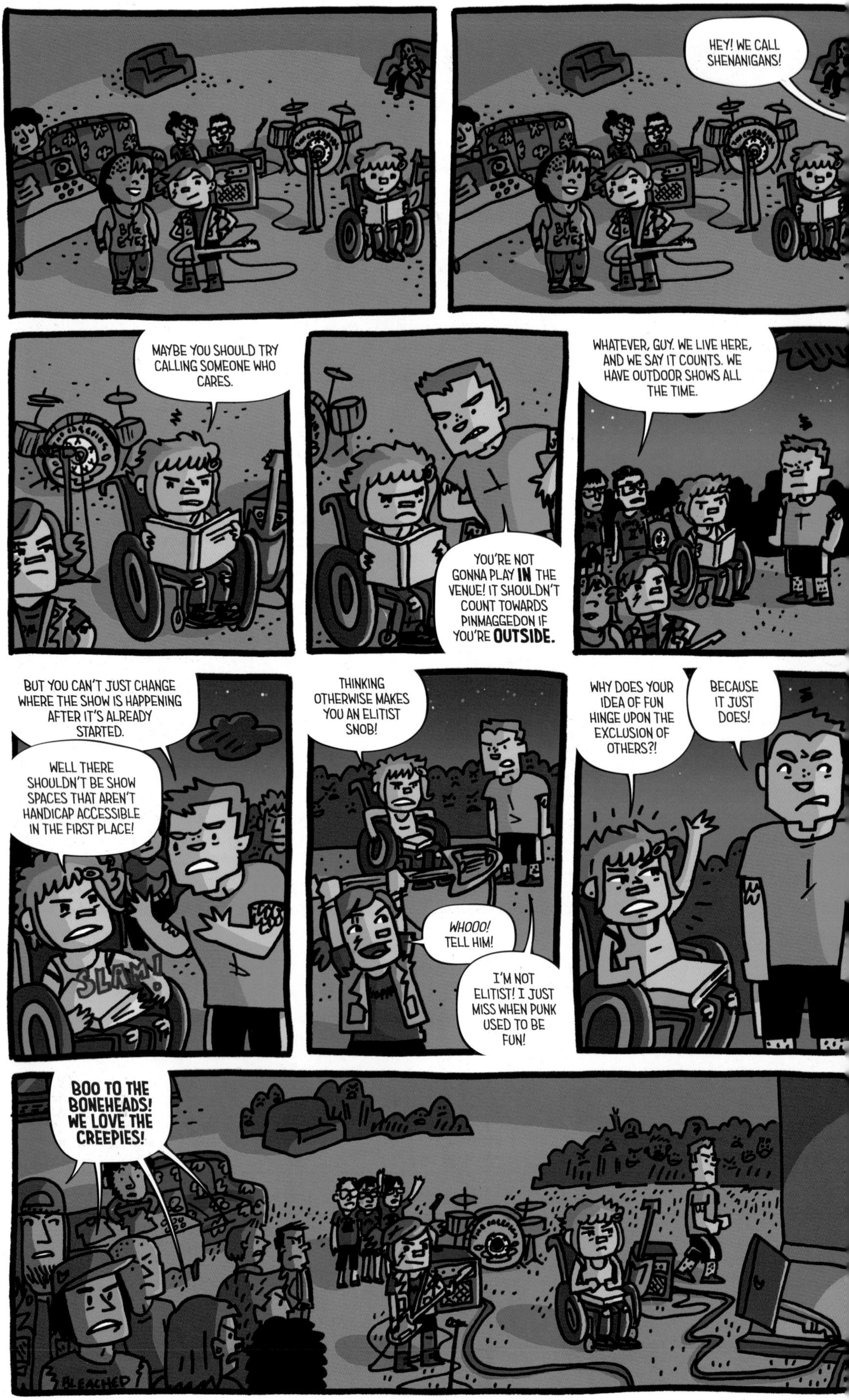
HEY! WE CALL SHENANIGANS!
MAYBE YOU SHOULD TRY CALLING SOMEONE WHO CARES.
YOU'RE NOT GONNA PLAY **IN** THE VENUE! IT SHOULDN'T COUNT TOWARDS PINMAGGEDON IF YOU'RE **OUTSIDE.**
WHATEVER, GUY. WE LIVE HERE, AND WE SAY IT COUNTS. WE HAVE OUTDOOR SHOWS ALL THE TIME.
BUT YOU CAN'T JUST CHANGE WHERE THE SHOW IS HAPPENING AFTER IT'S ALREADY STARTED.
WELL THERE SHOULDN'T BE SHOW SPACES THAT AREN'T HANDICAP ACCESSIBLE IN THE FIRST PLACE!
SLAM!
THINKING OTHERWISE MAKES YOU AN ELITIST SNOB!
WHOOO! TELL HIM!
I'M NOT ELITIST! I JUST MISS WHEN PUNK USED TO BE FUN!
WHY DOES YOUR IDEA OF FUN HINGE UPON THE EXCLUSION OF OTHERS?!
BECAUSE IT JUST DOES!
BOO TO THE BONEHEADS! WE LOVE THE CREEPIES!
BLEACHED

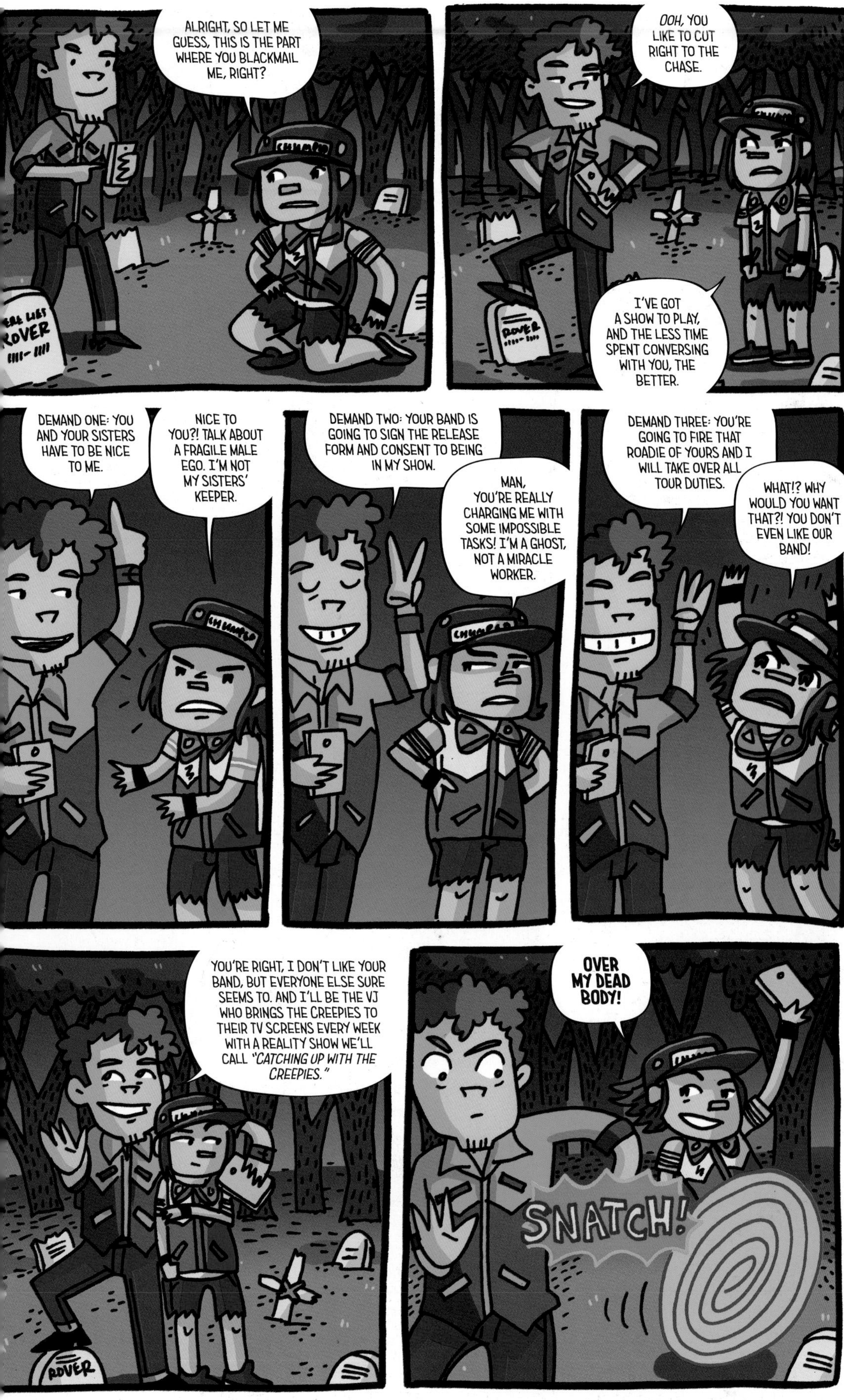
ALRIGHT, SO LET ME GUESS, THIS IS THE PART WHERE YOU BLACKMAIL ME, RIGHT?
HERE LIES ROVER
OOH, YOU LIKE TO CUT RIGHT TO THE CHASE.
I'VE GOT A SHOW TO PLAY, AND THE LESS TIME SPENT CONVERSING WITH YOU, THE BETTER.
ROVER
DEMAND ONE: YOU AND YOUR SISTERS HAVE TO BE NICE TO ME.
NICE TO YOU?! TALK ABOUT A FRAGILE MALE EGO. I'M NOT MY SISTERS' KEEPER.
DEMAND TWO: YOUR BAND IS GOING TO SIGN THE RELEASE FORM AND CONSENT TO BEING IN MY SHOW.
MAN, YOU'RE REALLY CHARGING ME WITH SOME IMPOSSIBLE TASKS! I'M A GHOST, NOT A MIRACLE WORKER.
DEMAND THREE: YOU'RE GOING TO FIRE THAT ROADIE OF YOURS AND I WILL TAKE OVER ALL TOUR DUTIES.
WHAT!? WHY WOULD YOU WANT THAT?! YOU DON'T EVEN LIKE OUR BAND!
YOU'RE RIGHT, I DON'T LIKE YOUR BAND, BUT EVERYONE ELSE SURE SEEMS TO. AND I'LL BE THE VJ WHO BRINGS THE CREEPIES TO THEIR TV SCREENS EVERY WEEK WITH A REALITY SHOW WE'LL CALL *"CATCHING UP WITH THE CREEPIES."*
ROVER
OVER MY DEAD BODY!
SNATCH!

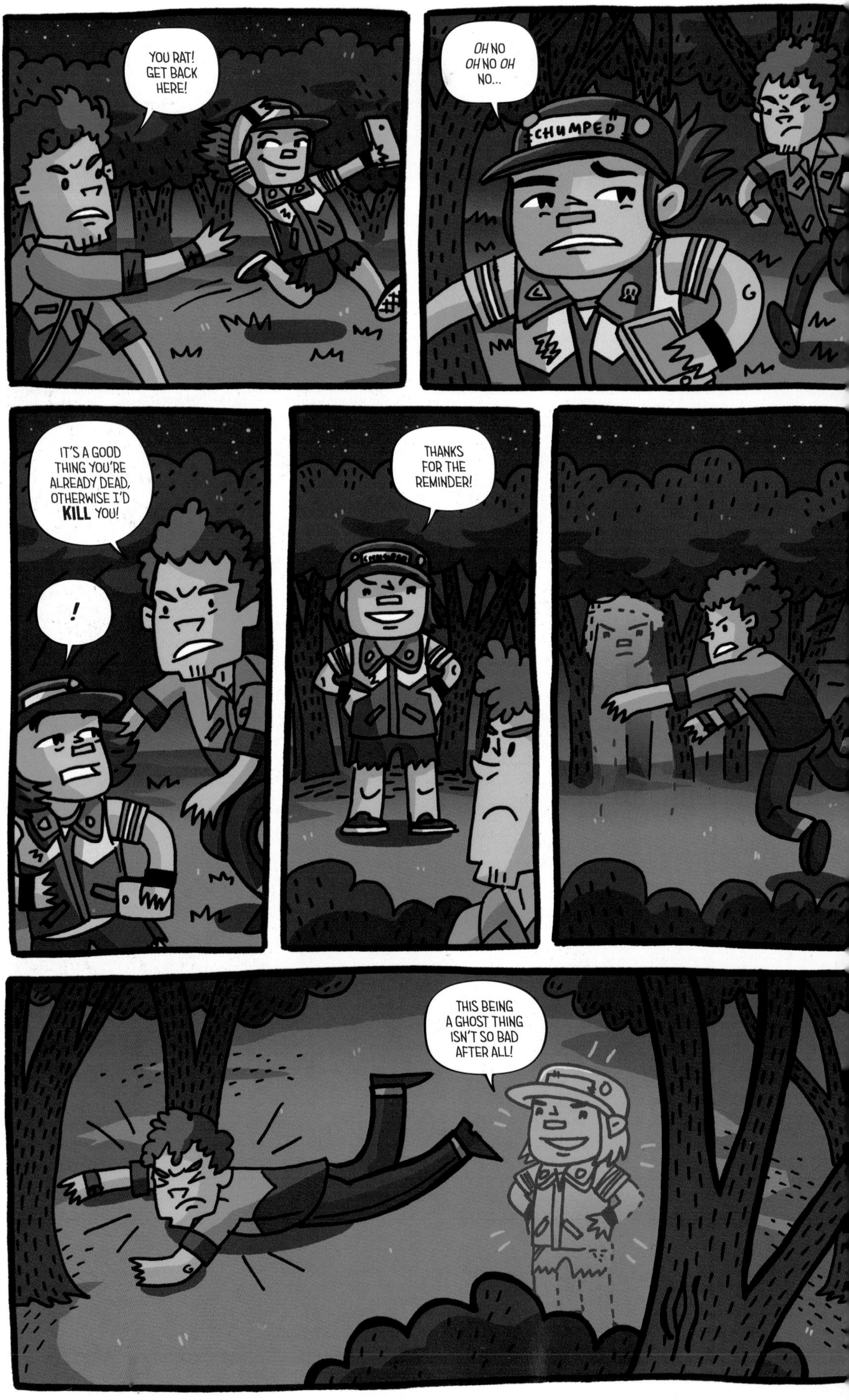
YOU RAT! GET BACK HERE!
OH NO OH NO OH NO...
IT'S A GOOD THING YOU'RE ALREADY DEAD, OTHERWISE I'D **KILL** YOU!
!
THANKS FOR THE REMINDER!
THIS BEING A GHOST THING ISN'T SO BAD AFTER ALL!

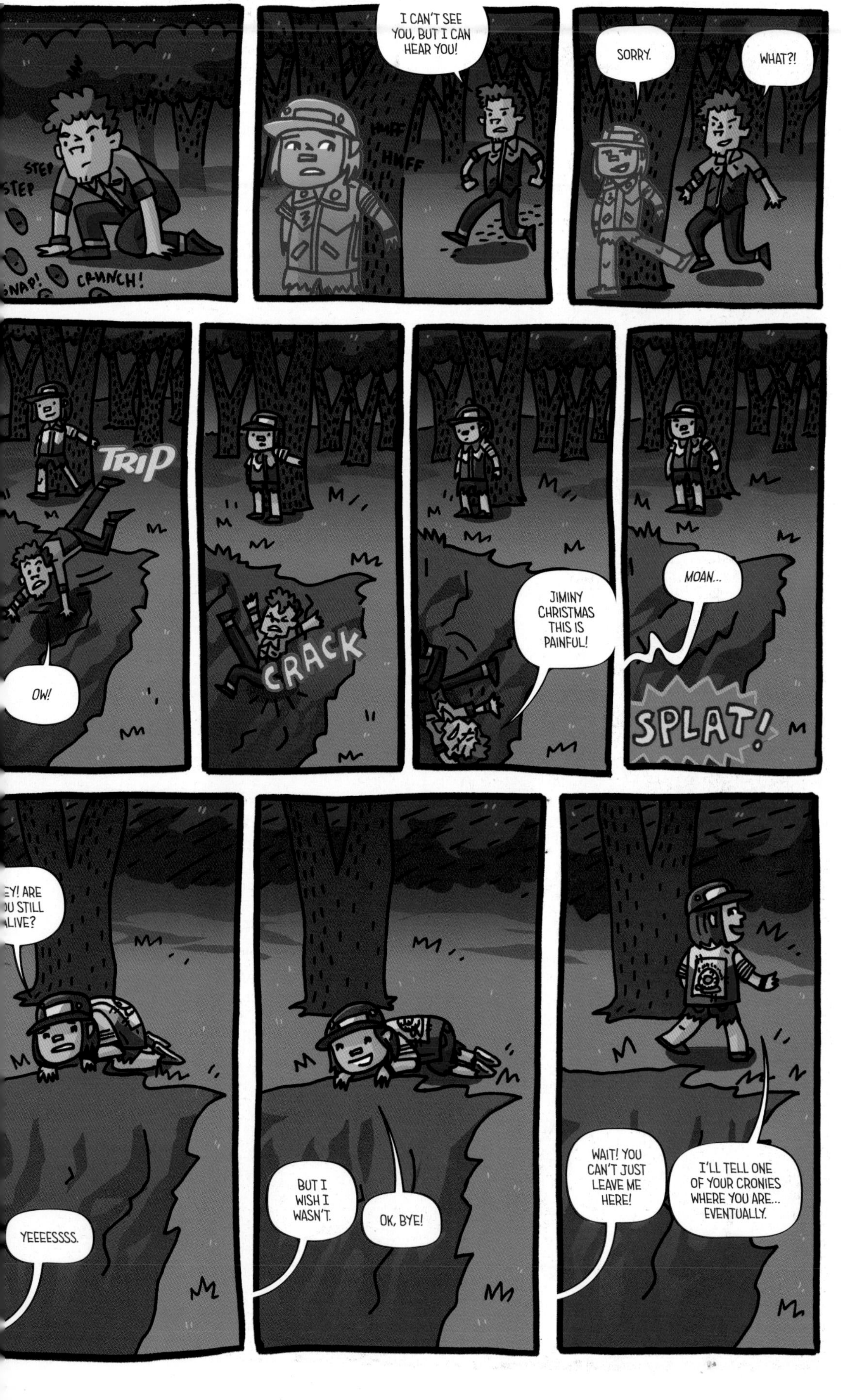
STEP
STEP
SNAP!
CRUNCH!
I CAN'T SEE YOU, BUT I CAN HEAR YOU!
HUFF
HUFF
SORRY.
WHAT?!
TRIP
OW!
CRACK
JIMINY CHRISTMAS THIS IS PAINFUL!
MOAN...
SPLAT!
EY! ARE
OU STILL
ALIVE?
YEEEESSSS.
BUT I WISH I WASN'T.
OK, BYE!
WAIT! YOU CAN'T JUST LEAVE ME HERE!
I'LL TELL ONE OF YOUR CRONIES WHERE YOU ARE... EVENTUALLY.

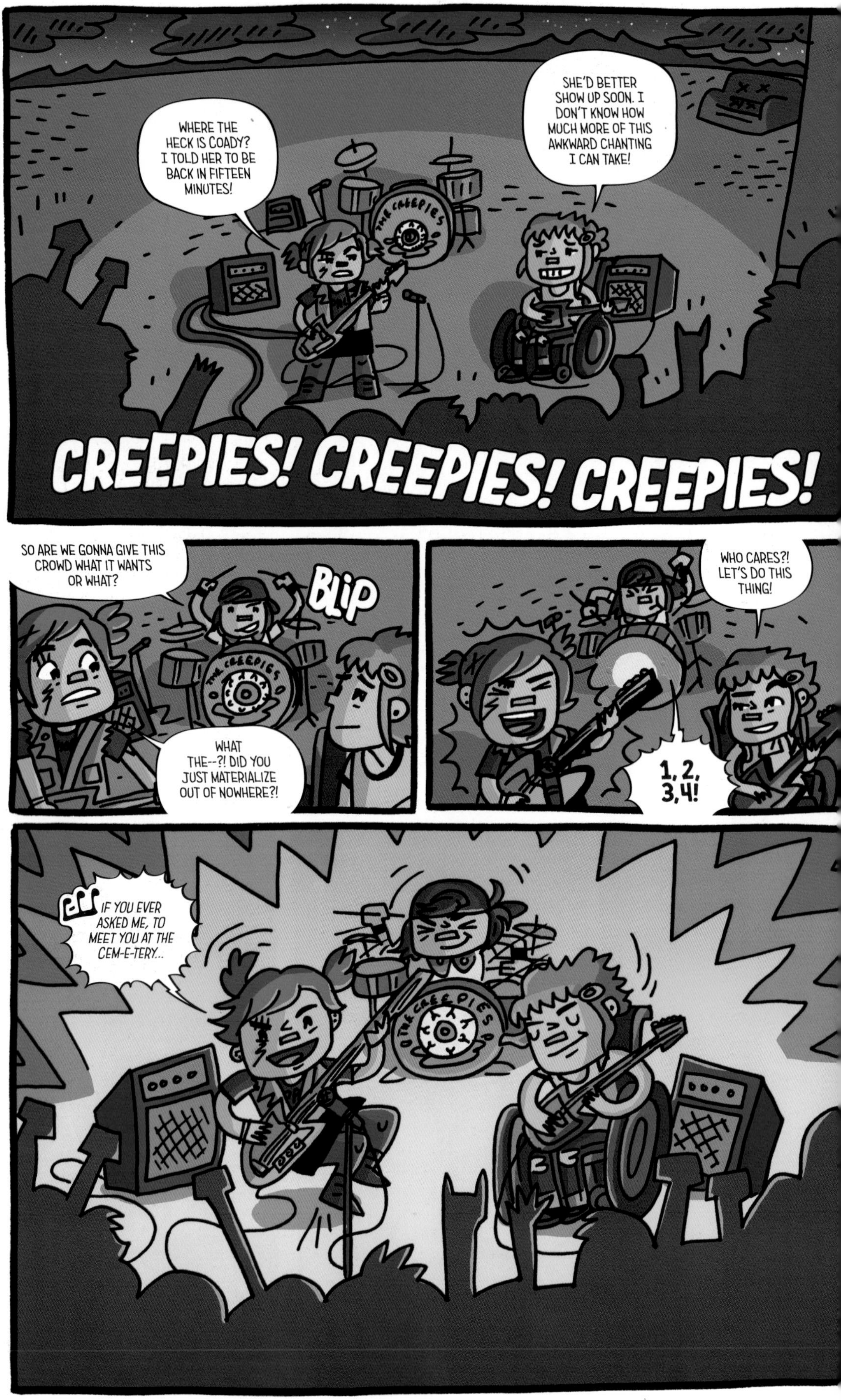
WHERE THE HECK IS COADY? I TOLD HER TO BE BACK IN FIFTEEN MINUTES!
SHE'D BETTER SHOW UP SOON. I DON'T KNOW HOW MUCH MORE OF THIS AWKWARD CHANTING I CAN TAKE!
CREEPIES! CREEPIES! CREEPIES!
SO ARE WE GONNA GIVE THIS CROWD WHAT IT WANTS OR WHAT?
BLIP
WHAT THE--?! DID YOU JUST MATERIALIZE OUT OF NOWHERE?!
WHO CARES?! LET'S DO THIS THING!
1, 2, 3, 4!
IF YOU EVER ASKED ME, TO MEET YOU AT THE CEM-E-TERY...

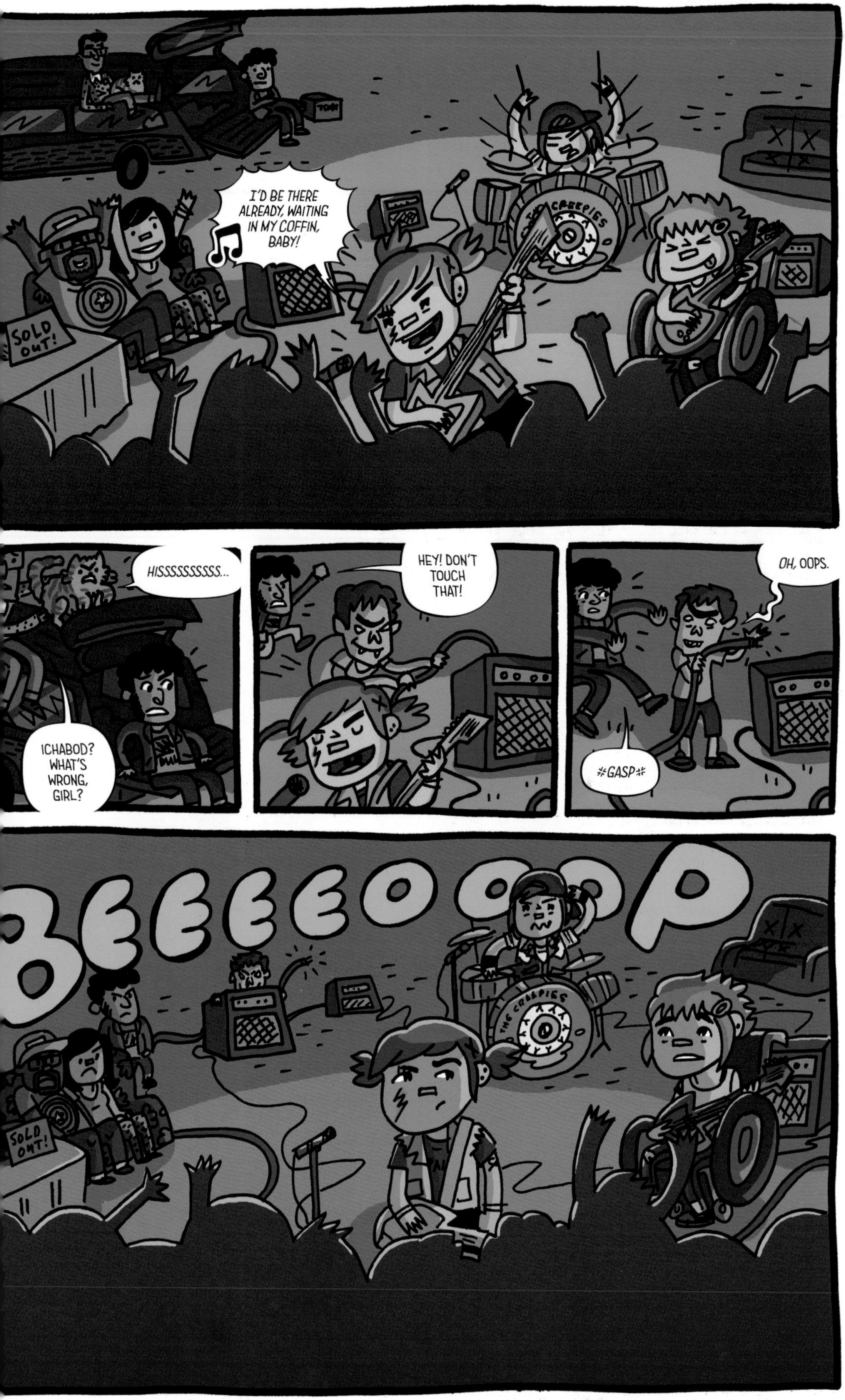
I'D BE THERE ALREADY, WAITING IN MY COFFIN, BABY!
SOLD OUT!
THE CREEPIES
HISSSSSSSSSS...
ICHABOD? WHAT'S WRONG, GIRL?
HEY! DON'T TOUCH THAT!
OH, OOPS.
GASP
BEEEEOOOP
SOLD OUT!
THE CREEPIES

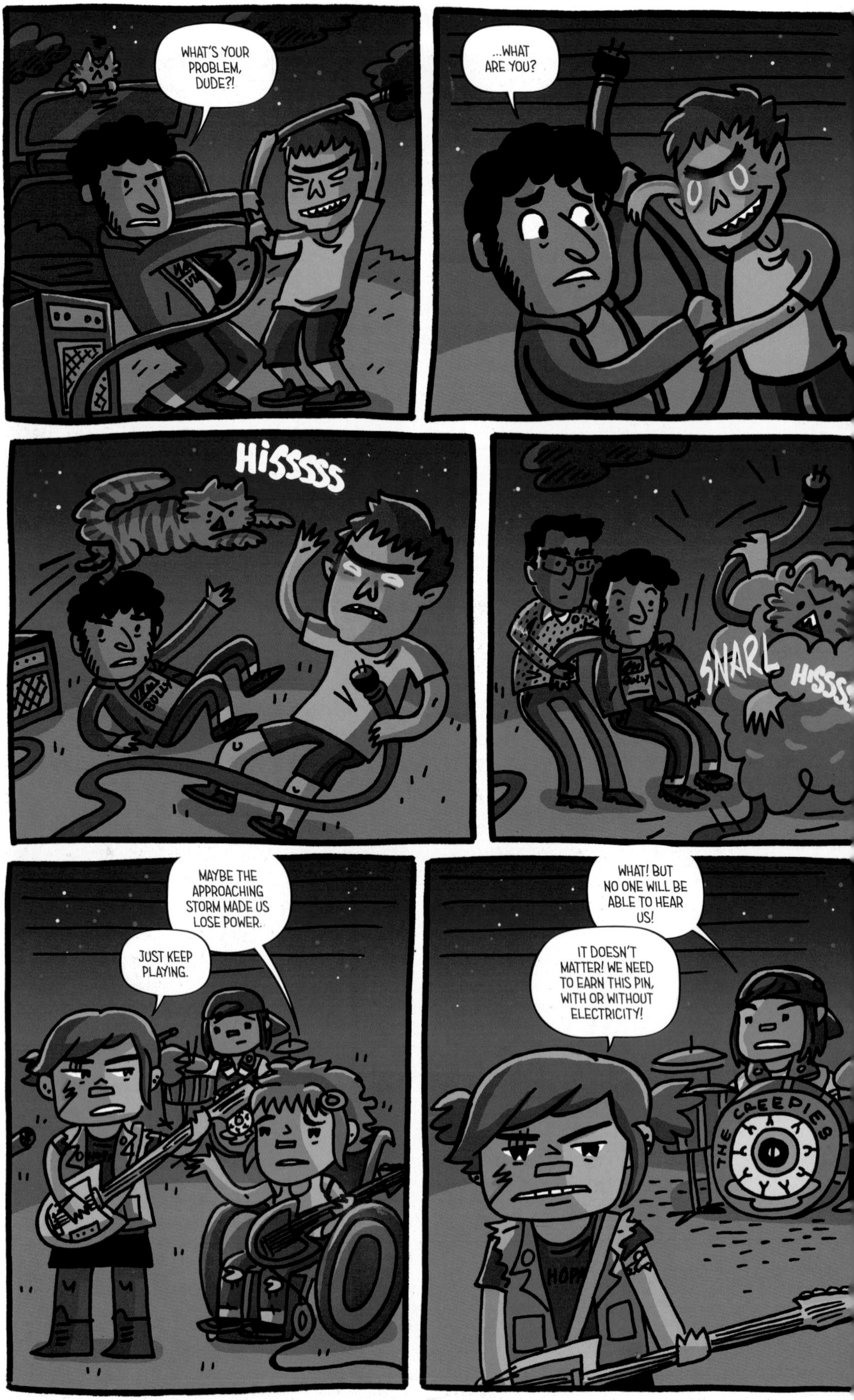
WHAT'S YOUR PROBLEM, DUDE?!
...WHAT ARE YOU?
HISSSSS
SNARL
MAYBE THE APPROACHING STORM MADE US LOSE POWER.
JUST KEEP PLAYING.
WHAT! BUT NO ONE WILL BE ABLE TO HEAR US!
IT DOESN'T MATTER! WE NEED TO EARN THIS PIN, WITH OR WITHOUT ELECTRICITY!
THE CREEPIES

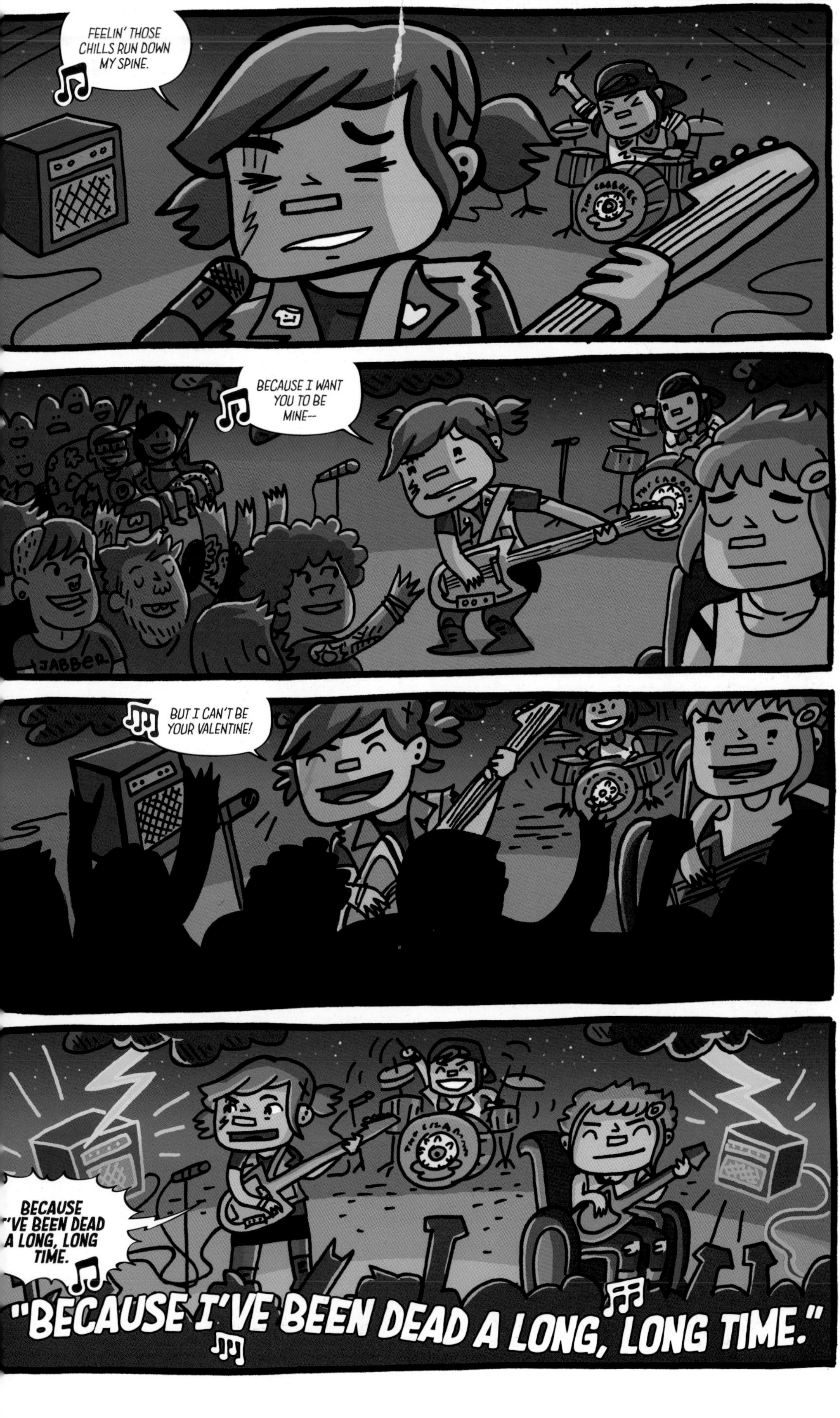
FEELIN' THOSE CHILLS RUN DOWN MY SPINE.
BECAUSE I WANT YOU TO BE MINE--
JABBER
BUT I CAN'T BE YOUR VALENTINE!
BECAUSE 'VE BEEN DEAD A LONG, LONG TIME.
"BECAUSE I'VE BEEN DEAD A LONG, LONG TIME."

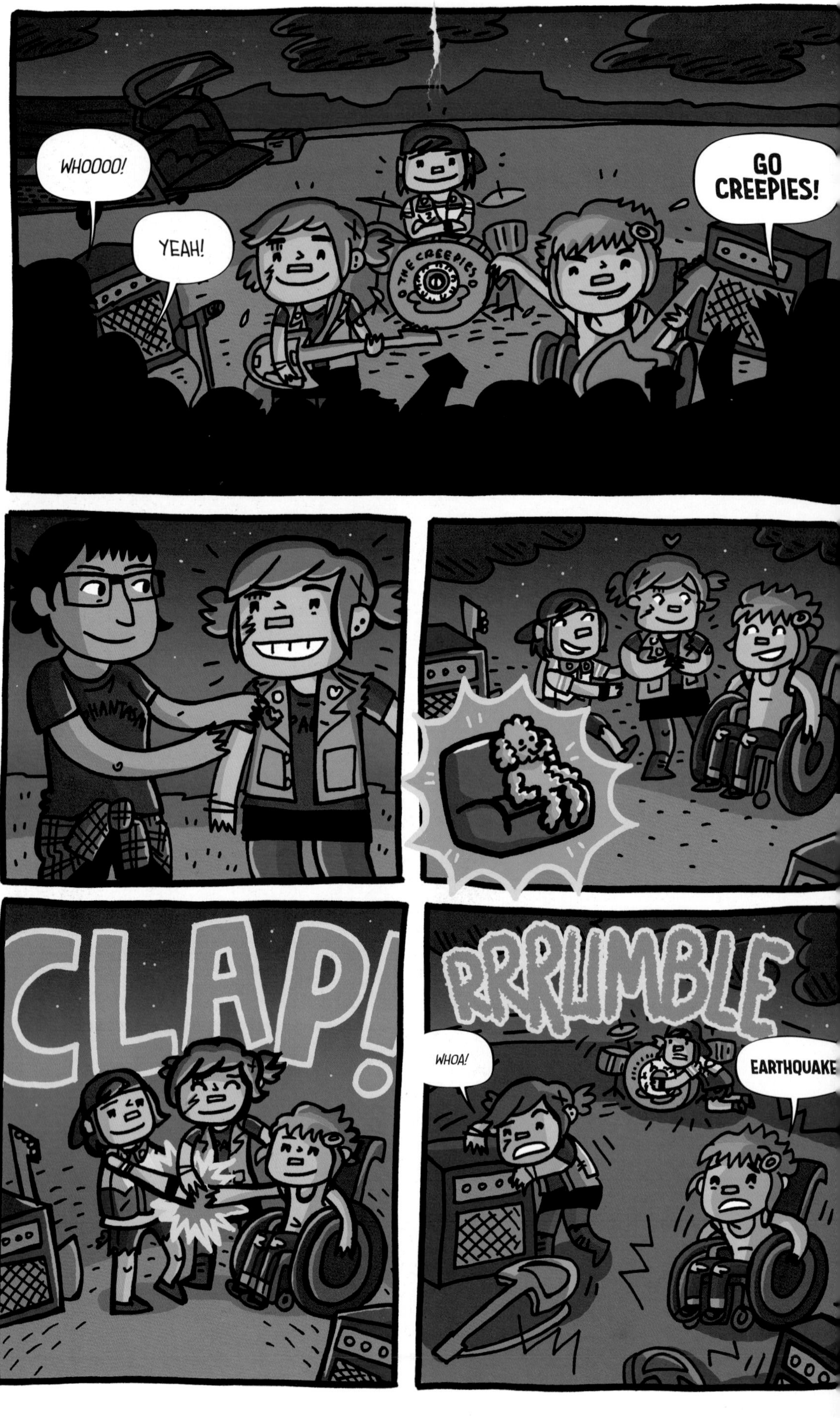
WHOOOO!
YEAH!
GO CREEPIES!
THE CREEPIES
CLAP!
RRRUMBLE
WHOA!
EARTHQUAKE

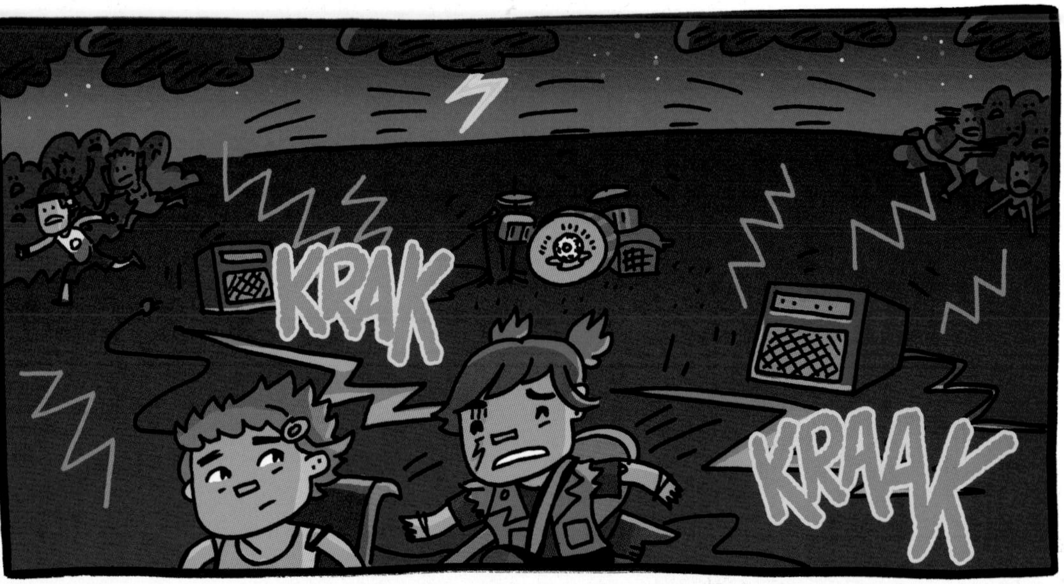
KRAK
KRAAAK

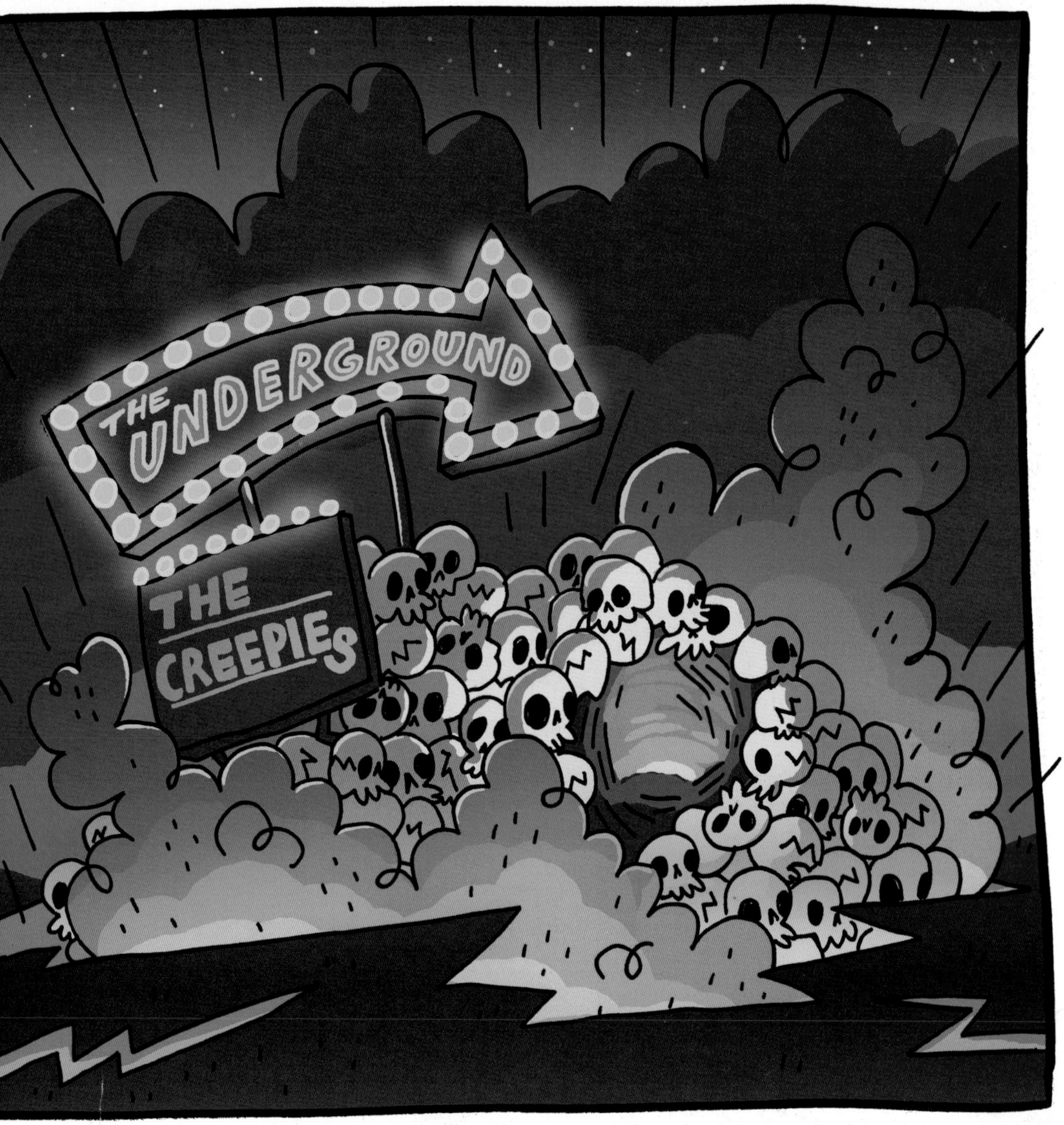
THE UNDERGROUND
THE CREEPIES

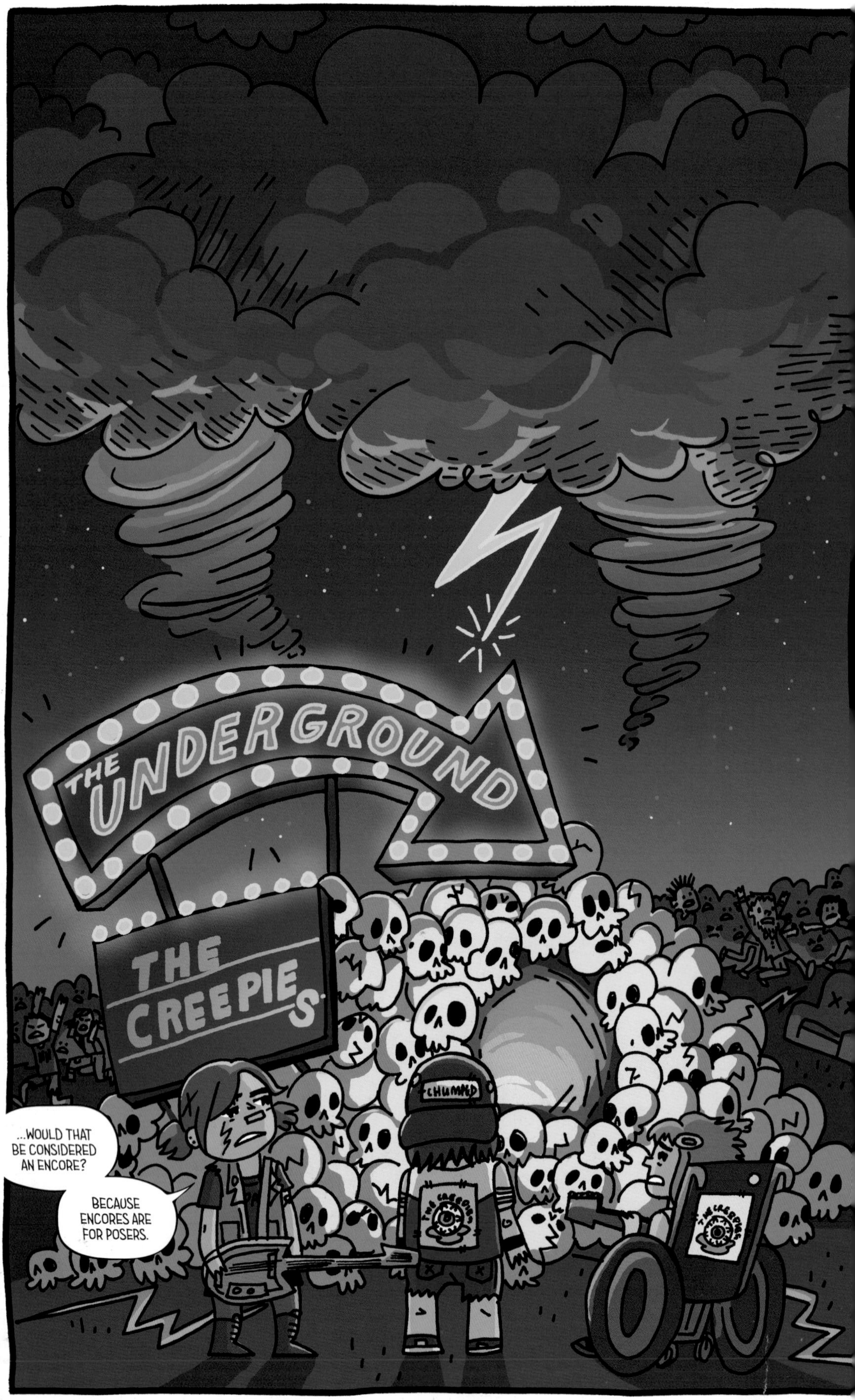
THE UNDERGROUND
THE CREEPIES
CHUMMD
...WOULD THAT BE CONSIDERED AN ENCORE?
BECAUSE ENCORES ARE FOR POSERS.

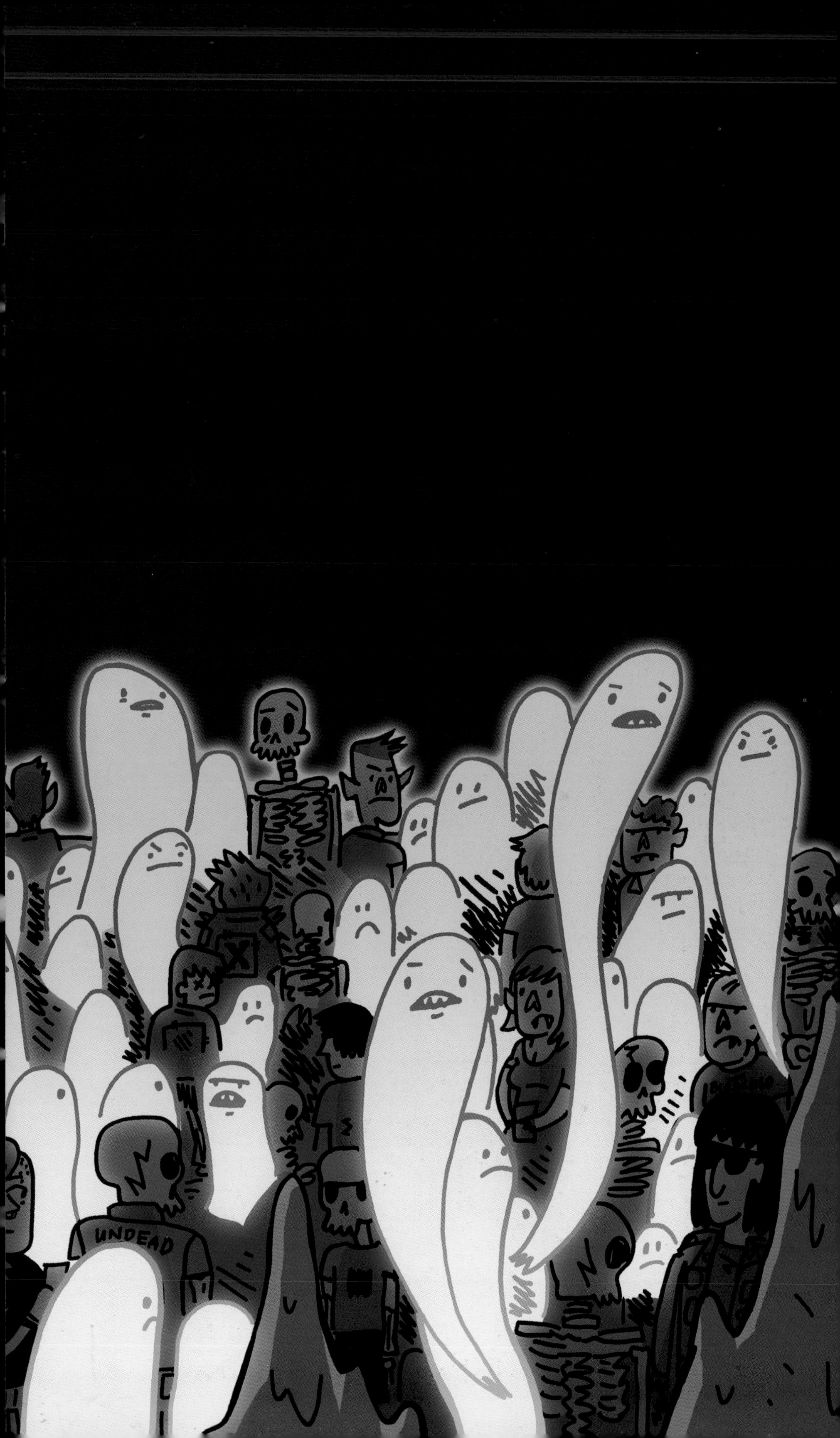
UNDEAD

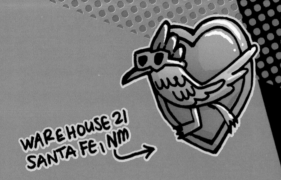

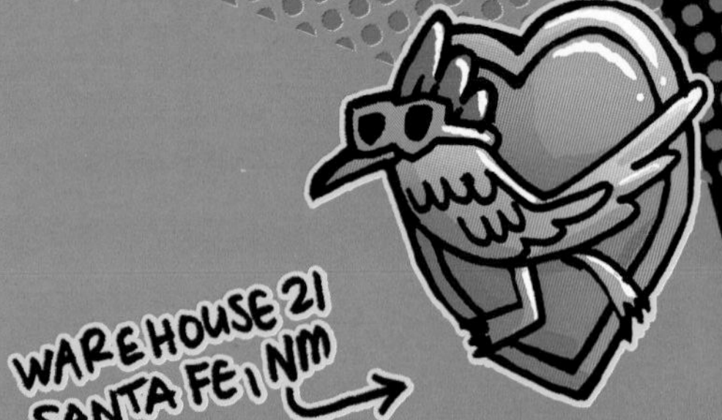
WAREHOUSE 21
SANTA FE, NM

CHAPTER FOUR

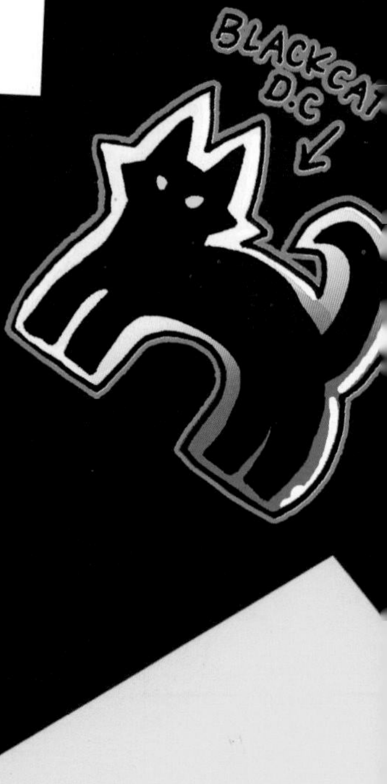
BLACKCAT
D.C

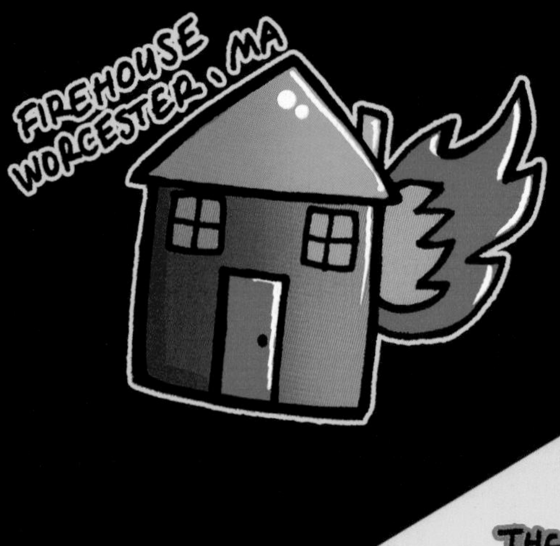
FIREHOUSE
WORCESTER, MA

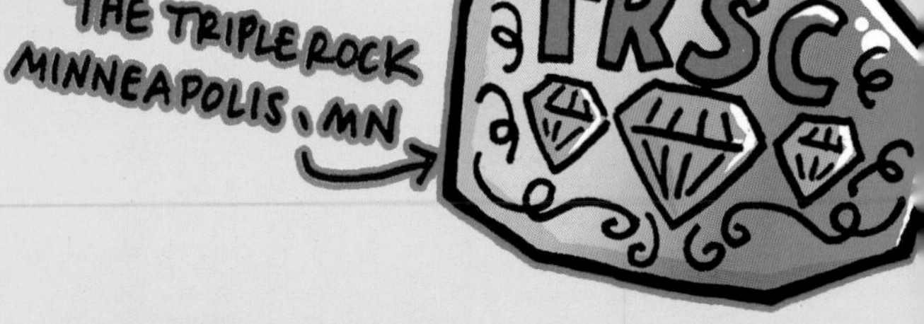
THE TRIPLEROCK
MINNEAPOLIS, MN
TRSC

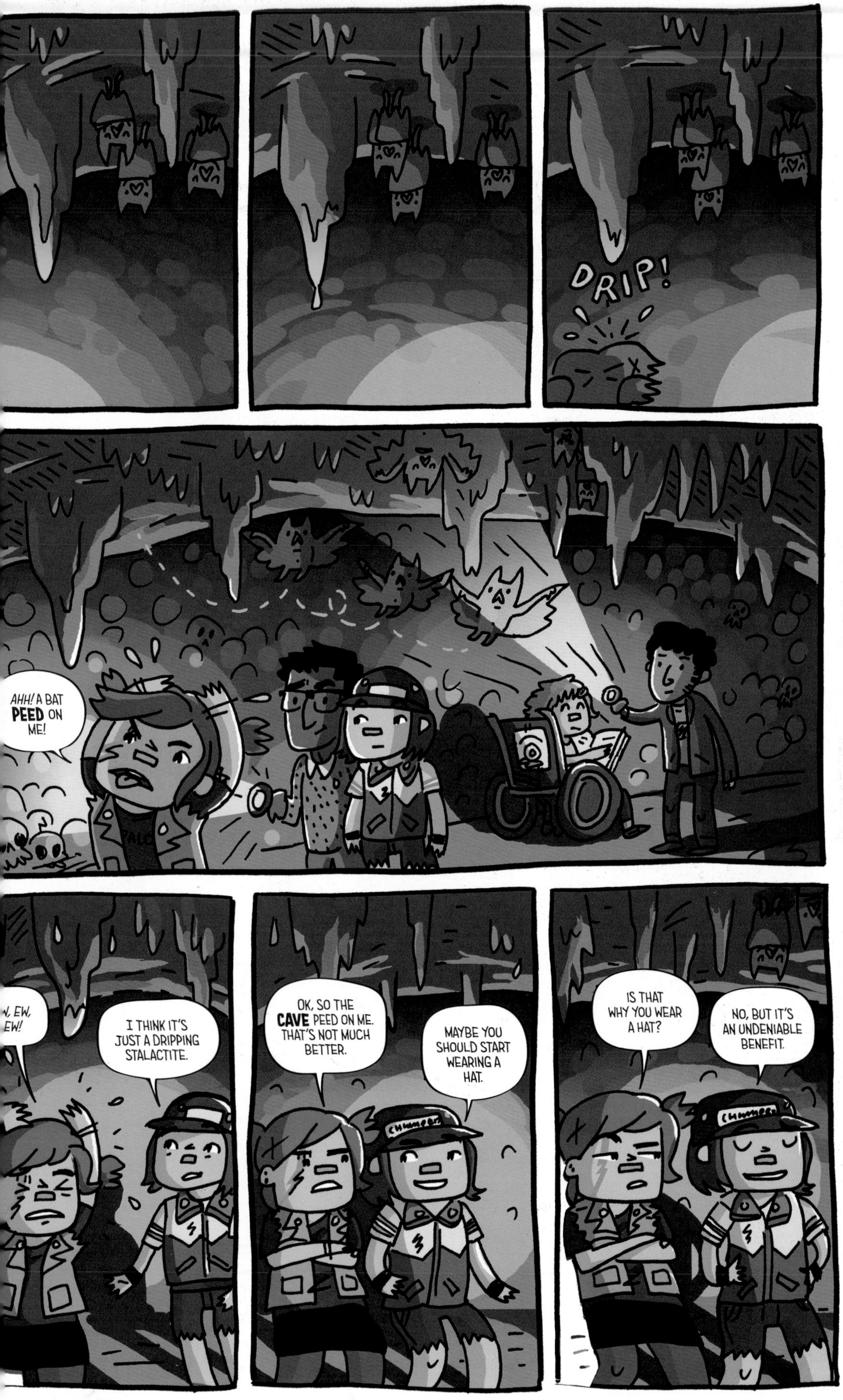
DRIP!
AHH! A BAT **PEED** ON ME!
EW, EW!
I THINK IT'S JUST A DRIPPING STALACTITE.
OK, SO THE **CAVE** PEED ON ME. THAT'S NOT MUCH BETTER.
MAYBE YOU SHOULD START WEARING A HAT.
IS THAT WHY YOU WEAR A HAT?
NO, BUT IT'S AN UNDENIABLE BENEFIT.

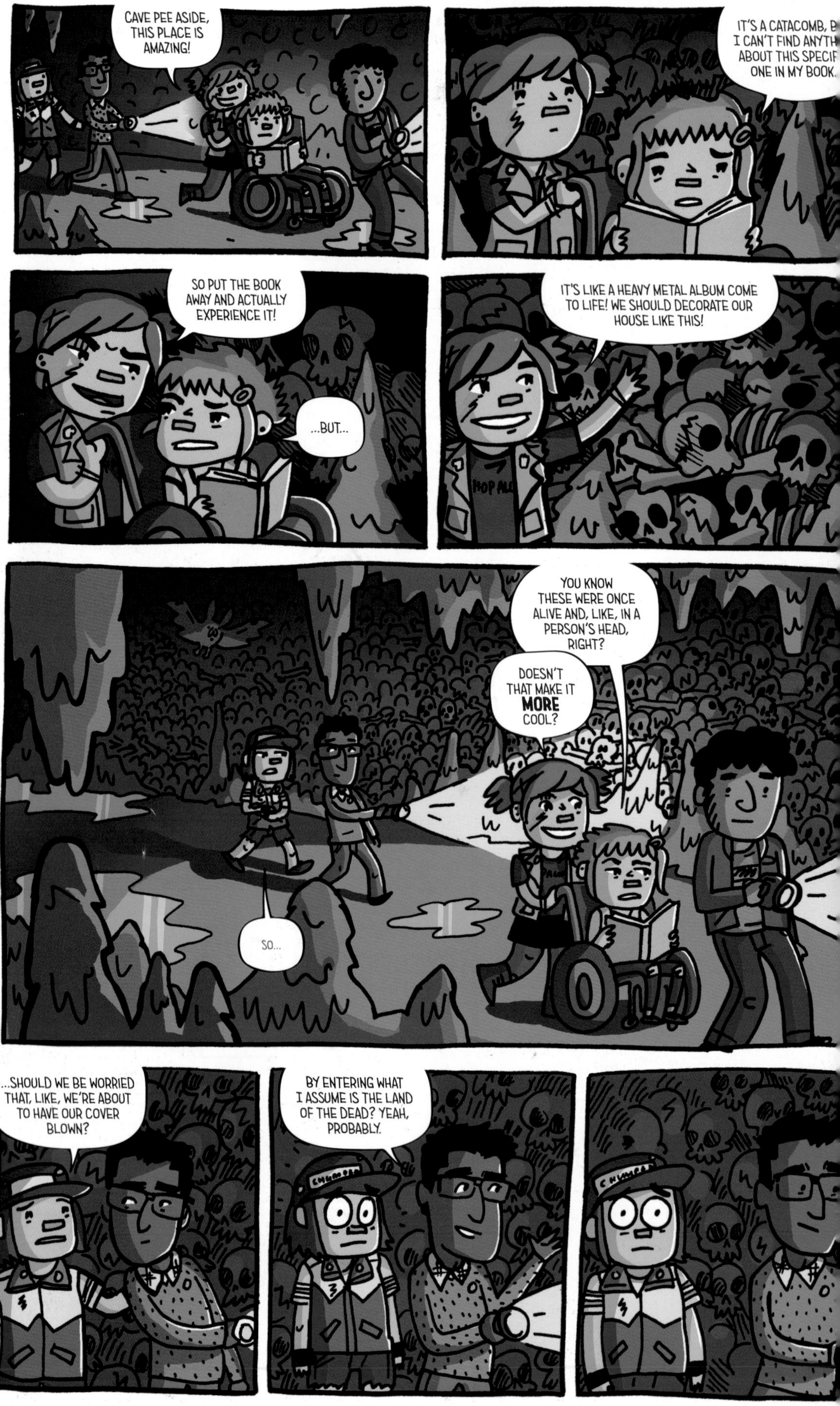
CAVE PEE ASIDE, THIS PLACE IS AMAZING!
IT'S A CATACOMB, B I CAN'T FIND ANYTH ABOUT THIS SPECIF ONE IN MY BOOK.
SO PUT THE BOOK AWAY AND ACTUALLY EXPERIENCE IT!
...BUT...
IT'S LIKE A HEAVY METAL ALBUM COME TO LIFE! WE SHOULD DECORATE OUR HOUSE LIKE THIS!
HOP ALL
YOU KNOW THESE WERE ONCE ALIVE AND, LIKE, IN A PERSON'S HEAD, RIGHT?
DOESN'T THAT MAKE IT **MORE** COOL?
SO...
...SHOULD WE BE WORRIED THAT, LIKE, WE'RE ABOUT TO HAVE OUR COVER BLOWN?
BY ENTERING WHAT I ASSUME IS THE LAND OF THE DEAD? YEAH, PROBABLY.

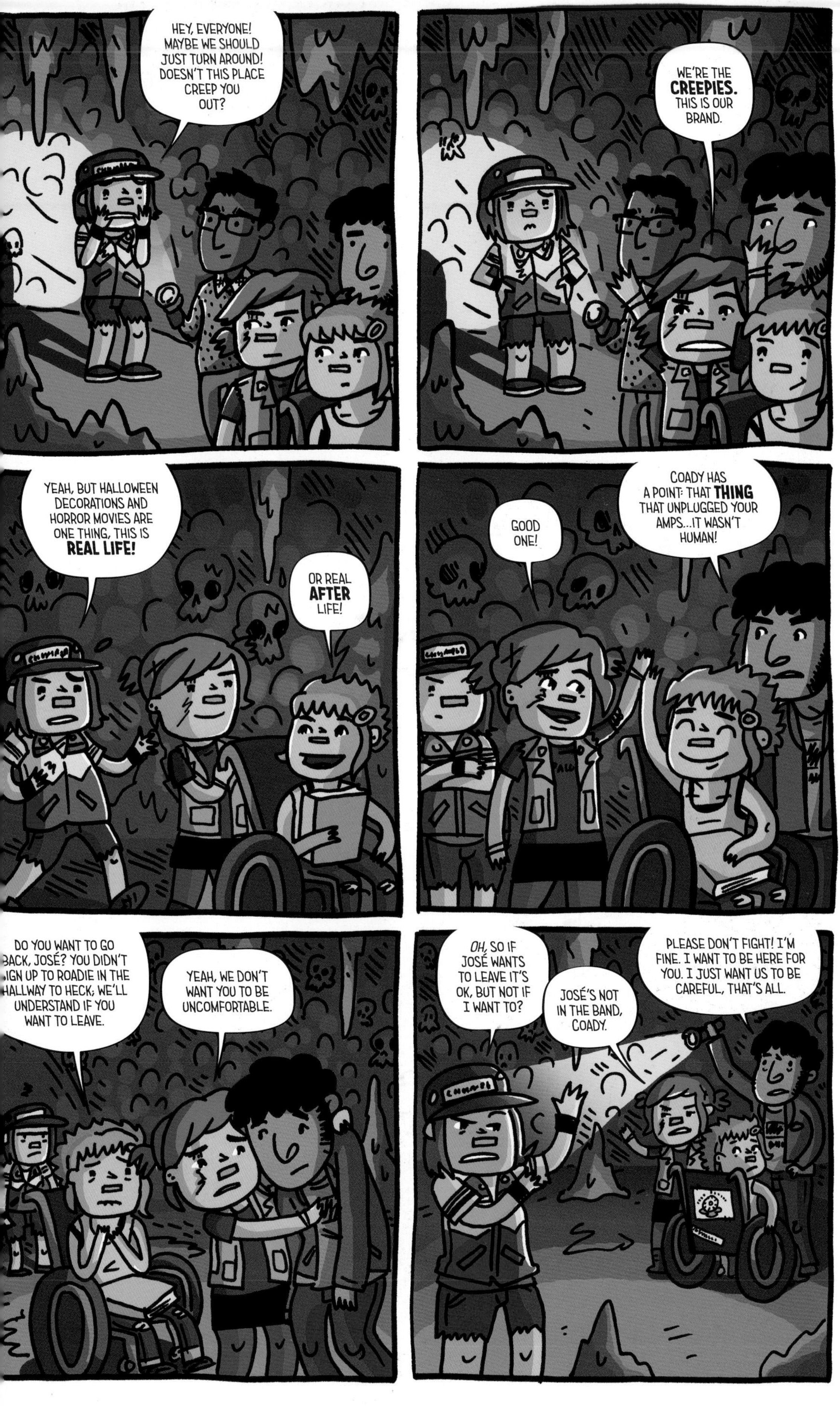
HEY, EVERYONE! MAYBE WE SHOULD JUST TURN AROUND! DOESN'T THIS PLACE CREEP YOU OUT?
WE'RE THE **CREEPIES.** THIS IS OUR BRAND.
YEAH, BUT HALLOWEEN DECORATIONS AND HORROR MOVIES ARE ONE THING, THIS IS **REAL LIFE!**
OR REAL **AFTER** LIFE!
GOOD ONE!
COADY HAS A POINT: THAT **THING** THAT UNPLUGGED YOUR AMPS...IT WASN'T HUMAN!
DO YOU WANT TO GO BACK, JOSÉ? YOU DIDN'T SIGN UP TO ROADIE IN THE HALLWAY TO HECK; WE'LL UNDERSTAND IF YOU WANT TO LEAVE.
YEAH, WE DON'T WANT YOU TO BE UNCOMFORTABLE.
OH, SO IF JOSÉ WANTS TO LEAVE IT'S OK, BUT NOT IF I WANT TO?
JOSÉ'S NOT IN THE BAND, COADY.
PLEASE DON'T FIGHT! I'M FINE. I WANT TO BE HERE FOR YOU. I JUST WANT US TO BE CAREFUL, THAT'S ALL.

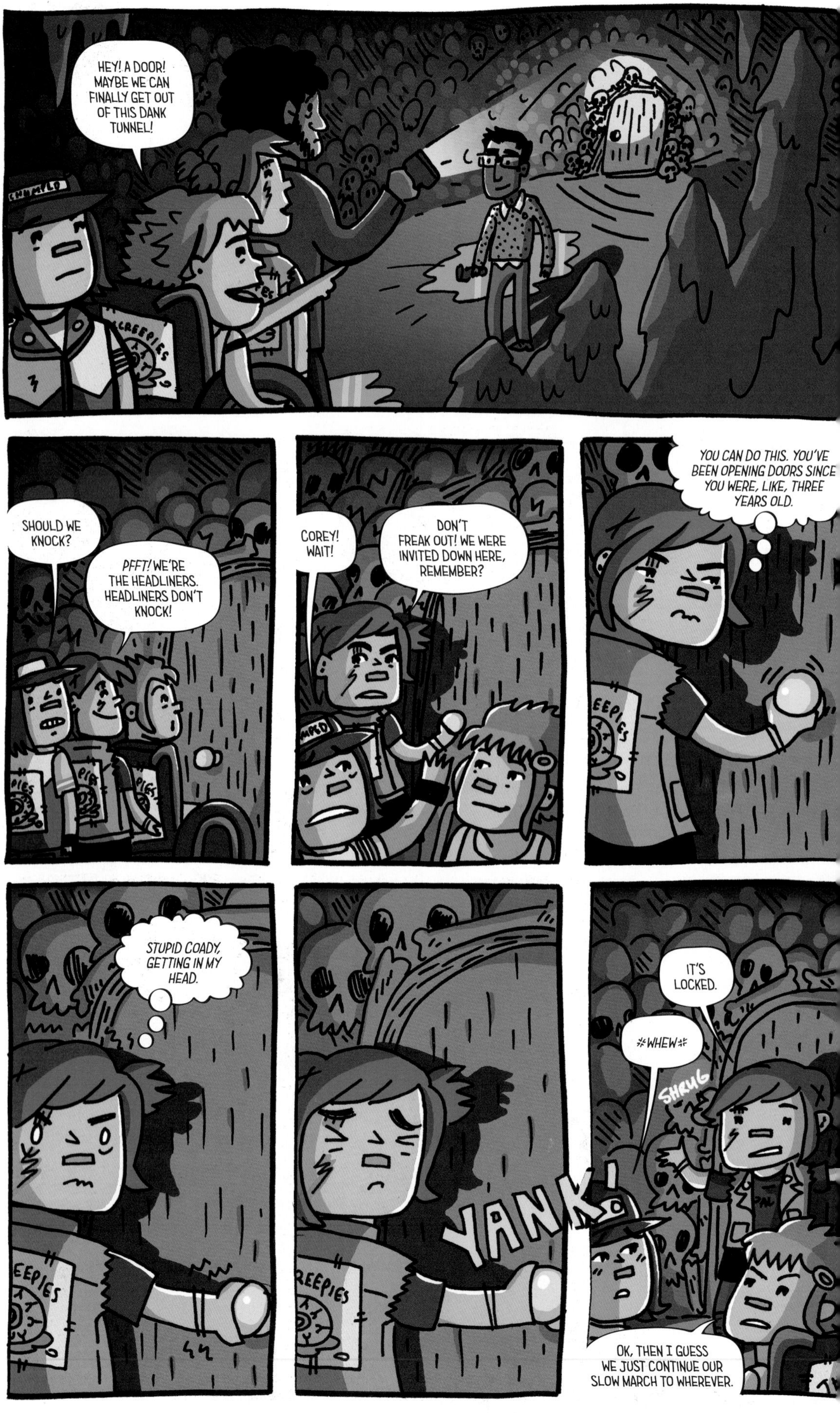
HEY! A DOOR! MAYBE WE CAN FINALLY GET OUT OF THIS DANK TUNNEL!
CHUMPLD
CREEPIES
SHOULD WE KNOCK?
PFFT! WE'RE THE HEADLINERS. HEADLINERS DON'T KNOCK!
COREY! WAIT!
DON'T FREAK OUT! WE WERE INVITED DOWN HERE, REMEMBER?
YOU CAN DO THIS. YOU'VE BEEN OPENING DOORS SINCE YOU WERE, LIKE, THREE YEARS OLD.
STUPID COADY, GETTING IN MY HEAD.
YANK!
IT'S LOCKED.
WHEW
SHRUG
OK, THEN I GUESS WE JUST CONTINUE OUR SLOW MARCH TO WHEREVER.

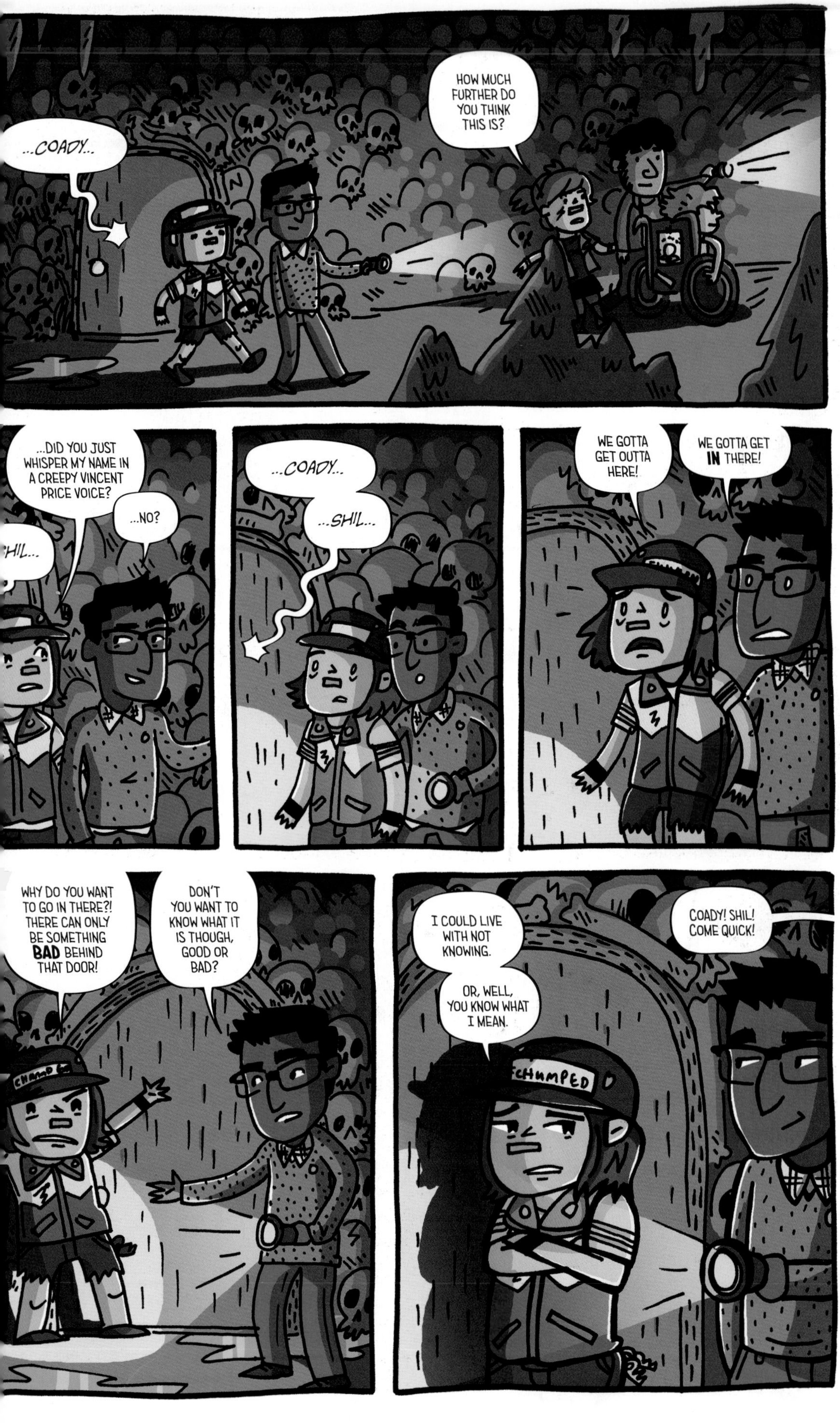

...COADY...
HOW MUCH FURTHER DO YOU THINK THIS IS?
...DID YOU JUST WHISPER MY NAME IN A CREEPY VINCENT PRICE VOICE?
...NO?
...COADY...
...SHIL...
WE GOTTA GET OUTTA HERE!
WE GOTTA GET **IN** THERE!
WHY DO YOU WANT TO GO IN THERE?! THERE CAN ONLY BE SOMETHING **BAD** BEHIND THAT DOOR!
DON'T YOU WANT TO KNOW WHAT IT IS THOUGH, GOOD OR BAD?
I COULD LIVE WITH NOT KNOWING.
OR, WELL, YOU KNOW WHAT I MEAN.
COADY! SHIL! COME QUICK!

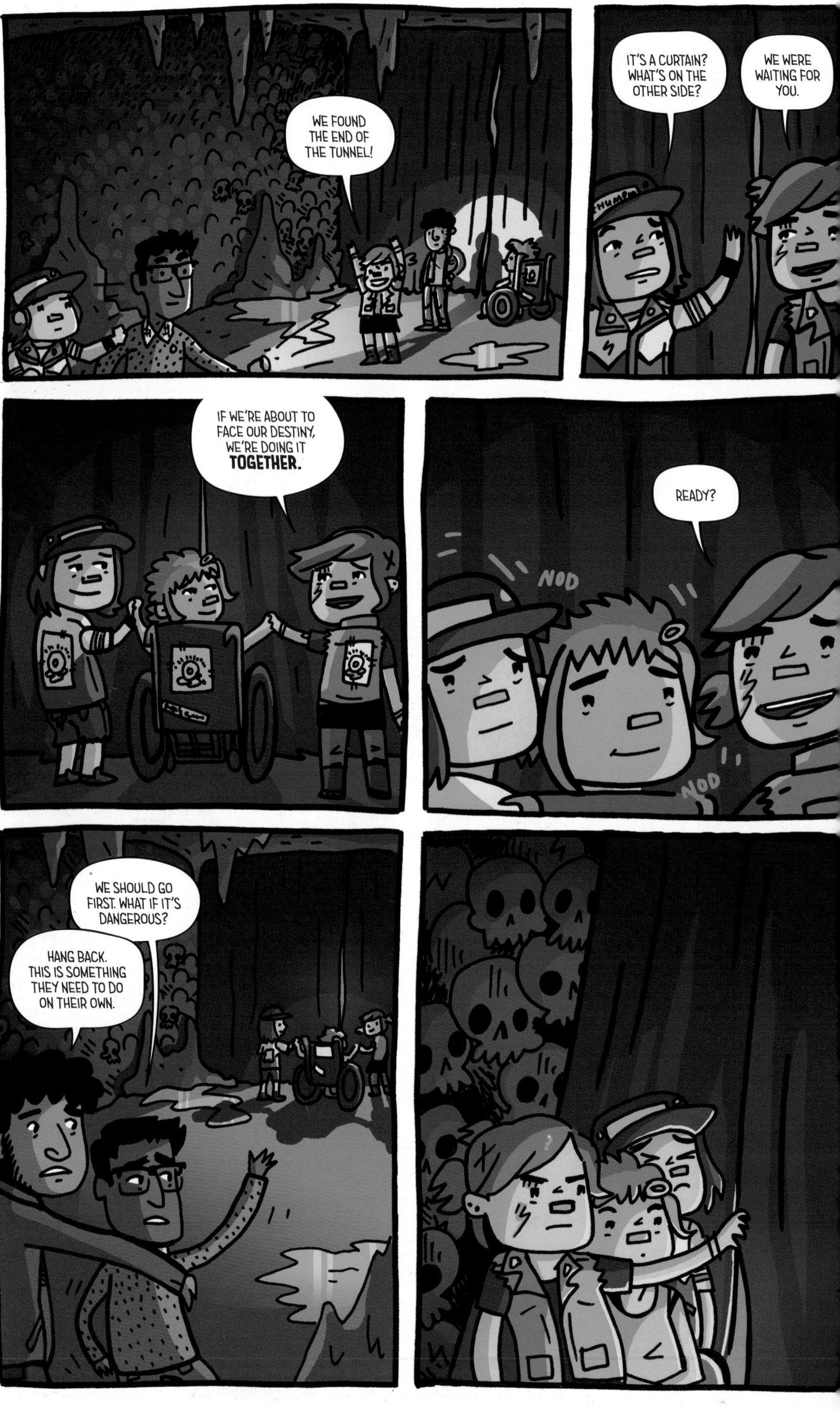
WE FOUND THE END OF THE TUNNEL!
IT'S A CURTAIN? WHAT'S ON THE OTHER SIDE?
WE WERE WAITING FOR YOU.
IF WE'RE ABOUT TO FACE OUR DESTINY, WE'RE DOING IT **TOGETHER.**
READY?
NOD
NOD
WE SHOULD GO FIRST. WHAT IF IT'S DANGEROUS?
HANG BACK. THIS IS SOMETHING THEY NEED TO DO ON THEIR OWN.

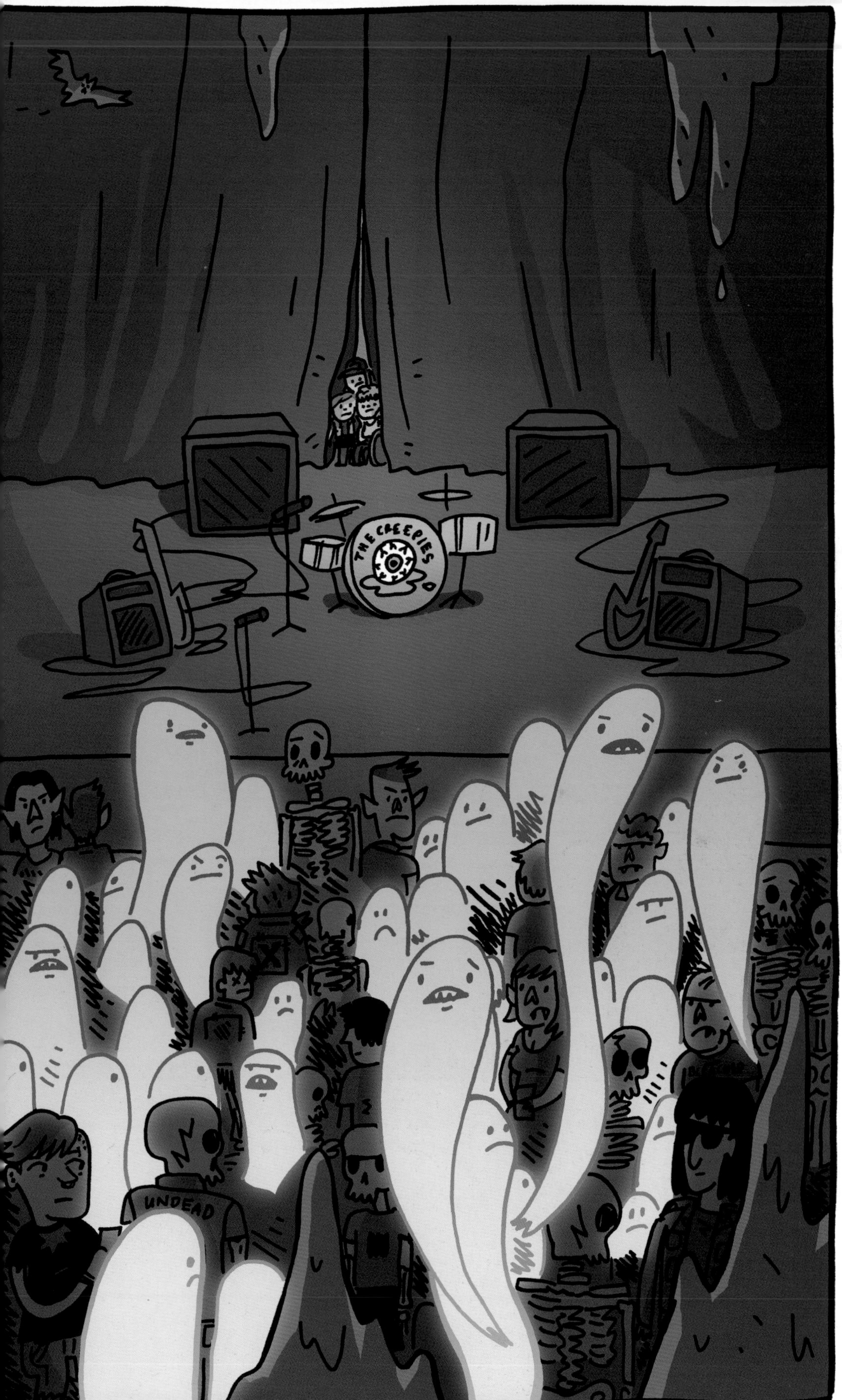
THE CREEPIES
UNDEAD

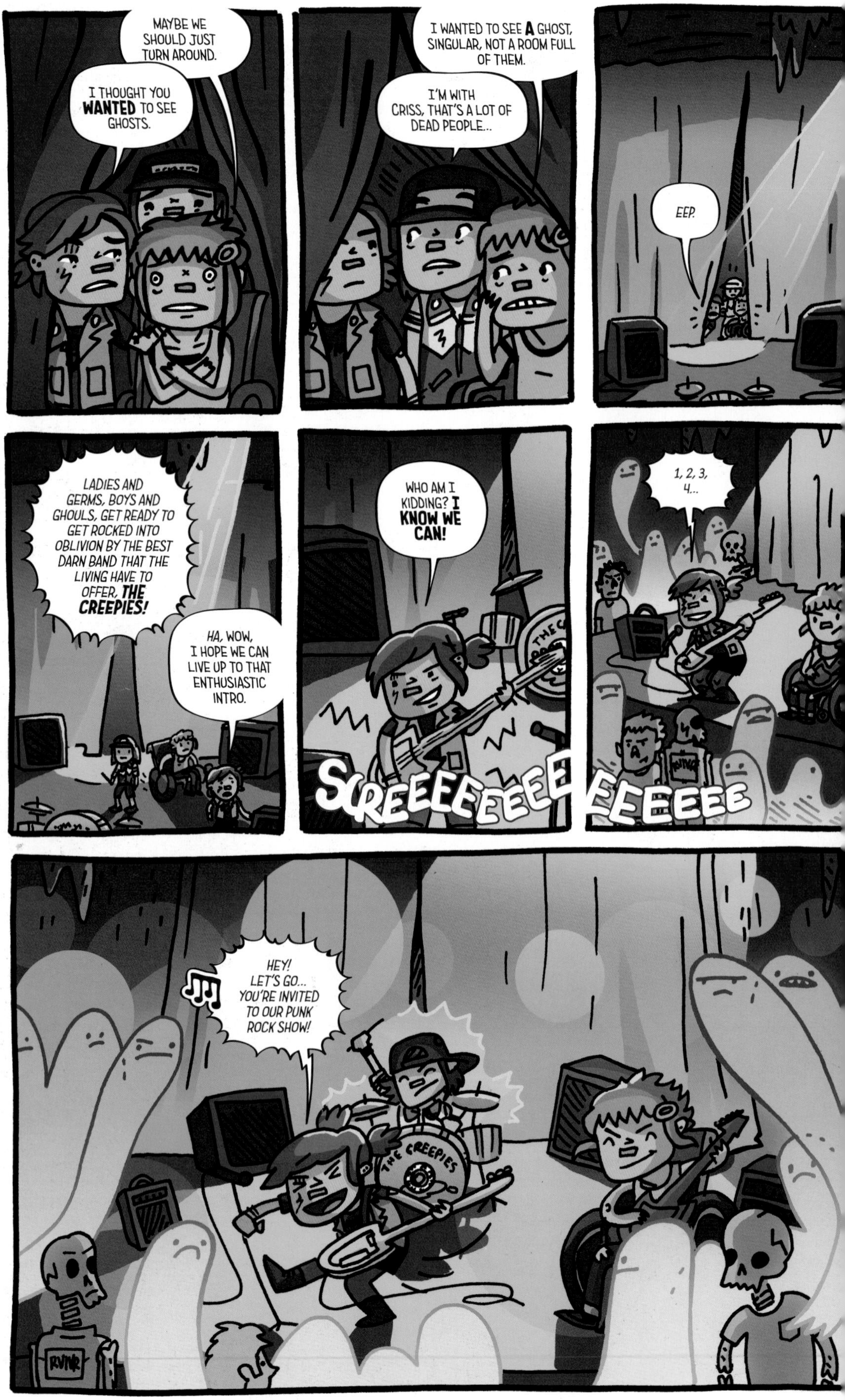
MAYBE WE SHOULD JUST TURN AROUND.
I THOUGHT YOU **WANTED** TO SEE GHOSTS.
I WANTED TO SEE **A** GHOST, SINGULAR, NOT A ROOM FULL OF THEM.
I'M WITH CRISS, THAT'S A LOT OF DEAD PEOPLE...
EEP.
LADIES AND GERMS, BOYS AND GHOULS, GET READY TO GET ROCKED INTO OBLIVION BY THE BEST DARN BAND THAT THE LIVING HAVE TO OFFER, **THE CREEPIES!**
HA, WOW, I HOPE WE CAN LIVE UP TO THAT ENTHUSIASTIC INTRO.
WHO AM I KIDDING? **I KNOW WE CAN!**
1, 2, 3, 4...
SCREEEEEEEEEEEEEEE
HEY! LET'S GO... YOU'RE INVITED TO OUR PUNK ROCK SHOW!
THE CREEPIES

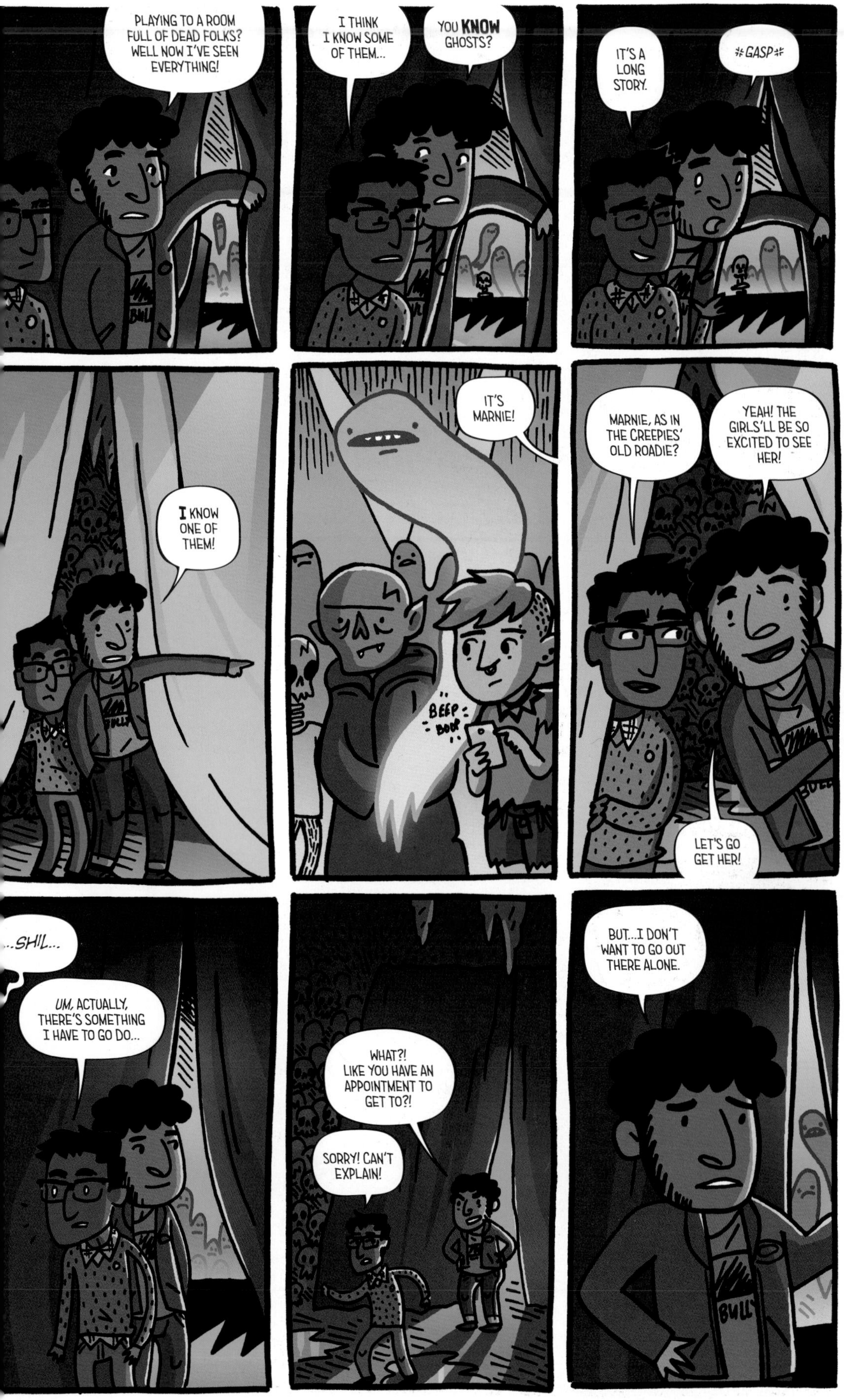
PLAYING TO A ROOM FULL OF DEAD FOLKS? WELL NOW I'VE SEEN EVERYTHING!
I THINK I KNOW SOME OF THEM...
YOU KNOW GHOSTS?
IT'S A LONG STORY.
#GASP#
I KNOW ONE OF THEM!
IT'S MARNIE!
BEEP BOOP
MARNIE, AS IN THE CREEPIES' OLD ROADIE?
YEAH! THE GIRLS'LL BE SO EXCITED TO SEE HER!
LET'S GO GET HER!
...SHIL...
UM, ACTUALLY, THERE'S SOMETHING I HAVE TO GO DO...
WHAT?! LIKE YOU HAVE AN APPOINTMENT TO GET TO?!
SORRY! CAN'T EXPLAIN!
BUT...I DON'T WANT TO GO OUT THERE ALONE.

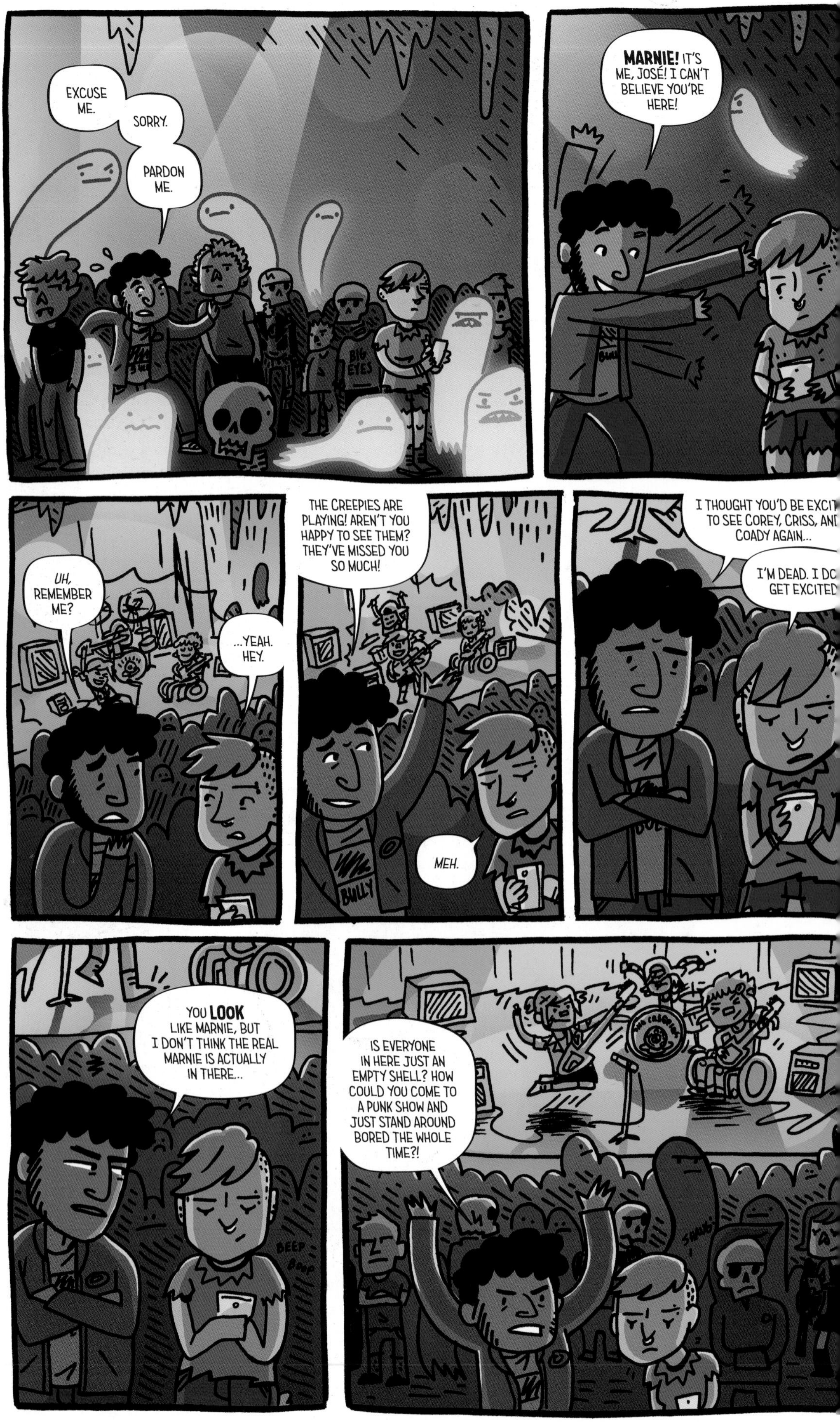

EXCUSE ME.
SORRY.
PARDON ME.
MARNIE! IT'S ME, JOSÉ! I CAN'T BELIEVE YOU'RE HERE!
UH, REMEMBER ME?
...YEAH. HEY.
THE CREEPIES ARE PLAYING! AREN'T YOU HAPPY TO SEE THEM? THEY'VE MISSED YOU SO MUCH!
MEH.
I THOUGHT YOU'D BE EXCIT
TO SEE COREY, CRISS, AN
COADY AGAIN...
I'M DEAD. I DO
GET EXCITED
YOU **LOOK** LIKE MARNIE, BUT I DON'T THINK THE REAL MARNIE IS ACTUALLY IN THERE...
BEEP
BOOP
IS EVERYONE IN HERE JUST AN EMPTY SHELL? HOW COULD YOU COME TO A PUNK SHOW AND JUST STAND AROUND BORED THE WHOLE TIME?!

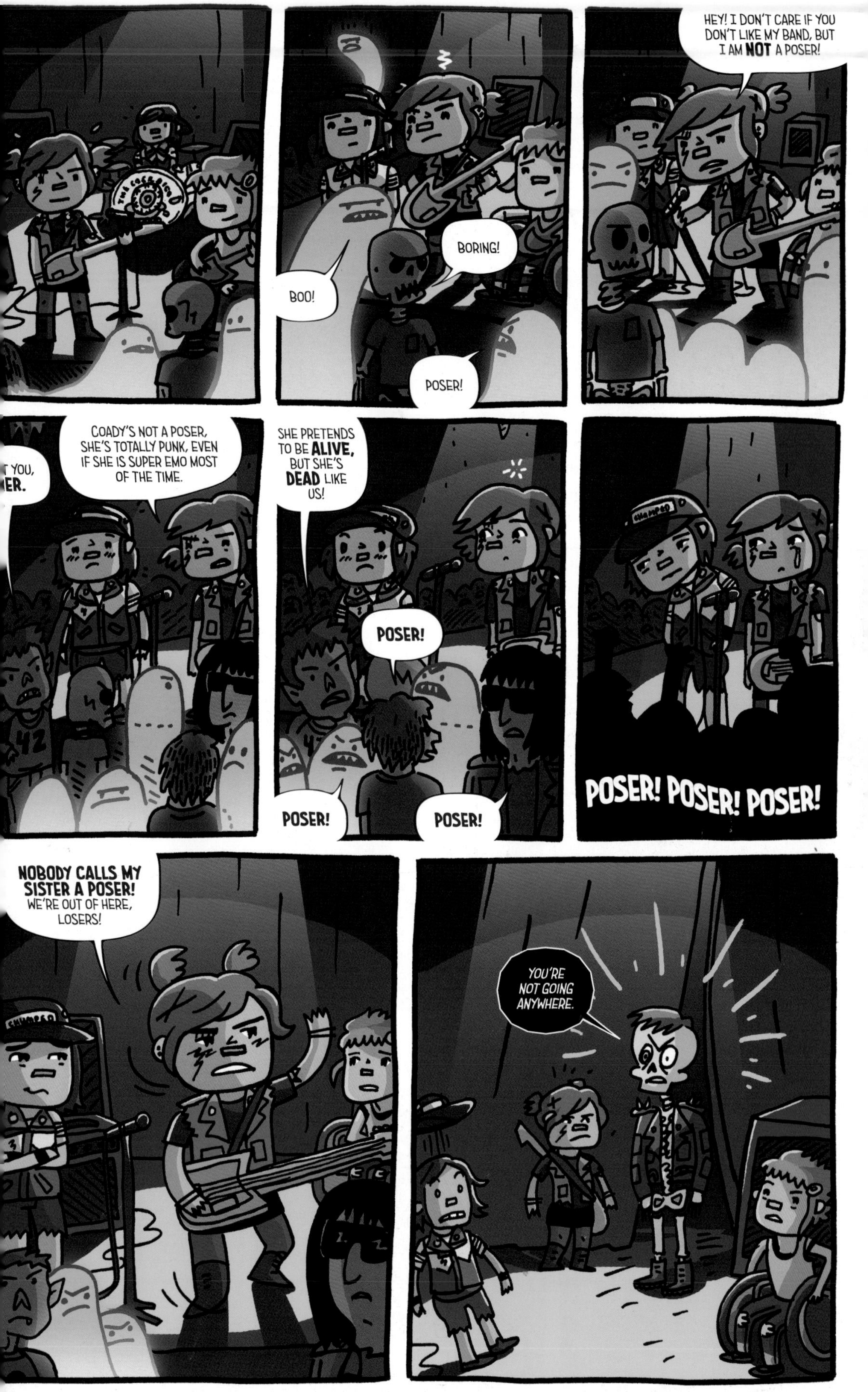
BOO!
BORING!
POSER!
HEY! I DON'T CARE IF YOU DON'T LIKE MY BAND, BUT I AM **NOT** A POSER!
COADY'S NOT A POSER, SHE'S TOTALLY PUNK, EVEN IF SHE IS SUPER EMO MOST OF THE TIME.
SHE PRETENDS TO BE **ALIVE,** BUT SHE'S **DEAD** LIKE US!
POSER!
POSER!
POSER!
POSER! POSER! POSER!
NOBODY CALLS MY SISTER A POSER! WE'RE OUT OF HERE, LOSERS!
YOU'RE NOT GOING ANYWHERE.

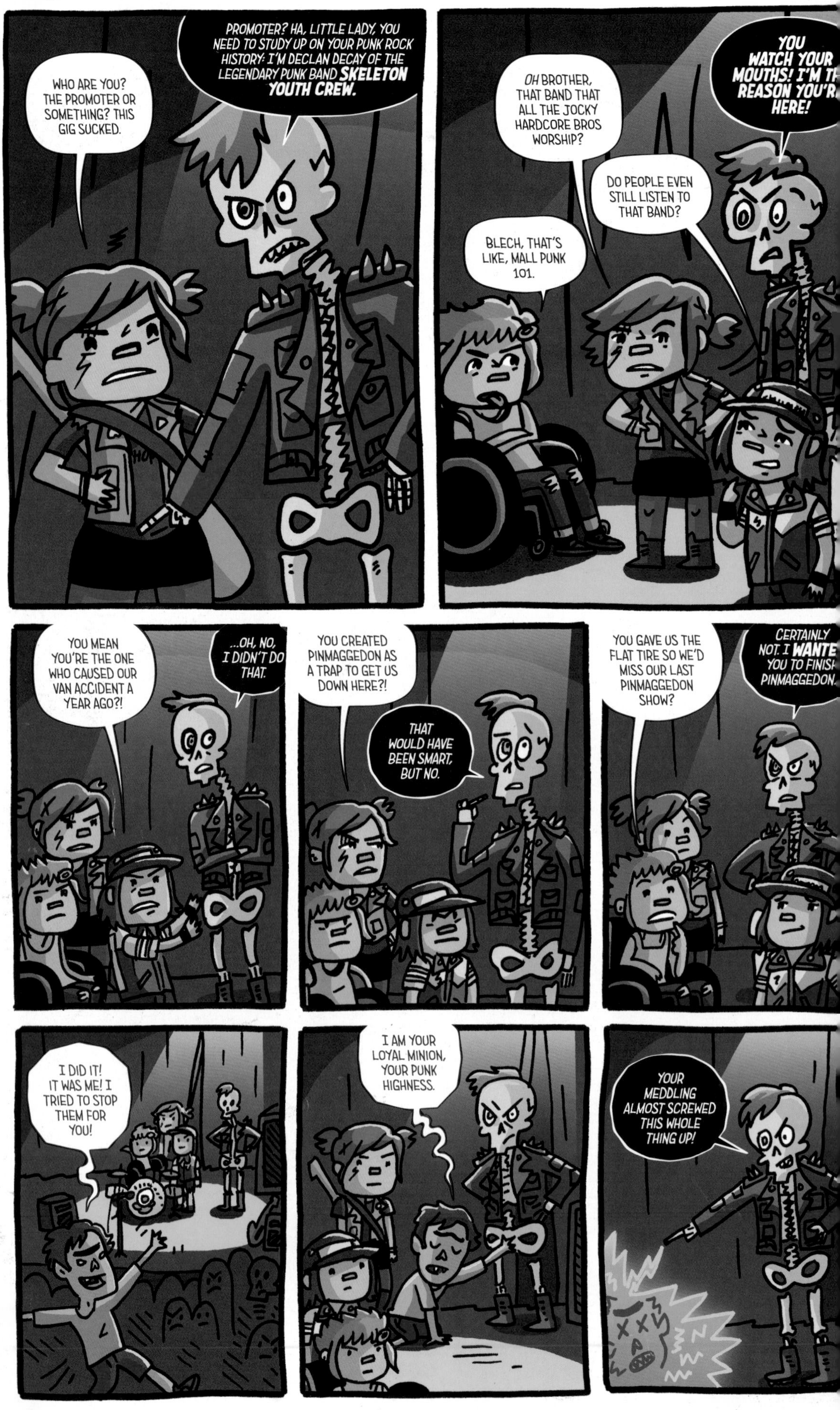
WHO ARE YOU? THE PROMOTER OR SOMETHING? THIS GIG SUCKED.
PROMOTER? HA, LITTLE LADY, YOU NEED TO STUDY UP ON YOUR PUNK ROCK HISTORY: I'M DECLAN DECAY OF THE LEGENDARY PUNK BAND SKELETON YOUTH CREW.
OH BROTHER, THAT BAND THAT ALL THE JOCKY HARDCORE BROS WORSHIP?
DO PEOPLE EVEN STILL LISTEN TO THAT BAND?
BLECH, THAT'S LIKE, MALL PUNK 101.
YOU WATCH YOUR MOUTHS! I'M TH REASON YOU'R HERE!
YOU MEAN YOU'RE THE ONE WHO CAUSED OUR VAN ACCIDENT A YEAR AGO?!
...OH, NO, I DIDN'T DO THAT.
YOU CREATED PINMAGGEDON AS A TRAP TO GET US DOWN HERE?!
THAT WOULD HAVE BEEN SMART, BUT NO.
YOU GAVE US THE FLAT TIRE SO WE'D MISS OUR LAST PINMAGGEDON SHOW?
CERTAINLY NOT. I WANTE YOU TO FINISH PINMAGGEDON.
I DID IT! IT WAS ME! I TRIED TO STOP THEM FOR YOU!
I AM YOUR LOYAL MINION, YOUR PUNK HIGHNESS.
YOUR MEDDLING ALMOST SCREWED THIS WHOLE THING UP!

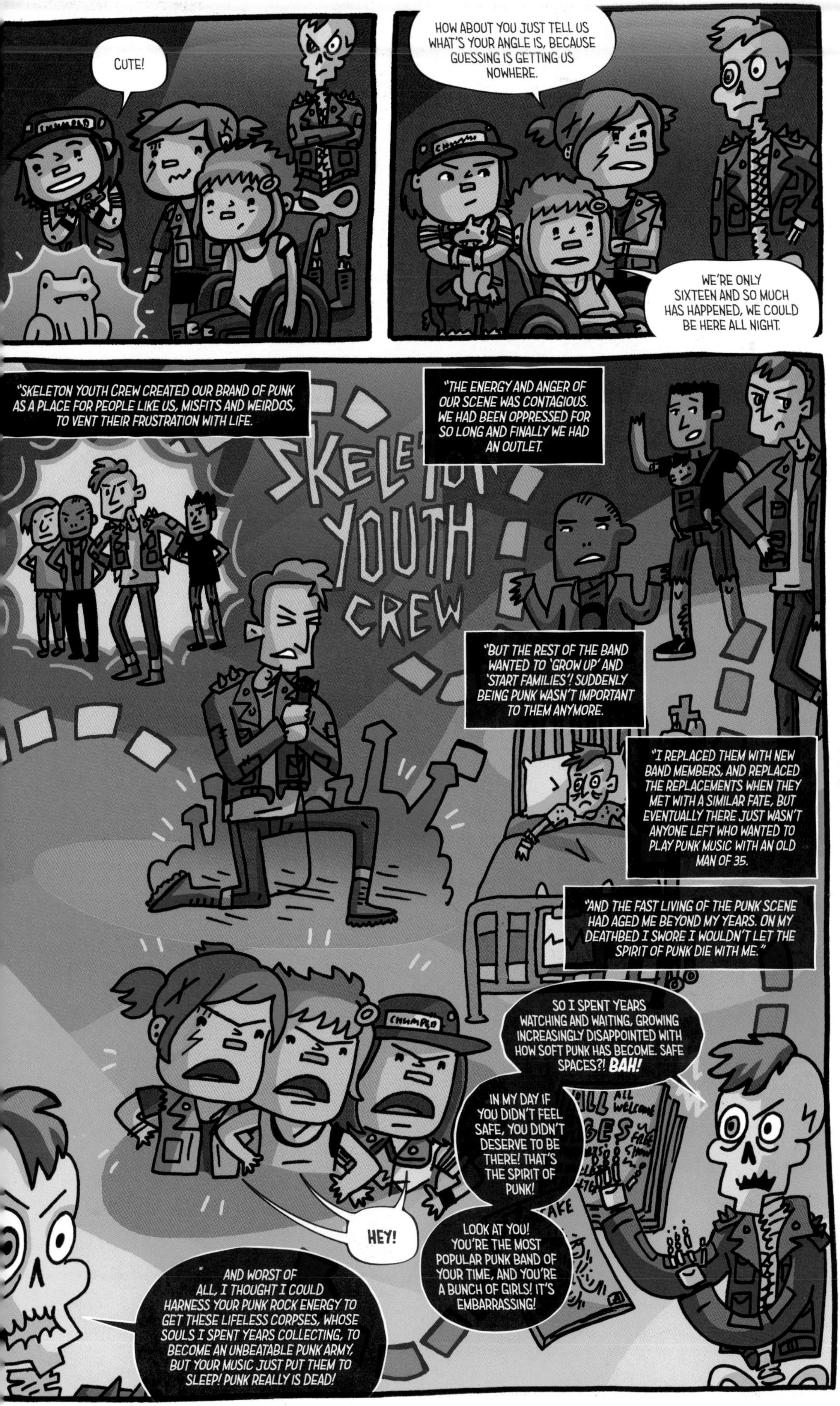

CUTE!
HOW ABOUT YOU JUST TELL US WHAT'S YOUR ANGLE IS, BECAUSE GUESSING IS GETTING US NOWHERE.
WE'RE ONLY SIXTEEN AND SO MUCH HAS HAPPENED, WE COULD BE HERE ALL NIGHT.
"SKELETON YOUTH CREW CREATED OUR BRAND OF PUNK AS A PLACE FOR PEOPLE LIKE US, MISFITS AND WEIRDOS, TO VENT THEIR FRUSTRATION WITH LIFE.
"THE ENERGY AND ANGER OF OUR SCENE WAS CONTAGIOUS. WE HAD BEEN OPPRESSED FOR SO LONG AND FINALLY WE HAD AN OUTLET.
YOUTH
CREW
"BUT THE REST OF THE BAND WANTED TO 'GROW UP' AND 'START FAMILIES'! SUDDENLY BEING PUNK WASN'T IMPORTANT TO THEM ANYMORE.
"I REPLACED THEM WITH NEW BAND MEMBERS, AND REPLACED THE REPLACEMENTS WHEN THEY MET WITH A SIMILAR FATE, BUT EVENTUALLY THERE JUST WASN'T ANYONE LEFT WHO WANTED TO PLAY PUNK MUSIC WITH AN OLD MAN OF 35.
"AND THE FAST LIVING OF THE PUNK SCENE HAD AGED ME BEYOND MY YEARS. ON MY DEATHBED I SWORE I WOULDN'T LET THE SPIRIT OF PUNK DIE WITH ME."
SO I SPENT YEARS WATCHING AND WAITING, GROWING INCREASINGLY DISAPPOINTED WITH HOW SOFT PUNK HAS BECOME. SAFE SPACES?! BAH!
IN MY DAY IF YOU DIDN'T FEEL SAFE, YOU DIDN'T DESERVE TO BE THERE! THAT'S THE SPIRIT OF PUNK!
LOOK AT YOU! YOU'RE THE MOST POPULAR PUNK BAND OF YOUR TIME, AND YOU'RE A BUNCH OF GIRLS! IT'S EMBARRASSING!
HEY!
AND WORST OF ALL, I THOUGHT I COULD HARNESS YOUR PUNK ROCK ENERGY TO GET THESE LIFELESS CORPSES, WHOSE SOULS I SPENT YEARS COLLECTING, TO BECOME AN UNBEATABLE PUNK ARMY, BUT YOUR MUSIC JUST PUT THEM TO SLEEP! PUNK REALLY IS DEAD!

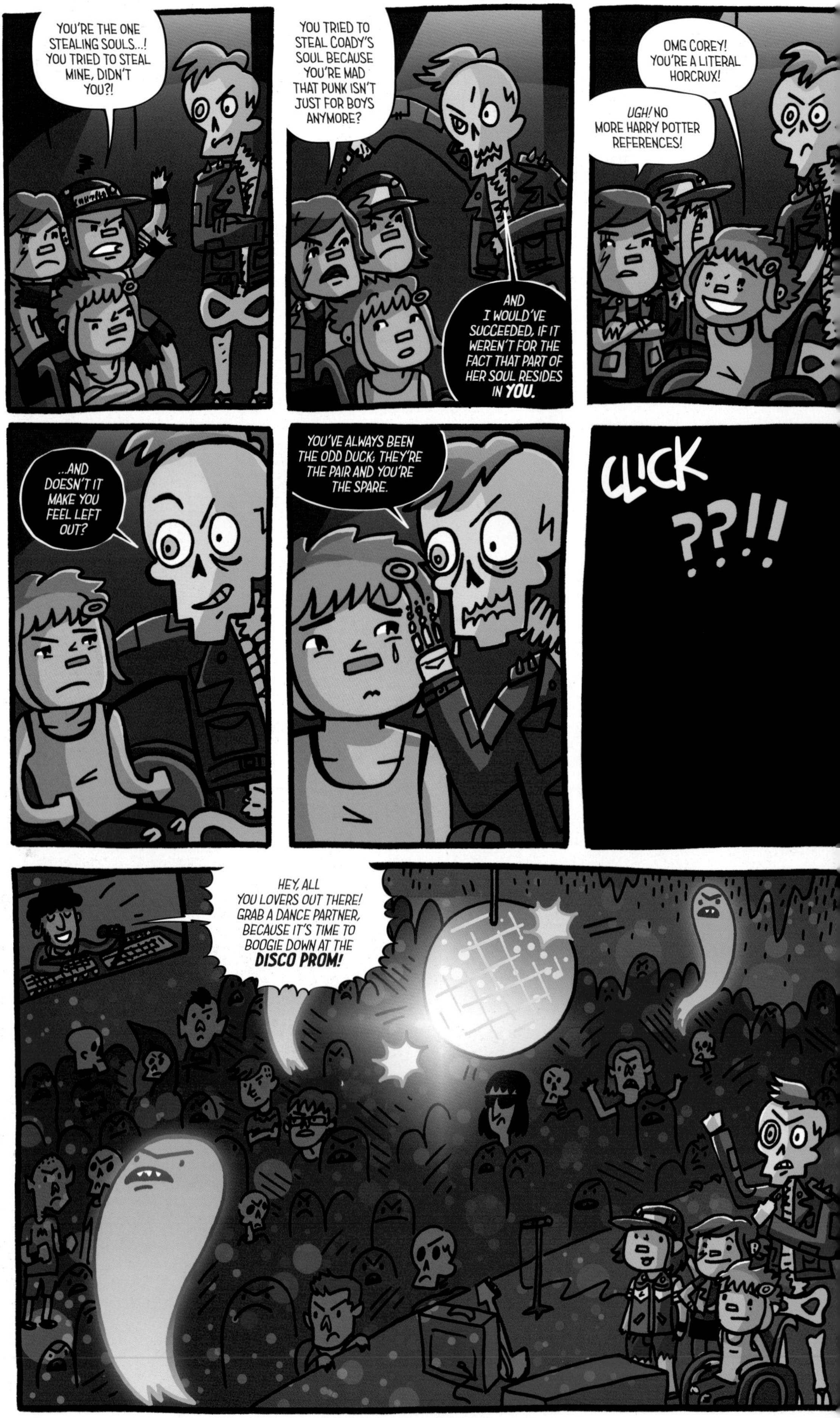

YOU'RE THE ONE STEALING SOULS...! YOU TRIED TO STEAL MINE, DIDN'T YOU?!
YOU TRIED TO STEAL COADY'S SOUL BECAUSE YOU'RE MAD THAT PUNK ISN'T JUST FOR BOYS ANYMORE?
AND I WOULD'VE SUCCEEDED, IF IT WEREN'T FOR THE FACT THAT PART OF HER SOUL RESIDES IN YOU.
OMG COREY! YOU'RE A LITERAL HORCRUX!
UGH! NO MORE HARRY POTTER REFERENCES!
...AND DOESN'T IT MAKE YOU FEEL LEFT OUT?
YOU'VE ALWAYS BEEN THE ODD DUCK; THEY'RE THE PAIR AND YOU'RE THE SPARE.
CLICK
??!!
HEY, ALL YOU LOVERS OUT THERE! GRAB A DANCE PARTNER, BECAUSE IT'S TIME TO BOOGIE DOWN AT THE DISCO PROM!

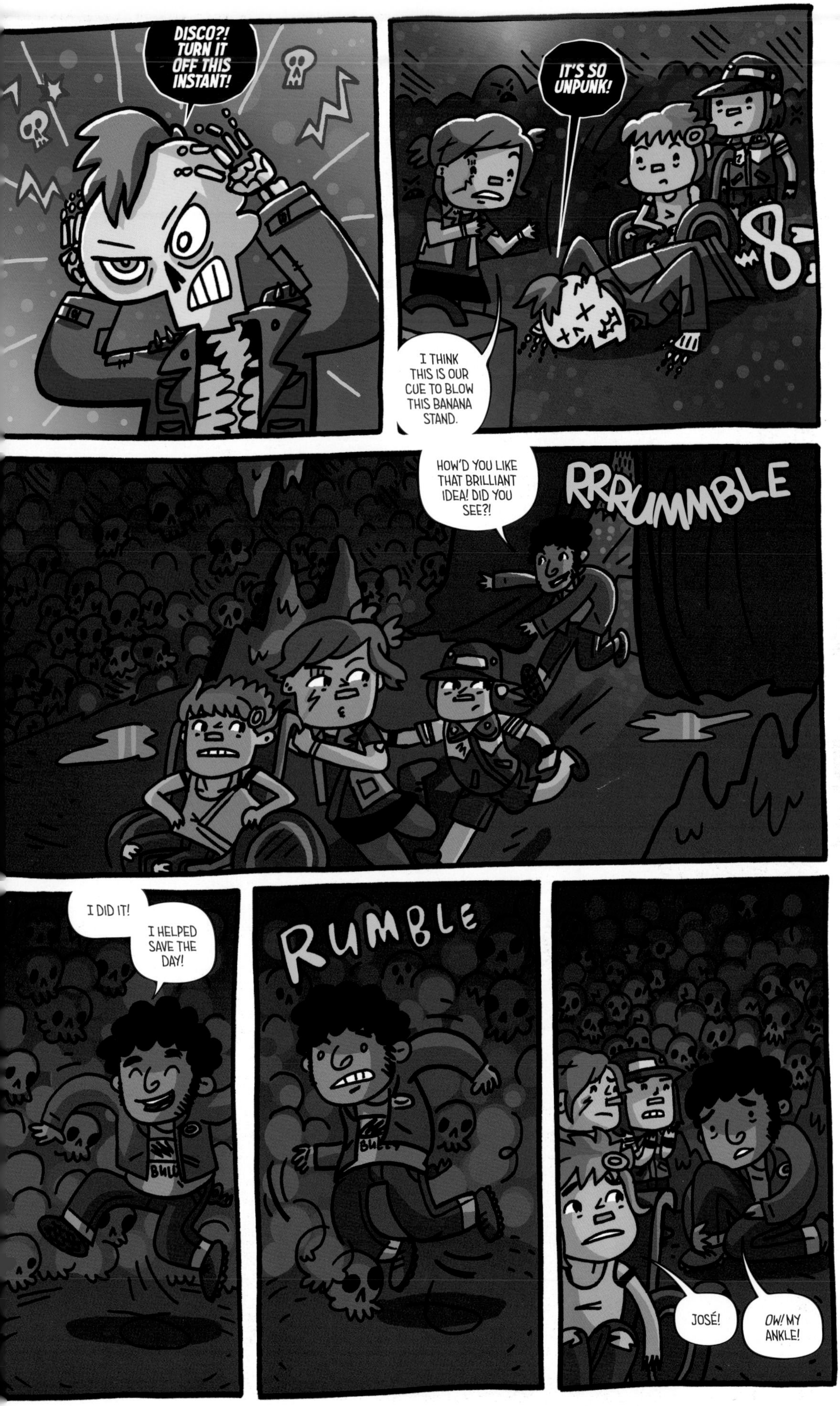
DISCO?! TURN IT OFF THIS INSTANT!
IT'S SO UNPUNK!
I THINK THIS IS OUR CUE TO BLOW THIS BANANA STAND.
HOW'D YOU LIKE THAT BRILLIANT IDEA! DID YOU SEE?!
RRRUMMBLE
I DID IT!
I HELPED SAVE THE DAY!
RUMBLE
JOSÉ!
OW! MY ANKLE!

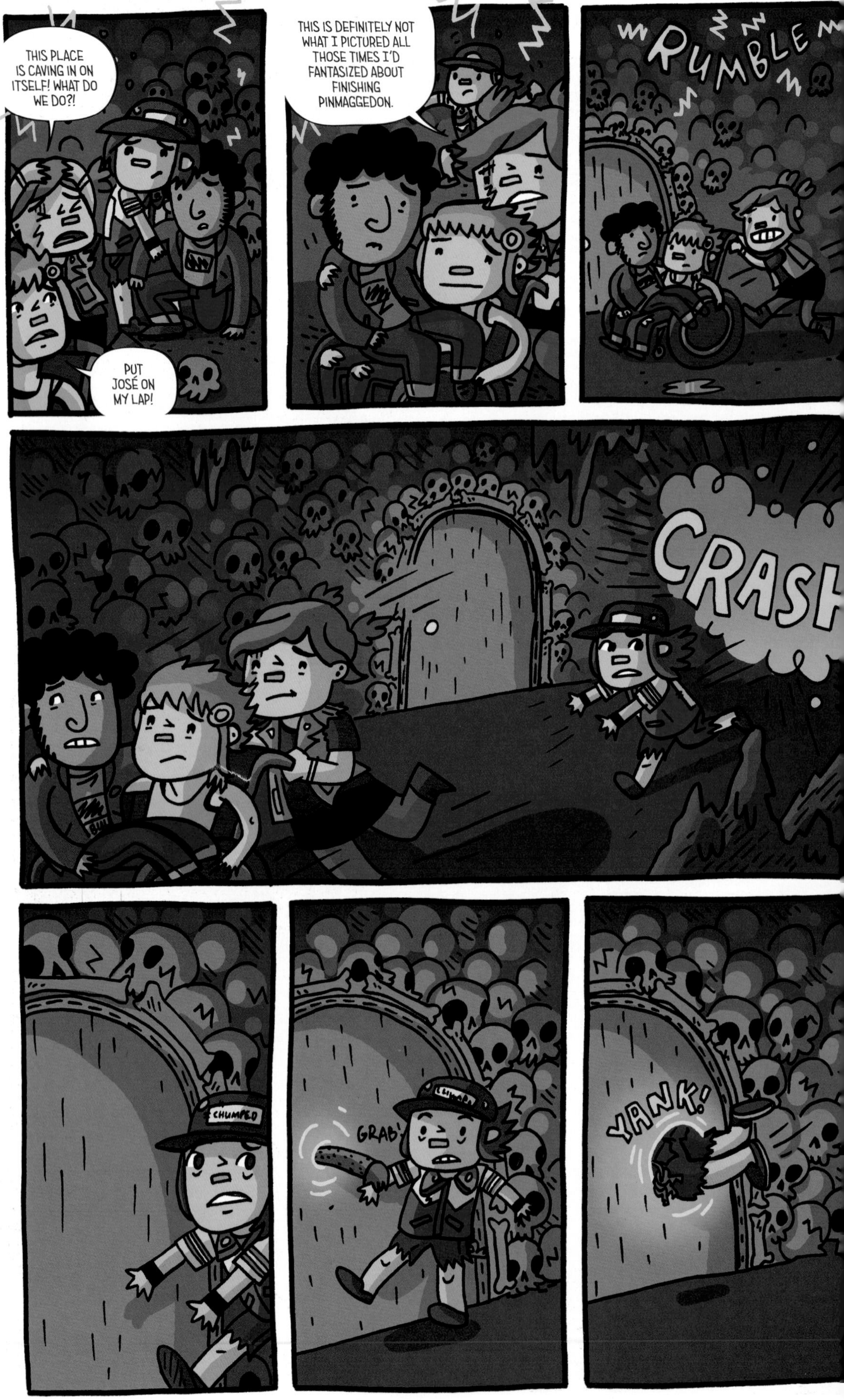
THIS PLACE IS CAVING IN ON ITSELF! WHAT DO WE DO?!
PUT JOSÉ ON MY LAP!
THIS IS DEFINITELY NOT WHAT I PICTURED ALL THOSE TIMES I'D FANTASIZED ABOUT FINISHING PINMAGGEDON.
RUMBLE
CRASH
CHUMPED
GRAB
YANK!

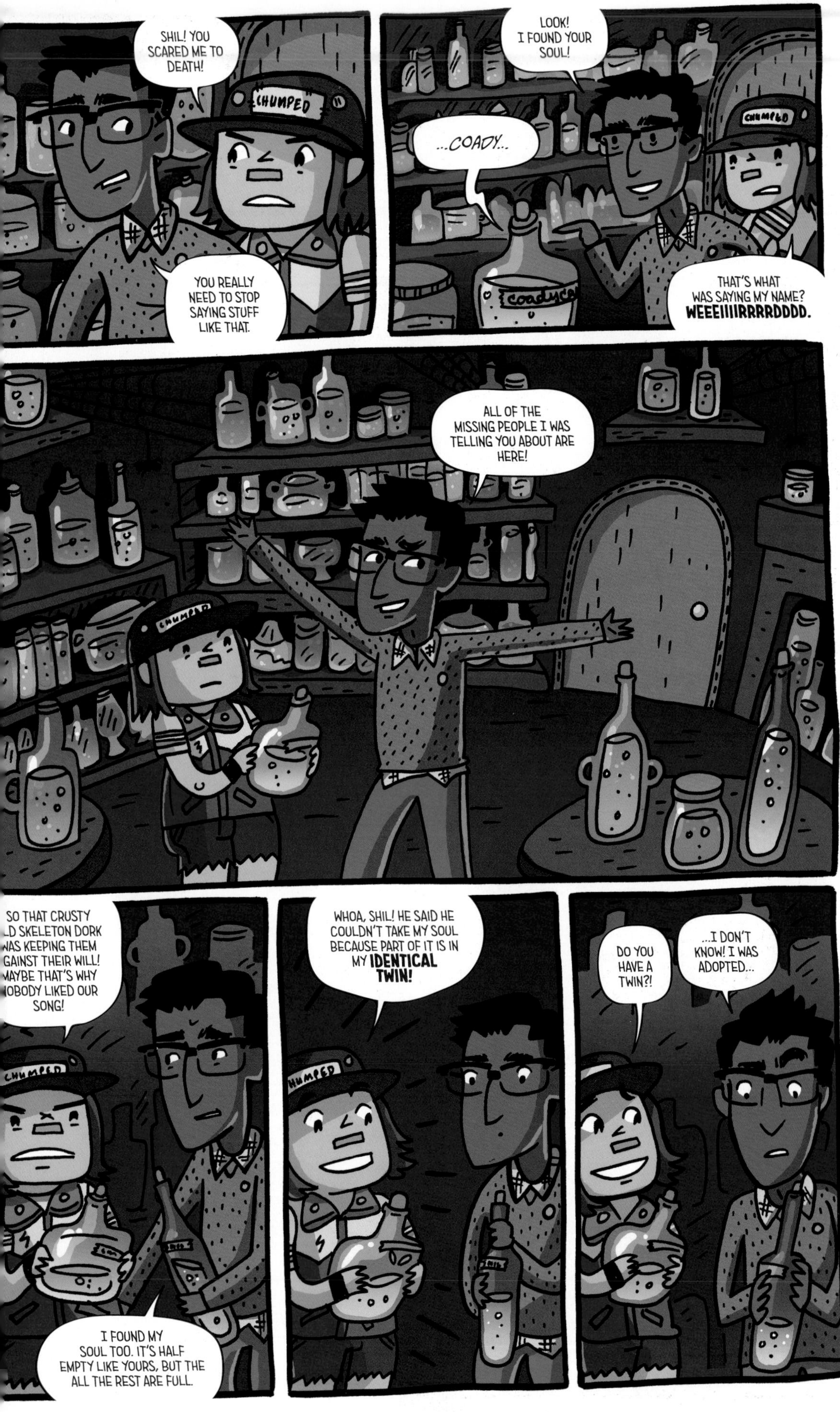
SHIL! YOU SCARED ME TO DEATH!
YOU REALLY NEED TO STOP SAYING STUFF LIKE THAT.
LOOK! I FOUND YOUR SOUL!
...COADY...
coadyco
THAT'S WHAT WAS SAYING MY NAME? **WEEEIIIIRRRRDDDD.**
ALL OF THE MISSING PEOPLE I WAS TELLING YOU ABOUT ARE HERE!
SO THAT CRUSTY
LD SKELETON DORK
VAS KEEPING THEM
GAINST THEIR WILL!
MAYBE THAT'S WHY
OBODY LIKED OUR
SONG!
I FOUND MY SOUL TOO. IT'S HALF EMPTY LIKE YOURS, BUT THE ALL THE REST ARE FULL.
WHOA, SHIL! HE SAID HE COULDN'T TAKE MY SOUL BECAUSE PART OF IT IS IN MY **IDENTICAL TWIN!**
DO YOU HAVE A TWIN?!
...I DON'T KNOW! I WAS ADOPTED...

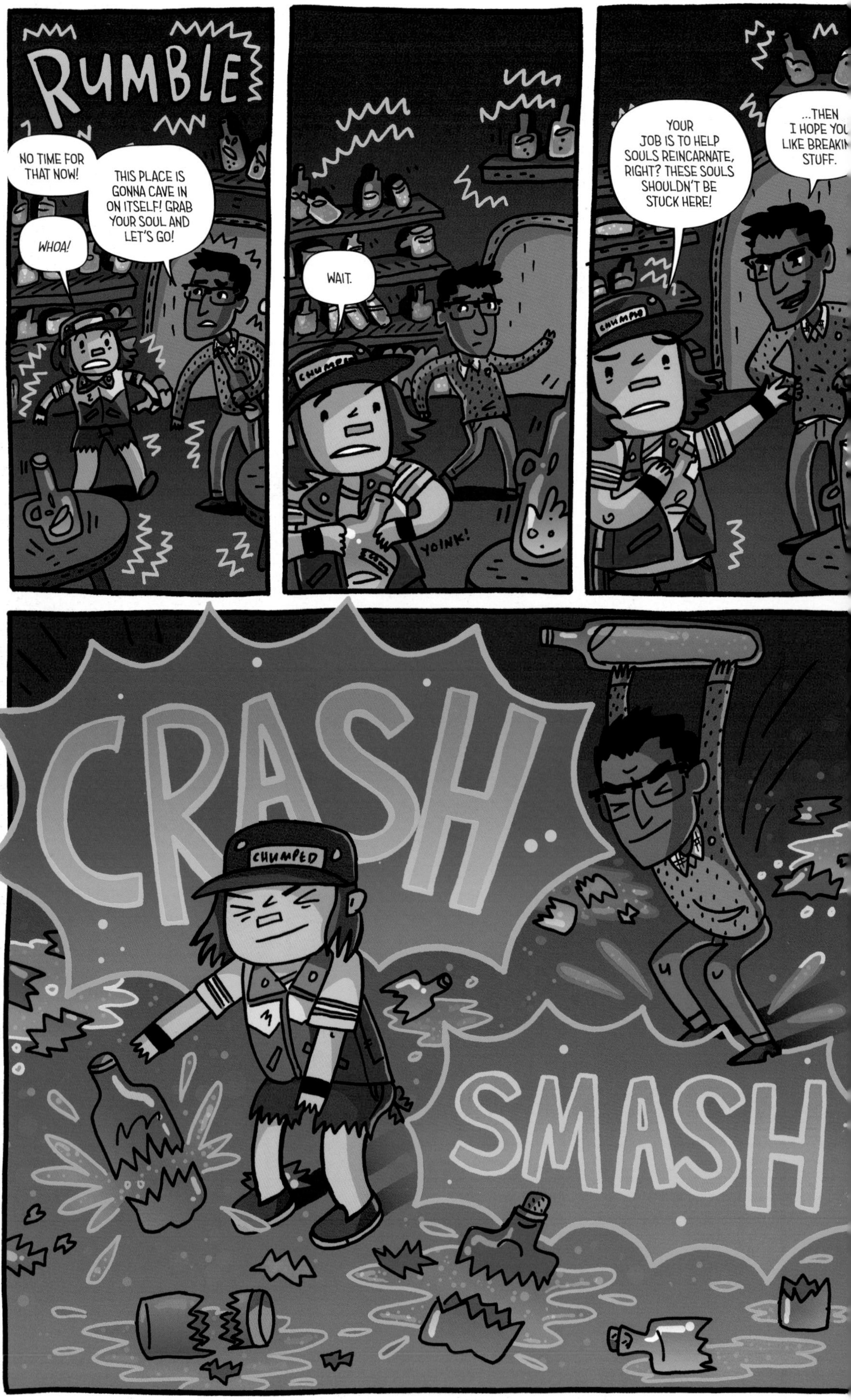
RUMBLE
NO TIME FOR THAT NOW!
THIS PLACE IS GONNA CAVE IN ON ITSELF! GRAB YOUR SOUL AND LET'S GO!
WHOA!
WAIT.
CHUMPED
YOINK!
YOUR JOB IS TO HELP SOULS REINCARNATE, RIGHT? THESE SOULS SHOULDN'T BE STUCK HERE!
...THEN I HOPE YOU LIKE BREAKIN STUFF.
CHUMPED
CRASH
CHUMPED
SMASH

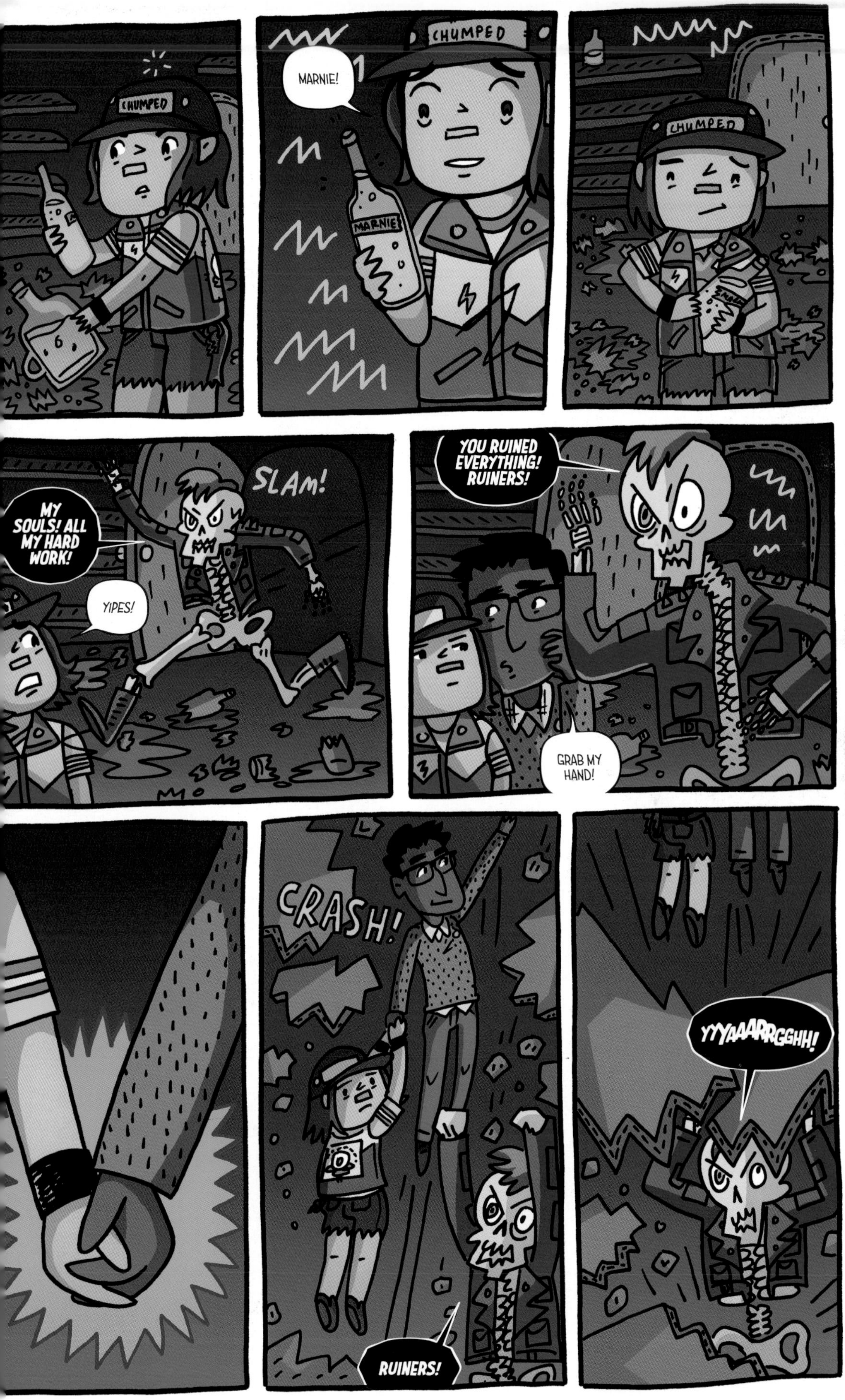
CHUMPED
MARNIE!
CHUMPED
MARNIE
CHUMPED
SLAM!
MY SOULS! ALL MY HARD WORK!
YIPES!
YOU RUINED EVERYTHING! RUINERS!
GRAB MY HAND!
CRASH!
RUINERS!
YYYAAARRGGHH!

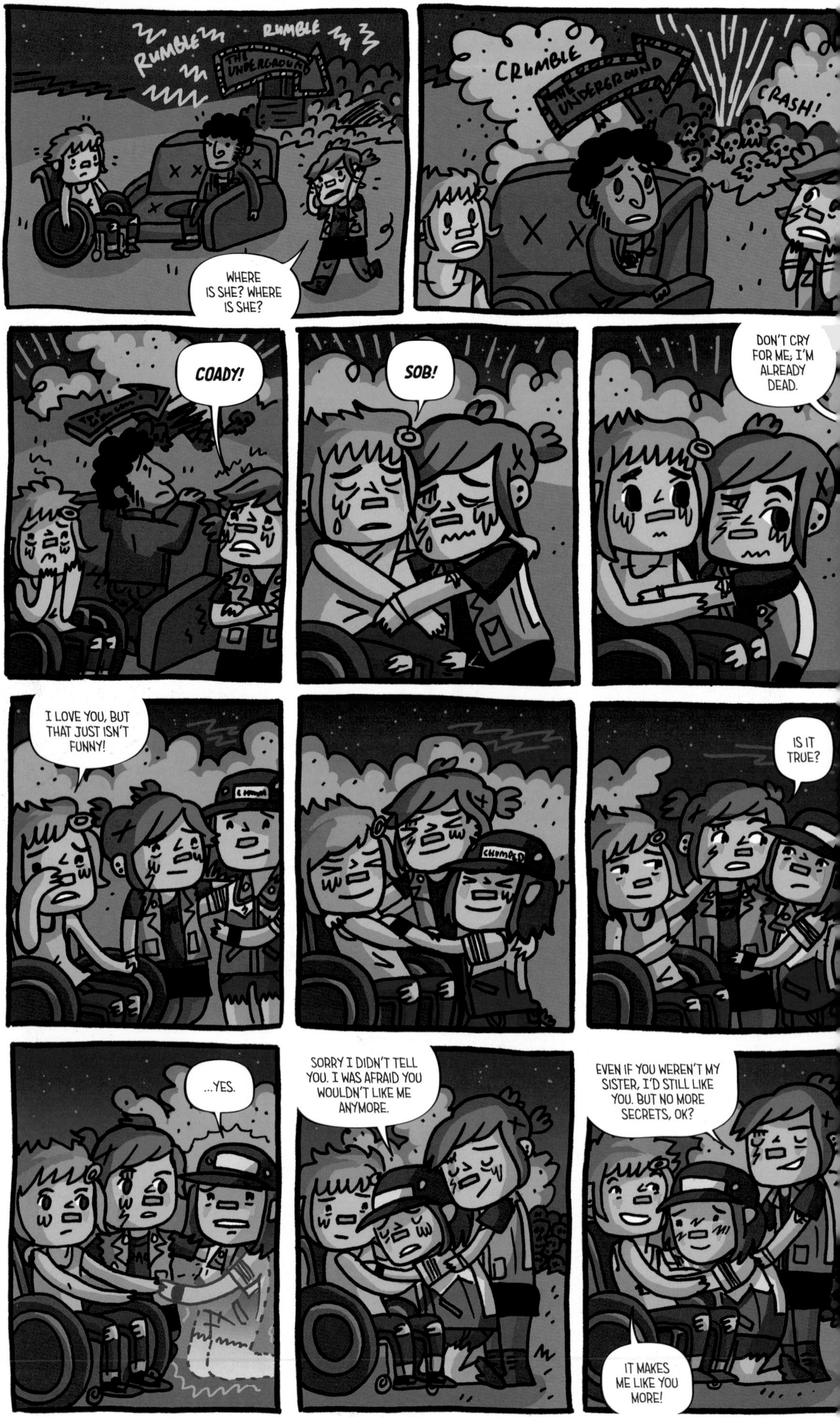
RUMBLE
RUMBLE
THE UNDERGROUND
WHERE IS SHE? WHERE IS SHE?
CRUMBLE
THE UNDERGROUND
CRASH!
COADY!
SOB!
DON'T CRY FOR ME; I'M ALREADY DEAD.
I LOVE YOU, BUT THAT JUST ISN'T FUNNY!
IS IT TRUE?
...YES.
SORRY I DIDN'T TELL YOU. I WAS AFRAID YOU WOULDN'T LIKE ME ANYMORE.
EVEN IF YOU WEREN'T MY SISTER, I'D STILL LIKE YOU. BUT NO MORE SECRETS, OK?
IT MAKES ME LIKE YOU MORE!

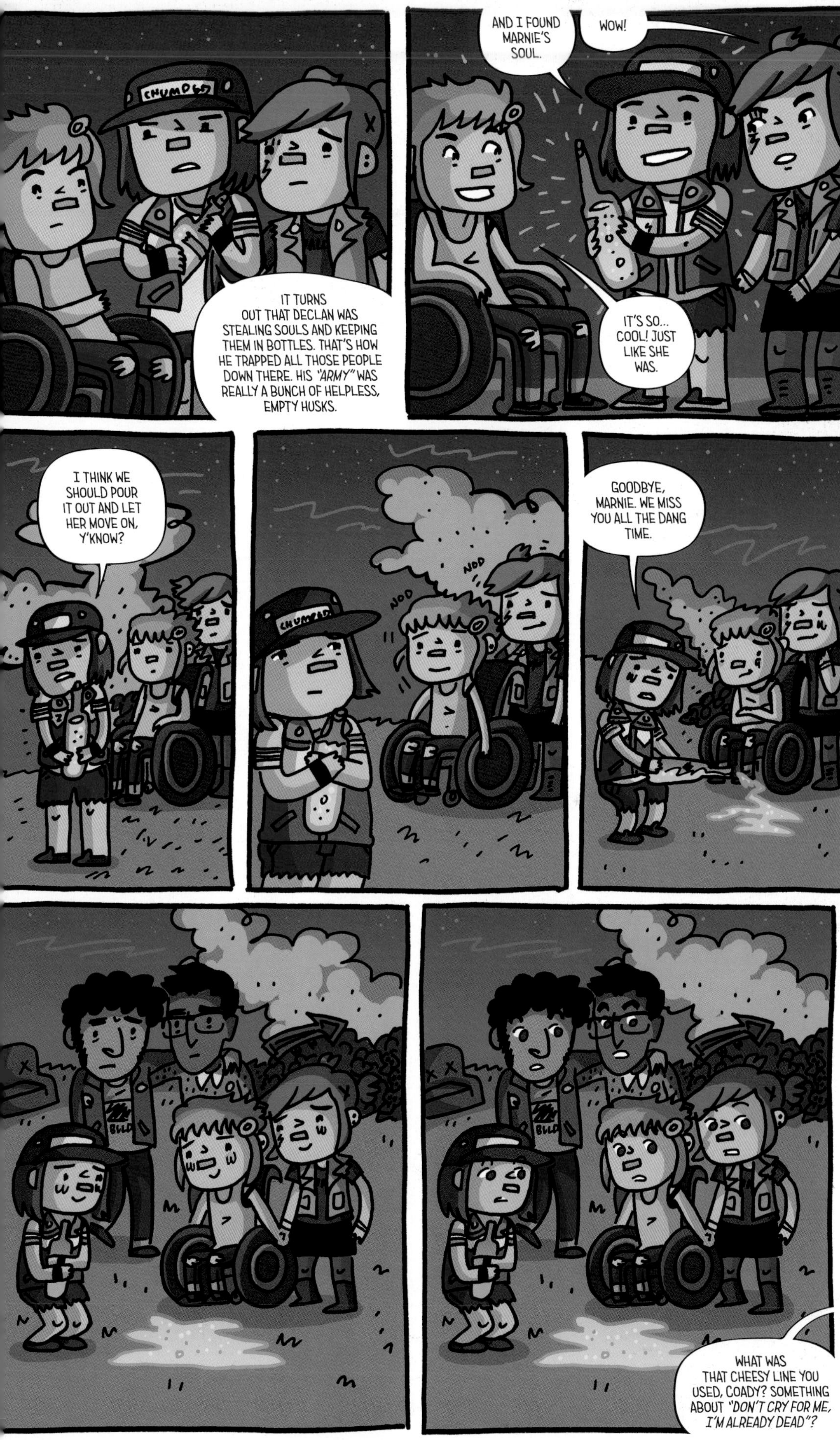
CHUMPS
IT TURNS OUT THAT DECLAN WAS STEALING SOULS AND KEEPING THEM IN BOTTLES. THAT'S HOW HE TRAPPED ALL THOSE PEOPLE DOWN THERE. HIS "ARMY" WAS REALLY A BUNCH OF HELPLESS, EMPTY HUSKS.
AND I FOUND MARNIE'S SOUL.
WOW!
IT'S SO... COOL! JUST LIKE SHE WAS.
I THINK WE SHOULD POUR IT OUT AND LET HER MOVE ON, Y'KNOW?
NOD
NOD
GOODBYE, MARNIE. WE MISS YOU ALL THE DANG TIME.
WHAT WAS THAT CHEESY LINE YOU USED, COADY? SOMETHING ABOUT "DON'T CRY FOR ME, I'M ALREADY DEAD"?

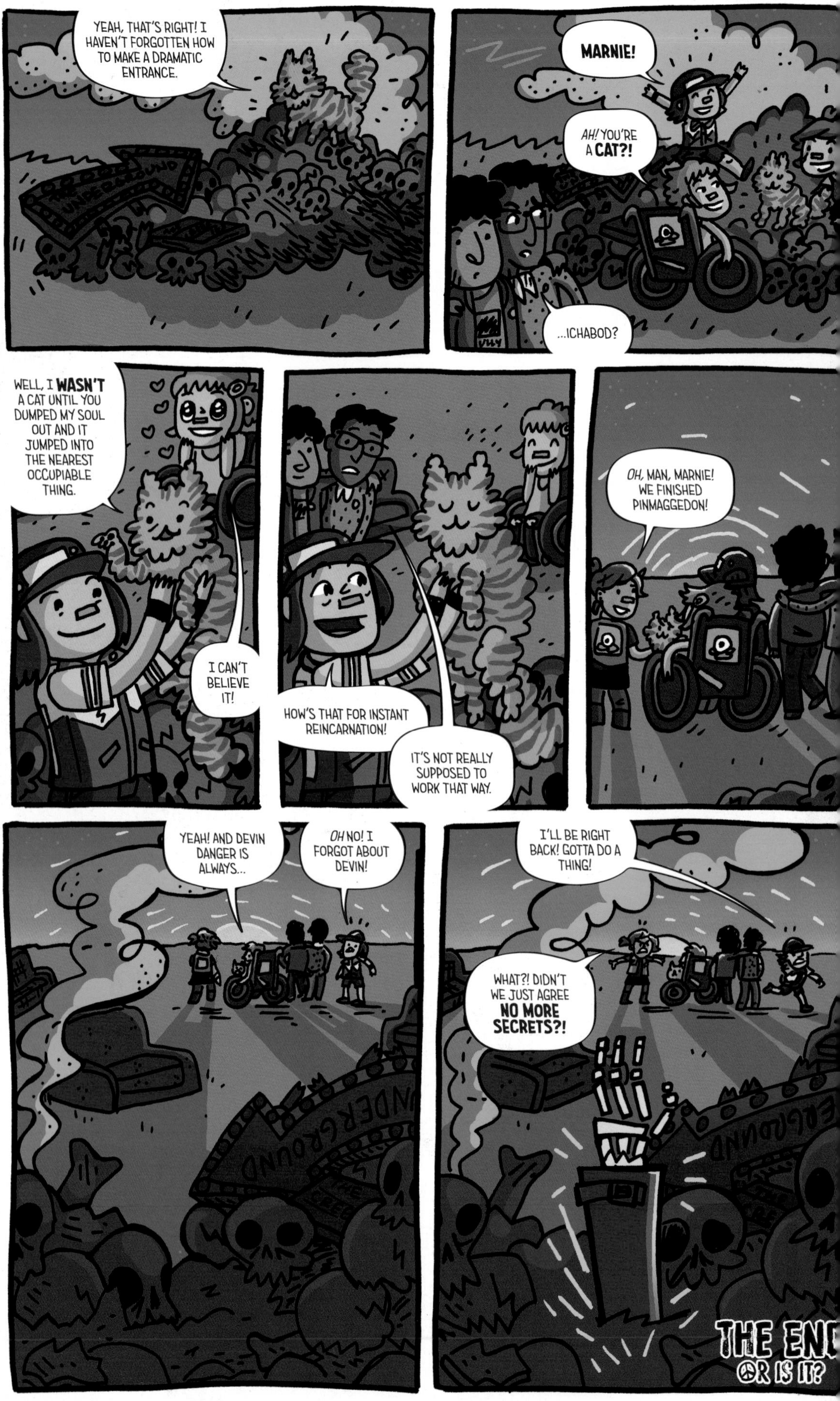
YEAH, THAT'S RIGHT! I HAVEN'T FORGOTTEN HOW TO MAKE A DRAMATIC ENTRANCE.
UNDERGROUND
MARNIE!
AH! YOU'RE A **CAT?!**
...ICHABOD?
WELL, I **WASN'T** A CAT UNTIL YOU DUMPED MY SOUL OUT AND IT JUMPED INTO THE NEAREST OCCUPIABLE THING.
I CAN'T BELIEVE IT!
HOW'S THAT FOR INSTANT REINCARNATION!
IT'S NOT REALLY SUPPOSED TO WORK THAT WAY.
OH, MAN, MARNIE! WE FINISHED PINMAGGEDON!
YEAH! AND DEVIN DANGER IS ALWAYS...
OH NO! I FORGOT ABOUT DEVIN!
UNDERGROUND
I'LL BE RIGHT BACK! GOTTA DO A THING!
WHAT?! DIDN'T WE JUST AGREE **NO MORE SECRETS?!**
UNDERGROUND
THE END
OR IS IT?

COVER GALLERY

Rock out to the original song "Creepies R Go!" here:

Issue One Main Cover by
KAT LEYH

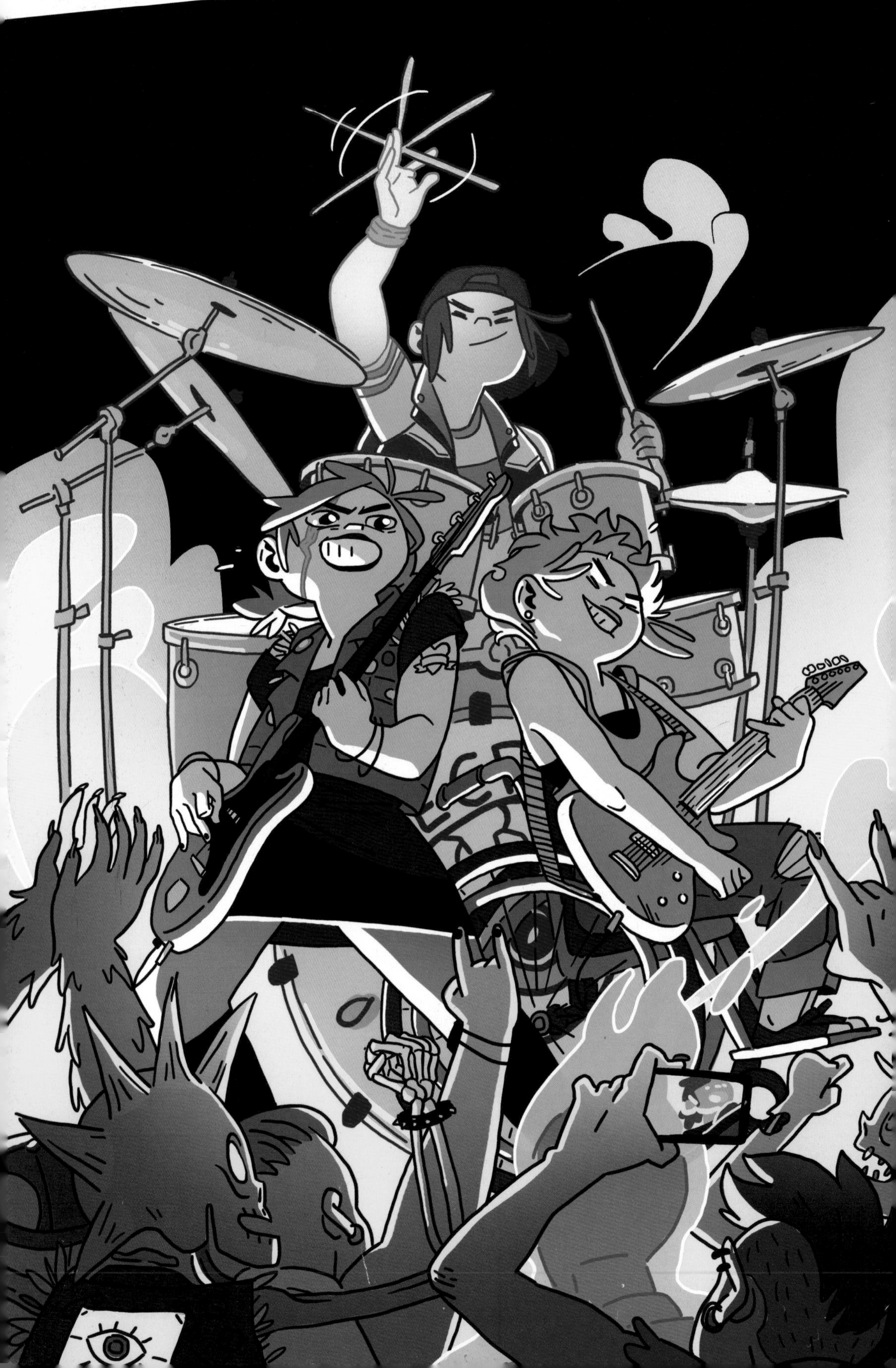

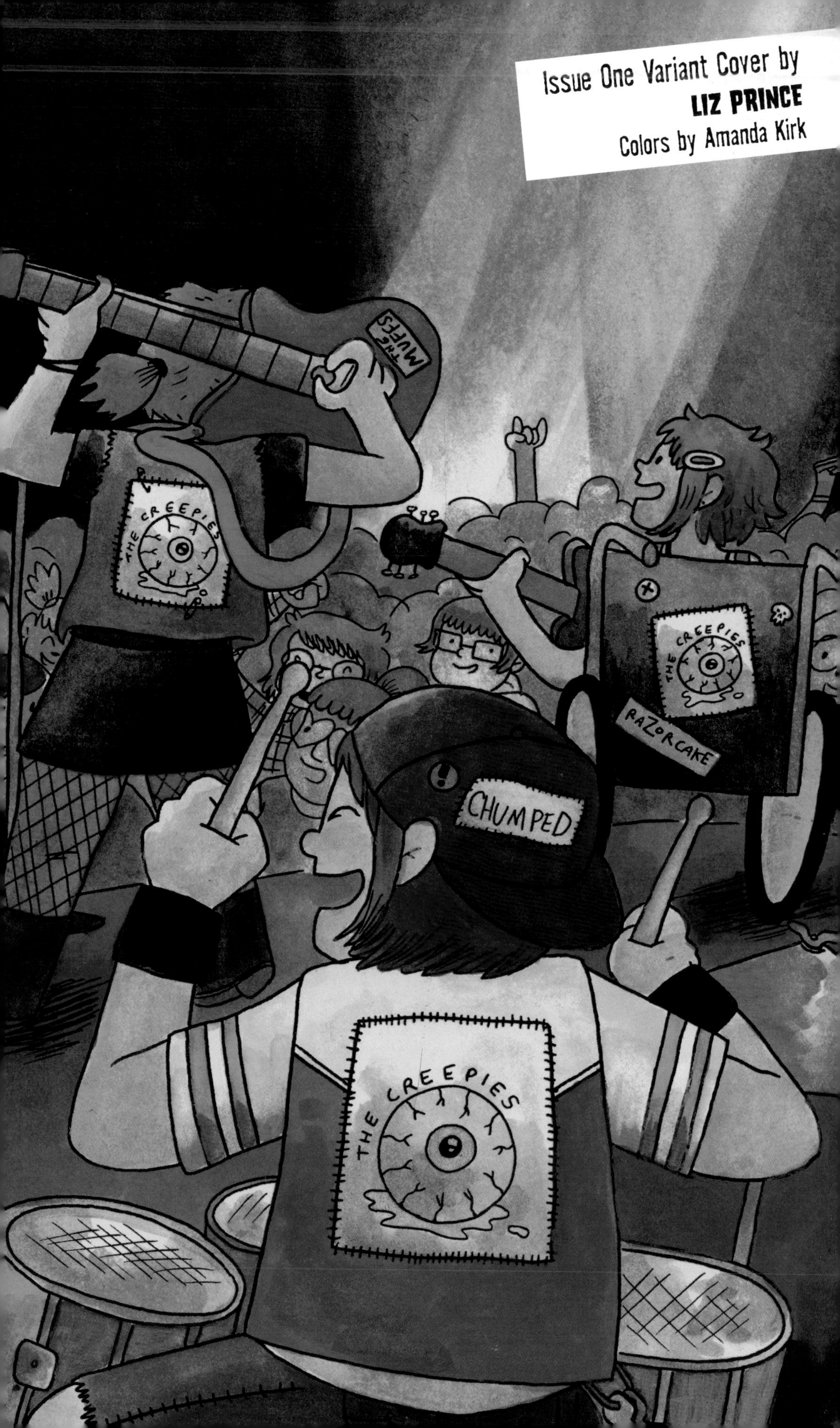
THE MUFFS
THE CREEPIES
THE CREEPIES
RAZORCAKE
CHUMPED
THE CREEPIES
Issue One Variant Cover by
LIZ PRINCE
Colors by Amanda Kirk

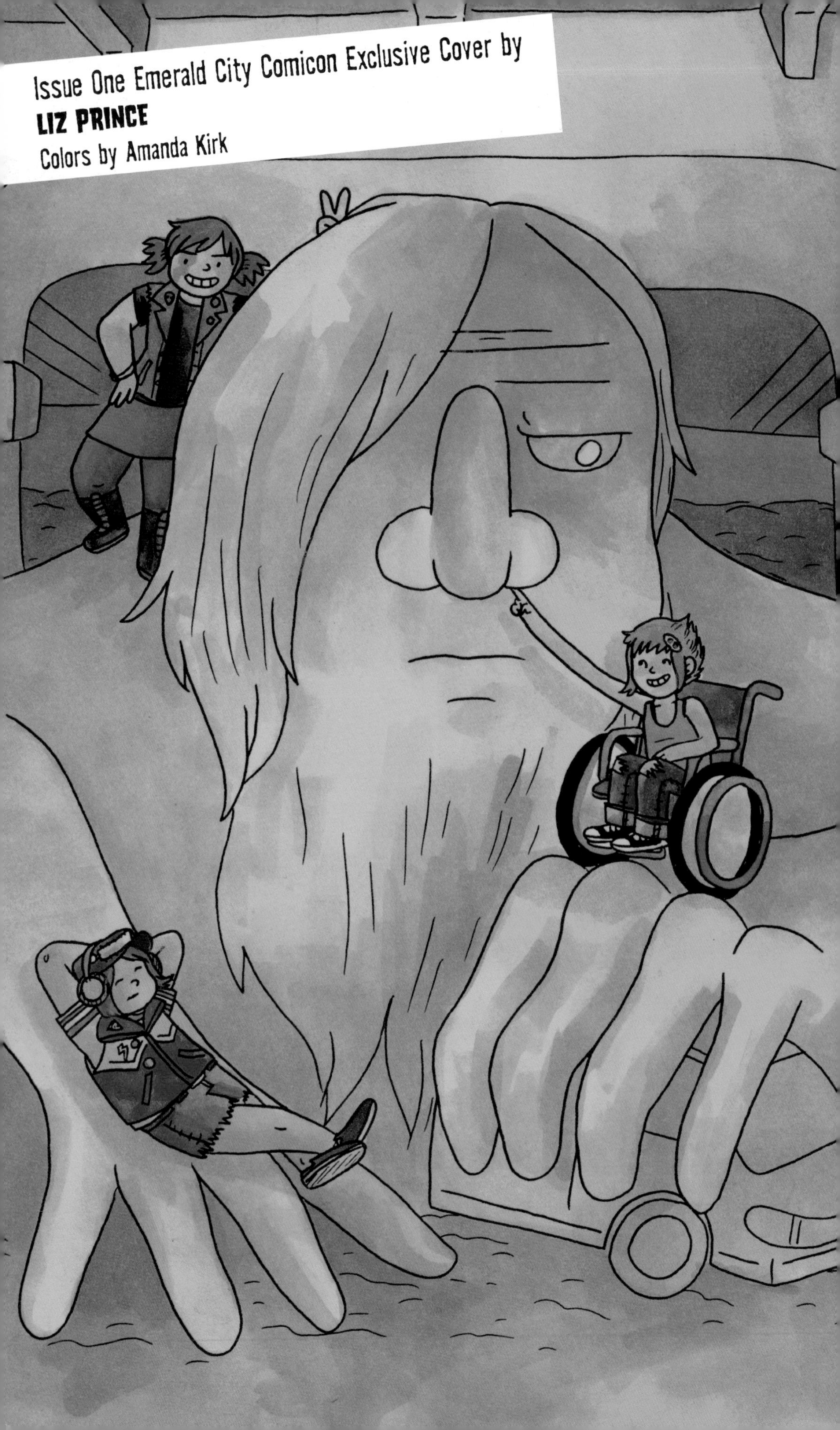

Issue One Emerald City Comicon Exclusive Cover by
LIZ PRINCE
Colors by Amanda Kirk

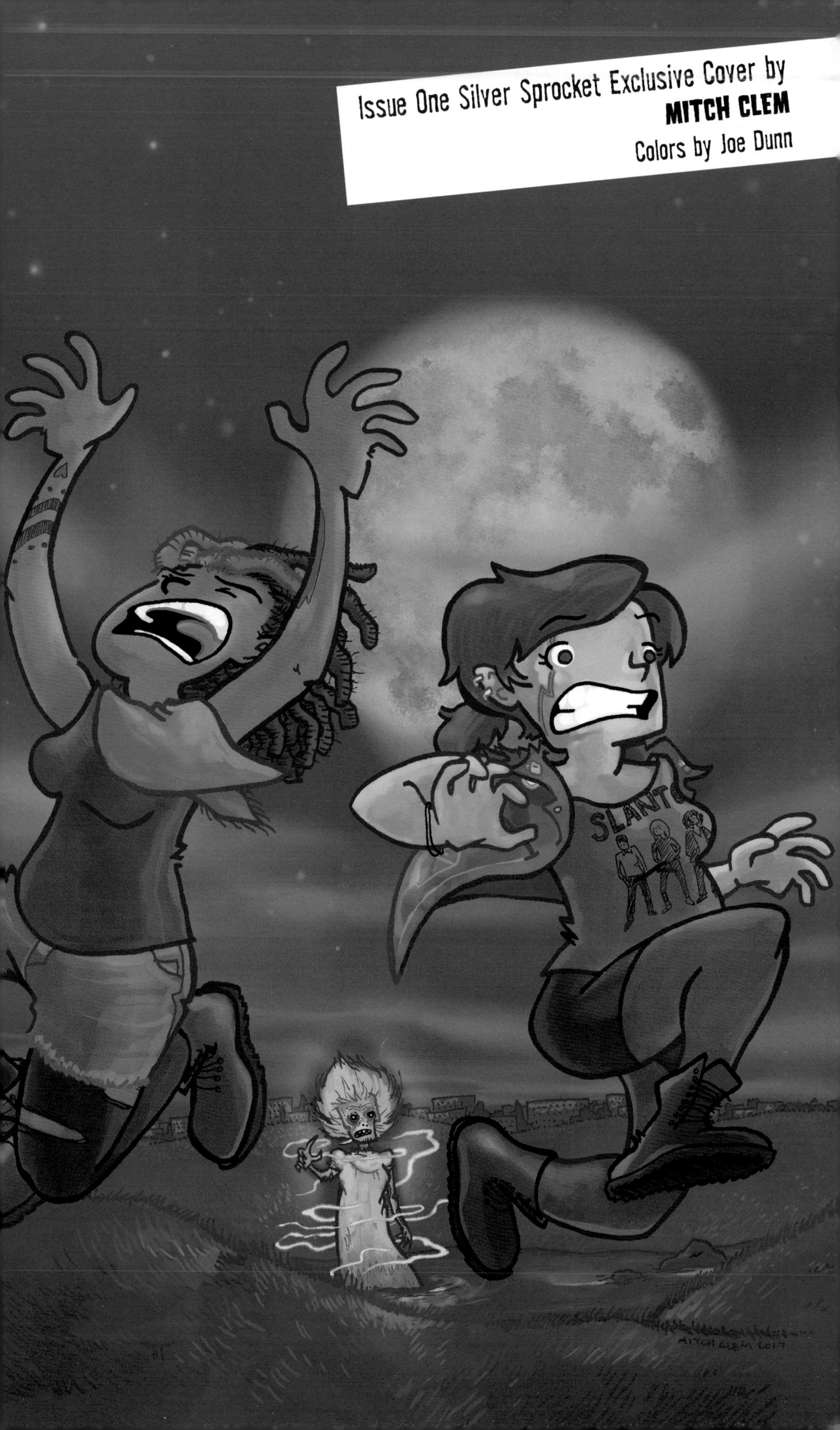

Issue One Silver Sprocket Exclusive Cover by
MITCH CLEM
Colors by Joe Dunn

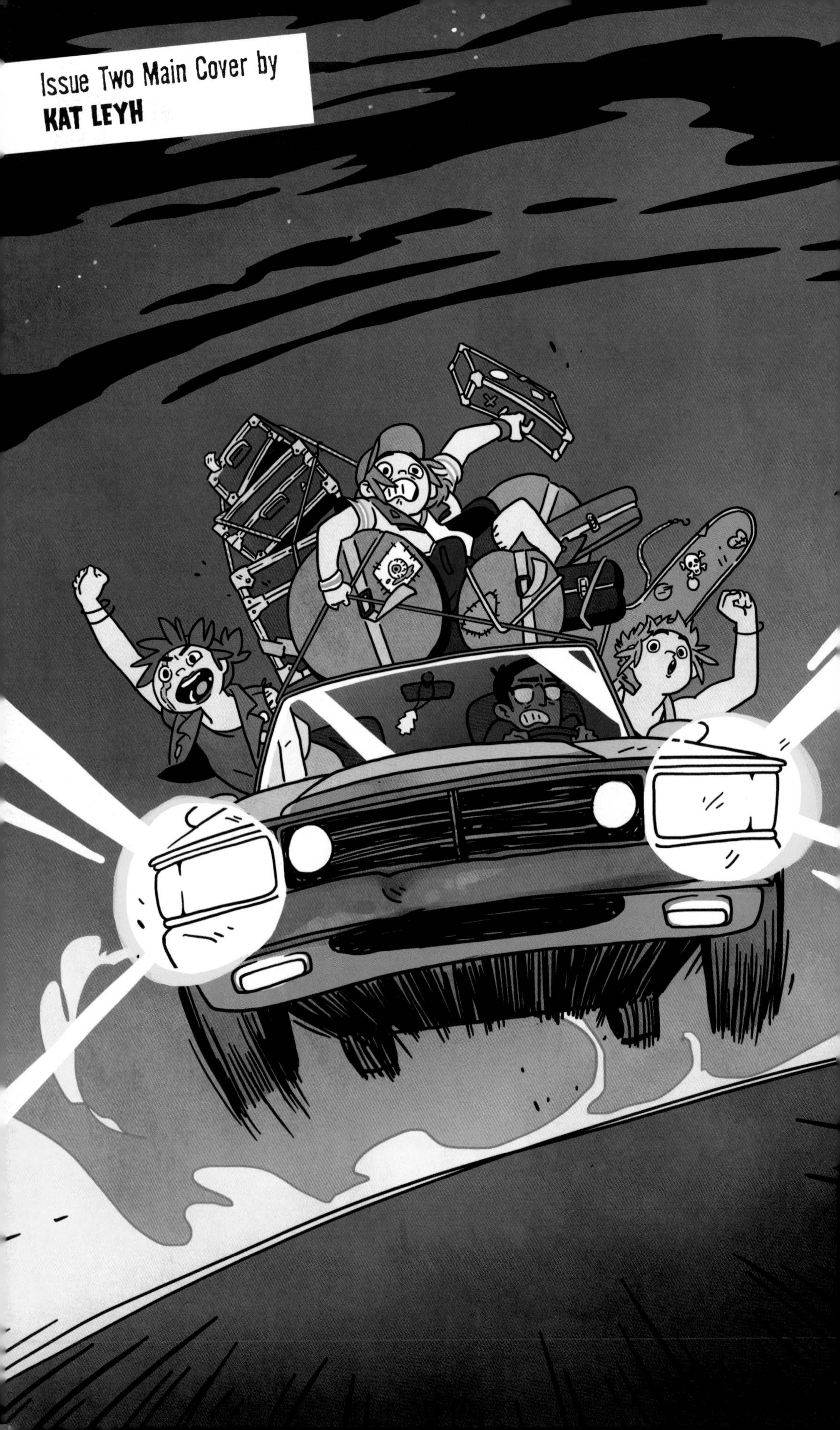

Issue Two Main Cover by
KAT LEYH

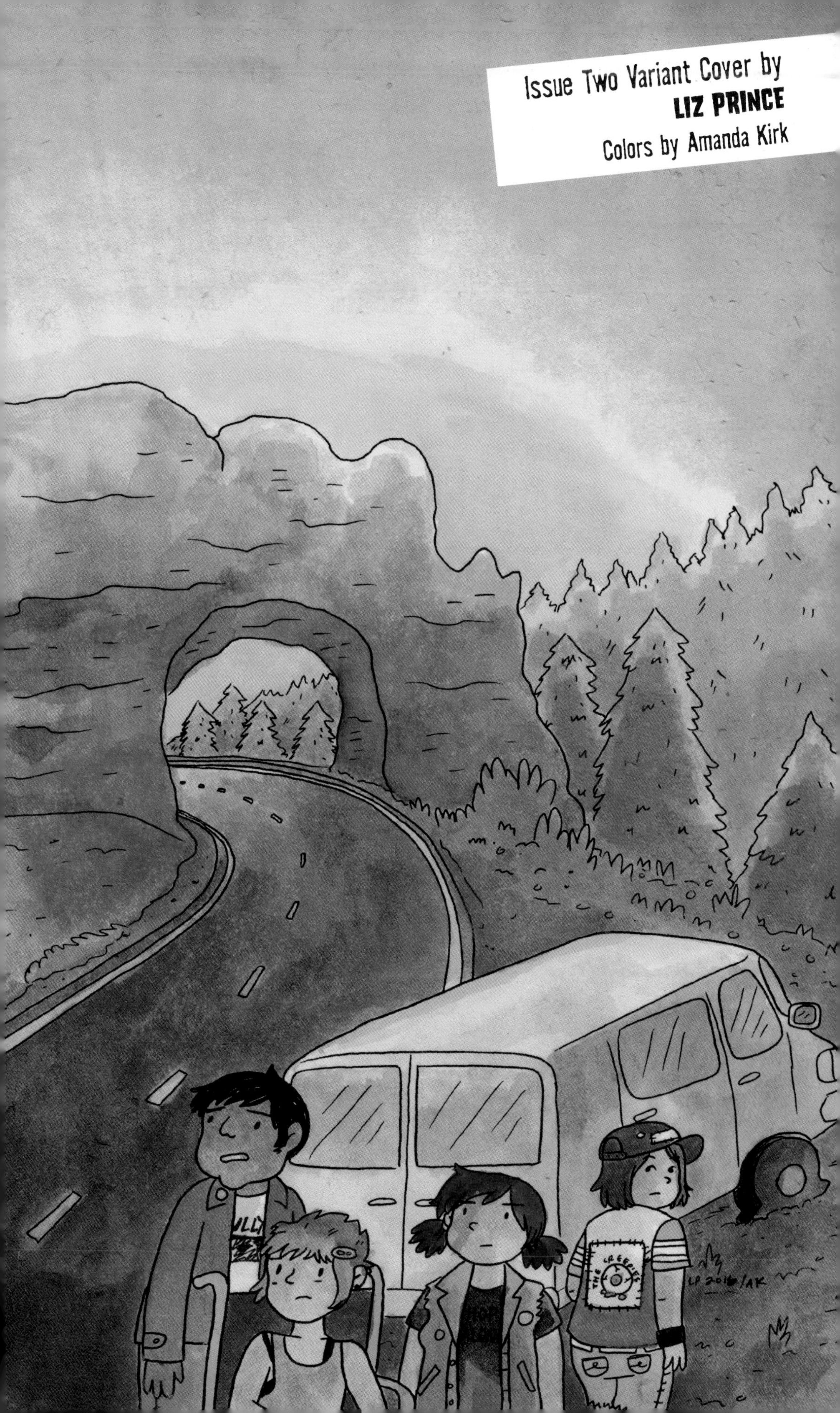

Issue Two Variant Cover by
LIZ PRINCE
Colors by Amanda Kirk

Issue Three Main Cover by
KAT LEYH

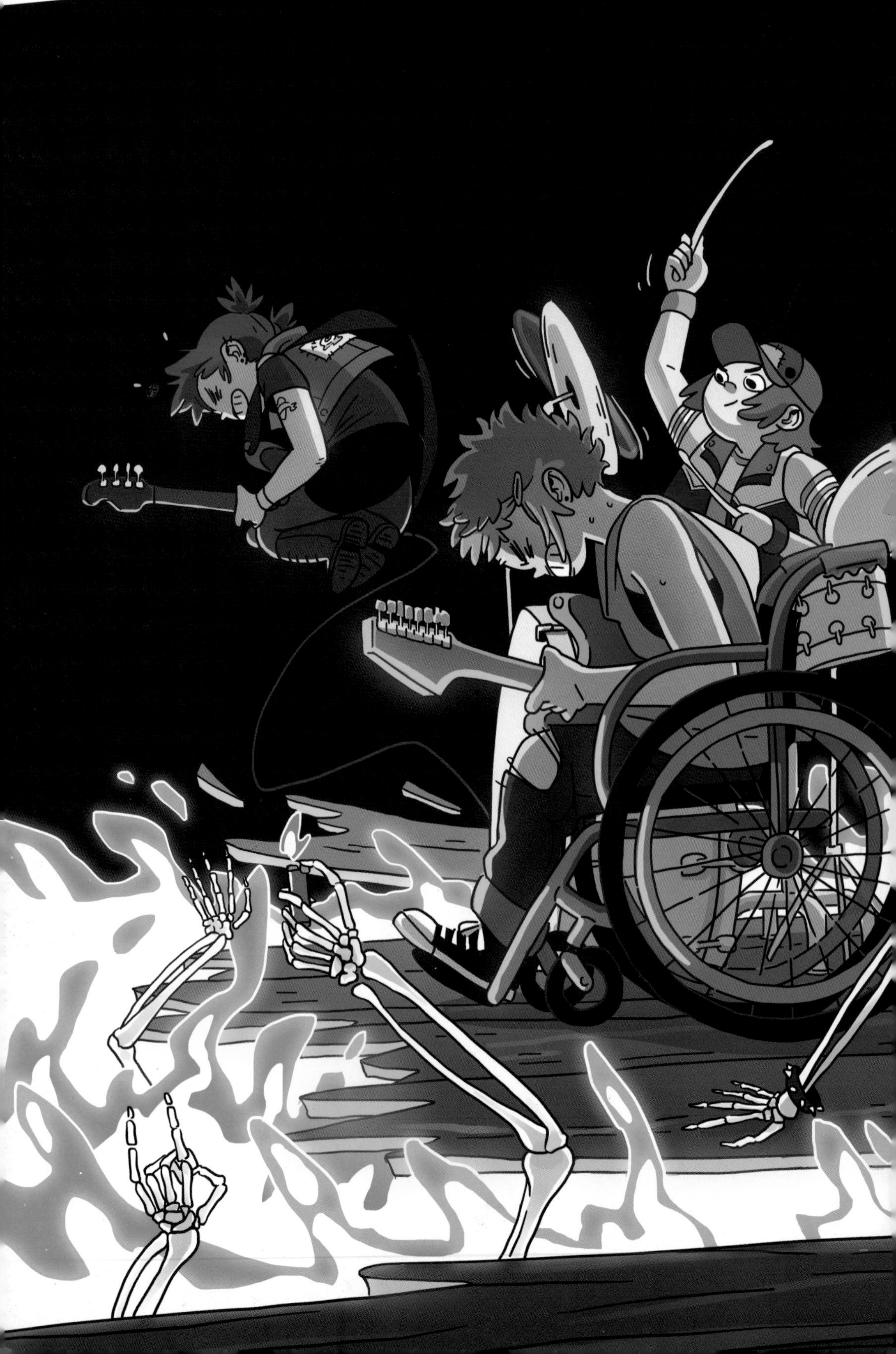

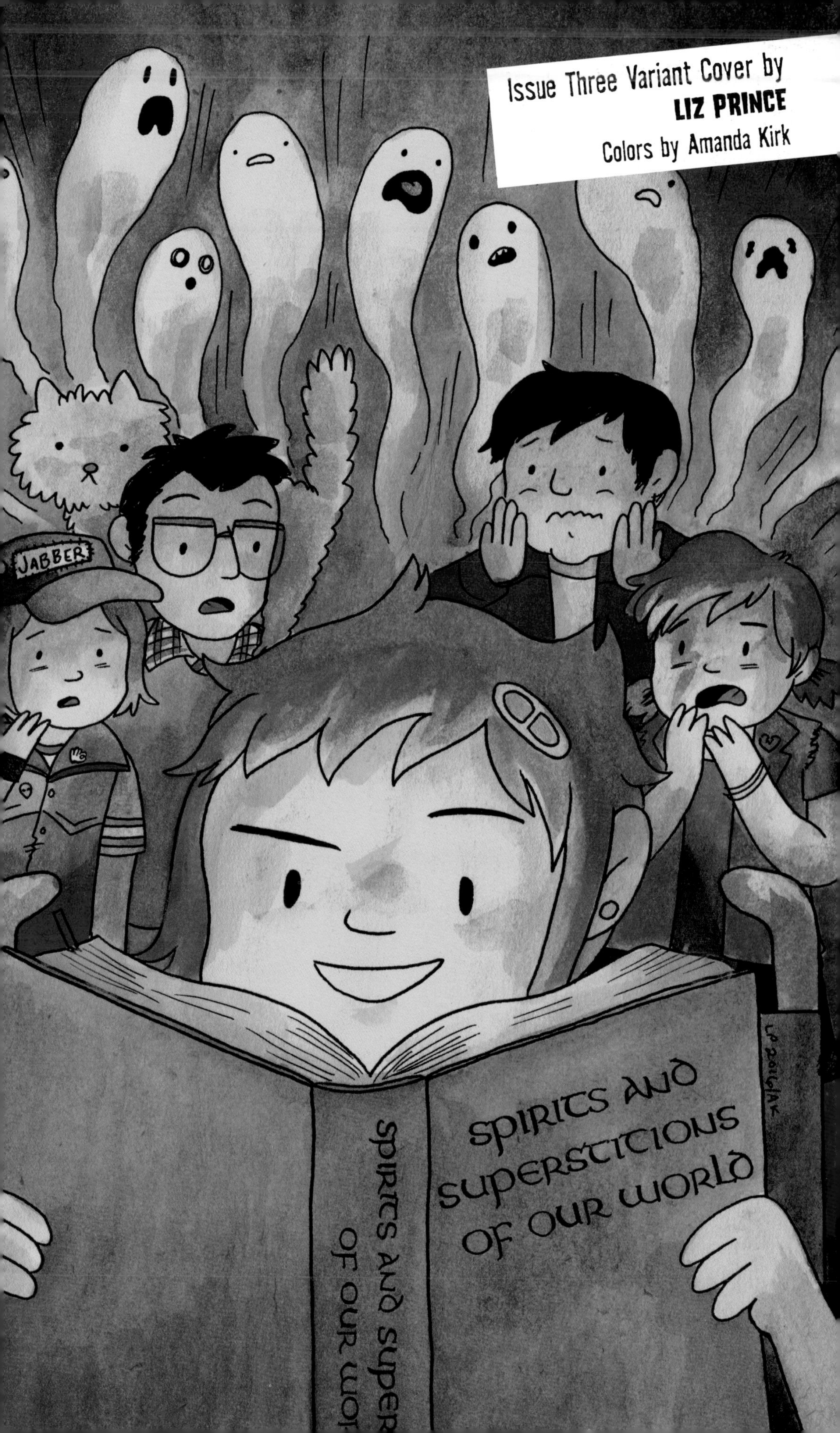
JABBER
SPIRITS AND SUPERSTITIONS OF OUR WORLD

Issue Three Variant Cover by
LIZ PRINCE
Colors by Amanda Kirk

Issue Four Main Cover by
KAT LEYH

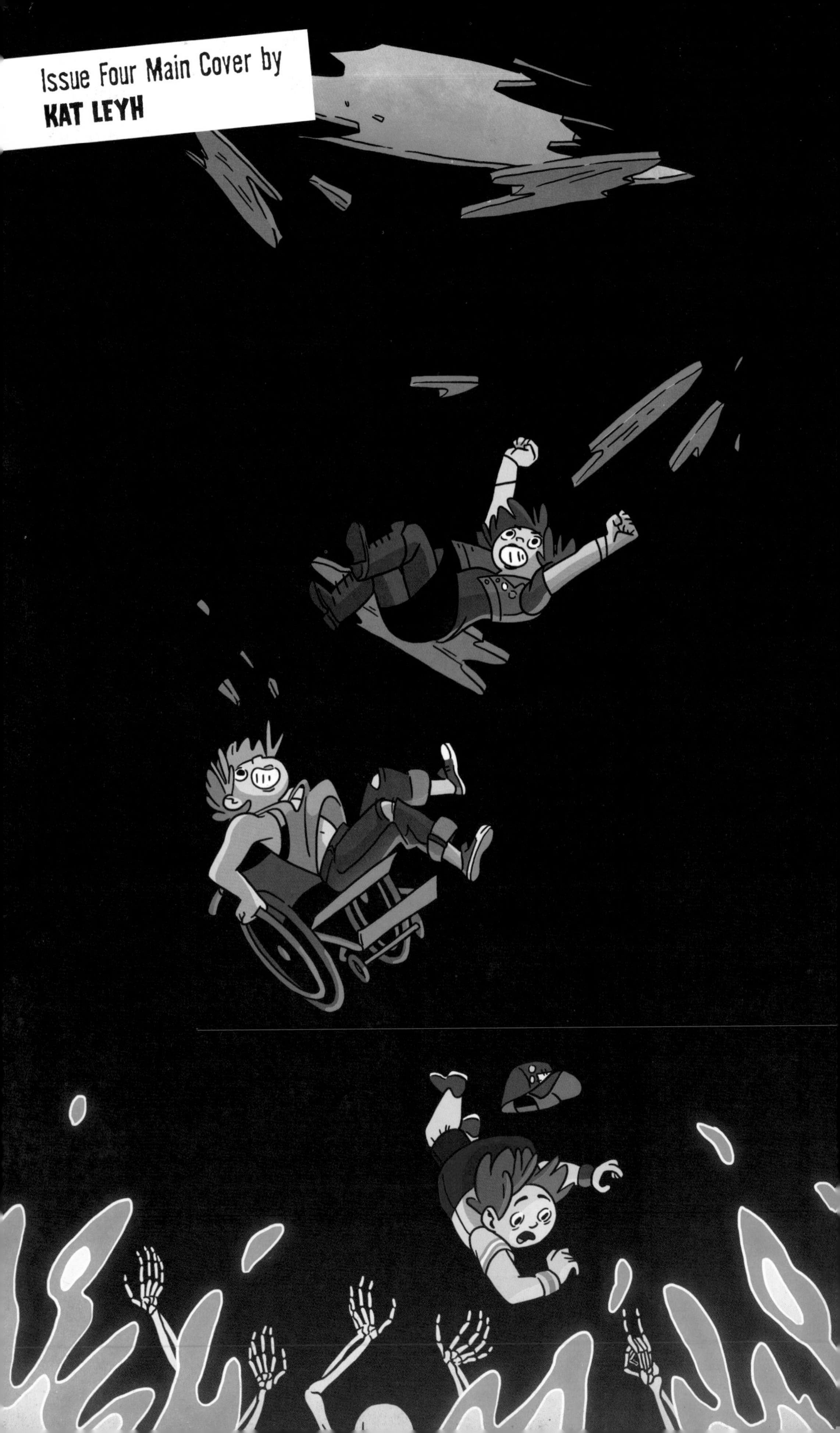

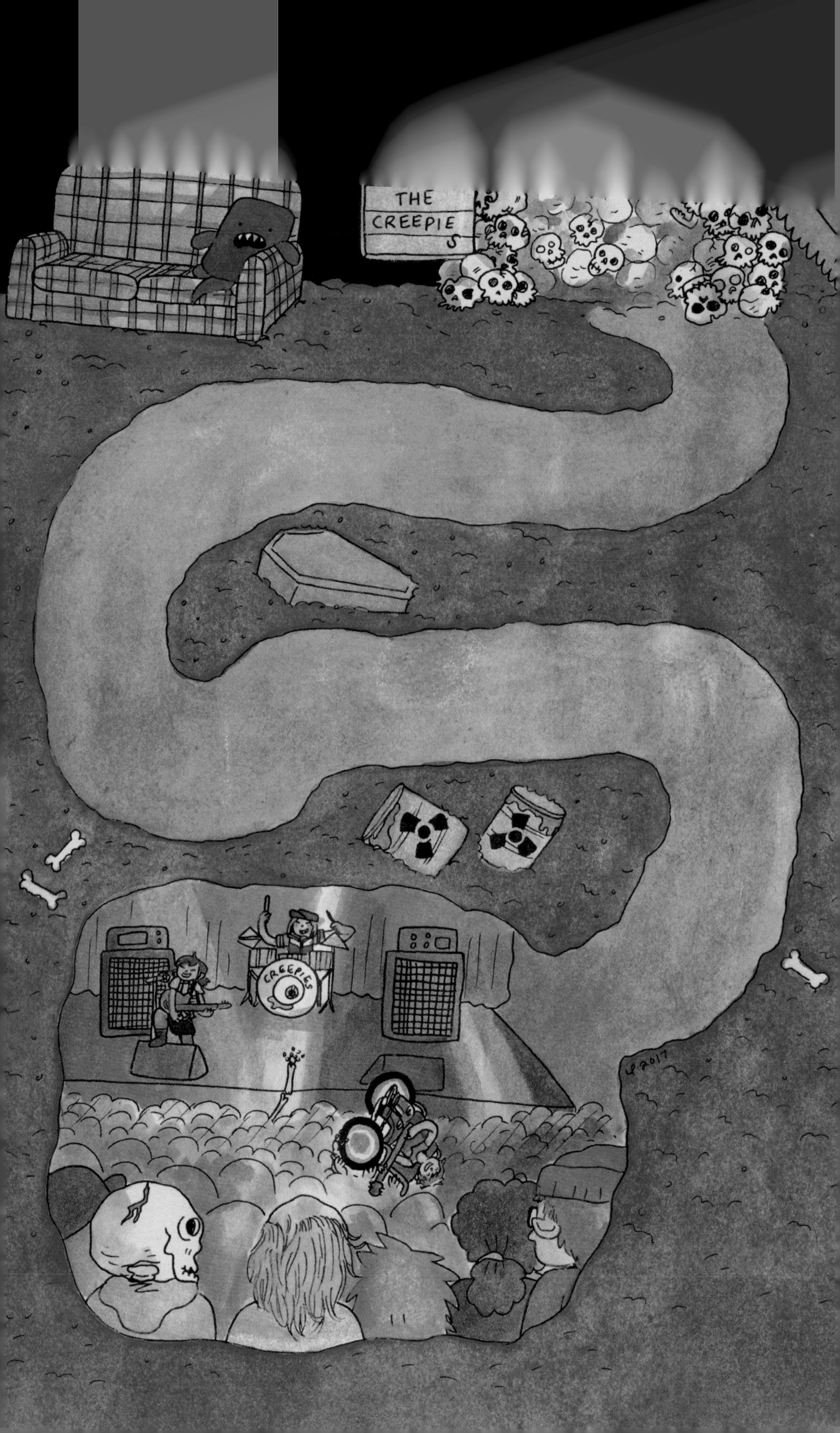
THE
CREEPIE
S
CREEPIES

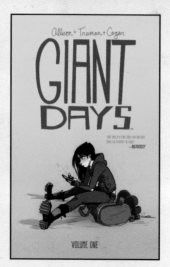

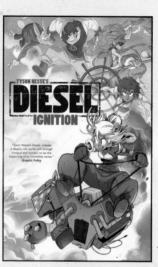